KISSING THE WARRIOR

"Kiss me."

"What did ye say?" he asked in a low, masculine rumble.

If I am going to die, she suddenly decided, *it will not be absent the kiss of this Irishman.*

She took his hand and moved it to her mouth. Shutting her eyes, she parted her lips and closed her teeth gently on his finger, letting the tip of her tongue trail against his warm flesh.

His body rippled slightly, like wind over waves. She felt every muscle in his body shift, very minutely, very definitely. He brushed his thumb over her jaw again, then once over her lips.

"Did ye tell me to kiss ye?"

"I did." Her whisper trembled.

His eyes searched hers. "Why?"

"Because," she whispered, "if I'm going to die, it will not be lacking all the things I am lacking at present."

"Ye're lacking a kiss, then?"

She nodded.

He bent to her. She felt warm breath on her cheek. Soft, teasing kisses danced across her cheeks, her eyelids. She sighed and he tightened his hold ever so slightly on the back of her head, as if holding her still. He cupped her cheek gently with his other hand and his lips finally settled over her own. He bent lower and nibbled her lower lip until, like he'd uttered a password, she parted her lips . . .

Books by Kris Kennedy

THE CONQUEROR

THE IRISH WARRIOR

Published by Kensington Publishing Corporation

The IRISH WARRIOR

KRIS KENNEDY

ZEBRA BOOKS
KENSINGTON PUBLISHING CORP.
http://www.kensingtonbooks.com

ZEBRA BOOKS are published by

Kensington Publishing Corp.
119 West 40th Street
New York, NY 10018

All Kensington titles, imprints, and distributed lines are available at special quantity discounts for bulk purchases for sales promotion, premiums, fund-raising, educational, or institutional use.

Special book excerpts or customized printings can also be created to fit specific needs. For details, write or phone the office of the Kensington Special Sales Manager: Attn. Special Sales Department. Kensington Publishing Corp., 119 West 40th Street, New York, NY 10018. Phone: 1-800-221-2647.

ISBN-13: 978-1-4201-0653-4
ISBN-10: 1-4201-0653-8

First Printing: June 2010

10 9 8 7 6 5 4 3 2 1

Printed in the United States of America

ACKNOWLEDGMENTS

I'd like to thank my husband, for always having the best comebacks when I tell him about the people who somehow imply writing (and reading) romance is a less-than-worthy pursuit.

To my family, none of whom read romance, all of whom read my book—I do love you.

Rachel, Courtney, Tatia, and Becky—Thanks for the blood-lettings.

To my editor, John Scognamiglio, who trusts an author to write the book she needs to write.

I'd also like to thank Jennifer Munson, my go-to girl for all things dye related. She was patient and thorough and never made me feel annoying when I asked things like, "Now, how dirty would my heroine's hands get? I mean, specifically. Wrists? Fingernails? And how long would it take to wear off? Specifically."

And to every reader who wrote me about my debut book, *The Conqueror*—I can't tell you how much it meant to me that you not only loved the book, but took time out of your day to tell me so. Go, romance readers!

Chapter 1

Early autumn, Northern Ireland, 1295 A.D.

"It's simple, really," drawled the voice from the shadows. "Submit, or men start dying. The choice is yours."

Finian O'Melaghlin, Irish noble, warrior, and chief councilor to the great O'Fáil king, finished his grim smile. Everything was going as planned. Or rather, as expected.

From the moment The O'Fáil sent Finian to accept Lord Rardove's long-standing but ultimately treacherous invitation to meet, Finian had been separated from his men, plied first with food, then with prison. Rardove was proving predictable. And dangerous.

Finian had argued against the meeting, but his king insisted. The Irish suspected Rardove was up to something. Something dangerous. Something related to the legendary Wishmé dyes.

Unfortunately, Rardove suspected the Irish were up to something as well.

Pain shuddered through Finian's body from the savage beatings he'd already suffered, but that meant nothing. All that mattered was finding out what Rardove knew and preventing him from finding out any more. For that, he and his men had committed to die if needed.

"Somehow, Rardove"—he angled a glance over his shoulder—"I don't feel I can trust ye."

The guards holding his arms eyed him warily. Shackled around the wrists, cast in a prison with a blade at his throat and a guard on both arms, he was scaring them half to death. He could see it in their anxious eyes, smell it in the stench of fear rising from their pores. He growled once, to warn them and amuse himself.

Iron chains bit into his wrists as one of the soldiers twisted his arm up and into his spine. Lord Rardove, baron of a small but strategically important fief on the Irish marches, stepped out of the shadows and made a slow circuit around the entangled foursome.

"Stop scaring my men, O'Melaghlin," he said, and deposited a disgusted glance on a soldier who'd backed up a pace at the feral growl. "Join with me and you'll be a rich man."

Finian laughed hoarsely. "Rich, is it? I'd have something different in mind than to be fettered in chains and thrown in a prison."

Rardove gave an exaggerated sigh. "You did not begin in chains, did you? We began in my chambers, with wine and meat. Now look at us."

Finian glanced around the small cell, where the stone walls wept rancid water from abovestairs and old blood from previous guests. "I agree. We've deteriorated."

A wan smile crossed the baron's face. "You will find me a most accommodating master."

"Master?" Finian spit the word from his mouth. Tall, ruddy-faced, blond, Rardove was the English ideal of noble handsomeness. Finian wanted to kick his teeth in.

"A hundred marks to you personally if you secure The O'Fáil's goodwill in this matter."

"Rardove," he said wearily, "ye've been here for twenty

years, and the land is dying under ye. The crops don't yield, your people die of ague, your cattle from murrain. Yer overlord can't stand ye, and neither can I. Why on God's good earth would I align with ye?"

The careful mask of calm covering the baron's visage cracked slightly. "Your king sent you here to parley, did he not?"

'Get inside the bulwark of Rardove Castle,' was actually what his king sent him here to do. Step one, accomplished.

"Parley?" Finian retorted. "Is that what ye call this?"

"I call this a necessary measure."

"My question is simple, Rardove, and has not changed since I knocked on yer door: what would ye get out of such an alliance?"

Step two: Ascertain what Rardove knew, how much he knew. And above all, stop him from learning any more.

The baron waved his hand through the air, a vague gesture. "Reduced threat of war on my borderlands. An end to an old feud." His voice slowed. "Perhaps, say, access to some of your Irish documents."

And with that, Finian had his answer: Rardove knew everything.

It was what he'd feared all along. Why would one of the most powerful lords in northern Ireland—powerful enough to seize these lands without his king's permission twenty years ago, then powerful enough to acquire the typically unforgiving Edward's royal dispensation afterward—now be begging for an alliance with the very people he'd conquered?

"Ye know about the dyes," Finian said slowly.

The mollusks, the Wishmés, had been forgotten for centuries, but their legends stretched back to the Romans. In a time when majesty was instilled primarily on the point of a sword, the indigo shade was allowed only for royalty, but it could make a man with the recipe richer than a king. Much richer. And more powerful. Disguise and rumor were half the game, and there was no disguise so rich, so stunning, so fueled by some inner blue-black fire, than the Wishmé indigo of the Western Edge. Ireland.

Rardove's lips stretched into an insincere grin. "I haven't the faintest notion what you're talking about."

Bastard.

The Wishmé dyes were truly the stuff of legend. Stunning. Rare.

Deadly.

Slowly, like climbing down a rope, Finian slid down the cords of his anger, fighting the almost overwhelming urge to smash Rardove's face with his boot. Then slit his throat.

"Does yer King Edward know?" he asked tightly.

Rardove smiled. "At the moment, you ought to worry more about me."

"Och, don't worry, *cruim*—inside, I'm shaking like a lamb," Finian retorted absently, his mind turning. The recklessness that would prompt Rardove to imprison an Irish nobleman on a mission of parley bespoke grave desperation. Urgency. Which wasn't surprising, because the Wishmés were generous with their perils.

As a color, they made a true dye that could drop a king to his knees. But that wasn't enough to make a lone English lord on the Irish marches goad his enemies with such abandon.

Weapons were. And the Wishmés could be made into a powder that would blow the roof off Dublin Abbey.

The question was, did Rardove know?

"Pretty, aren't they?" Finian said, testing. No use in subterfuge any longer.

"I do appreciate their hue," Rardove agreed, his tone musing. "But more, I like the way they explode."

Jesus wept.

Finian nodded coldly. "And yet, here I am. Ye might have the Wishmés, but ye don't know how to make the dye. Ye need the recipe. And someone who can read it."

Rardove smiled and spread his hands. "And thus, why should we not draw together, the Irish and I?"

Possibly because the Irish had lost the Wishmé recipe hundreds of years ago. Were, in fact, on a desperate hunt for the dye manual at this very moment. But Finian saw no pressing need to inform Rardove of that.

"You don't like the terms?" the baron inquired.

"Let's say I don't like ye."

"Tsk, tsk." Rardove shook his head. "You've to learn manners, O'Melaghlin, like all your kind." He snapped his fingers at the guards. A smelly hand reached up and grabbed a lock of Finian's hair, wrenching his head backward.

The sound of groans drifted in through chinks in the stone walls. Finian tried to turn but couldn't. It didn't matter. He knew who it was: O'Toole, one of his best men, whose leg had been broken in the attack.

Every member of his personal retinue knew this might turn out to be a death duty. Finian insisted each man choose it; no orders accompanied this mission except his own. But while his men may have been willing to sacrifice their lives for the good of Eire, Finian wasn't quite ready to give them up yet.

"And if I agreed?" he said quietly. Perhaps he could feign surrender, leave with his men.

"Why, you'd be free to go."

"And then?"

"Every day you don't return with an agreement from your king, I'll kill one of your men."

Barely able to see from the torturous angle, Finian freed his head with a savage jerk. He fixed the baron in a murderous glare, pausing barely a second to wonder on the wisdom of a God who would give a man so evil the face of a saint. "My men would come with me."

The baron shook his head in mock sadness. "You must agree I'd be a fool to release all of you, giving me no recompense were the terms of our agreement not upheld."

"I would agree ye're a fool."

Another thin, unwell smile lifted the baron's lips. "I think perhaps two a day," he mused, peering at his fingernails. "One in the dawn and one before bed. Like prayers."

"I'll sign the treaty," he said coldly. "Release my men."

"Release them? I think not. We sign papers, get witnesses, turn over the dye manual, all that messiness, before they leave."

Finian turned back to the wall in grim silence.

Rardove sighed. "Well, I didn't expect much wit from an Irishman." He turned to the guards. "Chain him to the wall and lay a few lashes against his back. We'll see if he thinks differently then."

They dragged him forward and shackled his hands in manacles dangling from huge metal braces bolted into the wall. A shield of dark hair fell forward as he dropped his head between his shoulders and braced his palms against the dank putrefaction, muscles contracted in readiness. He managed a brief prayer for survival, then one for vengeance, before the assault came.

It descended in screaming strips of leather, tearing open his flesh. Clamping down on his jaw, he scorned the agony, thinking only of what would happen to the spirits of his men if they heard him howling at Rardove's feet. Battered back, stomach, ribs; he'd been beaten into a bloody mess twice already. Once more couldn't matter much.

The assault was cut short on a shout from one of the baron's men, who came slipping down the moss-covered steps to the prisons.

"Good, my lord," panted the breathless courier. "Word has come. Senna de Valery arrives."

"Ah, my . . . betrothed." A pause. "Unshackle him."

Finian spared a brief prayer of thanks to the woman who had saved him from this beating.

"How long until she arrives?" he heard the baron ask. The guards began unlocking the heavy iron cuffs from his wrists.

"Soon, my lord."

"And?"

The simple but sinister question made Finian curl his lip in disgust. The soldiers jerked him around. A woman in Rardove's care? She wouldn't last a month.

"You will be disappointed in neither her face nor her form, my lord," the messenger said.

"Yes, I'd heard she's a pretty thing, if not so young. Twenty and five, if I recall."

The soldier flicked a glance at Finian, then looked away. "She has a great number of heavy ledgers with her, should that matter."

Rardove laughed. "It will not matter overly much, no. She will be . . . otherwise engaged."

She will be like a lamb to slaughter, thought Finian.

The baron turned back. "We'll have to continue our negotiations later, O'Melaghlin."

Finian shrugged. "We've more to say?"

"I do not. You do. There is a great deal for you to reconsider. I will enjoy watching it."

"I'll reconsider the terms of my mercy if ye release my men."

One graying, aristocratic brow inched up. "Mercy?"

Finian's slow grin stretched from ear to ear. "I can make yer death a quick one or slow, Rardove. The choice is yers."

The guards launched forward and flung him face-first to the ground. The weight of a heeled boot against his spine kept him pinioned as Rardove stepped over his legs and sighed.

"Would that these beatings worked," he said in a plaintive voice, "for I do appreciate their simplicity. But there you have it: they do not. One wonders whether it is due to the stubbornness or the stupidity of your people. Ireland is a strange land."

Finian shifted slightly, trying to ease away from the rock

gouging into his thigh. The guard's heel pressed down harder, and he stilled.

Rardove's voice drifted in from his right. "And Senna de Valery knows nothing of it, coming as she does from England."

Finian spared another brief thought for the woman. *To the slaughter.*

Scuffed leather boots paced an inch in front of his face then stopped, folding into thick leather wrinkles as the baron crouched beside him.

"I shall have to devise an educational welcome for her, don't you agree, Lord Finian? Perhaps a few Irish rebels dangling from the end of a rope?" He put his mouth close by Finian's ear. "I'll save you for the last."

Rage surged through him, red-hot and dangerous. He shoved his hips off the ground. The guard whose foot had been planted on his spine went somersaulting into the air. Finian swung around and kicked out with a boot, catching Rardove around his ankles. He went down hard. Finian leapt on top.

Four soldiers hauled him off and sent him flying through the air. He smashed into the wall, the back of his head hitting first. A knee in his stomach guaranteed he wouldn't rise again anytime soon, and one to his groin made him never want to anyhow.

The soldiers dragged him back to his feet. He stood, fighting the swaying tug of unconsciousness, his boots planted wide. Summoning what ebbing strength he could, he lifted his head and shook away the blood dripping into his eyes.

"Christ," Rardove snarled, his breath coming hard. "You're all savages." He jerked his head to the soldiers. "Make him pay for his insolence."

They did, and later, as the light from torches carried by the retreating guards faded to nothing, Finian lay spread-eagled on the floor of his cell, barely breathing. But he was thinking hard.

The Englishry were a plague, an infestation of stark naughts, Rardove being the best example of their descent into hell. Finian would not ally with them were he offered the lordship of *Tír na nÓg* in return. He hadn't wanted to come and even *feign* parley, but The O'Fáil wanted it done, and Finian could not refuse.

But now, even a feigned agreement with the worm would do nothing to save his men, only himself. Which was unacceptable. They would all leave, or none.

But either way, Rardove had best look to his back, for the Irish tribes were going to come down from the hills and besiege his castle from Lent until Yuletide. Then Finian himself would burn it to the ground, if he had to drag his bones out of the grave to do so.

Chapter 2

"This shouldn't take long," Senna de Valery murmured as she passed under the gates of Rardove Keep as the sun went down. It was four days after her ship had dropped anchor in Dublin and left her to her fate.

It had been a slow, long ride and Senna held her silence for most of its length, listening to the sounds of her new world: the host of riders accompanying her, creaking saddles, muffled voices, wind sighing over the Irish earth. Most of her time, though, was spent calculating how much money this business alliance would provide, if it came to fruition.

It was fresh hope, and that was practically priceless.

Forty sheep followed somewhere behind, the first installment of her bleating business proposition. Atop their sharp little hooves, her sheep carried the softest, most absorbent wool west of the Levant, a strain Senna had been perfecting for ten years, ever since she took over operations of the business from her father.

Wool was highly lucrative business. The fate of a dozen lesser crafts and a few minor princedoms rested on its commerce. Entire fairs in France were dedicated to the trade, sending coveted wool from England through the rich southern markets, straight to Jerusalem and beyond.

Senna wanted to nudge her way in to this market. If the wool being moved through the trade halls now fomented merchants' enthusiasm, Senna's strain would make them salivate. It was more absorbent, more silklike, more lightweight than any other wool out there, and required little mordanting to make dyes take.

She knew she had something special with her stinky, furry little sheep. She was simply running out of coin.

Rardove could give it to her. He had money that could save the business, the one Senna had spent the last ten years building up, while her father recklessly, relentlessly, inexhaustibly, gambled it away.

She stared hard ahead, trying to pierce the evening mists, eager for her first glance of Rardove Keep. Such purposeful peering had the added benefit of distracting her from the stench rising from her escort of burly, damp, leather-clad riders.

"Are the mists always so thick?" she asked the closest rider, pinching her nostrils as she moved closer to hear his reply.

He grunted and snorted back a sneeze. Or perhaps he said, "Most there's 'bout." Either reply was equally illuminating.

Senna lifted her eyebrows and said "Ahh," in a bright, cheerful voice, then reined a few paces upwind.

She could feel the eyes of the burliest soldier boring into her back. Balffe was his name, the captain of Rardove's guard. A block-chested warrior with a face like old sin, he hadn't taken his eyes off her for two days. And it wasn't leering, either; it was more like loathing, which was ridiculous, because she'd done nothing to him.

Yet. She passed him an evil glare over her shoulder. He glared back.

Never mind the soldiers. She turned forward. Lord Rardove was the only one who mattered. It was of no account that she'd heard he was lordly in his manner or fair as an angel in his face, because she wasn't in the market for a husband. She was in the market for a market.

As they drew near Rardove Castle, wraithlike villages began revealing themselves through the fog, first as pale splotches through the mist, then as dark splotches upon the earth. Small, huddling huts and waterlogged fields bespoke poverty, as did the thin villagers who stared sullenly as they passed.

She began immediately estimating the number of villagers per wattle-and-daub hut, calculating how much fatter and richer they would be if her scheme was successful. They might even become prosperous. She wished she had her abacus to hand. It was so much easier to tally numbers with the device.

It was so much easier to tally numbers than to calculate the goodness of building an alliance with a man who thought it wise to starve the people who fed him.

The horses' legs moved through low-lying evening mists as they passed under the portcullis into the outer bailey. The air was cool. Sunset flamed in fiery red sweeps across the horizon. Through the glaring haze, all she could discern was the single spike of the castle's tower and the offal dripping down the keep walls from the privy chutes.

As they passed under the gate, shouts rose from one of the dilapidated huts, followed by the sound of fists hitting flesh.

Well. First impressions can be deceiving, she reminded herself, nose pinched firmly in her veil, and she was determined to have this be successful. Get the contracts, build the flock, and she would be able to sustain herself. Never to rely on anyone else's inabilities again.

"A vision of my lord's justice, my lady," announced the knight at her side.

She pulled her mind from its reverie and glanced up to

behold a gallows. It took a moment to comprehend what she was seeing: a dog dangling from the end of a rope.

Her mouth dropped open. "My lord wreaks justice on *dogs?*" she whispered in horror, and crossed herself.

The soldier looked at her in confusion. "Lord Rardove stands yonder." He pointed to a broad-shouldered, blond-haired giant of a knight who stood gleaming in the setting golden light.

Wrenching her horrified gaze away, Senna looked to the condemned man standing beside him. His head was up, his face expressionless, next in line for the noose. She stared into his eyes and knew, with utter certainty, he was innocent of any crime.

Turning back to her prospective business partner's glittering eyes, Senna saw he knew it, too.

Her hand shot into the air. She pushed herself up in her stirrups, about to call out. The soldier at her side smacked her arm back down.

"Do not," he snapped, *"interrupt."*

A shiver of coldness unfurled inside her body, a thin banner of fear. She lifted her chin as they clopped dully across the cobbles and under the gate to the crumbling inner bailey. She barely noticed being helped out of the saddle and propelled toward the mossy round tower.

"Rardove Keep, my lady," said the knight as he escorted her up the covered stairwell.

"Yes, I see," she murmured as he ushered her over the threshold into a small antechamber. A maid hurried up. It was dim inside, damp and echoing. Cold. A long, shadowed corridor stretched away into the distance. There might be anything at the end. Kitchens. More stairs. A dragon.

Swallowing thickly, Senna fumbled with the brooch fastening her cloak.

"Welcome to Rardove Keep, my lady."

She jerked her head back up at the sound of the voice.

"I am John Pentony, Lord Rardove's seneschal."

Shoving back the hood of her cape, she peered through the dim light to find the speaker. Tall, thin, and gaunt, he was a ghostly, balding figure with almost lidless eyes, moving toward her.

She tried to step forward, but her feet were rooted to the ground, her tongue to the roof of her mouth. He pierced her with an unreadable gaze, then a smile creaked over his face, like a hinge unused to the movement. The maid blinked, her fingers frozen in a nervous twist before her waist. The jagged smile stayed on the seneschal's face and for half a minute they all stood, staring in silence.

Then his cold eyes marked a slow slice downward to the maid. She half curtsied and slipped between him and the doorframe. "I'll see to your rooms, mistress," she whispered.

The steward's eyes were washed of emotion as he turned back. "We are pleased you have arrived."

"Yes, I—I thank you." She flicked her gaze around the now empty hall. "We?"

The steward paused. "Your arrival was earlier than expected."

"Oh, well, not so early as to miss . . ." She faltered. "To miss what I saw at the gallows."

Empty, ashen eyes appraised her, level and flintlike. "They were Irish rebels, my lady."

"The dog?" she queried sharply, against her much better judgment. "The dog was an Irish rebel? He looked more Welsh to me."

One almost invisible eyebrow arched up, forming a ladder of small, upside-down crescent moon shapes across the steward's high, smooth forehead. Then he looked over her shoulder and nodded at someone or something in the shadows behind her.

A huge mastiff, Senna imagined glumly, growling and

slathering, waiting for the newest arrival to step wrongly and be thrown to him for dinner. That shouldn't take long.

A stone stairway disappeared into the gloomy distance behind Pentony's angular figure. Through the gray miasma of smoke and stale air hovering in the hall, the maid was returning, her slim shoulders pushing through the fog. In truth, the castle was a blurry echo of energy, reverberating in dim, cold pulses.

She shook off a shiver and turned back. "Where will I be meeting with Lord Rardove?" she asked briskly. "I have the account books here." She indicated a small chest by her feet, which the soldier had carried in.

"Lord Rardove asked that you be shown directly to the mollusk fields."

She drew back. "To the *what?*" She'd heard exactly what he said.

"The mollusk fields. The beaches."

"I know nothing about mollusks. Or their beaches." Which wasn't precisely true. Or true at all.

He regarded her somberly. "They're where the mollusks live."

"Why ought I visit them?"

Her high-pitched, startled responses finally gave the wraith-steward pause. "We were under the impression you knew something of dyeing, my lady."

She clutched her fingers to her collar. Another opening closed off. "I am here to discuss a joint venture in wool. I know nothing of dyeing," she assured him, in what she hoped were firm tones. Convincing tones.

"And yet, your mother—"

"I am nothing like my mother," she said sharply. "I know nothing of dyers or dye making." My, she was telling a lot of lies of a sudden.

Pentony's figure, already freed from excess movement, stilled further. "I will inform my lord of that."

"Please do," Senna replied in her haughtiest tone, perfected in dozens—nay, hundreds—of meetings with merchants and shippers and abbots of fair-towns. In general, it was intended to subdue anyone thinking bargaining with a woman meant easy terms. In this case, it hid belly-chilling fear.

Although why made no sense. She'd made no mention of being a dyer. Heaven forbid. Hard to believe anyone even knew that remote history.

It had nothing whatsoever to do with her. This was a business arrangement about wool. It had nothing to do with smelly little shellfish that, if crushed and mixed just so, by a true craftswoman, could create the most astonishing, wondrous shade of indigo—

Nothing whatsoever to do with her.

"Tell Mary"—Pentony's gaze indicated the trembling maidservant—"or myself of any needs you have."

With another slight bow, he turned to leave.

"And Lord Rardove . . . ?" she couldn't help asking, hating the quiver in her voice.

Angular ashen eyes glanced back to her, containing the expected chill. It was the faint glimmer of a genuine smile that surprised her.

"You will no doubt be joyful to hear he is to return soon."

The enigmatic Pentony left, cricking his neck to pass under the low archway, and Senna let the maid hurry her out a far door. She barely paid attention, instead enjoying a few moments of pointless rumination about Rardove's apparent proclivities for torture and very thin attendants, and what that might mean for her.

And the unsettling knowledge that someone thought she knew something of dye making.

They reached a small building.

She had her life's mission, and it was not about getting her skin discolored. It was not about coming in after days spent in a dye hut, sniffing out the trail of some new concoction that would create green the shade of ice, or a new red the hue of hot blood, with hair wild, huge smiles, and hugs and—

Nothing whatsoever to do with her. That was her mother's mad passion. Not hers. Senna had no passions. She had a business.

"The dye hut, my lady," the maid said, and swung a door open.

Senna came out of her reverie with a start. "Oh, no. I am not—I cannot—"

She froze and looked around her, peering at the trappings of a nightmare.

Chapter 3

The room was large and essentially empty but for one long wooden board laid across three trestles, creating a table like that in a great hall. Only this one didn't have trenchers and saltcellars on it. It had vessels and pots filled with bugs and mosses and drying seaweed.

Tall, narrow urns were scattered around the room beside squat, tublike clay containers, filled with dried flower blossoms and mosses—lichens picked gently off trees, their long spindly fingers stretching up over the lip of the urns. Roots. Tiny bugs, died and dried. Crushed shells. Light gray iron salts and brick red madder. Scales and sieves, and mortars for grinding. Only these did not grind flour. They were for making dyes.

Senna backed away, her hand at her throat. The room smelled like an old summer memory, rustling-soft and comforting. Potent, like garlic cooked too long at the bottom of an iron pot. Memories of Mama at her work, crafting dyes, but always a soft smile for Senna whenever she crept in to sit beside her. Mama's hair, braid coming loose and trailing down her back like a red stream, her cool hand on Senna's small, hot head.

Senna's breath came short and clipped, little choppy waves overtop an ocean of awfulness.

Her hand went unconsciously to the small, loose pages tucked into a pouch at her side. The only thing left of her mother's, this packet of letters. Senna had given up trying to recall her mother—given up wanting to—twenty years earlier, at the moment she'd understood what had happened: she'd been abandoned.

It beggared the imagination, then, the cost of understanding why these penned notes and sketches of her mother's were the only things she'd brought with her. And the abacus, of course. *That* held no surprises.

It struck Senna now that perhaps she ought not to have sent her small, armed escort back to England. But it might take weeks, a month, to complete the arrangements with Rardove, and she paid by the day for such men. She'd not even brought a maid; but then, that was because she didn't have one. Not anymore.

Even so, what good could her small escort have done? How many soldiers had she seen patrolling the walls? Far too many to resist whatever Rardove might wish to do.

Do not be foolish, she chastised herself. Foolish to think Rardove would endanger this highly lucrative business venture. The trunk of gold and silver coins she'd espied under the trestle table was not so valuable as the deal she was offering him: wool.

Still, such logic did little to allay the anxiety crawling through her belly. She started gnawing on her fingernails, her mind engaged in terrified pirouettes.

"Mistress Senna?"

She spun to the door, teeth at her thumbnail.

"Lord Rardove has returned. He wishes to see you in the hall."

Her hand fell limply to her side.

* * *

Muted revelry drifted up to the small bedchamber Senna had been shown to. A small, thinly cushioned bed mattress hung by straps of leather from the aging bedposts, for support. Two armless chairs, a table and a fireplace bespoke comfort, but in reality it was a small, unkempt room smelling faintly of rot.

This would not be her room for long, so it hardly mattered. She took a deep breath and ran her hand over her tunic. It was dark green with a mist green overtunic, designed to fit her upper body snugly. Ten years old, it had been worn for every contract signing she'd done in that time, and was starting to show the strain. The elbows were worn and the stitching at the waist and wrists badly frayed. Embroidery of pale hues bound the worst offenders, but still, it was old. Plain. Perfect.

A wave of raucous laughter came rolling up the stairs. Bawdy curses rode within like flotsam. "Are they always so . . . jubilant?"

The maid met her eyes. "Always, miss."

The maid stitched the thin sleeves tight, then pinned her hair up, creating a soft but complicated pile atop her head. She draped a veil of the palest green over the concoction and corded it with a slender silver circlet, and they stared together at Senna's dull reflection in a small, polished metal handheld mirror.

"You look as fine as a queen," avowed the maid, then added, a bit less firmly, "if you are a bit pale."

"I am as wan as an undyed tablecloth," Senna agreed sourly.

No matter her looks. This was about business. And that is what she did best.

She picked up the most recent ledger of accounts, cradled it in her arm like a babe, and swept down to the great hall, ignoring the way her breath came speeding out in unsteady little gusts. She had a great deal of experience keeping such panic at bay. She would do so now as well. Everything was manageable, given time.

She lifted her chin, crossed the threshold of the riotous hall, and froze like ice.

The room was smoky and crowded. A burst of laughter exploded from one of the crowded tables. A barely clad woman tumbled off a soldier's lap and the drunken group roared again. Arcs of mead curled into the air as their tankards crashed down on the rough-hewn tabletops. One of the coarse, leather-clad barbarians spit something wet and copious into the rushes, then leaned down to haul the woman up by her elbow.

Senna sucked in a breath. Numbers. Think of numbers. The number of coins Rardove was offering (a thousand French *livres*). The number of months left to pay off her shipping debts (not a one). The number of years she'd waited in an empty hall for someone, anyone, to walk through it and save her.

To her relief, a knight approached and, extending his arm, nodded toward the dais. Curious but detached faces watched, and the hum of activity dimmed as she passed. Blanching under the unfamiliar scrutiny, her step faltered. Angry with herself, she jerked on the arm imprisoned in her escort's grip, digging his ribs in the process. The knight grunted and released her.

Lord Rardove stood talking with his men at the far end of the dais. Even facing away, he was an imposing figure. Tall and wide-shouldered, he wore a midnight blue shirt and chausses that burned a dark background against his blood red tunic: the colors of Rardove. One hand went to the sword belted at his waist, toying idly with the hilt. Rardove might be nearing fifty, but any gray hairs were undetectable amidst the blond. He looked every inch the warrior lord.

She swallowed a ball of fear. Perhaps it was the Irish warriors shackled on the floor in front of the dais that made him puff out his chest and strut so. Please, God, let it not be for her.

Her nerve liquefied in her gut at the exact moment Rardove turned to her.

"Mistress Senna," was all he said, and his gaze held hers for half a moment, in a perfectly civil pause. But to Senna, it felt as if he were ripping apart her gown, assessing her like a mount, deciding if she was worth the cost.

Then a smile cracked the surface of his handsome face, and it was as if a window had splintered. He went into motion, crossing the dais.

"My deepest apologies I could not greet you myself earlier," he said, his voice rich and low with chivalrous smoothness. He took her fingertips. "I shall have to make it up to you."

She fought the crazed urge to slip her hand free and run screaming from the room. "There is no need, my lord," she murmured.

"I hope you have been made comfortable." He released her fingers. "Your trip was pleasant?"

"Quite." She tried to smile back. "The mists are thick."

He nodded. "Ireland." He spread out his hands, palms up. The smallest smudge marred his broad hands. It was dark red. Like dried blood. "Ireland holds many things behind a veil."

Her smile became more genuine. If he had the sensitivity to speak suchly, mayhap 'twas not all bad. Mayhap the Irishry *were* rebels, as Pentony said, unlawfully defying their overlord. Mayhap she could engage in business with this man without too much trouble—

"I hear you do not wish to see the mollusks."

Her smile faltered. "Nay, my lord. 'Tis just, I do not know that business."

"Is it not yours?"

Her smile collapsed entirely. "No, my lord."

Rardove said nothing.

"I deal in wool."

"Oh, I am interested in your wool, Senna. Quite. Exceedingly."

No sense of relief followed these softly spoken words. Quite the opposite: a shiver walked down her spine. So, he was a harrier, was he? One who preyed on smaller creatures. She had had ample experience with such men. Squaring her shoulders, she said firmly, "Well good, my lord. Just so we understand, then. I deal in wool. Not dyes."

"That is too bad, Senna. For you."

"My lord?"

"I need a dye-witch."

Chapter 4

The shiver became a cold chill down Senna's spine. 'Dye-witch,' people had said for a thousand years, as a way to insult. Or, depending on the whims of the local parish or lord, as a way to get a person killed. But, for those who knew such things, 'dye-witch' was a term of respect bordering on awe.

Senna so desperately wished she was not one of the ones who 'knew such things.'

"Oh, dear, my lord," she said briskly, "I believe there has been a misunderstanding. I am here about the wool." She extended the account ledger in her arm.

His gaze lowered briefly, then came back up. "There is no misunderstanding, Mistress de Valery. I have the Wishmé mollusks. I need the dye they create."

"Oh, my lord, the Wishmés are legend. Only legends." Ones she recalled her mother telling her by firelight. "Nothing about them is true—"

"They are real, Senna. Your mother's treatise clearly outlines that."

She practically recoiled. "My mother's *treatise?*"

Her mother? What did Rardove know of her mother? And what did her mother know of *treatises?* She'd known nothing but immoderation. Overweening fervor. Passion. She left the family because of it, ran away when Senna was five. Left Senna in charge of a one-year-old brother and a father descending into the vortex of heartbreak and gambling that had been slowly killing him all the years since.

She'd left it all to Senna and never come back.

Her mother knew nothing of documents, nothing about managing things. Corraling and harnessing the frightening forces of the world. She knew only about running away. And she *certainly* knew nothing about *documents*.

That was Senna's realm.

"And Senna?"

She jerked her attention back.

"The Wishmés are real. They are valuable. And I need you to make them into a dye for me."

She clutched the account ledger to her chest, feeble armor. She could not make dyes. They could offer her *chests* of gold that would save the business forty times over, and she would still not be able to dye. She'd spent her life avoiding it.

The question was: what would the stranger before her do when he understood that?

At the moment, he was simply watching her, but with a hawklike intensity that did not bode well for creatures smaller than he. Senna figured she would come to his chin. In slippers.

"Have you a suggestion on how to proceed, Senna?" His voice was calm, as if they were discussing the menu for the evening meal. Perhaps . . . her.

She wiped her free hand on her skirt. 'Twas time to prove herself reasonable enough not to be splayed and boiled as a first course.

"Have you attempted dog whelk? Or mayhap woad. Its colors are deep and rich, well suited to the fibers. Surely it can produce what you are looking for."

By the look on his face, Rardove did not agree.

"Sir, 'tisn't possible for any person with a will to craft the Wishmé dyes. Only a very certain few can—according to legend," she added hurriedly, then tacked on, even more hurriedly, "which I know only as a result of being in an associated business, you understand, and hearing such things. But even if I wished to dye, I could not do it, just so." She snapped her fingers. "Such craftsmanship takes years of study. I cannot fathom why you think I can make them—"

He snapped his fingers back, right in front of her nose, then grabbed her hand, overturned it, and pressed his thumb against her inner wrist, over the blue veins that ran beneath her skin.

"Your blood makes me think it, Senna," he said in a low voice. "They say 'tis in the blood."

Her mouth fell open. Terrified, she yanked on her hand. He released her.

Continuing to back up, she put her hand on the edge of the dais table for support, ledger clutched to her chest. Fast, frantic chills shot through her, like small, darting arrows, poking holes in her composure.

"Sir." She swallowed. "Sir." She was repeating herself. That could not be good. She never even quoted prices more than once. "Sir, you must understand—"

"I understand. You do not." He turned so his back was to the hall, reached into his tunic, and pulled something out. "This is what the Wishmés can do."

That was all he said, all he needed to say. Everything else came from the scrap of dyed fabric in his hand. Slowly, she set the ledger down and reached for it.

It was . . . stunning. Luminous, a kind of deep blue she'd never seen before, so brilliant she almost had to shield her eyes, as if it were emitting light.

Dog whelk could not create this. Neither could moss, or madder, or woad, or anything on Earth. This was straight from God.

"'Tis beautiful," she murmured, running her fingers almost reverently over the edge of the dyed weave. "On my wool, it would be something the world has never seen."

An odd look crossed his face. "Where will you start?" he asked, his voice hoarse.

She moved her hands in a helpless gesture. "I do not know."

But she did. A churning hot spot in the center of her chest seemed to be actually pulling her back to the dye hut, to the room with mortars and pestles, the lichen and bark that could be magicked into things of such beauty.

Just like her mother. Shame sizzled thin, hot rivers of self-loathing down her throat.

He pulled at the fabric in her fingertips. She let it go and pushed back her shoulders. "Lord Rardove, I deal in wool. That is what we discussed in our correspondence."

"Indeed. Just so."

"Just so, then. I am here to strike a bargain that will be lucrative for us both. Perhaps if I show you some of the accounts I brought with me, you will see the benefits. Or," she added, not liking the way he was looking at her and not the ledgers, "perhaps you would prefer to simply reconsider the arrangement, and I can hie myself back to the ship."

"Or perhaps we ought to take care of this other little matter straight away." Rardove gestured toward the shadows.

Pentony emerged from within them somewhere—*He is a wraith,* Senna decided—with a scroll of parchment in hand. Her response spoke to her shattered emotional state though, for upon sight of the steward's cadaverous figure, Senna smiled. He looked at her somberly, without a hint of recognition. She might be a table cover. Or a blot of wax on one. A mess.

She looked back to Rardove. "Other matter, my lord?"

He gestured impatiently to Pentony, who scanned the document in his hands, then began reading parts of it aloud.

"Senna de Valery, merchant of wool . . . Lambert, lord of Rardove, on the Irish marches . . . union in wedlock . . . banns posted . . ."

Senna's mouth dropped open and she almost fell to her knees.

Chapter 5

"That is not possible!"

He looked at her with something approaching mild curiosity. "No? And yet"—he pointed to the parchment—"here is the document, and"—he moved his fingertip her direction—"there are . . . you."

"Oh, no, this is not *possible.*"

"So you say."

Her mind spun away from coherent thought. This was madness. And yet . . . And yet, forced betrothals happened all the time. Simply not to her.

She'd spent the last ten years ensuring no one could do anything to her ever again. She'd built a business, created a world, where she would never be beholden again. Never need again. Where she was in complete control.

It was crumbling to the ground.

She could feel her heart beating, hard in her ears. *Thud, thud, thud.*

"I will not sign," she said dumbly.

He blew out a small breath, an impatient sound. "Certainly you will." He drew close enough for her to smell the leather of his hauberk. It creaked with newness.

"But why?" she asked, almost in a whisper. "Why marriage?"

"To ensure you stay. Or rather," he added in a fit of clarification, "to ensure my rights in retrieving you, were you to decide to leave." He took a step closer. His gaze slid slowly down her skirts. "And you must know, Senna, you are very beautiful."

"I—I cannot. Make dyes." It was fully a whisper now.

"Have faith." His body was almost touching hers. "You can do anything I tell you to do."

She smelled sweat and drink, ale perhaps. He lifted a hand to brush by her cheek. She jerked away. He stilled, then very deliberately rested one knuckle against her jaw. She stood rock still, but a strand of hair by her cheek trembled.

He smiled, very faintly. The moment stretched on. Sweat began to dribble down her chest. She had to actually will her gaze to stay on his, the muscles in her eyes straining to break free. She started to feel dizzy.

But something about the whole strange, silent encounter seemed to improve Rardove's humor, because he smiled. Taking her by the hand, he pressed his lips to her skin.

Senna stared at the back of his head, bent over her hand, stunned and reeling. She was saved the need for a response by a soldier approaching the dais.

"My l—lord?"

The baron paused, mouth still over her hand. "What is it?"

"We found a second contingent of Irishmen. Small, like O'Melaghlin's. Headed south. They appeared to be scouting out villages along the way."

Rardove's body stiffened. His pale eyes were blank as they passed hers and settled on the soldier, who appeared ready to empty his bladder in fear.

"Where is Balffe?" Rardove asked softly.

"He sent me, my lord . . . to tell you . . . we captured one, but there's something afoot. Balffe said to"—he gulped audibly—"to remind you we're not prepared to withst—"

"You've captured one?" the baron interrupted.

The man-at-arms nodded. The iron rings of his hauberk glittered dully in the firelight.

"Question him. Find the others."

"Aye, my lord."

"Then kill him and send his head back to The O'Fáil in a chest, to show what I *am* prepared for."

The soldier nodded and hurried out of the hall. Senna stared after, disbelieving her senses. This was lunacy. She could not survive here. She wouldn't last a month. A week. Another *hour.*

She slowly withdrew her hand from Rardove's.

He levered his gaze up to her face. "It doesn't do to let small insurrections grow into large ones, does it, Senna?"

It was probably for the best she was struck completely mute. She shook her head, her gaze riveted on his chin. An act of will made her lift her eyes to his. He watched her in silence. Predator. She felt like a creature *much* smaller than he, and the sensation made her angry.

"We understand one another, Senna?" he asked quietly.

She nodded.

Rardove gestured to the dais table. "Be seated, then, and indulge yourself. The meat was slaughtered just this day."

He barely inclined his head and a knight materialized at her side. Strong arms propelled her inexorably toward the table, where she seated herself and fussed with her skirts, her breath coming short and shallow.

The trestle before her was heavily laden. The scents of warm duck and butter with cooked greens wafted into her nostrils, but the thought of eating made her ill.

A goblet of wine was placed at her hand. *This I will drink,* she decided, desperate for something in her belly. She inhaled the ruby liquid, but the rich color belied its true nature. It was bitter and greasy, and she grimaced as she swallowed.

Murmured conversations buzzed through the hall, punctuated by bursts of gruff laughter, knives banged against wooden plates, and scuffling boots. She became aware of the prisoners standing shackled on the floor in front of the raised dais. Chains creaked as they shifted in their irons. The baron stood at the edge of the dais, talking to his guards and one of the prisoners below them.

Senna glanced down at the doomed Irish warrior standing with chains around his wrists and ankles. His beaten face held a handsomeness that could not be disguised by the bruises.

High cheekbones and full lips. Dark, dark eyes. Her gaze trailed down. Firm, contoured neck, broad shoulders, long, tangled hair. His muscular legs extended beneath the Irish *léine,* the short tunic he wore, and his feet were planted firmly on the rush-covered floor. Well-defined arms were folded over his chest, his shoulders thrust back defiantly.

But, most captivating of all, at the edges of his lips danced a smile. His mouth moved, and the baron scowled. The Irish grin grew.

Although nearly motionless, this warrior emanated energy and life. The intelligence and nobility brimming in his eyes made her want to cry.

No. This was not right. Nothing in this sordid castle was right and she wanted no part of it.

"Eat, Senna," Rardove threw over his shoulder.

And with that, something inside her snapped like the thin, frozen edge of a pond that has borne too heavy a boot, too many times.

She lifted her chin up the smallest bit. "No."

Chapter 6

Finian turned, his brows up, the corners of his mouth creased down. The angles of the Englishwoman's face were thrown into sharp relief by candlelight dancing through the hall. Oil lamps hung from the walls and amber rushlight glinted off her hair, making her glow in a gold-red halo.

This was the lamb?

He was impressed. Indeed, the entrance of the emerald angel was noteworthy enough, sufficient to draw his attention from the pain of his wounds and the baron's gloating. When she removed her hand from Rardove's sweaty grip, he'd been even more intrigued.

That she would now gainsay him was worth an exchange of shocked glances between him and the other Irish prisoners.

Certainly, here was bravado deserving of respect. It would not go well for her, of course, but that did not diminish the act, and was not what he would have predicted from the English, woman or man, foul race that it was. But here was spirit and defiance. And great beauty.

And she was no lamb. She was a *bhean sidhe,* glowing fire and defiance and wielding her disdain with a quiet dignity that made Finian blink. Twice.

How could God, in His infinite wisdom, have given the

worm Rardove a thing of such value? This must be due the devil.

But she was surely an angel, and seemed of immense value. Particularly as she stepped off the precipice of safety and plunged headlong into peril.

"No."

The low sound wafted to the edge of the dais. Rardove turned so slowly the pungent scent of a freshly extinguished wick could have dissipated by the time his angry eyes locked on hers. The entire room went still, English soldiers and Irish warriors alike.

He clucked his tongue. "Ah, Senna," he said softly. His gaze held no softness though. He could have shoved her backward off the dais with it.

Senna returned the glare, her eyes unwavering. Her heart, on the other hand, thundered a wild beat. This would never do. In a moment she would be lost to the terror wrapping around her heart. And that was unacceptable.

The backs of her knees hit the front of the seat and the bench jerked backward as she rose. She stepped out from behind the trestle table, her fingers still wrapped around the wine goblet's stem.

The scenes of her life unraveled in a flash before her eyes, but her contrary slippered feet propelled her forward. She was mad, she knew that now, and doomed as well. But whatever was to be would be, because she could be nothing other than what she was.

"I bid you a simple enough thing," the baron said. "Enjoy the bounty of my table."

"No." Again her soft voice wafted over the heads of the bloody warriors lined up four-deep on the floor.

His eyebrows shot up, then a sinister grin slid across his handsome features. "I see you've no aversion to the *wine*."

As if yanked by strings, she thrust out her arm. Holding the goblet in the air between them, she looked into the baron's eyes and slowly overturned the cup. Like a red flood tide, wine splashed across the floor into a huge crimson puddle.

Rardove's jaw dropped. Then his face contorted and he strode across the dais until he was only inches away from Senna. His shoulders blocked her view and she could smell him—sweat, leather, anger. His breath lifted her hair in small, hot drafts.

"That wine was precious," he said in a seething voice.

"As is my signature on a marriage deed, my lord—as precious as my blood."

He angled his head slightly to the side, as if considering her point. "Your blood is easily spilt, Senna, that is all," he replied, then reached out and smacked her backhanded across the face.

She reeled, cutting short a cry. Grabbing her hand, he yanked her forward again. "Do we understand one another?"

"I understand you, my lord," she said quietly. "But I fear you do not comprehend me a'tall." She pulled her hand free from his.

The anger seemed to wash out of him. A smile more terrifying than an outright assault spread across his face. Taking her chin between his fingers, he lifted her face. Faint blond stubble covered a chin that was not so square on close examination. He had a wide, sweeping forehead, hazel eyes webbed with thin red lines, and a well-shaped mouth that emitted such vileness it made her sick.

"If I need burrow into your very bones, Senna, you *will* heed me." His fingers tightened and his thumb stroked her cut lip in an idle, threatening caress. "If this be your insurrection, it stops now. Do you hear me?"

She tried to turn her chin away, but his grip was stronger. "I hear you, my lord," she said, her voice trembling.

He considered her a moment. "No, Senna. I don't think you do."

Without warning, he slammed her backward into the wall. She rebounded against the rock. He took her wrist and lifted it up into the space between their faces.

"Is this the hand you refused me?"

Low-pitched and sinister, the question froze her blood. She clamped down on her swollen lip to keep from screaming in terror and pushed her cheek flat against the stone.

He yanked her forward and slammed her hand down onto the dais tabletop. "You will learn right quick, Senna, *that I shall be heeded in all things!*"

This last boomed in a deafening roar. Grabbing a heavy, flat nutcracker, he smashed the instrument down on her hand.

Pain ripped a blazing path through her body, flashing out to every nerve ending God had created. She slumped to the ground at his feet, huddled and whimpering and fighting tears.

The Irishman lunged for the dais. His roar was silenced as the heavy chains jerked him backward and flung him to the ground. A soldier dropped on top of him, a knee wedged in his chest. Cursing, the soldier smashed an elbow into the Irishman's jaw, then hauled him back to his feet.

The disturbance drew a brief, furious glance from Rardove, before he swung back around. "I shed your blood now," he lectured in a calm voice from above, "to teach you the wisdom of heeding me in the future. I do not wish to maim your beautiful mouth, but if it causes more trouble, be you assured, I will." He dropped to a knee and bent close to her ear. "*Do you think I understand you now, Senna?*"

She sat perfectly still against the wall, clutching her hand to her neck. *Silence,* she thought wildly. *No more. Not tonight.*

So she nodded.

And that simple, surrendering effort took up more space inside her than all the losses all these years, more than she'd ever thought to hold inside her flesh and bones and blood. She was totally empty now. Filled with emptiness.

Rardove gestured to a servant. Gentle hands helped her from the floor. Her fingers throbbed, each wave a fierce, pounding hammer. Fighting the whimpers that *would* rise in her throat, she unfolded her body, her head held high. A length of hair wobbled free and dangled by her cheekbone.

At the far end of the hall a scuffle broke out and a courier dashed up the steps of the dais.

"My lord! A message has come."

The baron herded the messenger into a corner. They spoke in rapid whispers, Rardove's irritable voice rising occasionally to allow bits of the conversation to drift over those nearby.

"Curse the Irish!" Some faint reply came from another member of the group. A series of curses floated away into hushed tones, and the muted gathering waited. Finally the baron turned.

"Continue with the feasting, and take the prisoners back to the cellars. Except for the O'Fáil councilor. Lead him to my office after the others have been quartered." He leaned to Senna. "You will spend the night in the dye hut, or in my chambers. Either way, you will be working. Tonight, the choice is yours."

Without a backward glance, he disappeared from the hall.

Senna tottered sideways a step. The front of her skirts bespoke violence: a vivid ruby trail screamed across the emerald fabric. She walked to the long dais table, hyperventilating with pain, fear, and anger.

Anger won out.

She reached for a corner of the long table linen. The servants watched with wrinkled brows and wringing hands as she wrapped it around her palm twice and tugged.

One stepped up to her. He cleared his throat. "May I help bandage your wound?"

"No, thank you." She smiled sweetly, then jerked the tablecloth off the table with all her might.

Plates went spinning into the air and a tower of fruit and sweets tumbled to the ground. A large oval platter holding an eel dish spun around twice, looked as though it might stay centered on the table, then skittered off, joining the rest of the mess on the floor. The clamor and racket thundered through the hall, drowning the incredulous gasps and shouts of the gathering.

The jug of red wine, oddly, stayed put, heavy enough to withstand the quake.

"Praise God, my lord's wine is safe," she murmured. "'Tis a most precious spirit," she said.

Silence reigned. The servants, soldiers, and liege men gaped. Jaws dropped, heavy boots clomped on the ground as the men shifted nervously. What to do now? The baron had left no orders, although his last actions were clear enough indicators of how he planned to treat any disobedience on the part of his new "wife."

Still, watching her ramrod-straight back, somehow not a single man was man enough to approach her. A few servants scurried to pick up the downed items, and another ran to get water.

No one said a word to Senna.

The soldiers, after a spellbindingly long moment of indecision, went on with their task of rounding up the battered Irish warriors and leading them away.

Senna wrapped her bleeding hand in the cloth, leaving seven yards of fabric to trail out behind her, ridiculously excessive, as she walked to the window, a narrow, bailey-facing slit set at shoulder height in the wall.

She pushed open the shutter a hairsbreadth. Her hand throbbed with a fiery pain that made her breathing erratic. Blood seeped through the thick cloth. She was weary beyond words, and exhausted by the cold, hopelessness inside.

How had things come to this pass? All her efforts, to this end? It made one consider whether one ought to exert effort at all. Things went as they were meant to go, no matter how one fought against it. Destiny. Blood. Rardove had been right after all.

She lifted her unsteady hand to sweep back the hair that had escaped from the pins. Her gaze traveled dully over the room. It was arrested by the Irish warrior, the man whose eyes she'd met earlier, the one who had leaped to save her, a new seepage of blood his only reward.

Their gazes locked, and he smiled, a crooked, satisfying smile. Dark blue eyes sucked her into their depths. A surge of blood warmed her face. But more than that, the coldness inside her belly warmed, and the sounds of the hall faded away, so that the world became peaceful for a moment.

He lifted his head and jutted his square, stubbly chin. His smile grew, became mischievous, and he lifted his head another inch.

Senna almost smiled back. What was he saying?

Saying? Why would he be saying anything?

He pushed back his shoulders ever so slightly.

"Dear God!" She started in soft exclamation, her skin prickling. He'd read her thoughts. *'Don't surrender';* his silent message came as loudly as the baron's bellow had.

She glanced involuntarily to the door Rardove had exited by, then back to the beaten warrior. He inclined his head the briefest inch.

I will not give up. Chills raced across her skin. So be it. She would not surrender, not in this way at least. Not if this doomed warrior could attend to her need in the midst of his misery, and offer succor.

She pushed back her shoulders as he had done and met his eyes, acknowledging receipt of his gift.

* * *

Finian grinned. As if he hadn't known. As if he hadn't seen her head rise, watched the sparkle dance back into her eyes. As if he hadn't known the moment her drowning spirit was buoyed up.

And as he was led away, it gladdened him to know he'd had a part in keeping the flame lit in some small way, flickering in the beautiful woman he'd never met that night. He looked back, hoping for another glance of the angel fighting for her dignity in the slop of Rardove's hall.

He saw her eyes widen and, following her gaze, spied a knife lying among the litter the servants were cleaning up. His eyebrow lifted. She chose a dangerous route to rebellion. Then again, he decided, it seemed she would prove capable on most any path.

If the way were cleared. Would she be able to get her hands on the blade?

He was torn away from these musings by his captor's rough wrench, and shoved forward a few feet. Their progress was halted by a skirmish at the door leading out of the hall and the guard stopped, waiting for it to clear. Finian craned his head around again.

The chestnut-haired lady was bent over the ground, picking up a platter. She set it on the table and smiled at a nearby servant. This time his eyebrows almost met his hairline. Well, he hadn't expected her to help clean up.

Glancing around surreptitiously, she slipped the razor-sharp dagger into her pocket.

He grinned as he was hauled away.

Chapter 7

Throughout the castle, the story was passed mouth to ear. Soldiers and maidservants, livery staff and merchants on deliveries, guards and prisoners, everyone heard of Senna's defiance.

Foolish, they said. Reckless. Unwise. And in the end, hopeless.

But Senna was not without hope. Nor was she without a plan.

She appeared the next morning, utterly transformed. Docile, compliant, quiet and meek, she appeared on her betrothed's arm soon after the bells rang Prime, and seated herself quietly at the dais table.

Rardove grinned from ear to ear. "Eat," he laughed in a bellowing sort of way, gesturing to the hall.

The gathering shifted uncomfortably. Senna was a bruised and battered wreck. Her smashed fingers were tightly wrapped, but the cloth was stained a pale rose color, the dainty shade belying the violence of the wound seeping below. Her lip was swollen, her cheek black-and-blue. Her hair was pulled back softly from her face, but it was hard to miss the angry red line around her neck. Almost as if she'd been choked.

But whatever the castle prophets said as they stood around the wash buckets that dawn, Senna had hope and a plan.

But, as she stood over Rardove's prone, drugged body, where he'd fallen on the bed after leading her to his chamber, she wasn't sure it was the *best* plan, but as it was the only one to hand, it held great allure.

Had Rardove no notion how many uses some of these herbs had, aside from mixing agents for dyes? And he'd left them all within her reach.

For the rest of the day he would have terrible stomach cramps, and be in and out of a drugged state. Come morn, he would be enraged.

By then, though, she would be gone.

She meant to explore the castle from bailey to dog pens today. She would befriend every person, overcome every fear, crush every opposition, and find a way to the prisons. Then she would free the Irish rebel who'd given her strength in a moment of weakness and have him get her to the Dublin quay.

She had hope, determination, and a plan. What she was running out of was time.

Senna's younger brother, William, stared at the paper in his hand. "When?" He looked up at the servant, who cleared his throat before replying.

"Tomorrow 'twill be a sennight since she left, sir."

Will looked down at the missive again, an indefinable disquiet unraveling through his body. Senna had been running the business masterfully for ten years now, so he wasn't sure why he felt so uneasy. Yet he did. And after a year on the tourney circuit, and three hiring out his special services to lords with ambitions both noble and base, Will knew to heed such rumblings.

Still, this was simply a message from his quite-competent sister, outlining her current business venture. A much-needed one, in truth, after so much of the money flooding into the business went pouring back out again, to plug up the holes created by their father Sir Gerald's ever-increasing need for coin.

Their father had been cold and distant and for the most part *gone,* ever since their mother left, when Will was but a year old. Servants had been present for a while, on and off, but mostly it was Senna who had raised him. Senna who had saved the business. Senna who took on abbots and royal clerks and shipping merchants, and spun the faltering wool business their parents had founded into something with the potential for true greatness.

Senna could manage this matter with Lord Rardove. And yet . . .Will couldn't toss his uneasiness aside. It's what had brought him riding north after a servant sent him a message with a query about a collapsed roof on one of the barns, anecdotally reporting their mistress had abruptly gone to Ireland.

To Lord Rardove. How odd.

He lifted his head and looked at his knobbly-shouldered squire. "Well, we're off again, Peter," Will announced. "You've always wanted to see Ireland, haven't you?"

The boy blinked. "I have, my lord?"

"Good. Saddle Merc, put Anselm and Tooke on lead." Will tossed the message on the table and looked at his men, the small entourage he had assembled for various and sundry—often highly sundry—purposes.

"Roger, look lively," he said. One of the lightly armored men unraveled to his feet. "Find out what you can about Rardove's activities of late. Attend any rumors in particular. Meet us at the dock at Milford."

He glanced at the other men lounging about on stubby-legged benches while Roger tromped out, Will's squire hurrying behind. The small hall of the manor house was suffused with afternoon light, speckled with shadows from the riot of rose vines draped over the windows and shutters. Will looked his men over thoughtfully. They peered back, mugs of tepid ale hovering expectantly before their mouths.

"Did I ever tell you louts I have a small piece of land in Ireland?"

His men exchanged glances, eyebrows raised. "No, Will, you never did," said one.

Another grinned. "I don't believe it. You always said you were landless and wanted it so."

Will shrugged. "Did I? I talk a lot."

"Who enfoeffed you, Will?"

"'Twas a grant from someone appreciative of a job well done. How could I refuse? 'Twas after that business up in the north of England."

"That was Scotland, Will," one man pointed out.

"So it was. In any event, I think it's high time for a visit." He looked at them pointedly. "'Tis in Ireland. Across the sea." They just peered at him. "Get up," he finally said in disgust.

They did immediately, although one shook his head as he set down the mug of brown ale regretfully. "We heard you, Will. Just didn't believe it."

"Oh, believe it," he replied grimly, following them out the door. "Something is amiss in Ireland. I'm going to find out what it is."

Finian knew something was amiss the moment he heard voices coming down the corridor. One sounded drunk.

From out of the darkness, two soldiers escorted a stumbling third down the narrow corridor that ran in front of the cells. They wrenched opened the squeaking iron door to his right, tossed the mostly limp body in, locked the door, and strode away.

Finian waited until the flickering torchlight faded to nothing. Only a thin band of pale gold, sunset light came in through a high, slitted window, but it made the chamber glow with a stony amber aura. He turned to his new prison mate.

"What the hell are ye doing here?"

The soldier shook his head blearily, as if he was shaking off sweat. Or blood. He lifted the back of his hand to wipe across the corner of his mouth. Blood.

"'Twash fightin'," he mumbled. "And drinkin'. And sayin' shtuff about his lordship. And then I hauled off and slugged—"

"That's not what I paid ye for," Finian said coldly.

"Know that," he mumbled. "Wife left me t'day. For the miller. Sho sorry." He waved his hand unsteadily. His legs gave out and he slithered to the floor. His head dropped forward, chin onto chest, then his entire body tipped sideways. He was snoring by the time his skull hit the ground.

Finian tilted his head back until it touched the stone wall. He stared at the shaft of golden light coming in through the slit.

"Now how am I going to get the hell out of here?"

Chapter 8

The prisons. She had to find the prisons. And then what . . . ?

No *then whats.* Only right now, right here. Whatever was under her nose, in front of her toes, that is all she had to do.

Steal.

Under the guise of the new chatelaine, while Rardove slept and retched, that's what she did. Linen shirts, leggings, hooded tunics, food, rope, flint: anything she could lay her hands on. She also scooped four handfuls of pennies from Rardove's coffers, all she could carry without it being too heavy.

Then she shoved her booty into packs and stared at it glumly. Such a cache was meaningless if she ended up astray on the Irish countryside, well stocked to await her demise. She might have coin, but what she needed was the Irishman. Without him, she had as much chance of survival as a good notion in a tankard of ale.

She looked down at her injured hand and tried flexing it. Her fingers didn't hurt, which should have been mildly reassuring, except that they were numb. That could not be good.

The autumn day was growing weary of its task and stretched out in long shadows, when she spied a short, squat, red-faced villein who did odd jobs around the castle. He was pushing a creaking wheelbarrow. It was filled with old, rusted leg irons.

Senna stopped short.

The villein did too, his beefy hands frozen on the wooden handles. Senna stared. He stared back, then set down the barrow and scratched his balding head. She sighed. His hand froze mid-scratch, and his eyebrows lifted, but otherwise there was no change.

"Are you . . . milady?" he asked, lowering his hand.

"I suppose I am."

He dragged off his linen cap and gave a small—a very small—bow. "Milady." Then he deposited the linen back on his shiny scalp and levered the wheelbarrow onto its front wheel. "If I can ever be of service, then, milady. I'll be on my way, then? Milady?" His queries were sounding more desperate.

Senna's heart slammed against her ribs. There was nothing for it but directness. "I wish to see the prisons."

His eyebrows shot up, then descended into a thick black line, a startling slash across his red face. "Milady." He frowned disapprovingly.

"'Tis . . . a game," she declared.

"A game," came the flat, disbelieving reply. The black lines jogged into jagged curves.

She nodded. "A game. Lord Rardove devised it for me."

Something rippled across his sweaty face. It might have been disgust. Or sympathy. In any event, he set down the wheelbarrow. "Well, then. I'll show you the way."

He guided her down a dark hallway, out into another courtyard, back inside, through more doors and hallways, and down, ever down. The light dimmed, the air grew cold and dank, her fingers grew damp and chilled. She blew on them and hastened after. How in God's name would she remember all the twisting turns?

The villein suddenly halted in front of a thick wooden door. "I'll wait for you, milady."

"No."

Up went the thick black eyebrows. Passing her a look that spoke volumes on his opinion of the rich, he shrugged and pushed the door open. Two guards sitting at a small table leapt to their feet.

"Her ladyship is here . . . for a game. Methinks 'twill be great fun," he announced, then disappeared.

"Sirs," Senna trilled, sweeping into the small, dirt-walled room. She smiled brightly, completely pushing aside the terror about to close up her throat.

"My lady!" they exclaimed in startled unison.

"I am inspecting the castle," she explained brightly, as if it were the most natural thing in the world. "And I couldn't very well ignore this place, could I, where the ruffians who threaten my lord's peace are held, before being taught the folly of their ways? 'Tis here that the true peace is kept, and men like you ought to be honored for your role."

She concluded her patriotic little speech with sparkling eyes. The men stared at her, mystified.

"And how long have you been stationed here?" She wandered around the small antechamber, continuing the one-sided conversation.

The taller of the two cleared his throat. "Since Michaelmas."

"Do you enjoy the post?" she asked, seating herself at the small table and peering at them with interest.

"My lady," the shorter one mumbled helplessly. His thoughts were emblazoned across his face like an armorial crest: What was this cruel torment? What answer would suffice?

She got back to her feet and wandered about the room, tucking her injured hand close to her chest. The men stared, slack jawed, then jerked their eyes away. They shifted back and forth on their booted feet, their eyes darting to every point in the room but the brightest.

"The souls who do the hardest work are oft ignored by

those who receive the bounty of their labors," Senna said in a conspiratorial tone.

They nodded miserably. She could have said the king of England should be garroted and they would have agreed.

"I do not wish to be one of those who would benefit without giving recompense," she added, spinning around.

They jerked straighter and stared straight ahead. "Nay, my lady!"

"Some are," she breathed, soft again. Bending her head, she touched her hand gently, drawing their eye to the damage done by their lord.

"Aye, my lady," the taller one muttered uneasily.

"I wish to know all my people and to show my . . . *appreciation* to those who work hard in my service," she murmured in a low voice, and, in a fit of inspiration, trailed her hand along the curve of her bodice.

The guards' eyes practically bulged out of their heads.

"Aye, my lady," the shorter one stammered, wiping sweat from his brow.

She lifted her eyebrows ever so slightly. That particular tactic had never come into use in contract negotiations before. "And when do you leave your posts?"

"Prime," one croaked.

She smiled in relief. "So you shall be here later this eve?"

The taller one adjusted first. "As you wish, my lady." He stepped forward, his gaze raking her figure with an intense, hungry look.

Her mouth went dry. She stepped backward, her ankle turning slightly as she stumbled.

"Fine then. We understand one another," she murmured, her heart hammering. This was a remarkably dangerous game, but what other weapons did she have at her disposal? Few enough not to use those to hand.

"I will leave you to your posts and explore the remainder, as I have done with all the rest of the castle."

"My lady, those are the holes where the prisoners are kept," the taller one protested, stepping forward again.

She turned, her forehead furrowed in delicate disapproval. "Are you gainsaying me? My lord has it wished that I know every inch of his keep, as he will know every inch of me. Those were his exact words. I have found it unwise to thwart him."

She suddenly dissolved into tears, her shoulders bobbing up and down.

The soldiers herded her to the table, abashed. They sat her in a chair and knelt beside her, frantically soothing. No, of course they did not mean to oppose her. Yes, they understood how difficult it was to be married to a man such as the baron. Indeed they did. No, they did not want Lord Rardove to be angry with her. Yes, of course she must walk up and down every hallway as he'd bid her to do, and yes, she must do so alone, to test her memory of the maps.

However odd that last seemed, neither man seemed willing to bicker with her tearful ladyship. Not with the delicious promises she'd hinted at ringing in their ears.

She left them at the table, their heads close together, and pushed open the door to step into the hallway of the cells.

Chapter 9

The sniffles stopped. Her body assumed a different posture: watchful, alert, capable. The corridor was dark, the air rancid and old. She followed the guards' instructions to stay by the left wall, farthest from the "holes."

Her slippers made gritty, grinding sounds on the floor. Small rays of light poked in through chinks set high in the walls. By this dismal illumination she made her way, peering through the bars into each cell, praying she'd find the one she sought.

It smelled of decay and urine, and she moved through a blanket of eerie quiet, peering sideways into each cell as she passed. Every one, empty.

If her mouth had been dry before, 'twas nothing compared to the woolen clump of fear she had to untangle now. Four Irish soldiers had been chained in the hall the night she was beaten. Where were they now?

Please God, don't let *him* be gone.

The only sound was the thundering of her heart and her raspy, shallow breathing. As she crept along, she saw one prisoner, slumped and snoring in a cell, but it wasn't her Irishman. Then, out of a far cell, separated from the others, trailed a length of familiar black hair. Her heart leapt. She left the wall and came over to crouch in front of the cage. The figure was slumped in a sitting position, his side pressed up against the bars.

"Sirrah," she whispered.

Nothing.

"Sir," she whispered again, more loudly.

Nothing. She reached in and poked at his shoulder.

A hand whipped out and grabbed her wrist. She stifled a scream. Her slender bones were trapped in the firm grip of the prisoner in the cell. All breathing stopped.

The prisoner slowly turned his head.

"Thank God 'tis you," she exhaled, icy relief dripping into her blood.

His eyebrows shot up. "And who am I?"

"You are you. How am I to know?" she said in an aggravated tone. She tugged at her wrist.

The Irishman grinned into the darkness. "I've here in my grasp a female who comes floating out of the darkness of a prison, smelling of sweetness and light, for all the world as if 'tis a garden stroll she's on. She pokes at me, and praises God that 'tis myself, although she doesn't know who that would be, and growls when I ask. Being a witless man, at least when it comes to fragrant ladies, I'd say I've died and gone to heaven, and am staring at an angel. Although why she'd be here in hell with me, I've no notion. Can it be ye're to answer my prayers, sweet angel?"

She was surprised by the tumble of feelings evoked by his little speech, spoken in a rough but pleasing voice. There was a smile and gentleness in his tone, but rock-hewn power lay repressed in the hand that still wrapped itself around her wrist.

She tugged a little, and he released her.

"I need your help." Leaning closer to peer into the cell, she could discern his outline. There was only the glitter of bright eyes and the gleam of white teeth as he grinned at her.

He smiled more grimly. "'Tis as if ye read my very mind.

But sweetly as your request is spoken, 'tis little succor I can give, as I hope ye can see."

"If I free you, will you help me?"

The gleam from his smile disappeared and his gaze grew sharp and intent. "Aye," he said slowly, regarding her. "And why would ye be doing that?"

"I need a guide when I leave."

"Is that so?"

"'Tis," she replied in a firm whisper.

"I thought ye only just arrived to be made a baroness."

She leaned a tiny bit closer. "I do not fancy his wine."

"Aye, I noticed that."

"I do not mean to shock you, but Rardove tells lies. I am not his betrothed."

He gave a slow grin. "Ye are surely not."

"And I need a guide to the Dublin quay when I leave."

"Couldn't ye find another Irishman, or better yet a Saxon, who would be pleased to do such a task, and better able, too?"

"Mayhap. I have not looked."

"Really?" He sat upright to regard her. A small smile lifted the edges of his lips and a tremor of unnamed excitement traveled through her body.

"Really," she breathed, lowering her voice. She was entranced by the way his body curved over itself, his muscles tightly corded and tensed beneath what looked to be silky skin. Even in this decrepit prison he was filled with sunshine and fresh air.

"Now why would ye be doing such a thing as that, angel?" he inquired in a low tone.

"In the hall . . . you made me hold my head up. I think you would be best." There was nothing more to say.

A genuine, pleased smile brightened his features before a grimace of pain took over. "Aye, then, lady, I'll be awaiting yer coming, but ye'd best work quickly, as my head is being fitted for the stakes out front."

Senna glanced over her shoulder. The guards would grow suspicious soon. "Tonight, after dark."

"How?" he asked swiftly, his gaze suddenly hard and appraising.

Senna picked up a handful of rocks and ran her thumb over the jagged edges. "Rardove is thrashing on his sheets at this moment, clutching his belly. I expect it to last the night. Some mysterious infection of the gut."

His eyes gleamed in the darkness. "Och, they're terrible mysterious out here. Hit without warning."

She gave a miniature smile. "This one did. I didn't give him any warning a'tall."

"I'll owe ye my life."

"You will be helping get back mine."

He smiled and when she smiled in return, he sat back on his heels. "Ye're a fair measure of beauty, ye are," he whispered.

"What, with my bruised cheekbone?" This time she did laugh, very softly. "You must fell a great many ladies with such lies."

The smile this earned was all charm and self-assurance. She shook her head, looking away. That would not help *at all.*

"Finian O'Melaghlin."

"Senna—"

"De Valery," he finished, his gaze traveling slowly over her face, the smile fading.

"You know my name?"

His eyes lifted back to hers. "If ye can get me out of here, I'll have it put in a song."

"If you can keep me alive once we're out, I'll write it myself," she whispered back.

His smile returned, and her heart tripped over another beat. "I'll remember yer name forever, angel, song or no."

Her eyes fell into his deep blue ones and for a fleeting moment she felt as if she were floating. His rough voice and gentle manner pleased her greatly. For heaven's sake.

"I will return," she whispered, rising to her feet.

"I'll cancel all my other engagements," he pledged, his voice rough and solid.

She smiled over her shoulder, startled at how calm she felt with her life resting on what they planned. It was like the peace she'd felt in the hall when he made her lift her head, when the world had receded except for his endless blue eyes.

And all he'd done then was smile at her.

Will de Valery spent all of a day preparing to leave England and did so with a vengeance, securing the services of a few additional for-hire knights, promising good terms in lieu of the plunder he could not offer. Yet. But one never knew what might be around the next bend in the road.

Thirty-three weapons-bearing others, men-at-arms and attendant squires, made for a goodly force. Two cooks, eight servants, a marshal and a mason completed the ensemble—his grateful proprietor had intimated the manor house was in grave disrepair when he enfeoffed Will with it in the first place, and that was likely much the reason for his largesse in any event.

They took to the seas in the middle of a storm, all staring askance at their lord, who stood golden haired at the bow of the ship as if he could drag the Irish coastline closer by force of will.

When the troop arrived in Dublin, the marshal would stay with the others in the walled city to arrange for the needed horses, wagons, and provisions, then march for the keep.

Will would take the five men he trusted with his life—despite their abiding affection for brown English ale and their desire to stay in England to drink it—and arrange a meeting with Lord Rardove.

He planned it all out in his head, to the last detail, while the wet winds blew across the ship, and Senna was beguiling the guards with sweetmeats and lies.

Chapter 10

Moonlight cut through the slatted shutters, creating just enough light for her to see by. It clawed its way over the window ledges and grasped at the stony walls, thin fingers of chalky light.

Creeping over damp stone and gritty floors, crunching over stale rushes, stumbling and slow hurrying, Senna moved through the castle, dodging the occasional nocturnal servant and bleary-eyed soldier returning from a tumble in the brothel. The castle was rock under moonlight.

She wore a pair of boys' hose and a belted tunic that hung to midthigh, overtop a soft linen shirt. Over everything she wore a loose over-tunic gown, barely girdled, just enough to look the part should anyone stop her.

In her hands she carried the packs. Her hair was banded loosely with a strip of leather and hung in a long braid down her spine. Her eyes were bright, her head spinning, as she crept to the cellars. Setting down the packs, she stared at the solid oak door. Stretching out on either side was a narrow, endless corridor of chunky stone and eerie echoes.

The sound of furtive sniffing jerked her gaze down the hallway. A pair of small, round eyes, glittering flatly in the gloom, met her startled gaze; a rat snuffling at a pool of fetid water. What nourishment could it gain from that bracken watering hole? She shivered and looked back at the heavy door. Now or never.

Planting her palm against the iron handle, she pushed it open.

The soldiers leapt to their feet exactly as they'd done earlier. She smiled through the flickering candlelight.

"Sirs." She inclined her head as if she were arriving at a social gathering a few moments early.

They goggled at her exactly as they had earlier.

"My lady," the tall one gasped, fumbling to pull out the small bench he'd been seated on. Exactly as he'd done earlier.

If only their wits are as dim as earlier, Senna decided, *I shall be fine.*

She lifted her skirts and sat. Their mouths hung open half an inch. Easy prey. She closed in for the kill with absolutely no sympathy for what they might suffer as a result of the escape: they had helped to hang the dog.

She thumped down a flask of whisky on the table, filched from the baron's cellars, and looked up with a smile. They smiled back, gap-toothed.

In almost no time, they were well sodden and stupid, not a far cry from where they'd started the night. But this drink had an added spice, a powdered tincture of valerian root filched from the herbalist, which would ensure they slept for a long time. It took three swigs, maybe four, before they crumpled to the floor, leaving Senna standing, legs braced, breathing so fast her head spun.

No turning back now.

Plucking the keys off the taller one, she crept down the hall toward Finian's cell. A single torch lit her way.

"Angel." His rough voice drifted down to greet her.

"I am come," she announced in a low whisper, as if it were needful, completely ignoring the fact that his voice made her smile in the dark.

He was standing tonight, and Senna was a bit awed by his height and strength. Firm, corded muscles were tensed in the darkness and his voice had to travel some distance down to her. She'd picked a strong one.

They fumbled through the keys, found the one that fit, and after swinging open his cell door with an ear-piercing screech that would have awakened the dead—but not the guards—they crept back along the dank corridor.

"What happened to them?" she whispered, gesturing to the empty cells.

"The Irishmen who witnessed your kindly welcome in the hall were all killed soon after, lady, and in intriguing ways, too, rest assured," he replied gruffly, following her up the hall.

Looking back, she found his jaw set hard, his eyes dark and impassive. She turned forward again, her fingertips trailing along the slime-ridden wall. Were her men to have been killed, she would be spitting for blood. Waving a sword and howling. He was so . . . restrained.

She repressed a shudder and pushed open the door to the antechamber.

He stared at the crumpled guards. "Ye have gifts I would never have suspected."

She frowned a little. "I have a few hidden talents."

He regarded her sideways, briefly. "Aye."

He nodded his thanks when she handed him bread, then they swung the packs onto their backs. They were off, creeping across the shadowy courtyard. All they needed to do was steal a few weapons, sneak through both baileys, and scramble over the castle gate without being spotted by the guards.

Senna tried not to consider anything other than the next obstacle. Thinking too far ahead made her nauseous.

Crouched and watchful, she guided them to the blacksmith's hut. It was an elaborate affair, made of stone, two stories high. They stared up at the window on the second floor, far above their heads.

"It didn't look that high in the daylight," she muttered.

Finian's hands closed around her hips. A startled breath whooshed out of her. "I'll boost ye up," he murmured, and his fingers tightened as he lifted her up against the side of the stone building.

She reached as far as she could, stretching, aware of the power of him through his thick curled fingers, his shoulders, the steady strength holding her body up in the air. She curled the tips of her uninjured fingers around the window ledge, and that was as far as she got. The injured hand was still strangely numb, and therefore, while it did not hurt, it did not seem to have strength either. It certainly would not help her scale the side of the building.

"More," she whispered.

"I haven't got any more."

She scrabbled silently, panting and scraping her elbows and knees, but she wasn't a fly, and there was no way she could climb up the side of the wall.

"Stand on my shoulders," he said, a gravelly command.

She stilled, then bent her leg back. She must have kicked his chin or something, because he grunted. She slowed her movements and nudged her toe backward, felt for the ledge of his shoulder. She planted her foot on it, then did the same with the other. It gave her just enough lift to get her elbows on the ledge.

She pushed at the shutters. Locked. Stifling the urge to smash them, she felt around in her pack and pulled out a strip of dried meat. Working it between the two shutters, she lifted upward, unhooking the latch that held them closed. A small metallic *clink* rang out, loud as a shout, and the shutters creaked in opposite directions, one in, one out.

Quickly, she shoved them inward and shimmied through. Thrusting her arms out, she dropped to the ground. Her palms hit first and the rest slithered behind, until her knees hit the floor with a muted thump.

She scrambled to her feet. Her vision quickly adjusted to the deeper shadows. A black opening gaped straight ahead. The stairway.

Another black gaping hole appeared to her right. The blacksmith's bedchamber.

She swallowed dryly.

She hurried down the stairs, weaving her way between tables and anvils, and tiptoed carefully around the oven, which was still heated to a pale orange glow. She swung the latch up on the door and inched it open. Finian stepped inside.

They crept back up the stairs, where the items in for repair and new works of deadly art were stored. Where the blacksmith was stored, along with his wife and children, but, praise God, no dog. After tonight, there would be one for certes.

They worked swiftly, without words. Within minutes, Finian was garbed in the powerful protective covering of an Englishman's mail hauberk, flinching just slightly as the weight of it settled on his back. There was none to fit Senna. She picked up a knife that looked the right size for Finian, which he immediately strapped around his thigh. He grabbed another one and she belted it for him, around his left arm. She grabbed one for herself, a long, wicked thing that looked just right.

At that moment, the blacksmith spoke, muttering a few garbled phrases. They froze, staring at each other. Silence, then a murmured, "Move over."

Good heavens. The smithy's wife was awake.

Coldness spread across Senna's chest. A few feet away, Finian extracted the blade from its arm-sheath. She shook her head wildly, silently. He tipped his head to the side, one palm up, looking at her like she was crazed.

She gestured adamantly to the sheath on his arm. He just lifted his brows, but, as the silence extended, he slowly redeposited the blade. She smothered a sigh.

It felt like hours before they moved again. First Finian, then she, slunk back to the stairs, hunched over and breathing fast.

Senna spied something out of the corner of her eye. She moved closer.

A broadsword, in a beautifully adorned sheath stitched with bright threads resembling fantastical shapes of animals and lettering in an unknown language. It looked like a warrior's sword, a king's sword. It looked like Finian's sword.

Without another thought, she lifted the massive weapon, staggered down the stairs, and hissed at his back.

He spun, his eyes glittering in the darkness, his body reflexively crouching into a fighting stance. The fire-glow of the oven lit up dark shadows on his face. He looked wild and dangerous, and she was about to hand him the hugest sword she'd ever seen.

"Here," she whispered.

"My blade," he murmured, stepping close.

"Yours? Truly?" She'd only thought it *looked* like a sword he might have.

"Aye." He took the weapon and held it reverently, handling its weight as if it were a dinner platter. He slid it halfway out of its scabbard. The flat glitter of steel flashed in the firelight. "The scabbard, too," he whispered. "I thought 'twould be quickly assumed by another, although the spells woven in it would not work well for any other. And never a Saxon." He lifted his gaze to hers. "I am doubly indebted."

They left the smithy's building and crept along the side of the open exercise field, a labor in madness which frightened her into a dry mouth and prevented her from talking for a good three minutes. Finian seemed impressed. They ducked between the buildings, silent moving shadows: one-room cottages, a chapel, the stables.

As they passed the kitchen gardens, Senna stumbled in a rutted furrow and muttered a curse. It sounded like a shout in the quiet nighttime. She snapped her head up.

Finian stared at her, frozen.

Then, keeping time with her hammering heart, the boot steps of a soldier drew near.

Chapter 11

They threw themselves against a wall, barely breathing. The soldier walked by, striding on a path perpendicular to them. Senna held her breath. He kept walking, never looking over, and finally disappeared behind another building. She rolled her head to the side and looked at Finian.

"I think—" she whispered, so quietly she could barely hear herself.

He shook his head sharply. Another five minutes of silence, then another soldier came by. Senna pushed the back of her head into the wall and focused on looking like a pile of refuse. The guard passed.

Ten more minutes and no more soldiers came. Finian let his body relax off the wall. Senna followed suit. She opened her mouth. Swiftly, and in utter silence, he cupped the back of her neck and pulled her forward.

"Patience and silence, lady," he murmured. "For God's and my sake, patience. And silence."

Now, why on earth did her body warm up at his words?

Nodding curtly, she swung away, leading them to a corroded section of the inner bailey wall, an easy ascent of some eight feet. Gripping the loose, crumbling footholds, she scrambled up. A small stream of rubble broke loose, and she went sliding halfway back down the wall.

Finian stopped her with his shoulders and arms. They froze, holding their breaths, completely still, his hands firm and warm on her ribs, her buttocks resting on one of his shoulders. She tried to ignore the startling rush of heat his touch brought to her face and other, less moonlit regions of her body. Nothing moved in the night. She looked down, he looked up, then he cupped her bottom with both hands and pushed her the rest of the way up the wall.

Flinging herself to the top, she spun and crouched down, hand extended. Finian leapt up without effort and without touching her hand. He smiled as he came up, just the slightest all-knowing, roguish lift to the corner of his mouth. *That* was about how he'd touched her when he hoisted her up the wall. She ignored it and turned, still in a crouch, to peer over the other side.

He crouched beside her, his body hot and strong. Ten feet below was a small pile of clippings from the castle garden. Ten feet was nigh on two of her.

"'Tis a long way down," she whispered tautly.

He turned in her direction. His face was shadowed. "Not so far, lass."

"Far enough." Could he hear panic in her voice? It had frozen her fingers to the lip of the wall.

He nodded slowly. "It seems far."

"I don't think I can." Shameful, shameful fear. Was she to crouch here on the bailey wall then, until someone spotted them?

"Would it help if I pushed ye?"

She almost laughed. "Aye, that would help immen—"

He put his hand on her shoulder and pushed her off the wall. She didn't have time to scream or even feel scared, before she landed with a soft bump on the mound of rotting flora. She scrambled to her feet just as he dropped down beside her.

"You've lost your wits," she hissed.

In a flash, he towered above her. The heat from his powerful torso shimmered between them, hovering at the edges of her tunic. Senna threw her head back, startled.

"Mistress, I'm fairly certain ye're a few stones shy of a full load yerself." He lightly touched her upper arm for emphasis. "Now, hush."

She shivered at the rush of *something* his fingers created. She could not rip her eyes from the sight of him, so close. His torso was long and lean but sturdy, wide shoulders tapered in clean, muscular lines to trim hips and powerful thighs. Corded muscles in his neck and arms were defined by the moonlight, and tangled black hair spilled down past his shoulders. His face was carved in moonlit angles, his chin square and firm. The growth of hair on his face made him appear rough-hewn and wild, but then there was that heart-stopping smile.

The Irishman was sinfully handsome.

Her breathing grew shallow, but the rush of heat to her face was simply a result of the drama of the escape. Surely.

It was the rush of heat to her loins that was so bewildering.

His dark eyes flicked back to hers in question. "Which way?"

She looked around. The castle grounds, while tumbling into disrepair, were enormous, built over the years into a veritable village within the castle walls, filled with twisting turns and dead ends. Keeping an eye on the buttressed main gate was only minimally helpful, because they could not take a straight path toward it, across the wide-open training fields. They must keep to shadows and corners.

A series of low, thatched buildings ran in a fairly straight line away from them just now, and would provide some concealment. But beyond that dubious shelter, there could be anything. Guards, swords, battle.

"This way," she said firmly, starting off, then hesitated. "I think."

His eyes gleamed in the moonlit dark. "As ye say."

"But I am not certain—"

"Ye've a better sense of the keep than I," he said shortly. "Do not doubt yerself."

She marched off. "You'd best be alert, Irishman, for I've no idea to what end I lead us."

"I am ever alert. There is no need to caution me in that." His soft voice wafted through her hair, and her skin prickled in unwelcome response.

Soon the main gate loomed before them, black and bone-like. Finian gripped her arm and, to ensure her silence, put his finger over her lips. She inhaled sharply at the touch. His eyes darted to hers. He shook his head in silent warning. Her head dipped in a nod.

He disappeared for a few moments, then his hunched form reemerged out of the darkness. "The sloth of the guards is inconsistent. The gate is occupied, although perhaps not guarded too well." She looked at him. "There is a fine argument brewing. Something about gambling. And a woman. They are drinking."

"A fight and liquor will bring even more puppets to the gatehouse," she predicted glumly.

"Well, then," he murmured, "let us have a hope they are all as inept as their lord."

That was a dim hope. These were the baron's men, fed on his evil, and while they might not be bright, they did not need to be particularly accomplished in their wits to notice two people slinking around the castle gates long after Lauds had rung. Especially not when one was a six-foot Irishman who was supposed to be shackled in the baron's prisons.

The cloud of gloom beginning to billow over her must have been noticeable even through the darkness, because Finian considered her a moment, then leaned close.

"Courage," he murmured.

"I haven't a bit of it," she whispered in reply.

"Ye're made of it."

She almost laughed. "Hardly. What I am is reckless and headstrong and I don't listen particularly well—"

His arm wrapped around her shoulders. "I don't need to be told those things, lass," he whispered directly into her ear. "Ye're the candle at night, nothing to hide. Ye also talk a great deal, and were ye to find it in yer heart to save a poor Irishman's life, please do so now by shutting yer lush mouth a few moments."

Her tongue was nailed to the roof of her mouth as she stared into the dark Irish eyes inches from her own.

Just then the outline of the two patrolling soldiers walked by in a circuit around the castle walls. Finian froze. The weight of his muscular arm, slung over her shoulders, was oddly comforting. They heard a rough laugh, then there was silence.

Senna inhaled a shaky breath and her life slowed to the pace of a languid breath of air on a hot summer day. She wanted to stand just as they were for a very long time. She wanted his hand to dangle, just as it was, barely brushing against nipples grown tingling hard.

How odd and strange everything was. Here she was, in a foreign land, fleeing a man who wanted to force her into marriage. Here she stood, shivering outside a prison wall, tucked under the arm of an Irish warrior, her body behaving as it never had before.

Strangest of all, this didn't seem strange.

He removed his arm. She shivered, suddenly noticing the chill. They started for the gate, only to hurl themselves against the side of a building a moment later when a clamor of shouts and curses rang out. The two guards ran back to the guard tower, now ablaze with lights. Out on the rampart stood several dark figures.

"Bollocks," came a hushed, almost reverent whisper, at

odds with the crude curse. The penitent was bowed almost in half over the edge of the stone tower, gazing into the shadows below.

"By your balls indeed," another agreed, his harsh voice bouncing down the ramparts to them. "The pricker threw Dalton right over the battlement!"

The shouts grew louder. Finian and Senna looked at each other.

"Break it up," one voice broke through the mêlée. Balffe, the huge captain of the guard, waded through the mess evident at the top of the tower and stared over the wall. "Christ Almighty, Molyneux, you've killed him dead." He looked back up and glared at the perpetrator. Hairy forearms folded over his chest as he waited for the pathetic explanation.

His patience was not tested. "He lost the wager and wouldn't pay up." The murderer's voice lifted and fell unevenly, clear evidence of his overindulgence.

"And you've got more balls than wits or not enough of either, and I'll not be paying for it. Go get him," Balffe ordered, unfolding his beefy arms and striding forward, a mountain in motion.

"What?" The guard hooted and staggered backward out of the captain's reach. "And be made into mutton by the Irish who stalk the castle walls?"

"Which would make you a sheep, you bastard." The mountain took a step closer. "I don't care if the godforsaken Saracens have left the Holy Lands and landed in Ireland." He took another step forward. "I don't care of they're sharpening their scimitars and grinning at you, you rotting piece of dung—you're going out there."

Grabbing the man's gambeson and mail covering between his thick fingers, Balffe hauled him up to eye level, a not average feat of strength. "You drag his body back inside, *now,* or I'll hang you by your balls." He flung the hapless guard down and pointed to several others. "You, and you, and you," he ordered, "go with him."

Muted curses followed the reluctant volunteers down the winding staircase.

"Come," Finian whispered in her ear.

He gripped her wrist and tugged her to hover in the shadows by the crenellated barbican tower as the monstrous portcullis was raised. Creaking chains sounded and a dog barked. The men hauling the gate up grumbled contentiously—night duty was supposed to carry its own rewards, most notably an absence of tasks requiring attention.

The iron grate was finally high enough for the four men to pass under it and over the lowered wooden draw. What with their grumbling and cursing, and the gory interest in their morbid task from those above, neither the soldiers nor the watchers from atop the tower noticed the two hunched and hooded figures who glided out behind them. Nor did they espy the shadowy shapes as they turned away and dropped into a dry but remarkably noisome defensive ditch.

Senna felt Finian's hand on the back of her head, pushing her down the side of the drop-off. She fell flat on her stomach. He dropped on top, covering her body with his.

"Hummphh," she groaned as all the air was pressed out of her.

"Silence," came his hissed reply.

"I can be nothing but, as you are lying on top of me—"

His hand snaked under her, sliding over parts of her body in the most startling ways, and came up by her mouth, which he overlaid with a broad palm.

She lay quietly as, above them, the soldiers grumbled in their efforts to retrieve the dead man. Grasping an extremity in hand, the foursome carted the mangled body over the draw and into the castle. The creak of heavy chains sounded again, and the barred gate clanged back into place. Silence descended.

"Up. Now, before their attention turns back." Finian knelt

between her legs and looked down at her flattened body, half submerged in the dirt. He pulled her out and turned her over.

Her face was covered with a fine film of dirt, her nose and cheeks red and creased. She was so covered with grime that the front of her tunic was barely distinguishable from the ground beneath her.

“That was close,” she whispered.

Finian held out his hand to help her rise. “Quite.”

He stood beneath, pushing her up over the side of the ditch. She finally curled her body over the lip. “Next time, all I ask is that I be on top.”

Finian, with one thigh thrown over the top, his arms flexed to support his weight, froze. An enormous grin spread over his features as he hauled himself up.

“As ye wish it, angel.”

Their hunched figures were but small, dark spots on the darker landscape as they crawled away from the castle. Finian led her to the edge of the road and they sped away into the night, disappearing into the vast Irish wildside.

Chapter 12

They halted briefly an hour later beside a wide, rushing stream, a tributary of a larger, more riotous river flowing some fifty steps away, behind a long, narrow copse of trees.

Finian knelt at the water's edge and adjusted his tunic. His arms burned from the effort of lifting them overhead. By chance, his eye caught Senna. She was staring, her lips slightly parted.

"Ye might want to turn away, lass," he suggested quietly.

She spun so quickly her braid lifted in the air, then thumped against her back. The curls poking out at the bottom bounced in small, ruddy ringlets at the dip of her spine. He looked at them a moment, then turned back to the river.

"I'll need but a trice."

"Take all the time you need. And I've seen men before," she added sharply.

"Umm."

He tore off his *léine,* the traditional knee-length tunic, and tossed it over the boulder beside him, then waded into the frigid stream. Kneeling, he gave his body a rough but thorough scrub with the small, sand-like pebbles that covered the riverbed, washing away the stink of the prisons. His skin rippled prickly-hot at the freezing temperatures, and he dunked his head under the water. Coming up again, he shook himself like a dog, spraying water droplets. With the palm of his hand, he flipped his hair off his forehead and turned.

A tunic and pair of leggings came sailing over and landed on his face. He dragged them off. Senna's back was still conspicuously toward the river, as if she were aiming it at him. But her head was turned in his direction slightly, so that her chin sat on her shoulder.

"You'll want something clean and English-looking to put on," she mumbled.

"My thanks."

"And in any event, I didn't have one of"—her hand waved vaguely in the direction of his hips—"those."

Even from this distance, even through the moonlight, he could see her cheeks flush pink. And he did not have to see anything at all to know this was due the fact she was not fully turned away. She'd been watching him.

He pulled the tunic over his head. Once his leggings were on and laced, she turned. Her gaze didn't quite meet his.

"Are we quite ready?" she asked in an imperious voice.

"I am ever ready, Senna. Why don't you take off yer skirts?"

Her jaw dropped. Everything about her shone in the moonlight. Her bright, wide eyes, her lower lip, now wet as her tongue slipped along its fullness. That long, chestnut brown braid, which trapped the wild, rampant curls.

"M—my gown?"

He stepped closer. "Ye have leggings on under? And a short tunic? Aye. Then, off with it."

Her cheeks flushed so brightly he could see it through the moonlight, but she was already pulling it over her head, huffing something incomprehensible while under its folds. He took it and threw it away, next to his *léine,* halfway behind a large rock on the streambed. It looked as if the clothes had been hidden, but poorly.

Quickly he took a head-to-toe appraisal of her—it was

impossible not to, with leggings that skimmed her thighs so snugly—then he turned away and shouldered his pack again. But in the time it took to make the visual sweep of her body, he heard a small, quick breath slip out from between her parted lips.

"Let's go, then," he said.

She spun on her heel, took her very pink cheeks, and stalked away down the path they'd been following for the past hour.

"This way, Senna," he called out softly, turning back the way they'd come.

Stones crunched as she spun. "Back that way? Why?"

"I've a mad notion to throw them off our scent." He rubbed his palm across the back of his neck. "We've a long way to go, lass, and I haven't the time to explain myself to ye."

She stepped up beside him with an impatient stride. "Then we walk. Can you not walk and talk at the same time?"

He looked down coolly. "Not so well as you."

As they hiked quickly back up the creek side, he gave a brief synopsis of their next few days. "We have two rivers to cross—"

"A river?" She sounded deeply shocked.

"Two."

"Two rivers?" she clarified, as if his meaning had somehow been unclear.

"Then a town, and—"

"Friendly?"

"Hostile."

"Hostile?"

"Then leagues of open land before we reach safety."

She walked silently and seemed to be figuring, determining which was the most important thing to focus on just now. "You mean Dublin," she finally said. "We're making for Dublin."

He grunted. No, he did not mean Dublin.

He meant Hutton's Leap. That was the most important thing right now: getting to the town of Hutton's Leap before Rardove figured out what the Irish were up to, and went there himself.

The mission had been two pronged from the start. Finian's task was to probe Rardove's cunning, as well as take on the hazardous job of providing a distraction while another Irish warrior was sent to Hutton's Leap to retrieve the dangerous, coveted dye manual that contained the secret of the Wishmés.

Finian now knew that warrior's head was being sent to The O'Fáil in a box.

No time for grief or rage. Just focus on the mission. Someone had to retrieve that dye manual before it fell into the wrong hands. Rardove's hands.

Finian was the only one who knew the mission had failed. Therefore it had just become his mission.

Senna, of course, did not know this, as she had no idea they were actually *on* a mission.

"Is that . . . is that one of the rivers?" she asked, her words tentative.

A slim, pale finger pointed at the sparse tree cover that separated this tributary from the main rushing river, perhaps forty paces off, as the slip of land they were on slowly narrowed until it became but a diving board into the raging river.

"Aye. That one."

"And how wide is this riv—*what was that?*"

A low howl rose up through the dark air, like the nighttime was haunting itself. Another howl came, filling the darkness with its mournful sound. She looked at Finian, her eyes wide and frightened.

"A wolf," he explained gently.

"We haven't many of them in England anymore," she whispered back.

Another low howl came and Senna tripped backward, until her back was pressed to his chest. A startlingly attention-getting maneuver. He was vaguely impressed such an unconscious move should imbue such sensuality. "Are they close?"

"Aye." It was always harder to detect panic within a whisper, but Finian was fairly certain the telltale tremble was there. "Are ye ready to go now, lass?"

"Quite."

They didn't say much as they retraced their steps to the banks of *Bhean's* River. Woman's River. It was well named, for it was wild and stunning in its beauty and ferocity. Dangerous, with wicked currents. Deep, an onrushing power to it.

It was autumn, though, and the summer had been dry. While the farmers lamented the fact of it, tonight Finian gave thanks to all the gods he could think of, old and new, because it meant they could cross without needing the bridge at *Bhean's* Crossing, which was only half a mile from Rardove Keep.

Still, the *Bhean* was deep. Deep enough to warrant caution. Deep enough to drown in. Especially if one cracked his skull on the rocks when he fell. Or she fell.

He stopped at the edge. The moon was bright. "How are ye with rocks, Senna?"

Confusion marked her face until she followed his pointing finger. It cleared, into fear. A jagged row of boulders of various sizes zigzagged across the river like huge stepping stones.

"Finian. You cannot be in earnest." She considered him suspiciously. Then she looked back at the river. "You're asking us to jump those? *Those* rocks? Those rocks."

Nothing had changed about his original query, but her voice became more flatly incredulous. "Why, Finian, some are as widely spaced as my body is tall. The force required . . ." Her voice trailed off. "And the rate of the current . . ." She trailed off again, looking across at the dark, rushing river.

She was probably reckoning rate and velocity at this very moment, he realized dimly.

"If ye're too frightened, Senna—"

"I'm not frightened," she snapped. "I'm never *frightened.* I'm . . . figuring."

"Ah." He held his breath. If she said she couldn't do it . . .

Her chin came up. "I can do it," she said, rather loudly. "I used to climb them all the time, you know."

He smiled as a little warmth flared in his chest. "I didn't know, Senna," he murmured, shifting the pack on his shoulders. "But I'm glad of it. Now, do as I do, just as I do it."

He hopped onto the closest rock. It had a low, broad surface. He quickly hopped to the next one, not two feet away, and turned. "Now yerself, Senna."

She closed her eyes and leapt. Finian lifted a hand in protest, but by then she'd already landed, knees bent. She opened her eyes and looked up triumphantly.

"Well done," he said, giving her the congratulations her self-satisfied, never-climbed-a-rock-before smile required. After which he added, "Never do that again. Eyes open, always."

He turned to the next boulder. Fifteen. Fifteen to cross. Not so many, except that they kept getting higher and more steeply pitched as you went, until the last one towered like an armored sentinel on the river's western edge.

"Do they seem to get bigger as we go?" she suddenly asked.

"Not a bit of it. 'Tis the moonlight. Tricks the eye."

"Oh."

He pushed off, propelling himself to the next boulder. This one wasn't far at all, but it had a steeply sloped top, like a barn roof. He landed, one foot on either side of the pitch. Arms out, swaying, aware of every whipped muscle in his legs and back, he balanced himself. He blew out a long breath and leapt again, leaving the boulder free for Senna.

Behind him, he heard a small sound over the quiet rush of water. A prayer, spoken in a whispered, feminine voice. "Please, dear Lord."

He turned just as she jumped. For a moment she hung in

space, both legs bent, as if running in midair, then landed with a thump, knees sharply bent, but with a foot planted firmly on either side of the rock.

Standing atop two boulders, in the moonlight, their eyes met. Finian nodded firmly. Senna, panting just a little, from exertion or fear or both, gave a small smile. Almost as if *she* were encouraging *him*.

A corner of his mouth curved up. He turned to the next one.

And so they made their leaping, slipping, flying way across the boulders of *Bhean's* River. Until the last.

A full four feet away, and easily a foot higher than the one Finian stood upon, it required a running leap. Which they had no room for.

"Come, Senna." He gestured with his hand, stepping to the side to give her room to land beside him on his boulder. He grabbed her hand as she landed, pulling her up beside him.

The rising moon lit up the currents of the river below like small, steely gray snakes. On either side of the water lay low, flat land. To the west stretched the perils of the king's highway, but beyond that, the safety of hills Finian had known since his youth. To the east flowed English lands. North, lay Rardove. And four feet away hunkered the biggest boulder on *Bhean's* River, renowned for its sentinel-like granite edifice.

He could tell Senna's face had paled, even through the moonlight. "Do ye think ye can jump it?"

"Of course."

"Senna."

She started to protest, then shook her head slowly. Silver, moon-cast glints gleamed in her eyes. "I don't know, Finian. 'Tis a long way. I cannot say for certes."

He nodded. "Then I'm going to throw ye."

Her mouth fell open. "What?"

"What's yer other plan?" he asked sharply.

"I—" She shook her head. "I haven't one."

He didn't even pause. He swept a boot behind her, shifting to stand sidewise, facing her. Her lithe body trembled. Small, fast pants shot out of her mouth. Finian spread his legs wide, crouched down, grabbed under her arm, and slid his other hand between her legs, lifting to her crotch.

"Don't try to help," he ordered. "Do not push off. Don't move. All ye have to do is land on yer feet. Aye?"

The contours of her profile were frozen. "Aye."

"Ready, girl?"

"Jésu, Finian," she whispered. "I'm ready."

He focused all his attention and, tensing his already wearied legs and arms and shoulders, and tightening every muscle along the length of his burning back, he flung her across the churning water straight at the boulder.

Chapter 13

Senna couldn't help it; she pushed off, too.

That may have been what threw her slightly off course, offset the trajectory of Finian's mighty toss. Whatever it was, she landed with a sickening thud chest-first, almost to the flat, top surface of the boulder, but not quite. Instead, she clung to its slanting side, like a fly on a wall.

Her cheek was planted into the rock. She clung to the hard, impermeable surface of the stone, her good fingers clutching desperately for any small crags. She found them aplenty, all jagged, knife-sharp things. Her benumbed, wounded fingers weren't necessary for gripping, but their incapacity seemed to sap the strength from the others.

But her blood, that was hot and ferocious. It pounded through her body. Everything coming out of her—breath, effort, curse—was hot, panting fury as she lifted her legs and arms, scrabbling up the side of the stone face.

She gained the summit and flung herself over the lip, sprawled out like a dead thing. Her arms and legs were on fire, her knees bruised and torn, arm muscles screaming, her lungs burning. She lay for a moment, feeling the cool face of the stone under her feverish cheek. Then she pushed up to her elbows and peeked over her shoulder.

Finian was crouched, fingertips on the stone between his knees, his body rocked forward, staring at her, his mouth moving silently.

"Bonny toss," she called softly, lifting her voice just above the rush of river currents.

His head dropped and for a moment, she couldn't see his face. One broad hand lifted to wipe across the features she could not see, then he pushed to his feet, shaking his head.

"If ye hadn't pushed off when I told ye not to—"

"Oh, indeed. 'Tis my fault."

They stared at each other. A corner of Finian's mouth lifted into a grin. "Get off the damned rock, Senna."

She stepped to the side.

"Off."

"But—"

"I want ye on the ground," he said sharply. She looked at him in surprise. This was the first hint of harshness from him. "On the ground. I want ye on the ground. Where ye're safe."

The ground, where she'd be safe, was about fifteen feet below. In truth, it wasn't even ground; it was water, and, while shallow, still churning. "It's an awful far way—"

"It'll be longer if I push ye. I cannot jump with ye standing there. There's no room. There are handholds on the far side, and cut-outs. Use them. Go."

She did. As she slithered down the angled rock face—the rock widened at its base—using the copious number of footholds Finian had predicted, wiggly tendrils of weeds and roots scratched at her cheeks, but all she was attuned to was whether she heard Finian's boots hit the boulder or the water.

At the hard clatter of bootheels on stone, her feet felt more solid in their footholds. She looked up just as Finian's face appeared over the edge, peering down, long dark hair swinging beside his face. She smiled.

"Go," was all he said.

As if she needed him to tell her to 'go.' The giddy truth of it hit her—the admission—and swirled in her belly like a miniature cyclone: all she'd wanted to do her whole life was *go.* Go somewhere, anywhere—anywhere other than home, watching the world sweep by through expensive leaded windows, alone but for servants and account ledgers, dying inside.

But should she require a reminder of the importance of taking care in her prayers, Senna thought as she scrabbled down the boulder, placing a foot just so, using her good hand wherever possible—here was her giddy life on the go: fleeing for her life with an Irish rebel, out on the wildside, beyond the Pale, past rescue, past safety, past any future she'd ever dreamed of.

In the end, the footholds gave out, and she was forced to hop into shallow water. Quickly she sloshed to dry land. Finian landed a moment later, splashing to the shore.

He stopped, the heel of one palm pressed against his ribs, his brow furrowed, his jaw tight. She waited silently, quelling a moment of panic. He'd obviously been beaten, and might be seriously injured. How would they make it if . . . ? How did he find the strength—

He straightened, and any thoughts of physical vulnerability were swept away beneath her awareness of his total maleness. A chest firm with plated muscle, arms cut and carved in that defined musculature, legs thickly corded with sinew and strength, he was a specimen of raw masculinity. But her attention lingered longest on the sculpted features of his face, how they looked more haunting in the moonlight. Dangerous.

His gaze swept the land around them, plotting their next move. His eyes swept over hers once, unseeing, then came back again. He smiled faintly, but she could see the unrelenting steel behind the gentle gesture.

"Ye did fine, Senna."

Some ridiculous pleasure rose up in her. Bubbly, like the

small creek behind her manor house. "You weren't so bad yourself, Irishman."

No, not so, indeed. Dark hair fell back alongside his face to frame the easy, damaging smile he sent her way. The steel in his gaze was sheathed deeper for a moment, behind a roughish, seductive glint. "Ye've seen nothing of what I'm good at yet, Senna."

Heat raced to her cheeks. "Well," she retorted, "I know 'tisn't tossing women across rivers."

He grinned as he shifted his pack, the muscles of his body rippling even under that slight movement. "Senna, if ye can't guess what I do well by now, I haven't a hope for ye."

That started the shivery ribbons through her belly. The look in his eye before he turned away started the heat in her groin.

"All we have to do tonight is make it across the king's highway," he explained, "and far enough into the hills on the other side."

"Cross the king's highway? That doesn't sound prudent."

"'Tisn't," he said as they headed into the woods.

"It sounds dangerous."

"'Tis."

She kept imagining Rardove's rage when he discovered she was gone. Could Balffe have realized it already? And if so, wouldn't they gallop directly to the highway, run like mad for Dublin, just as she was doing? Straight down the king's highway.

"Isn't there some other way?"

Finian skirted a tree trunk. "No other way now, Senna. Forward or back. Nothing in between."

Chapter 14

They came to the edge of the king's highway and ducked low. A breeze rustled the reeds, a low, seething sound, like a hiss through teeth. They stretched on their bellies side by side, peering out at the puddle-strewn, rock-encrusted, narrow, muddy path that marked the main passageway from the north to Dublin.

"'King's highway' has a rather overstated magnificence," Senna murmured.

"So does most of what the English say and do." He pushed forward on his elbows. "The way is clear. We're off."

They hurried across, staying low. The highway might only be wide enough for two wagons to pass, but it ran straight as an arrow-shot in either direction. It would be easy for them to see anyone coming. And easy for anyone to see them. There was also a ridge a few yards back that lined the far side. Anyone could be up there waiting with arrows. But apparently they had no choice. They had to cross the highway.

"Why is that?" she asked when they were safely across and striding up a steep, narrow, almost imperceptible path that Finian had found on the hill beyond. "Why did we have to cross the highway? Could we not have kept to the east side and headed south for Dublin? This *is* the way to Dublin, is it not?" she added after a long moment of silence ensued.

He still didn't reply. The hill was long and steep, and as climbing was beginning to take all Senna's strength, she was just as glad to have the conversation halt momentarily.

They climbed swiftly, ducking under sloping tree branches that dripped with moss maybe a hundred years old. Silvery light slanted through their feathery veined fingers, making the world glow with greenish gray light. It smelled fresh.

They finally crested the ridge. The path, while still only wide enough for one at a time, at least leveled out. Senna stopped and bent over, breathing hard. Behind her, Finian was breathing slightly heavier than usual. Very slightly.

She looked back. He was mostly a silhouette of power, standing upright, looking down to the road below. With the moonlight washing over him, his body was cut clear, like something hewn from rock. Dark hair spilled down to his shoulders. Impatiently, he raked it behind his ear, revealing the dark outline of a square, stubbly jaw and chin. She could see the thick hilt of his sword rising up above his left shoulder.

"Ready, Senna?"

She straightened and nodded, although another hour of rest would not have been misplaced. Keeping account ledgers at a copyist's desk did not tend one toward physical exertion. Still, she rode and fished at times, and of course had to practice every day with—

"Senna?"

But being a merchant did not quite prepare one for rabid barons, or raging rivers, or nighttime flights across a foreign frontier.

It was not often she was faced with a situation she did not have a ready reply for, an answer that could be written in ink, tallied in rows, stamped and scrolled and signed by witnesses who could prove and ensure no one could ever take away—

Warm fingers crooked under her chin. "Senna?" He angled her face to his, his eyes searching. "Are ye with us?"

The feel of his fingers, strong and thick, solid and real,

funneled some measure of calm back into her. She nodded. He nodded along with her and dropped his hand. Her chin felt cold where his fingers had been.

"Forward, then, angel. We've a far way to go."

She started walking. "To Dublin? A long way to go to Dublin? I may be off in my reckoning, Finian, but we seem to be headed west, not east and south."

"*Baile Átha Cliath.*"

She paused. "West."

"*Baile Átha Cliath.* Keep walking."

"Is that intended to mean something?" she asked after a moment of trying to ascertain his meaning. Which she could never do, because firstly, she was being baited—growing up with a brother provided sufficient experience to know when she was being toyed with—and secondly, Finian was speaking Irish. The low-spoken syllables were strange and evocative, as if he were chanting an incantation, murmuring spells.

"It means Dublin," he said shortly.

"Bally cle, cle—" She sailed an irritated glance over her shoulder, even though she knew better than to expose a weakness such as irritation—again, the experience born of being a sister, even if she was the elder. "Why not just call it by its name?"

"'Tis its name. Dublin is what the Northmen used to call it. And now the Saxons *gall* call it that as well. But her name is Baile Átha Cliath."

Not Vikings, not English foreigners. Irish.

She glanced over her shoulder again. He didn't appear angry, or any less imperturbable than he had thus far. He was walking as steadily as ever, obviously adjusting himself to her pace, because again, he barely appeared to be exerting effort. His eyes caught hers.

She faced forward. "Oh."

The trees to their left opened slightly. She could see the road below them, winding its silvery outline under treetops, hugging the hillside. From out of the silence came his rough-edged murmur, "And, nay."

The trail had narrowed to a rather alarming degree, so Senna didn't bother to look around this time. "Nay, what?" she asked, as calmly as possible.

"Yer query, Senna. Nay, this isn't the way to Dublin."

She stopped so short he walked up the back of her heels. "What?" she whisper-shouted, trying to turn around on the sinuous path. "You promised to take me to Dublin."

"I ne'er promised such a thing, lass."

She glared over her shoulder. His chest was barely inches from hers, and she contemplated elbowing him over the side of the ridge. "You did!"

"I did not. Becalm yerself," he added quietly.

She glared. She was practically crackling with fury. She was also being quiet. Angrily quiet. *Vehemently* quiet.

"I will be calm when you—"

His hand snaked out and closed over her mouth, silencing her.

"Riders." His gruff voice was a notch above silence.

And like that, Senna's orientation shifted. No longer was she aware of her leaden, weary limbs, nor her desperate situation, nor the fear that had been marking its way up the back of her neck like the tip of a knife. She wasn't even terribly aware of the riders on the highway, some forty feet below. She was aware, only, of *him.*

His fingers gently held over her lips. The touch of his wide wrist against the side of her neck. His thighs just behind hers, pressing heat onto the back of her legs.

She drew a steadying breath and inhaled the scent of him, the river and the wild, stones and pine.

"Fimiam?" she puffed against his hand.

"Can ye not hush for a single second?" he whispered back, but his words were made of breath, his jaw an outline of heat beside her ear. Her back and buttocks were warm from him.

She could hear the men on the road far below, muffled voices and shuffling hooves.

Riders? What of it? What did this man taste like?

She trembled, from fear, surely, but more, from the power of this new, reckless desire. The root of her mother's evil. Reined in for years, bound by books and ledgers, *now* being released? While she was on the run from a madman? The onrushing strength of it shocked her.

He must have felt her trembling. The hand covering her mouth slid to her cheek, and his thumb stroked gently by her jaw. His other hand skimmed up her back and rested warmly between her shoulder blades. She shivered, not whatsoever from fear.

"Nothing to fear, lass," he murmured. "'Tis but a messenger and his man. They are not seeking us. All we have to do is let them pass."

All I have to do is taste you.

Senna jerked at the thought. No, not a thought, an *urge,* rising out of something so deep inside her it pulsed with each heartbeat.

He put his mouth by her ear. "Easy, now, Senna." His thumb stroked her jaw as if he were gentling a wild thing. His sculpted body was hot behind hers. "Be easy."

"Stop touching me," she pleaded in a whisper.

His thumb stopped moving. "What?"

"Kiss me."

The rest of him went completely still.

Oh, please, Lord, deliver me from this. But it was too late. His body was too hot. She was too far beyond the Pale.

"What did ye say?" he asked in a low, masculine rumble.

Her heart started a strange thudding. Their voices were so quiet that the breeze blowing over them nearly drowned them out. Both were held paralyzed by the riders on the highway below. No one was going anywhere. In fact, it might all be over in a matter of minutes. And all she wanted was his touch.

If I am going to die, she suddenly decided, *it will not be absent the touch of this Irishman.*

She touched his hand and slid it across the mere inch back to her lips. Shutting her eyes, she trailed the tip of her tongue over his warm flesh.

His body rippled slightly, like wind over waves. She felt every muscle in his body shift, very minutely, very definitely. He brushed his thumb once over her parted lips. Her breath shuddered out.

"Did ye tell me to kiss ye, Senna?"

"I did." Her whisper trembled.

"Why?"

"Because," she whispered, "if I'm going to die, it will not be lacking all the things I am lacking at present."

A pause. "Ye're lacking a kiss, then?"

She nodded.

For a moment, everything held suspended. Then he cupped the back of her head and turned her to him. His eyes were unreadable, with no hint of a smile, but something else was there. Something dark and masculine.

Each inhalation she attempted was short, chopped. Each exhalation came out long and slow and hot. It made her head spin. He bent to her.

She felt warm breath on her cheek. Soft, teasing kisses danced across her cheeks, her eyelids. She sighed and he tightened his hold ever so slightly on the back of her head, as if holding her still. He cupped her cheek with his other hand and his lips finally settled over her own, whisper light, coaxing her: *Remember you are a woman.*

He bent lower and nibbled her lower lip until, as if he'd uttered a password, she parted for him. He slid his tongue between her lips, a single hot swipe. Ribbons of desire uncorded between her thighs.

He pulled back and whispered through her hair, "Is that what ye were thinking of?"

In the distance, the riders passed down the highway. Finian said nothing. She heard nothing. Leaning forward the barest inch, she grazed his full, warm lips with hers. He exhaled lightly. She liked that.

Her tongue slipped out and glided across his lips and another deep, masculine groan rumbled out. Her body quivered. Repositioning herself on her feet, she tasted him until she felt the tip of his questing tongue. Pushing boldly, she slipped her tongue inside his hot mouth.

A flash of touching, a swipe of tongues, then she withdrew, barely capable of drawing breath. Panting and enflamed, she whispered in his ear, "Oh."

Her word came on a hush. Indeed, a squirrel in the tree above would not have heard it. But Finian did. Finian felt her warm, sweet breath against his cheek, drifting into his ear. He shifted, as the hardness between his legs stiffened further.

He was not on a mission of seduction, but there was nothing to be done about this moment. It was happening. And he was suddenly powerless to be the one to end it.

They stood together without touch; there was only the exchange of heat and breath between their bodies. Such closeness was highly erotic.

"The riders have gone," he said reluctantly, waiting for her to step away.

But she didn't. She stayed, her breasts barely skimming his chest. One heartbeat, then another. "Have they?" she whispered.

With deliberate slowness, he splayed his fingers around her ribs, then slid them down, to the curve of her waist.

"Have ye had yer kiss, Senna?"

"Have you?" she murmured against his ear.

The breath shot out of Finian's lungs as if chased by a demon. No, he had not had his kiss.

Gently, he ran his fingers up her back, breathing steadily in her ear, the tip of his tongue teasing the skin just below. She shivered and clasped her hands hesitantly behind his head.

Heaven, these sweet womanly curves, this arching spine, this feminine breath grown ragged.

He entangled his fingers in the braided knot at the base of her skull and with a few swift tugs, pulled it loose. Her hair tumbled over his hands and wrists. He groaned at the softness sliding between his fingertips and buried his face in it, murmuring sweet, approving words. He slid his other hand ever downward, to the dip in her spine, pulling her closer, until her breasts pressed against him, and he bent to her mouth.

When her lips parted, her tongue met his, and the sigh she surrendered shot another bolt of desire through his groin.

His kiss intensified, his tongue no longer slow and dancing, merely coaxing her to flirt with danger. Now he demanded, laid claim. He pushed her for more, hotter, deeper kisses, using his carnal knowledge against her innocence, until she gave him his response; she whimpered and pressed up to him, offering her curving body, her mouth open wide, her tongue wet and hot in his mouth. And he took. His hands roamed her back, her ribs, coming close but never touching the soft rounded breasts so close to his thumbs. She shifted and shimmied, wanting the touch.

Lust churned through him, dark and purposeful. He slid his hands down in a bold move and cupped her bottom, his hands spread wide, almost lifting her.

"*Oh,*" she whispered into his mouth, moving with reckless, wanton little pushes. He molded a hand down the back of one thigh and exerted a small pressure, urging her to lift her leg for him. She did, bending her knee into his hand, shifting so his erection pushed against her, long and thick.

She threw her head back and bit off a cry.

Finian knew the feel of surrender, felt the bending of her spine and, battling the roar of lust surging through his blood, he pulled away. She was completely untutored in her body, that was obvious. The only thing more obvious in all the world was that if the sun rose, it also set, and until tonight,

Senna de Valery had known nothing of the shuddering glories her body was created for.

She'd just been awakened.

With no choice in the matter. No real choice. She hadn't known what was coming. And he couldn't imagine anything more despicable than doing, with the best of intentions, what he suspected so many others had done with the worst: use her as a means to his own ends.

He let her go.

She stumbled backward, her cheeks flushed, her hair in wild, glinting disarray, her fingers reaching up, touching her face, as if amazed to find herself still there.

He bent over, hands on his thighs, and stared at the ground. "We'll not have any more of that," he said to the dirt.

"No," she gasped. "Certainly not."

He looked up, palms still pressed on his thighs. Even through the darkness he could see her lips were slightly swollen from his kisses. Her hair was mussed and looked like a dim halo, loose sprays of red star-tails around her nose and cheeks. Her chest was fluttering up and down, her breath unsteady, rapid. Aroused.

He straightened. "Let's be off."

"But, what of Dubli—Bathy Clee," she whispered, trying to pronounce the Irish word.

"Whether we're going to Dublin or hell, Senna, we first have to go up that hill." He jerked his head in its direction. "Travel near the highway is unsafe. So," he added when she opened her mouth, "is talk."

"Oh?" she retorted, unconsciously gathering a collar she didn't possess closer to her neck, in a protective feminine gesture. "But kissing is allowed?"

"I don't know, Senna. That'll be up to yerself. Is kissing allowed?"

Without waiting to see if she replied, followed, or began ripping her clothes off, a fairly slim likelihood, Finian admitted, he started off, deep into the Irish woods.

Chapter 15

They walked throughout the night, weaving their way deeper into the countryside. Finian kept watch, gently correcting her when she was about to tread into a tree or a hole, but otherwise said little, unless she asked a question, usually shrilly, usually about a sound.

"What was that?" she whispered once, huddling close to his back as they trekked swiftly up an exposed hill.

"A nightjar." He looked down. "A bird, Senna."

A few moments later she threw her hand over her heart when they entered a clearing and an owl hooted loudly, swishing overhead. She ducked.

"Ye've owls in England, haven't ye, Senna?" He knew he sounded irritable, which he wasn't. Not with her. But he was highly irritated with the way his body behaved every time she pressed near.

"I wouldn't know," she retorted, sounding just as irritated. "I'm hardly out walking at night a great deal, now, am I?"

He just lifted an eyebrow and kept going. They reached the edge of the clearing and ducked beneath the trees. A flutter of wings and brush exploded beneath their noses. A covey of birds shot into the air. Senna tripped backward and landed on her buttocks.

"And that?" she demanded in a whisper.

"Birds, Senna. Some are ground-dwelling, build their nests in leaves and rocks and such. We disturbed them."

She scrambled back to her feet and brushed her bottom off with her uninjured hand, grimacing. "I suppose we did."

Grayness was slowly overtaking the black of night. Even beneath the forest canopy the darkness was lightening. He pointed to a wall of long-clawed brambles just ahead. Some of the thorns were as long as a toe. Senna studied them.

"You jest."

He started forward. "I never jest about things that bite."

They pushed through slowly, Finian holding aside the worst offenders with his mailed forearm and sword. The brush crowded back into place behind them with eager rustlings and clickings. They finally emerged, slightly scratched and breathing heavily, on a meadow near the crest of a ridge.

"We rest here," he said shortly. "We have until twilight."

A fervent orange glow pulsed along the edge of the horizon, bringing light and heat to their chilled fingers. Finian threw himself on the ground, absorbing the respite for all it was worth. He closed his eyes and flung out his legs and arms, letting the fresh air and morning dawn flow over him like water.

"When you look like that, Finian, I can see you as a boy."

He opened his eyes and stared at the dark blue-black sky overhead, still pricked by a few stars, then shifted his gaze down. Senna sat, arms hooked around her knees, considering him.

He cocked an eyebrow. "Is that so? A lad? In what manner?"

She smiled. "In the stubborn sort of manner."

He snorted. "We're two of a kind, then."

Her smile faded. "No." She shook her head. "Not so much." He watched from beneath his lids as she got to her feet and stumbled, head down, to the edge of the ridge, one hand pressed to her spine as if for support.

Small birds trilled and chirped. Fresh pine scents filled the air. The weak but fiery sunlight warmed his bruised legs as he lay, arms crossed under his head. Sleep crept in, dragging his eyelids shut.

The sudden sound of pebbles kicking out snapped them open again, but it was just Senna. Although now her body stance was entirely different than a few minutes ago. Her chin was up, her shoulders back.

He pushed to his elbows. "What is it?"

"That"—she turned to him with a smile—"is a beautiful sunrise." She gestured to the horizon. Though hushed, excitement carried her words clear across the meadow. She sounded like she'd made a discovery.

He glanced briefly at the sunrise, then back to her.

"Aye, beautiful," he agreed slowly. "'Tis a powerful draught you've sucked on."

The sun had expanded from a pulsing orange to a warm golden orb. Their shadows had shortened a quarter inch. Dew sparkled in flashes of green and sapphire in the chilled air. And she stood at the forefront of it all, a dark, curving figure, but the fiery glints of her hair picked up copper and gold from the sun.

She touched her cheek as if trying to feel what he might be referring to, then gestured to the horizon again. "'Tis a beautiful day."

"Aye," he agreed. "A mighty tonic, that fact."

If Senna could see him as a lad, he could see her as a young lass, all wide-eyed and wondering, sending men into madness even at that age. The cliffs around her home were probably littered with the bodies of unsuspecting knights who came to find a wife and ended up hurtling themselves off bluffs to escape her bewitching, obstinate beauty.

"I admit, I don't think I've been out for a sunrise in . . ." She paused, figuring. "Three years," came the final report.

"Been hunched over a desk, have ye?"

She half shrugged. "Something like that."

A good merchant. And yet . . .

Untutored passion practically pulsed from this woman. Their kiss on the ridge proved it. She was packed with something molten, and it spilled out in everything she did, from removing her hand from Rardove's grip to flinging herself over boulders. To kissing him.

He frowned. What did that matter? He had no time for things of the heart. No interest. No capacity.

Women's bodies, though, he had interest and ability there. But much as he could not live without their curving bodies and pretty smiles, they had never captured anything more enduring than his attention. Noble or peasant, dainty or voluptuous, he loved them all equally: not enough to matter.

He had nothing to give. He paid it little mind. For what reason dwell on the truth that he would always be alone?

Better than becoming what his father had: ruined by a woman.

That was not his path. His duties for The O'Fáil, foster father and king of the greatest *tuatha* in Ireland, were endless. Chief negotiator, councilor, and diplomat, Finian's position occupied him constantly, by desire and design and great, pressing need.

At present, that need was simple and dire: find the secret recipe of the Wishmé dyes before Rardove did. Or else their lands, their lives, and possibly large tracts of Ireland would be lost to the English king, Edward I.

There was nothing left for women, nothing meaningful, and certainly nothing moving.

Which is why he was surprised to find that, notwithstanding his current, dire circumstances, and their direct connection to those consequential duties, he was enjoying the distraction Senna provided, with her bright eyes and bright wit and the bright, surprising things she kept saying and doing.

"Why do ye do that, Senna?"

She flipped open the flap of her pack and knelt carefully upon it, as if it were a small table linen, then started rebraiding her hair. As her fingers twirled in and out of the reddish-yellow silk, he kept remembering how it had felt, crushed in his palms. How she'd arched her body for him, and—

"Why do I do what?" she asked.

He dragged his gaze from her hair. "Accounts. Ledgers. Hide yourself from the sun."

He'd never known a woman who kept accounts. And he could not imagine why she would choose to be bound up in a line of numbers, clicking wooden markers across a stone, when she could be out in the sunrise she just admitted to missing for the *past three years.*

"The books need to be kept."

Ah. Well, then.

She adopted a look of exasperation. "The business is large, ever expanding," she explained in a tone of . . . was she reprimanding him? "You've no idea the work it takes, Finian."

He stretched out on the ground, head resting on his crossed palms, grinning a little. "I'd know if I loved sheep as much as ye do."

A moment of shocked silence ensued. "I do not love sheep. Not a'tall. I love—"

Then, mystery of mysteries, she faltered.

"Money?" he suggested.

A pale flush slid up her cheeks.

Which is why, even if he had been inclined for more than a tumble—which he most certainly was not—her all-but-admission that money ruled her world should have been enough to cool his ardor. His experience with women said only that Senna was more honest in admitting to it.

It didn't make her any less mercenary. But it definitely made him less interested.

Or should have.

"'Tisn't funny." She was all about reprimand now. The edges of her mouth puckered around disapproval. She picked up a stick and began shredding it. He could see the light of determination in her eye. Or mayhap it was something not so nice.

It mattered naught, either way. Mercenary or saint, she was not his.

"Wool is highly lucrative business," she declaimed. "I have been building it for . . . I know every penny that comes in and goes out . . . I am in charge of everything. I hire the carters and wagons. I ensure we've stalls at the fairs. I negotiate the contracts. Barns, ewes, safe conducts, I arrange them all. *I* charter the ships. *I* hire the laborers. *I* pay the creditors. I—"

She must have hit some internal sea wall, for the deluge of instruction on the merits of the wool business—or perhaps of her—came to an abrupt halt.

He waited.

A moment later, staring at the ground, she said in a quiet voice, "I'm awfully good at it."

He was certain she was. The best. But her face looked as if it had been carved from wood, and her voice was hoarse, like sand had swept over it in a storm.

"Awfully, is it?" he echoed.

She stared at the stick in her hands. "You've no idea."

She said it so quietly he might not have heard, her words like moths fluttering away from a light extinguished. Then she tipped her chin up with a sudden shove, as you might if you were preparing to lift a heavy weight.

"I know about awful things," he said, surprising himself. He did, indeed, know of dark things. He simply never spoke of them.

She considered him out of the corner of her eye. "Do you?"

"Aye. I know two things." He held up two fingers.

An infinitesimal smile tipped up her mouth. "Which two?"

"I know they are sticky, and I know they are always behind us."

"Sticky?"

"Aye. They stick, if ye let them, like pitch."

First one cheekbone, then the other rounded and lifted into a much larger, genuine smile. "Indeed. They stick," she echoed softly.

"But I also know they are not here. Not now."

Her eyes were on his. "No," she agreed. "They are not here, now," and the husky, considering tone of her agreement was the most beautiful thing he thought he'd heard in decades of tossing awful things over his shoulder and walking on.

Morning sun lit up the side of her face. In the prisons, in the bailey, even in Rardove's candlelit hall, she had been all reflected light and shadow. But here, as the sun rose and the shadows shortened, she was like a drop of dew on a flower, bright and glittering.

"Rardove is likely ruing his error in judgment about now," he remarked, mostly to himself, for in the daylight, one could see what a jewel had been tossed aside.

She snorted. "For certes. He could have had a lucrative showing in the wool trade. Instead, he speaks to me of marriages and dyeing." She shook her head.

Finian sat up straight. "Rardove spoke of dyeing?"

"Aye. Some mad notion of his."

"The Wishmés?"

She was mid-nod before she stopped, abruptly. She looked at him with a new, considering regard. "The Irish know of the Wishmé indigo?"

"We know," he said in a flat voice.

"Legend." Her words tumbled out quickly. "Rumors, all. Wishmés. The Indigo Beaches. Rardove lands are not the

Indigo Beaches of legend. Pah." She pushed a length of hair behind her ear and picked up another stick.

"*Now* Rardove lands," he said quietly, tamping down on the churning in his gut. "Upon a time, they were Irish lands."

Indeed. Upon a time, they were *his* lands. His family's.

Still, he ignored the urge to grab her by the shoulders and demand to know how much she knew and why she knew anything at all, because when it came to the Wishmés, the more one asked, the more one revealed. And it was worrying enough that this lick of English flame knew of them at all.

He resigned himself to saying simply, "The Wishmés have been forgotten for many years now."

"But they are just legend." Oddly, it sounded like a question.

Even more oddly, he answered it. "What do ye think, Senna? Do ye think Rardove would cause all this trouble for a lie?"

"I think Rardove is past mad."

He laughed. "Be they truth or no, Senna, the Wishmés have a way of ruining people, and ye're better off far away."

She looked over at him. Her eyes shone in the morning sunlight. "I've seen them," she admitted in a low voice. "I have seen the Wishmé dye."

His heart sped up. "Have ye?"

She nodded. "Rardove had a sample, a piece of linen dyed with the indigo. Have you ever seen the color, Finian?" she asked, her voice low and eager. "'Tis the most astonishing shade of blue . . ."

"'Tis alchemy," he replied, unable to stop himself.

Something like enthusiasm was wending its way into her voice, lightening the dark sternness that occurred when she spoke of her business. "I can hardly describe it. If someone could recreate that color, it would be . . ."

He waited for the last word to slip from her lips, wondering what she might say. He'd grown up near these beaches, listened to the tales of the old dyers and their lost, secret recipes. Like alchemists of beauty, the wizened old Domhnall and sharp-tongued Ruaidhri were as legendary to Finian as Fionn mac Cumhaill, Tristan and Isolde.

Upon a time, the dyers of the Indigo Beaches had wrought such stunning shades of royal blue that the Roman Caesars heard of them. In the end, though, the Caesars were unconvinced a trip across the Irish Sea would be worth the additional warfare. And right they were, Finian thought grimly.

So the Irish dyers had worked their art in peace; but, growing wary, they closed the circle of initiates, allowing fewer and fewer to practice the craft, or even see the color, until finally the eye-shattering indigo was crafted only for the High Kings, only upon their coronation on the rock at Tara, a rare and royal privilege. Over time, the Vikings came, and the Normans, and the secrets were lost.

Until Rardove came. Twenty-one years ago, when Finian was ten, Rardove came and stole everything, including the title—although not the secret—of the Indigo Lands.

And now, for the first time since the Roman Empire fell, word was leaching out again: rumor of the Wishmés and their magnificent, consecrated colors.

So Finian waited to hear the words fall from Senna's lips, seeing the color of blue in his mind's eye. He felt a kinship with her, for her appreciation of their beauty, a feeling of connectedness he had not known for a long time. How would she choose to describe the shade his ancestors created in secret? Glorious? Astonishing, again? Pretty? Simply, 'blue'?

He did not for a moment expect the word that *did* fall from her lips.

"Lucrative."

He felt like someone had stomped on his chest. He lay down and shut his eyes. "Go to sleep, Senna."

Throwing his forearm over his face, he hovered in the familiar state of half repose, half alertness, his mind wandering over paths of the past that were not restful at all.

* * *

Senna sat at the edge of the ridge. Blue-gray shadows still stretched long, but a russet-gold, grainy dawn light was nudging its way farther into the corners of a small hamlet far below.

She cast a furtive glance over her shoulder. Finian's hands were crossed behind his head, his head resting on his palms. Long black hair spilled out over his wrists and onto the grass. The skin on the underside of his arms was paler than the rest, the faint outline of carved muscles beneath pressed into the silky skin. His long body stretched out across the spring grass, his powerful legs crossed at the ankles. His breathing was deep and regular.

She crept closer and lay down, near him but not touching. She cradled her injured hand to her chest by habit more than pain. She put her head on the hard ground and smelled the cool dirt and pale green points of grass. She looked up into the sky and watched the day take its bright, wild shape. It was endless and blue. Mayhap too endless, too blue. Too much for her.

Even so, she was unable to still the excited pounding in her chest.

For the first time in a long time, she *knew* she was alive.

Chapter 16

"I will kill her. I will flay her skin into strips and toast them over the fire."

The steward Pentony watched impassively as Rardove, recovered from his sudden gut affliction, had been on his way out for a morning hunt when the maid brought the news that Senna was neither in her room nor the dye hut. A minute later, the guards from the prison came up as well, holding their bashed heads and groaning.

Rardove had flung his gloves to the ground and taken a few enraged spins around the room, shouting and cursing.

It was still dark inside the hall, a dreary, damp darkness. A thin sheen of moisture smeared itself across everything: musty bits of straw scattered across the floor, wary faces, a hound's glistening black nose, poised quivering in the air as the rumor of violence entered the room.

A faint gray dawn light shouldered its way through the windows slitted high along the walls, but the ashen illumination only accented sullen shadows lurking within the pits of the jagged stone walls. In the fireplace, a fire flared up in occasional bursts of enthusiasm, but even these flashes of brilliance finally succumbed to the raw dampness pervading the hall.

Rardove's roar drew his attention back. "Goddamned *bitch!*"

Pentony's hand surprised him by lifting to scratch at a phantom itch on his scalp, then along his inner arm. He stared down at it as if it were possessed. Restless movement connoted nervousness or agitation, both of which were as foreign to him as naïveté.

He forced his hand to hang at his side, its proper resting place. For nigh on thirty years his body and heart had been frozen, stilled from such dangerous revelations of emotion.

Such efficient invisibility had once allowed him entry into the highest places. Bailiff in the king's service and then cellarer for the abbot of Tewkesbury, the most powerful obedientiary in the abbey, he'd been in charge of the lands revenues and church patronage. He had overseen every aspect of the abbey, from the kitchens to the brewery, from maintenance of the buildings to provisioning of foodstuffs, fuel, and farm stock. All lay brethren, servants and tenants, had come under his direction. All monies were at his discretion.

Both positions had been prestigious and lucrative. His fall from the grace of God—or at least the prior of Tewkesbury—had been almost as great as his sin, but he regretted nothing. Certainly not parting company with men of God who wielded their piousness like a weapon.

He glanced down at his wayward hand again. It hung deceptively still, but he could feel the urge toward movement prickling up the inside of his wrist.

"And goddamned Irish *savages!*"

The baron's bellow bounced around the room, followed by a wine goblet. Pentony watched as he turned his rage on a more likely and responsive victim, wincing as Rardove's boot thudded against a dog's ribs. The hound leapt up, yipping, then slunk away. Another pewter cup bounced off the wall and sounded a flat *clang* before it fell as quiet as the dog.

"As God is my witness," Rardove said into the sudden silence, "I will kill them both."

"My lord," Pentony murmured, "I have readied the men to search."

Rardove barked in harsh laughter. "How in God's name did she do it?"

"The men are at the gate, ready to be gone on your command."

"She is a goddamned *sorceress,* I tell you, bedeviling plans years in the making. I had O'Melaghlin right here"—an angry flick of his finger indicated the cellars below—"and I would have had that damned recipe. Now he's gone, and he's got my dye witch." Rardove cursed again. "Search her room. And send a contingent north to find them."

Pentony took a step forward. "They may not be going north, my lord."

Rardove rounded on him. "Not go north?" he shouted. "In which direction does the Irish king O'Fáil live? His foster father?"

"North." Pentony said it flatly, as if not a single emotion was present. Which none was. It had been too long. "I am simply saying we ought not to underestimate O'Melaghlin. If you send a few men sou—"

"And where did they find that scrap of O'Melaghlin's tunic?"

"Along the Bhean River. To the north."

"Exactly. O'Melaghlin is chief councilor to the O'Fáil. He's their spy, their negotiator, their goddamned battle commander. He's their *fycking head.*" He flung his gloves on the table and snatched up a jug of wine. "He went north."

He didn't even bother pouring it into a cup, just lifted the fluted lip to his mouth and drank, then slammed the vessel back on the table.

"And if he finds out who Senna is, that she is the last in the line of Wishmé dyers . . . ?" He smashed his fist on the table again, making plates skip. "And if King Edward finds out?"

This was asked rhetorically, Pentony assumed, or else he'd have given a reply. But they both knew quite well what the king of England would think if he found out Rardove had been keeping secrets. That he'd found a dye witch and was trying to make the recipe without the king's knowledge.

Seeing as Edward had granted Rardove the land twenty-one years ago for this express purpose, on Rardove's express promises, he would not be pleased at all.

Rardove never should have let King Edward in on the secrets of the dyes. Royalty was best enjoyed from a distance.

But then, without the promise of the dyes, King Edward would never have granted Rardove the land in the first place, not after the renegade Rardove had marched in and seized the land without royal permission. The promise of perfecting the Wishmés into weapons was the only thing that stayed the king's hand and invested Rardove with the barony.

Now matters had turned desperate for the English king. The Scots were showing their rebellious side. Banding together, signing treaties of mutual aid with France, they were all but declaring war. The old inducements—burning, plunder, swords through the heart—all seemed to have lost their persuasive power. Edward needed a special weapon to herd the Scots back into the fold. Rardove was to give it to him.

The Wishmés were a battle commander's alchemy. Awe-inducing in shade, they were also violently incendiary. Powdered and heated, they created an explosion that could burn so fast and hot it would incinerate a man. Or a building.

Or . . . Scotland.

There was no way Edward could win a long-lasting military victory against the Scots, not if the barbarians kept fleeing to the hills at the first sign of pitched battle.

But he *could* start blowing things up, in small batches,

things like recalcitrant nobles and native aspirants to the throne of Scotland.

He would not be pleased to discover Rardove was trying to perfect them as a weapon behind his back.

"What do we know about that other contingent of Irish?" Rardove snapped. "The one we captured?"

"He broke," Pentony reported with distaste and, to his surprise, realized he didn't know if the distaste was more for the breaking, or the means by which he was broken. "It seems that while you were . . . meeting . . . with O'Melaghlin, he was on his way to a rendezvous with Red. The outlaw."

Rardove's head snapped around. "While O'Melaghlin was here."

"Drawing your eye."

"You are suggesting he was here to *distract* me?"

Pentony shrugged. "Perhaps."

Rardove emitted another series of foul curses, then turned to the matter at hand. "The Irish were to meet with the spy-bastard Red? About what?"

Pentony didn't bother to comment. How could they possibly know the purpose of the meeting? And in any event, Red was not the outlaw's true name. No one knew that. But Red's intrigues were renowned, for all that they usually concerned faraway Scotland and England, and the man had been like a phantom for almost twenty years, foiling plans of King Edward in his campaigns against the Scots. Now Red was turning his attention to Ireland? That could not be good. For King Edward.

"Where were they to meet?"

Pentony shook his head in reply. "We do not know. The Irishman died before he could say."

Rardove shook his head, perhaps disgusted at his soldiers' inability to moderate the severity of their beatings with more finesse. He snapped his gaze to Pentony. "What are you waiting for? Send for Balffe. He goes north, to capture O'Melaghlin and the bitch."

The soldiers were gone within twenty minutes, draped in armor and swords and their lord's rage. The huge, hulking figure of Balffe, riding at their head, was the last thing Pentony saw as he watched from atop the gate tower.

Thick-quilted gambesons and a layer of boiled bull-hide provided the first layer of protective bulk for the men. Then came the mail hauberks, small, overlapping iron rings that covered the torso and hung to midthigh, slit along the sides to allow for movement. Overlaying this they wore steel breastplates and backplates, riveted in place. Steel helms covered their heads, saving for the ominous slitted eye openings. Steel greaves and poleyns for covering legs, shins, and feet completed the ensemble.

They were outfitted for war.

Pentony watched until the only upright figures on the landscape were the trees on a distant plain. He wondered what Senna had been wearing when she snuck out of the castle last night.

Chapter 17

The gaping tear in her tunic was the first thing Finian noted through his half-opened eyes. The next thing he saw was the rounded tops of her breasts.

She was kneeling beside him, leaning over him, close to his face. Her hair, freed from its braid, tumbled down like a silken, if slightly dirty, curtain. Instinct kicked in and he stretched his arm out, to pull her down.

"Don't you think it's time we start for Dublin?" she asked.

His arm fell away. "What?"

She sat back, knees bent, feet beneath her buttocks. She was bright, her cheeks a bit reddened from the sunshine of the day. "Dublin. Oughtn't we be on our way?"

He pushed himself up on his elbows and looked around, getting his bearings. Almost evening, closing in on Vespers. He took a deep breath, yawned, and pushed his fingers through his hair.

"We're not going to Dublin, Senna. I thought I told ye that."

She gave a clipped nod, as if she were barely up to the task of humoring him. "I recall something of the sort. I thought you were in jest."

"Is that so? If someone disagrees with ye, they must be joking?"

One pert eyebrow arched up. "When they say ridiculous things, indeed, I suspect a jest."

He leaned forward until their noses were barely a foot apart. "Listen well then, lass, for 'tis no joke: we're not going to Dublin."

She practically flung herself backward. "But why not?"

He sat back. "Use yer fine-looking head. Do ye not suspect the king's highway is exactly where Rardove will go looking for ye?"

"Well, I—" she began, then paused. "It might be where he'd look for me, Finian, but do you not think *this* way, deeper into Irish lands, is exactly where he'll go looking for *you?*"

He considered her a moment. "Ye must have been a sore trial to yer mum, Senna," he said, then lay back down and shut his eyes.

"I was a sore trial to me Da," she snapped, mimicking his Irish accent.

"We're not going to Dublin."

"You are serious."

"As mortal sin."

She was quiet, but in the ominous way a powerful wind might be, on the other side of a ridge, before it rushed over the top and bent trees beneath its fury.

"My business cannot manage without me," she warned.

"Then I suppose ye oughtn't have come to Eire."

He thought if she could have stabbed him in the heart just then, she might have. "I came for business," she explained icily.

"Ye came for money."

She sputtered, which he suspected was more due to an overwhelming excess of responses, rather than a lack.

He kept his eyes shut and tried to sleep. Tried to recapture the half-resting state of repose that marked his nights and substituted for sleep.

He'd been up for regular reconnaissance throughout the day, and Senna had been awake, too. He knew, because every time he'd risen, her gaze followed him, although her body never moved, rigid as a post kicked to the ground, arms clamped to her sides. She ought to be tired. But just now, she may as well have been pounding on his chest with her fists, for all that her energy had abated.

He finally sighed. "Ye're like a spring wind, Senna. Ye never stop pushing. We're not going to go tripping down the king's highway to Dublin. Ye're mad to think so."

"No. I'm mad to have ever believed you."

"I never said I'd take ye to Dublin."

"But I asked you to!"

"Och, well, ye ought to have found another guide, then. One more well suited to being ordered about."

She drew back. "I do not *order about.*"

He watched as she ripped her gaze away and stared across the small clearing, her hands twisting around each other with great, unrelenting pressure. The edges of her palms turned white from it. She suddenly sat forward, her spine rigidly straight.

"I *shall* go to Dublin," she announced imperiously. "At once."

"Is that so?"

"'Tis."

"Ye'll be going alone, then."

She swallowed but did not shift her gaze away from the no-doubt fascinating profile of a tree trunk. "How much will it cost?"

He gave a short bark of laughter. "What?"

"How much money do you want?"

He sat up slowly. "To take ye to Dublin?"

She gave a clipped nod, still staring away from him. But he

stared at her very hard. The back of her hair was starting to glow from the dipping orange sunrays.

"Whatever ye've got, Senna, it would not be enough to make me go to Dublin." He threw himself down again, coiled anger pushing through him. "English," he muttered. "And their coin."

She sighed in a resigned way. He felt hope.

"So be it, Finian," she said in a reasonable, therefore highly suspect, voice. "I understand your reasons for not taking me. I accept them."

He examined her more closely. She looked exhausted, like she'd been . . . escaping from a violent, enraged baron. Her eyes looked wide awake and alert, though. Quite alert. A bit too alert. Hectic, in fact.

"What are ye saying?"

"You cannot take me to Dublin, and I cannot traipse about the Irish countryside. I must get home."

Indeed, her eyes were far too bright. She was losing her mind.

"Ye've lost yer mind."

She scowled. "I know where the highway is."

"Oh, ye do, do ye?"

She nodded. "I have that sort of mind. It remembers things."

"Oh, aye? And do ye also remember where the quicksand is?"

She looked startled. "Quicksand? I don't believe I encountered quicksand."

"Och, well, it'll be hard to find then. And the wolf den? Do ye know where that is? And how about Rardove's village, a few miles south, the one you'll pass through when ye're marching down the highway?"

She looked rattled, but determined. "I wasn't going to walk down the middle, waving my arms about," she said sourly.

He wiped his palms over his face, a few vigorous strokes,

to bring blood to his head and help him sort this out. "Senna, ye've lost yer mind." He got to his feet. "I cannot go to Dublin. And therefore *ye* cannot go to Dublin. And I think ye know that."

She stared away from him with great purpose.

He sighed. "Ye look determined."

"A bad habit."

He leaned his buttocks back against a large rock. It was warm from a day of sunshine, heating the backs of his thighs. "I'd have to bind ye if ye tried, Senna," he said in a reflective tone, "and that would slow us down considerably."

The smallest flicker crossed her face. More determination? Laughter? The urge to haul off and hit him? He rubbed his hand over the back of his neck, then flung it down.

"Fine, then," he announced curtly. "Go. The way to Dublin is fair lined with swords. What road does every Saxon knight use? Upon what highway does yer fine king's governor travel? And tell me, which is the easiest road up north? Soldiers, merchants, *cows* travel the road to Dublin, Senna. And the first two would spit and roast a monk as quick as turn ye over for the reward Rardove's sure to put out on ye."

"They'll never recognize me," she insisted. "I can blend in."

He eyed her head skeptically. "With that hair?" Her hand shot up to touch her scalp. "Och, not a bit of it, Senna. That sort of magnificence will mark ye like a scent across the path of a fox. And a ship? Ye think ye'll gain berth on a ship?" He snorted, ignoring the bright pink blush rushing over her cheeks. "Ye'd be raped before ye hit the end of the quay. And anyhow," he added, more mildly at her shocked gasp, "I like yer company."

She jerked, startled, he was sure, by the rapid succession of compliment, threat, and veiled admission of . . . something.

"Cannot yer father manage your terribly important business for a bit?" he demanded irritably, to shove off the . . . something.

"*I* manage the business."

"Och, ye've made that abundantly clear, lass. And what does yer father do, while ye're managing his business so awfully well?"

"Gamble."

Finian felt his mouth opening in amazement, not so much from the news, for that was common enough, but from witnessing the brittle pain it nailed onto her spirit like a stake. Her body had gone stiff. Hard, no dents, she suddenly looked impermeable, like stained glass. Many bright colors, all seared in place.

He pursed his lips, then said gently, "Ah, Senna. That bug stings hard."

A blindingly bright smile ripped up the corners of her lips. "I know."

His heart did a little tumble. She was a woman-child, and whatever hurts she spoke of now, he was certain many more lurked in the shadows of her heart. Every penny that came in, counted in her silent ledger, must have been a coin measured against the rest of her life.

And her father was a fool.

"Senna," he said carefully.

Woodenly, she looked over, the edges of her mouth still tipped up in that false smile, like a painted marionette.

"Men are fools," he said in a low voice. "Ye're to remember that, above all other things."

She was quiet for a moment; then, to his surprise, she laughed. And such a laugh it was. Quiet. Pretty. Natural.

"Truth, Irishman, I suspected as much," she said, a smile dipping into her words like an oar, pushing them along. "But 'tis good to have it confirmed by one of their kind."

Ah, this one was a keeper. For someone.

"I suppose I can spare a few days," she allowed in a regal tone, as if it were up to her whether they came or went from

Dublin. "But I can't spend too much time with you, traipsing about these hills. My reputation, you understand."

"Before the next full moon, I'll have you bundled on a ship, Senna. My reputation cannot stand the strain of it either. Being seen with an English wool merchant?" He gave a little shudder.

She laughed, but his gaze lingered on her dirty face and limbs, her hair, long free of its confining braid, and her bright, intelligent eyes. A cord of worry unraveled in his heart. This woman had more wits, more bravery, more ingenuity than most battle commanders he knew, yet there appeared to be no one to seek her out, worry about her.

Just someone who, in all likelihood, wanted to kill her right now. And the man who'd abandoned her to him.

And Finian was to sail her away to England? To what end? Her father's home couldn't be an option any longer, not after this escapade. Neither was wandering the Ulster hills for twenty years. Travel, then? To where? With what money?

With no resources, no family to hand, and no connections, she was in a more precarious situation than if she'd stayed in the squalor of Rardove. She belonged nowhere.

Still, he decided as he reached for the leather straps of the bag she'd shoved on his back before leaving the prison, to say she was without resources was to be more foolish than the swiving bastard who had beaten her beautiful and burning body.

"Now, tell me, lass," he said, hoping to entertain her, whatever was required to keep her smiling, because it was a travesty what someone had allowed to be done to her, so that she could ice over with such chilling efficiency. "What have ye put in these bags ye've made us carry all these miles?"

She moved through the springy turf, her footsteps soft and muted. She stopped in front of him. He looked up, trailing his gaze over her filly-long legs, hugged tight by the hose, over her curved hips, and up the length of untamed curls.

"Rocks?" he asked. "All yer pretty baubles?"

One chestnut eyebrow arched up. Indomitable. He grinned.

"I don't believe in baubles."

"One doesn't believe in them," he said, amused. "They simply are."

Her other brow arched up, as doubtful and pretty as the first. "I wouldn't know."

He snorted. "I'll show ye, one day. Now, what's this?" He reached in and extracted a lump of putty soap. "Soap?"

She crossed her arms over her chest with one eyebrow hitched a little higher, silently inviting him to continue his survey.

Next out was a pair of breeches and a tunic, and he barked in laughter. "Ye've had us lug around clothes?" He was indescribably touched. "'Tis the epitome of a womanly thing to do," was all he said.

"A womanly thing?" Her voice was deep with suppressed laughter.

She stood with her hands on her shapely hips, her hair tumbling down around her, and he was shocked at the jolt of commingled desire and tenderness that coursed through him.

She was smiling, her teeth bright white against the dirtiness of her face. But her lips were still rosy and aching to be kissed, her breasts still full, her legs still strong and primed to be wrapped around his hips, he thought helplessly, running his hand through his hair as he bent back to the bag.

"What else might a man have brought?" she pressed.

"Och, mayhap weapons—"

"But I did. Did I not find you your very own sword, master? And a knife for us both, and a belt full of arrows?"

"That ye did."

"Tell me, then: what else would a proper-thinking man have provisioned for?"

"Foodstuffs," he suggested, a dark eyebrow arched in vague warning.

"You'll find them there," she said sweetly, tilting her head to the side. Her tunic slipped farther down her arm.

"But ye might have fit more, had ye not brought the clothes," he tried to explain.

"Mm." She tipped her head to the side. The sight of the pale smooth skin of her shoulder drew his eye briefly, then he looked back to her decidedly mischievous eyes. Mischief suited her. "Anything else, man?"

"Nay. A man would be traveling lighter, there's the difference," he grumbled.

"Then dig farther and see what else a woman brought." Her voice danced with laughter.

Out came, as she had said, dried berries and meat, bread and cheese. There was flint, some toiletry items, rope, and several clean linen squares. Then his hand alighted on a cool, hard surface. Realization dawned before he even saw it. He threw his head back and laughed as he lifted the flask of whisky into the air.

"Praise God, 'tis *uisce beatha!* Senna girl, I promise to never judge yer decision-making again."

He laughed, and she laughed, too, so for a moment she was scared by neither the people hunting her nor the people who would never hunt for her. He could see it in her bright energy, the simple happiness pouring out of her.

She dropped to her knees next to him. Digging eagerly through her own pack, she pulled out a twin flask of the drink, which she held in her bandaged hand. His eyes dropped to the sight. He dragged them back up when she spoke.

"I saw these flasks, and the whisky. Rardove mentioned it was his best. Some I gave to the guards, laced with valerian root. These, I brought for us." She grinned and tapped her flask to his.

Hearing her tale of small defiance, watching her face dissolve into laughter, Finian was gripped by a sense of affection and something else.

"Ye're a brave woman, Senna," he said gruffly.

"Not a bit. Although, with enough of this," she indicated the flask with a tip of her head, "I suppose I could become brave." She lifted it higher and looked at him, a smile playing at the edges of her mouth. "Shall we?"

He grinned. "Indeed. A little bravery might go a long ways, Senna." Holding up his flask, he uncorked it. "To my savior." He tipped it in her direction, then downed a huge swallow.

"Warrior," she said, lifting the flask toward him, returning the toast. Raising the bottle to her lips, she threw back a draught. Her shoulder tipped back as she arched her throat to swallow. Long reddish hair fell to the top of her rounded buttocks, which were pressed into her heels as she knelt beside him. He gritted his teeth. Strong, long legs. Bright, dauntless eyes. Passionate spirit.

This woman had not been crafted by God to run ledger rows.

He threw back another portion, then smacked his lips. "Aye, 'tis a good drink, but my brewers do a better job," he claimed. "'Tis smoother than this."

Her eyes were spilling over, her reply a wet sputter. "I hope that is so, Irishman, for this is harsh to my tongue."

She smiled at him and the pace of his world dropped to a slower beat. Her hand was on her waist, thumb behind her back, slim fingers curled over her ribs. Where he suddenly wanted his fingers to be with strong, surprising force.

He shoved to his feet. "Time to go, lass."

Chapter 18

They walked through most of the night. The moon was high and lit their way. Mostly they skirted the edges of fields and farms, staying just inside treeline, small, shadowed figures no one would notice. They hardly spoke, until they finally stepped out onto a path rutted from the passage of generations of people and sheep and cattle.

"No choice now, Senna," he murmured. "We've got to follow the road awhile. Stay to the edge, and help me find something." He was already bending low, looking into the ditches.

"You lost something out here?"

"I didn't lose anything. I know right what they are. Yarrow and comfrey root. And a bit of your valerian dust should do us well, if ye've any left."

"For my hand," she determined glumly.

"Just yer fingers," he said, scanning the ground. "We'll leave yer hand be."

"You could leave me be. My fingers, my hand, the whole lot of me."

"Do not be afraid, *a rúin*. I've healed wounds before—"

"I am not. Afraid."

He looked over his shoulder. She was staring at him coldly. "Ah. Ye sounded it."

"You misheard." He returned to his searching. "Yarrow needs to be made into a tea," she pointed out a moment later. "Comfrey wants hot water, too. We'd have to build a fire, and that would be unsafe."

He crouched beside the ditch and gently pushed under the delicate ferns, brushing them aside. He'd found what he was looking for. "I can make a fire ye wouldn't see till ye stepped in it, Senna."

"Oh."

They followed the narrow rutted path for maybe half a mile, before they skirted back into the forest. They walked until the moon was dipping below the tops of the trees before he stopped them for good. Senna bent her knees and dropped to the ground, unconsciously cupping her injured hand in her good one.

Finian knelt beside her, bending over her hand, pulling it gently from her grasp with soothing, wordless sounds. After a moment, he looked up. "'Tis poorly set."

She bit her lower lip and scowled. "What does that mean?"

"It means ye can leave it as 'tis and it will heal crooked, if at all. Or I can reset it." He sat back on his heels and regarded her levelly.

"That doesn't sound pleasant. What do you know of such things?"

"Nay, 'tisn't pleasant."

"What do you know of setting bones?" she prompted sharply.

He lifted a shoulder and let it fall. "Ye learn many things, living as I have."

"That is your answer?" She scowled. "Pah, you probably know nothing of it."

"I know more than ye."

She sniffed.

He sat back. “I suggest ye leave it, then. What does it matter if yer fingers cannot move as ye want them to, and are misshapen without need? Or mayhap oozing pus.”

He settled himself on a hummock beneath the branches of a nearby tree, watching her out of the corner of his eye.

She sat, stiff as a wagon spoke, glaring at a bush some ten paces off. Without her bright, engaging chatter, sleep layered quickly into his blood. Thick, heavy waves of it. He closed his eyes.

“Finian.” Her plaintive voice curled across the meadow.

“Aye?”

“I lost my comb.”

“Ah,” he replied slowly, unsure what response was called for.

“My hair is so tangled.”

There was quiet for a few moments. She played with the hem of her tunic.

“Finian,” her small voice called out again.

He raised his eyebrows, waiting.

“I need a bath.”

He rolled his eyes. “My apologies. I forgot to carry yer tub with us.”

“I do not like how you Irish folk place your rivers and streams. They are most inconveniently arranged. In England, there is one every few yards, at the least.”

Unlike the one they’d crossed yesternight, he supposed. “I’ll be sure to take ye to one as soon as I can.”

She was quiet a moment. “Promise?”

“Aye,” he replied gruffly. He closed his eyes.

A few moments passed. “Finian?”

“Senna?”

He opened his eyes and looked up. The leaves of the giant oak tree were dark above, and all around, stars dotted the sky.

“Did you say we were going to a town?”

“Aye.”

“Oh.” A bit of silence. “Does that seem wise?”

"Not in the least. Is that how ye think I make decisions?"

"I stand corrected. But . . . a town?"

"I haven't a choice. I've to meet someone."

"Oh." She sniffed. *"Someone."* Pause. "I hope she's pretty."

He closed his eyes. "Hard to be prettier than ye."

That brought another round of silence. 'Someone' had been rather a massive understatement on his part. His contact, the spy Red, had taken a grave risk contacting The O'Fáil, letting them know he had located the precious, lost dye manual. Whoever had the manual, and a dye witch, could make the weapons. Could blow up buildings. Could win a war.

At this point, Finian would be five days late, but five days or five years, he would still follow through. And he knew Red would wait. The payoff was enormous. The risks, including death, were negligible in the face of it.

"Finian." Her soft voice lifted again. "What were you doing in Rardove's prisons?"

He shifted his head against the gnarled bark, finding a more comfortable spot. "Walking through a muddy river."

"Oh. I suppose you do not mean the dampness of the cellars."

"Nay."

Another few moments ticked by.

"Finian?"

He dragged his eyes open. He'd been seconds from sleep. "Aye?"

"I need food."

He bestirred himself. Grabbing their bags, he knelt at her side and rummaged through them, then handed her a hunk of bread and cheese. He watched her chew without interest. She laid her hand on her lap. The food slipped to the ground.

"Finian?"

"Senna—" he interrupted, thinking to stop her scattered, hesitant talk. Talk, or sleep. Or passion, he thought languidly, but one or another fully. He was so weary he could almost hear sleep calling to him.

"My hand hurts. Help me with it, would you?"

"Aye." He reached for a flask. "Here." Tugging the cork free with a muted *pop,* he held the vessel in front of her face.

She wrinkled her nose, pushing it away. "It stinks."

He furrowed his brow. "Ye drank well enough earlier."

"That was then."

He sat back on his heels and exhaled noisily. The hair over his forehead lifted and lowered with the breeze. Senna watched with some interest.

"Drink," he insisted, holding the flask closer to her mouth.

She sighed as if enduring the torture due a martyr, then swallowed and sputtered.

"Another." His hand touched hers, his wide fingers curling around hers as he made her hold the flask and lift it to her lips.

She drank.

He coaxed her to take another couple long draughts; then, while waiting for it to take effect, he dug a deep, small hole and built a small fire in it, then prepared the herbs. He pounded out the root with the hilt of a blade while he boiled the water that he'd procured, then made up a poultice and a tea; then, finally, he removed the stained linen bandage from her broken fingers. It was caked with dried blood, stiff and thick and dirty.

"Ye haven't been at washing it," he scolded gently, his eyes not leaving her hand.

"*You* haven't taken me to water," she accused unsteadily.

He glanced up briefly. "We crossed a river last night."

She gave him an evil look. "On rocks. We crossed a river by leaping on large rocks. That hardly counts." She hiccupped. "Hardly."

"'Tis a grievous wrong I've done, mistress. I'll right it as soon as I'm able," he murmured, not paying attention to his words, only her beautiful, wrecked fingers.

"I'll remember that," she continued through gritted teeth as his sure fingers probed hers. "I stink to the high heavens. We both of us need a bath, and instead, we jump over rocks," she lamented in a singsong voice, then reached for the flask again, hiccupping quietly.

A smile lifted his lips, but his worried eyes and confident fingers never left her hand, feeling with his hand and his mind, seeing the bone. Let her prattle on, and let her drink.

"And after lying in Rardove's ditch," she went on after swallowing again, "I must smell worse than the leavings under the rushes. Why you tried to kiss me, I'll never know."

"I didn't try."

She shook her head sagely, as if lamenting the passing of chivalry. "'Tis a sad day, I tell you."

"Sadder than ye know. And ye asked me to kiss ye."

She glared from beneath lowered eyelids. "You're laughing at me."

"Never," he murmured, dusting his touch up the length of the ring finger of her left hand. This, and the little one beside it, they were the damaged ones. They'd not been set properly. Sinews were already threading themselves wrongly, roping themselves like snakes where they didn't belong. The bones would knit askew, and she'd never use these fingers again.

Rardove had known what he was doing. He hadn't shattered the bones—just a nice, clean break. And she could still function without these two fingers. Sick bastard.

"After scrambling around in the dirt with you," she slurred derisively, then hiccupped. "And without bathing—"

"Back to the bathing, are we?"

"—and you think I asked you to kiss me?" She shook her head. "You, who know so much about women—"

"Who said I know anything about women?"

"—should know a woman does not *ask* a man to *kiss* her." She looked at him triumphantly, her torso weaving slightly.

"Here." He shoved a large stick between her teeth. "Bite."

She took it but glared. "Moo, ambove all ufferz, fhould know a woman preffers—Ahhhhh!" she shrieked as he abruptly rebroke her fingers.

She flung herself backward, howling in pain. The stick tumbled to the ground. Rolling over onto her belly, she held her now-straight fingers in her good hand and rose to her knees, then staggered to her feet. Finian sat back and watched. She stumbled forward a few steps before falling to her knees again, clutching her hand and biting back screams of pain.

Finian was surprised it took as long as it did—perhaps a minute—before she found her voice. "Irishman," she vowed hoarsely, "come a time, I will hurt you as much as you just hurt me."

"I'll be counting the days," he drawled, pleased she showed fire. He must keep her in this angry state, for he still had to set the bones, lash them to hold them straight.

She was kneeling but no longer rocking. In the distance, a chorus of frog songs bubbled out of the creek. She sniffled.

"Ye're wailing and complaining in a childly way," he remarked coldly, to give her anger, and thereby strength.

She glared. "I neither wail nor com*plain*—"

"Come here," he ordered roughly, reaching out his hand, done with placating. There was a bone to be set and sleep to be had. He yawned hungrily and turned his palm up.

She staggered over, weaving as she came. She lowered herself, swaying slightly as she sat, her knees bent, legs kicked out to the side. Her hair was free of its confinement, a tumbling chestnut wave that spilled over her shoulders and down her back. She looked like she belonged in some sultan's palace. Or right where she was, on the hills, with him.

She shook and cried out as he worked on her fingers—first whisky, then poultice, then cobwebs, then strips of linen torn from the spare tunic in her pack. She kept him informed of every bolt of fiery pain that shot through her body, but she did not move her hand until he was done, by which time she'd become utterly quiet. He lifted his head to encounter a small, shocked, tearstained face.

With a muffled curse, he held out his arms. She fell forward into them and he wrapped her up, stroking her hair and murmuring soft, soothing words for a long time.

"The yarrow should start to dull the pain soon," he murmured eventually.

"'Tis a'ready."

"I'm sorry."

"You should be."

He held her tighter. Her faint words rose up some time later. "I am left breathing, which was more than I hoped for a few moments ago. My thanks."

"Aye, angel."

Her fingers throbbed with pain, but she suspected this was because Finian had shifted something back to right, and now the messages were flowing between her body and mind as they ought: *Attend. This hurts.*

In fact, many things hurt. Her fingers, her knees, due to the small jagged rock she was kneeling on, but she didn't move. Because more important than the pain was the feel of Finian's arms around her, the soft, gentling words he was murmuring in her ear, designed to comfort and calm. They did both.

After a while, with great reluctance, she disentangled herself from the solid warmth of him. One could not lie in a warm embrace indefinitely.

"I'm fine now," she said stiffly. He released her silently.

Throwing herself down on the ground, she tried to sleep. She punched the sack serving as her pillow and turned on her side. Ouch. Muttering, she flipped to the other shoulder. No, that was not helpful. She flung herself on her back, feeling the earth bite into her bones, and hummed until her own off-key tune annoyed herself. She tried imagining the sounds of a waterfall, hoping that would lure her into sleep. It didn't.

She stared up at the sky, which was lightening into predawn. It was no good, nothing helped. Tears loomed.

She heard a small movement in the grasses, then his arms were around her, pulling her backward into his warmth. He lay on his side and tucked her into his chest. As if she'd been waiting for just this, she relaxed.

"Rest, angel." His soft, rough voice rumbled through her hair, onto her neck.

His lean, hard body was stretched against hers, heating every inch of her from neck to knees. One powerful arm was slung over her hip, the other stretched on the ground above their heads. She sighed deeply. This was beyond goodly, and more than enough to hold her pain in abeyance. Now, how had he accomplished that?

"Thank you," she whispered just as sleep stole over her.

"Thank ye," he murmured back. She snuggled in and his hand tightened on her hip. She fit right in.

Chapter 19

When Senna awoke, Finian was already up, standing a few feet away, kicking more dirt atop what had been their firepit. Each time his foot moved forward, the rest of his body adjusted for the movement, muscular arms out slightly, the hair beside his face—that not trapped in its binding at the nape of his neck—swaying slightly. His chiseled face was dusky with beard growth. His gaze was intent on the pit.

She sat up. He looked over. His eyes dropped to her hand. "Yer fingers?"

She thought about them, then realized the fact that she needed to think about them with purpose was a good sign. "They do not throb so much, and there's no pock."

He nodded appraisingly. "Aye, no swelling. Here's yer chance to wash." He pointed to a small creek she hadn't noticed last night.

She looked at it without moving. There was absolutely no way she was going to undress in front of him.

"Now, lass. We leave as soon as we're done." He pointed again.

"I do believe a good rest was all I required," she said brightly. "Sleep," she added when he looked confused. "Not a bath."

His face cleared. One dark eyebrow slanted up. "I will not watch ye, Senna." Was he amused? It certainly appeared to be a smile threatening to break free on his face.

"I simply do not think 'tis wise to dampen my hand," she said coldly. "All your leech craft would have been for naught."

A small smile did curve up a corner of his mouth at this, but he didn't say any more. He finished with the fire and started unbuckling his hauberk. Its flap fell down over the soft undertunic and he dragged the armor over his head.

"I don't want to hear any regrets later," he said, his voice muffled.

She didn't reply. She was too busy staring in amazement: the Irishman was going to undress right in front of her! The armor came off, and he pulled up the bottom of his tunic. He was going to remove it. She couldn't rip her eyes away. Excitement flew around her belly like birds coming out of a nest, swirling and fluttering. He tugged up, revealing his flat stomach. Senna lurched back into speech.

"You shall hear no regrets," she said sharply. "Although it seems quite likely that you knew of this stream last night when I wished to bathe, and did not mention it . . ."

Her words trailed off. There was simply nothing more to say on the subject, and the tunic had gone up and over Finian's head, dropping onto the ground beside him.

Tangled black hair fell down around his smooth, muscular shoulders as he rotated each one in turn, stretching his head the opposite way and groaning in appreciation, apparently unconcerned that she was watching him undress. Staring. She wrenched her gaze away.

He stepped over to the far side of the creek that ran in the gully, an easier access point than the side Senna stood on, and ducked his head under the water. He came out wet, and shook his head, sending water droplets spraying into the air. He pushed his hair off his forehead with a swift push of his palm, then looked at her.

"So tell me, lass, why are ye the one managing the books for yer father's business?"

She watched as he splashed more water over his face, then took one of the cakes of soap and clumped its misshapen lump in his palm. He spread it over his cheeks and jaws. Reaching into the belt lashed to his waist, he pulled out a blade.

"You shave!" she exclaimed in surprise.

"Aye."

She watched in utter silence. When he was done, he plunged his head into the water a second time, threw his drenched hair back, and revealed his unbearded face for the first time.

Long dark hair slicked back, revealing the sharp, fine lines of his jaw and cheekbones. His mouth still held the grin that so beguiled, the one that made her heart thump, but now the full sensuousness of his lips was fully revealed, and it set her heart hammering as she recalled what he'd done to her with them.

Thick fingers entwined in his hair as he shoved the hair off his face, and before Senna's eyes flashed an image of them tugging through her own. The sculpted definition in his arms, bent above his head, exposed curves and lines that her eyes followed with greedy intensity. A dusting of dark hair covered his flat, ridged belly, which narrowed to trim waist and hips, then widened again to thick, corded thighs.

Her gaze devoured his body as if it were a meal, mindless of the fact that he was watching her watch him. Finishing, she lifted her gaze and encountered his wolfish grin.

"A woman who looks at a man like that, Senna, is a very tempting thing."

God save her, the Irishman knew every turning in her wicked thoughts, every depraved notion and erotic wanting that had flickered through her mind. She blushed. He cocked an eyebrow. Her flush met her hairline. She ripped her gaze away.

Apparently satisfied, he knelt back by the stream. "The accounts," he said, prompting her to recall his question.

She half turned her head, trying to ignore the sight of the bunched muscles of his thighs as he crouched beside the stream, splashing water over the cake of soap in his large hand, then rubbing it over his wet arms and chest.

"I manage the accounts because I am quite good at it."

"I didn't so much mean how ye came to it, Senna, as how yer father came to *not.*"

"Oh. Indeed. As I said, Sir Gerald gambled. Come a time, he would wager on anything. Horses, tourneys, raindrops, anything. Once he bet my mother's brother whether King Edward would choose Balliol or The Bruce to rule Scotland."

Finian picked up his tunic and rubbed it over his damp hair. "And which did yer father choose?"

She gave a bitter smile. "One of the few times he was right, and the only time he was not pleased. Gambling became his passion, after my mother left."

His gaze flicked over, but he didn't ask the question begging to be asked: *What do you mean, "after your mother left"?* Senna hurried on before he could. "Sir Gerald regularly raided the coffers. He has incurred debts to rather . . . unsavory men."

"Your father has dealings with unsavory men?"

"My father has dealings with whomever will feed the beast. Noble thugs or dock workers, what matters that?" She flicked him a glance. "You are not afflicted by it, so you would not understand."

"Unsavory, of what sort?"

"Of the manly sort, that comes to the house at night, sometimes in noble finery, sometimes plain as dirt." She was distracted by his undressing and washing and his glistening, wet body and such, but beneath the glory of Finian, she realized she was speaking of things she hadn't for many years. "The sort who visits late at night, and you hear their angry voices, but all in whispers, as if they are sharing great, angry secrets. The sort that is gone the next morning, your father along with them. Unsavory, of that sort."

He crumpled his tunic into a ball. "Ye call yer father Sir Gerald."

"Oh," she said, flustered and irritated. Why did he need to be perceptive as well? Could he not be lacking in *some* regard? "I'm used to referring to him thusly. Our contractors. Business, you know."

"Well, I'm fair surprised to find such a spirited lady coming from his seed."

"Me?" she shouted in laughter. "You must mean some other."

"Och, ye're right, now. I'm talking about all the other fine ladies who stole me out of prison."

Straightening, he stepped back across the stream and turned to reach down for his armor. The movement drew her eye. What she saw drained all the blood from her face.

"Mother of God," she whispered, all of it an exhale.

His back was shredded. Long, deep lacerations whipped in a jagged orbit around his body, bisecting one another in a red fire and tortured map of brutality. Some were scarring, some spoke of more recent acquaintance with a leather strap. She rose slowly to her feet, her eyes fixed on the horror.

"Jésu, Finian."

Gladiator muscles slid beneath his satiny skin as he turned to her. She could almost feel the razor-sharp whip snapping through the air, ripping open his flesh, tearing into the awesome strength beneath, like a knife cutting through a pear. Her trembling fingers passed a hairsbreadth above the ravaged flesh and she lifted her head to meet his steady gaze.

There are green flecks in his eyes.

"Ye suffered too," he murmured, his eyes lingering on the fading bruises of her cheekbones.

"Oh, Finian," she exhaled, feeling tears prick. Dropping to her knees, she dragged her pack over. "I've unguent," she reported in a shaky voice, digging through the bag. In wild arcs everything came out, scattering on the ground around her: a brick of hard cheese, three small pouches, linen scraps, a rope, strips of leather.

She lifted her head, holding up a small container as high as she could, which reached to the middle of his chest. With an utterly unreadable look, he took it, and she scrambled to her feet. "Have they festered?"

He shook his head, resettling the damp hair across his shoulders. "They don't feel to have."

"Well, I'll see about that," she said in a clipped tone. The pricking of tears a moment ago was nothing, of course—simply understandable concern for the wounds of the man she needed healthy to ensure her survival. She put her hand on his arm to turn him around. "Stand fast."

He allowed her to turn him, and she allowed herself to ignore the feel of his warm, wide shoulder beneath her hand. Clamping her tongue between her teeth, she began applying the thick lotion in slow, gentle movements that sent his muscles shuddering in response.

"Am I hurting you?"

"Aye," he said gruffly.

She paused and peered over his shoulder at the profile of his square jaw. "Much?"

"Aye, that ye are."

"Well," she retorted, then said it again. "Well."

He stood quietly under the painful repair work. When finished, she stepped back and looked with a critical eye at her handiwork. "I think I've got them all," she muttered, angling her head to the side to see if the light had tricked her and she'd missed one. *No,* she decided, straightening, *I've got them all.*

His dark eyes were waiting for her.

"I've another debt to pay, mistress."

His gaze dropped to the unguent still coating her fingertips. A stride of his muscle-corded legs brought him close enough to catch her hand in his.

Her lips parted around a hot rush of breath. Almost thoughtfully, he placed the pad of his thumb on her lower lip, curling it down, his rough, clean skin on the fleshy inner side. Hot coils unwound through her body.

"How shall I repay it? What do ye want, Senna?"

"All I want," she whispered, "is to go home."

Home, where there were no wolves baying or soldiers hunting. Where the biggest river to be crossed was the murmuring brook between home and the stables, and the hardest bed she ever had to sleep in was the one she'd made herself by booking passage with the more expensive shipping merchant for last autumn's Flanders drop.

Home, where the sun slipped away each evening through leaded glass windows, spilling dull green light across the ledgers at her copyist's desk.

Where months passed with only the servants to talk to, until she had to let them all go too, when the debts grew too large.

Home, where silence reigned and even the 'lucrative sheep' were simply bright white specks on the sodden brown landscape of her heart.

His hand was warm curled around hers. "Is that truly all ye want, then? To go home?"

No, her heart cried. *No, no, no.*

"Aye," she said dully.

He dropped her hand, and she barely remembered how to lift it again. They shouldered their packs and silently slipped under the cover of trees as twilight spread, leaving neither sound nor trace of their passing.

Chapter 20

"Praise God. A boat."

Senna had the exact opposite reaction. "Oh, dear Lord. A boat."

It was the third noontide after their escape from Rardove, and they were crouched above a river. On a small isle in the center of the rushing currents was a small village. Perhaps five little tear-shaped boats bobbed at the edge of their side of the river.

"A boat will make travel much faster. And easier."

"We're stealing a boat," she clarified flatly. As if thievery was the reason for her protest.

"Aye, Senna. We're stealing a boat."

He started down the hill, hunched low, until he was near the riverside, then ducked down into the tall reeds and rushes. No one was to be seen on this side of the water, but on the other, villagers went about their business. A few women were washing clothes in the stream. A child in bare feet ran from one hut to another, calling someone.

Senna followed glumly in Finian's wake. They couched amid the grasses, *something I find myself doing with great frequency of late,* she thought sourly.

It was still risky to travel during daylight hours, but

not nearly as risky as traveling by boat in the dark, and apparently, travel by boat they must.

They watched as the villagers on the small island moved through their daily paces, keeping Senna and Finian trapped in the rushes. She felt like a young child, playing hoop and hide with her brother Will. Just the two of them, running around like wild things, Mama gone, Father may as well have been.

What grand games they had played, not realizing how their voices echoed back to them across the empty meadows. For a while. But soon, Will was taken—sent, she corrected swiftly—to be fostered as a squire, trained as a knight, a privilege and expense she herself ensured once she took over the accounts at age fifteen. Will's education had lacked for nothing.

The boats bobbed as a gust of wind whipped down the river. She swallowed. *Will had probably even been taught to swim,* she thought sourly.

She rooted around in her pack and came out with the flask. Uncorking it, she threw back a swallow. It burned the whole way down. Finian flicked a glance over.

"I can't swim," she said.

"That should help." He looked back at the river and the bobbing, sickening boats.

She took another scorching swallow and aimed a glare at the side of his head. He had a very attractive side of his head. "Why ought I know how to swim? What good is that?"

"'Tis helpful when you want to cross a river."

She took another sip of the whisky. "I do other things."

"Aye," he agreed, not looking over. "Make money. Drink firewater. Talk a great deal."

She gave a wan smile. "I can use a weapon, too, should that interest you. It ought, if you intend to go on in that manner."

He turned then and studied her, those blue eyes trailing over her face. Then he smiled his dangerous smile and settled back amid the high, swaying reeds. The low drone of flying things going about their business—butterflies, gnats, flies—settled over the heated earth.

"Is that so?" he said. "A weapon? Who taught ye that?"

"My brother, Will. He taught me many things. How to climb trees. Use a short bow. And a knife." One of his dark eyebrows quirked. She nodded. "Oh, we were wild, for a time."

Finian snapped a reed stem in half and chewed at the tip. "Good Lord," he said mildly. "Ye were rough stuff. I'm surprised that's not a crime."

"Teaching a woman to use weapons?"

"No. Teaching ye to."

He watched her with a teasing half smile, the long, lean length of him stretched out, resting back on an elbow, waiting patiently for the villagers to move out of sight, for her to tell her tale in a low murmur.

"How can you be so calm? When all this"—she waved her hand generally at the world—"is happening. Has happened. Will happen. How can you be so . . . at ease?"

He tipped the grass stem away from his lips and smiled full on. It was as if the sun just came out. "There are worse things I could be doing just now, Senna, than sitting here with ye. For the moment, I am at ease."

Just as if the sun came out, indeed. She grew warmer. Everywhere. Lowering her eyes, she toyed with one of the tall, waving reeds, then snapped one off like he had done. She popped the tip in her mouth. She immediately took it out, grimacing. "I see why we put these on the floor."

He nibbled on his stalk again, smiling. "Yer brother, Senna, and his criminal acts, teaching ye to use a bow and knife."

"There's been no damage done yet. I'm not terribly good with a bow."

"Och. I'm sure if ye set yer mind to a matter, it'll come out a good-looking thing in the end."

They were speaking only in murmurs, hidden in a pocket of reeds and heat and his smile. There was something about the quality of how Finian lay stretched out on the earth, something about his breathing that said all his attention was on her. Although why she should care about that was utterly inconceivable.

She pushed an intrusive cattail out of her face.

"I'm surprised yer Da let it happen, though," he said. "The weapons."

She gave a bitter little smile. Why did they seem to touch upon the topic of her father so very much? She hadn't spoken of him in years, save brief conversations with Will, where one or the other would report they hadn't seen Sir Gerald in weeks. Months. Years.

"My father was gone a lot. I rarely saw him."

His regard of her grew a little closer. "And what did yer Mam think, ye learning to use weapons?"

"My mother left. I believe I was five. I do not know my mother."

He chewed his reed-tip in silence for a moment. "Do ye remember nothing of her?"

She shook her head vehemently, in direct opposition to the strength of the lie. "Not even what she smells like."

Roses and green. Fresh, new green. And the yellow roses from out back, the ones she'd let overgrow with vines.

"Ah." A dragonfly hovered silently by Finian's shoulder, a quivering, iridescent arrow. Then it shot off. "Just ye and yer brother then, raising each other?"

"Just us. Until it was time for him to leave."

She knew the wistfulness in her voice revealed as much of her as the words themselves. She looked over, loathe to find what she expected: scorn. Or worse, disinterest.

Instead, she found dark eyes considering her. The filtered sunlight made shadows of his serious regard. And when he nodded, slowly, gravely, she felt as though she'd been accepted.

And, with that, a breath of a new wanting brushed past her consciousness.

Finian's eyes stayed on her, directly, a level, listening gaze, as if the things she spoke of were not shameful a'tall. Which they were. Highly shameful. The things her father had allowed to be done, the way he went through the world, a river of potential, a tepid pool of yield, after the gambling began. After Mama left.

And the shame of Mama, that could not be calculated if she used every abacus in France. Even as a child, Senna had felt it seeping out of those around her like frost heaves, icy remnants. Slippery and treacherous. Never look down.

And of course, all that was in Senna as well.

She tilted her chin up, a move she'd perfected years ago whenever shame threatened a coup. "I took over the business after . . . when I was fifteen. My father was never to home. Will works for coin. I do not know exactly what he does. He will not speak of it; something for various lords, I think. He hasn't married yet. That cannot be good. He doesn't look as if 'tis good. He looks rather . . . hard."

"And what did yer hard brother say about ye coming to Ireland?"

"He doesn't know."

A companionable silence stretched out between them. Finian glanced at the river. Not a villager in sight. He rose to his knees and fingertips, then unraveled to his feet.

"Let's go, lass."

The sun burned hot on the top of Senna's head and upper back as they hurried forward, crouching at the waist. Everything seemed bright and close to hand. The world smelled fresh, like warm, clean dirt and pine, hot flowers and river-stirred air. Ireland's beauty was beyond her words, vivid and brilliant, like a drop of ink quivering on a manuscript.

The tall grasses closed behind them, rustling like eager, buzzing conspirators. Small puffs of breeze coasted down the river, which was such a shattering, smashing shade of blue it almost hurt her eyes. The thought of getting in a boat hurt her stomach.

She plodded forward, looking neither left nor right, resigned to the fate of sickening all over the indescribably beautiful land of Ireland. Or its waters.

Closing her eyes resignedly, she put her hands on the edge of a worn wooden boat and threw her leg over.

"Senna, no!" Finian hissed behind her.

She turned, startled, half in the boat, half out.

"Not that one." He gestured once, rising slightly out of his crouch. "Come. This one." He pointed to a smaller teardrop-shaped craft, tucked amid the cattails, hard to see.

She sighed and lifted her foot back out again. She did not, though, remove any of her weight from her hands, which rested on the lip of the boat. In fact, she was quite used to leaning on things, things that didn't bob. Being incautiously unaware that her previous experience with one's leaning tendencies and the movability, or immovability, of things upon which one leaned, did not apply in the present situation, she pressed down on the boat, which was, by nature, a bobbing thing. Her foot was in the air.

The small craft sailed out into the river. The rope tugged it immediately and snapped it back to shore, but it had to bounce off Senna, who had fallen in the water with a hearty splash. One ankle still remained hooked over the lip of the boat.

She flailed as soundlessly as flailing in water can be done, trying to get her footing. Water lapped over her belly as she arched backward, her hands sinking into the soft, silky mud, one foot in the water, the other hooked over the edge of boat.

How she hated boats.

She tried to kick her leg high enough to free it. Her body having only so much bend, each kick up with her foot forced her head in the opposite direction which, in this case, was under the water. Her fingertips sunk deeper into mud. How long before the owner of this boat heard her racket and came to investigate?

"What do ye tink ye're doin' with me boat?"

Not long at all, apparently.

She tried to crane her neck around to see whom she'd perpetrated her highly embarrassing but not-yet-criminal behavior upon.

Finian's legs walked into view. She tilted her face up to look at his, which appeared to be filled with disgust, if she was reading it properly. She *was* upside down, of course. Perhaps she was interpreting it wrongly.

He put an arm behind her back, which gave her the leverage to get her foot out. He helped her slosh to shore where she stood, dripping wet, a length of sea grass stuck to her neck. She peeled it off, looking at the sullen, yet-surprisingly-unsurprised, aged face regarding her.

"Me boat. Why're ye climbing all over her?"

"I was only climbing there at the bow . . . the prow, the . . . edge," she said chirpily. "She's a bit wetter, but none the worse."

Finian and the old man scowled at her. Then Finian turned to the old man.

"Grandfather," he murmured, bending his head, and that was the last word she understood, because Finian lapsed into the most evocative, lyrical, deep-throated plumage of language she'd ever heard. Irish. It almost took her breath away. Finian surely did.

Watching his body, so powerful, restrain itself to bend into a pose of respect for an elderly man. Listening to him, whom she knew not at all, transform into some spellbinding creature before her eyes.

Wild, his language was. Wild, he was. Wild, she wanted to be.

Without warning, Finian was moving again, tossing a few heavy bundles onto the boat she'd almost capsized, speaking so she could understand again.

"We'll take these to *Cúil Dubh* for ye, grandfather. And ye've my thanks."

The old man stood impassively. He must have been sixty if he was a day, and more fit than men half his age. Compact, sinuous, and suspicious, he did not look happy, but he wasn't arguing. Finian was moving swiftly, tossing another sack into the craft, muttering for Senna to get on board.

She hesitated. The old man was watching her with a canny regard. His eyes were bluer than the water, his eyebrows as wild grown as the grasses they'd crawled through, and his face was cragged enough for plants to take root. Old curmudgeon. She smiled. She'd once had a curmudgeon in her life, a laughing bear of a grandfather she hadn't seen since her mother disappeared. Senna liked curmudgeons.

Slowly, the old curmudgeon smiled back.

"And we're off, Senna," Finian said lightly. But underneath, he sounded rushed. As if he was worried. As if, at any moment, this old man might turn and start shouting to others. Younger, armed others.

Without thinking, Senna scooped deep in a pouch tied around her neck and lodged between layers of her clothes, and dug out a few coins she'd taken from the trunk under Rardove's table. She dropped them into the old man's hand. A few pennies gone from her future, but they were owed.

"My thanks, grandfather," she whispered, then held a finger to her lips, suggesting silence. She smiled at him over its tip.

His hand closed around the coin, probably sufficient to sustain him and his eight neighbors for a decade. His smile didn't grow an inch, but slowly, one eyelid came down in the most extravagant, flirtatious wink Senna had ever been the recipient of. She blushed to her hairline and got in the boat.

They floated off, the old man watching them, until the tall grasses swallowed him up and the only thing to be seen was the blue bowl of sky and the long, outstretched wings of a dark, silent cormorant that flew overhead.

Chapter 21

"Ye gave him coin?"

At Finian's sharp tone, she looked down from the bird and nodded.

He snorted. "Ye bribed him. That's something ye English like to do."

She smiled loftily. "And something you Irish like to do is assume you understand the meaning of things. 'Twasn't a bribe. And if you cannot see that, then I am at a loss for words."

He snorted again. "That'll be a rare day in hell."

"You snort a lot," she pointed out.

He stared at her. "Lie down."

"Pardon?"

"An Irishman in an Irish *curaigh* floating down an Irish river with a sack of skins is unremarkable. Ye, remarkable. Lie down."

"How am I remarkable?" she asked, already lowering herself.

He just looked at her.

She did insist on disrobing somewhat, rather than lying in wet leather, to be baked like a cod in the sun. He grumbled but she was resolute, and in the end, he relented.

A brief, disagreeable delay ensued, wherein she hitched and yanked at various wet clothes, disrobing down to a thin linen shift. Then she lay down in the bottom of the boat.

The sacks of skins were not down here with her, she realized irritably, although they would have made perfect bedding. But they were perched on one of the benches, sunning themselves. Finian's sword and bow were down here with her, of course, out of sight but within easy reach. They were also poking her.

She shuffled around, trying to fit into the small cramped hull of the boat, which really was not where she wished to be, not even for a moment. She was squished, her arms tight up against her sides. It smelled. It was mucky. It was wet. Wet, as if a small pond held a secret life down in the basin of the curmudgeon's *curaigh*, or whatever Finian had called it.

"Finian."

"Mmm?" He didn't look down. His powerful arms kept up a powerful paddling. She could almost feel the river skiffing away not an inch below her body.

"I think there's fish down here."

"Aye. This river has many fish."

"No. I mean this boat. Swimming around me. Little tiny fish."

His lips twitched.

"If you laugh, I'm getting up," she warned.

"Hush." His voice went low, his lips hardly moved. Senna barely had time to feel a tingle of concern before she heard the shouts of men at the shoreline. The rush of panic came flying for her. Englishmen. Soldiers.

They'd been found.

"Heave to, Irishman," one of the soldiers called.

Finian shoved the paddle deep into the mud of the riverbed, keeping the boat from sailing any farther, which would have sent the soldiers shouting for whatever others were billeted on the people and patrolling the lands. It also kept the *curaigh* from going any closer to the shore.

"That looks like O'Mallery's nubbin' boat," one of them said.

"That's so," agreed Finian easily. "He let me use it."

"Not bloody likely," muttered the shorter one. The two stared at each other a moment, then the taller one snapped his fingers.

"O'Mallery don't let his wife use his pecker," he growled. "Come over here, boy."

Senna could almost feel Finian rise up in the boat, like a huge wave uncoiling itself close to shore. She grabbed his boot. His steely gaze snapped down. With her free hand and an open palm, she mimed going softly down. *Sit* down, *calm* down.

"For me," she whispered.

He fired his gaze up again. "There's only two of them," he said, not moving his lips.

"*Now* there's only two," she whispered. "You said you enjoy traveling with me. I enjoy traveling with you. Let it go."

"I've let a lot of things go," he said in a calm voice. That worried her. He was still squinting toward the shoreline, locked, she supposed, in mortal eye combat with one of the English soldiers.

"I'll make it up to you," she whispered urgently.

The faintest trace of a smile lifted his lips.

"Boy, git over here."

It was the whisky that made her do it. She was fairly certain of that. The hot, uninhibiting flush the drink had sent coursing through her limbs simply floated into her brain and melted her wits.

She took a deep breath, gave her tunic a harsh tug so it tore further, exposing an immodest curve of her breasts and the valley between. Then she sat up. Unraveled, really. Or so she hoped.

Finian's jaw dropped, but not so far as the English boys' did on the shore.

"Jay-sus!" one of them shouted, jumping back as if she were one of the *fey.*

She smiled as lustily as she could and draped her arms over Finian's thighs, her face close to his groin, implying she'd only just lifted her mouth away.

"Hello, lads," she said in a confident, husky tone. Or did it sound like she was sick? She didn't quite know how to sound seductive, and hoped this would do. "Are we disturbing ye?"

She tried to sound as much like Finian as possible, the rocking cadence of his speech, the slow, seductive dropping off of the sharp-pointed ends of words, as if he couldn't be bothered to stab so at a thought.

The soldiers gaped. Finian adapted immediately. He put his palm lightly but possessively around the back of her head, exerting the slightest pressure downward, bringing her lips just slightly closer to what was now, partially, an erection. He was obviously familiar with the move. A fiery rush shot through her body, down to her womb.

The young soldiers turned their gapes to Finian, then burst out laughing, smacking each other on the arms, as if they'd accomplished something great and worthy. All pretense of being on opposing sides fell away in the face of getting a woman to suck their—.

Holding her stiff smile, Senna said through unmoving lips, "You may attack them now."

Finian didn't remove his gaze either. "Shall I? And yet, we like traveling together."

"Let's try this, then." She lifted her voice. "Have a good day, lads," she sang out, lifting one hand to wave. "I know we will."

Finian yanked his paddle up and the boat began slipping downstream. One of the soldiers stepped forward, a concerned look on his face. He raised a hand, half roused from his voyeuristic stupor.

Again, it was the whisky that gave her the idea. She was quite certain this time.

She bent her head and brushed her lips over Finian's erection.

The soldiers' jaws dropped, then they exploded into whoops and hollers, jumping up and down like they were standing on a beehive. Nothing about Finian changed, except that his hand tightened almost imperceptibly around the back of her head.

The river sluiced away beneath the boat, but Senna, to her own dim surprise, did not move. The bottom of the boat was hard and wet, with a rib bone-like wooden beam jutting into her as she knelt between Finian's legs. But she didn't feel a thing.

All she was aware of was Finian's hard thighs beneath her arms, the heat of him engulfing her chin and cheeks, the hot sun on the top of her head, and the powerful rising up of his chest. His was looking down, his face shadowed, his dark eyes unreadable but watching her. And his hand was still on the back of her head.

She must never drink whisky again.

"I'm feeling reckless," she murmured. Reckless indeed. She felt like she was flying.

"That is a very bad idea," Finian replied tightly.

He took a moment to say it, trying to compose himself, but every moment of looking at her unraveled him further. Her hair was still damp, tangled and drying in small, dangling curls, like a rainstorm of burnished amber gemstones beside her face. Her lips were plump and wet, and her mischievous eyes worried him. He removed his hand.

"A very bad idea," he said again.

"But there it is," she replied. Was that a smile underlying her words? Was the clerical virgin from the English Midlands teasing him?

No, he thought gloomily. The sharp-witted goddess who'd freed him from prison was teasing him.

"Don't, Senna," he said in a warning tone.

"But . . . why not?"

"Ye're playing with fire."

"Maybe I want to play with fire."

"Then ye'll get burned."

"What if I kissed you?" she asked in that low, sultry voice.

As far as he could tell, Senna was no maven. She did not use her body for much beyond getting her quill-holding fingers from one contract to another. Surely, she did not *negotiate* with it. When she spoke in this husky-throated manner, she was probably just being innocently aroused, and discreet.

It sounded like she was sending him sex on her tongue.

"If ye kissed me, Senna," he ground out, "I'd lay ye out on the grass and have ye howling to the sky, if all the soldiers in Ireland were riding for us."

She blinked. Her mouth rounded into an *'O.'* Then she said it. "Oh." She sat back at the other end of the boat.

"Are ye still feeling reckless?" he asked with grim satisfaction.

She stared out at the shoreline, at the passing trees and meadows. She shook her head.

"No. Yes. I mean, yes. I'm feeling highly reckless, but recklessness has not served me well." He held his silence, thinking she'd probably never acted reckless in her entire life. "It doesn't seem the best of plans, does it, to go about being reckless?"

He disagreed. He thought it a fine, fine idea, perhaps the best in years. But all he said was, "Then see ye don't toy with me, Senna. I'm not a boy."

"I didn't think I was toying."

He started paddling. "Now ye know."

"Now I know."

The autumn sun was feisty, hot and bright. It was like a

golden stage. It shone behind her so brightly it was as if she were floating in gold, *was* gold. She turned to him and he felt desire pulsing off her, onto him.

"And yet, Finian, I feel *quite* reckless."

He set down his paddle very deliberately. How was a man to fight this knowing innocence?

"Really?" he ground out. Her face flushed. His heart slowed into a hot-rushing, sluggish beat. "I wonder."

"What?" Her voice was unsteady, but her eyes were locked in his: she wanted what he had.

He went hard like he hadn't in a dozen years. It was the waiting. The torment of wanting her all this time and not being able to have her. (*It hasn't been fully three days* some dim recess of his mind pointed out.) There was nothing special about her or the arousal she conjured, he assured himself. Just a woman with a staggering mind, a blade-sharp wit, and a body men would lick dirt to touch.

"If I asked ye to do something," he said in a low voice, "would ye do it?"

"Aye," she exhaled.

"Run yer hand up yer leg."

A hot whimper trailed out of her. She looked down at the hand she had draped over one knee. So did he. Her fingers fluttered, then she trailed them up her inner thigh so slowly he could count to ten. It was the only way to avoid complete embarrassment, counting was. One of her feet slipped forward, and she braced it against the rib bone of the hull. He felt himself slipping into the churning vortex of lust.

She stopped her lazy travel north just below the juncture of her legs. Her slim fingers hung there, knuckles slightly bent, in what he knew would be hot space, high and tight between her thighs.

He raked his gaze up her body, which was now slouched back against the prow of the *curaigh,* her forearm draped over her belly, her lips parted, her eyes waiting for him.

"Now what?" she asked breathlessly.

A taunt, a test, a true question? And if he answered, then what? Take her virginity and break her heart? Because that is all he had in him. He was capable of nothing more.

He smashed his fingers through his hair and almost dropped the paddle. He grabbed it just before it fell in the water.

"Now, naught, Senna."

She struggled to sit straight. "What?"

He started paddling. "Sit back. Note the view."

"But—"

"And put them on."

"What?" Confusion marked her voice. "Put what on?"

"Every stitch of clothing you've got. And possibly a few of mine as well," he added in what he hoped was a firm, no-negotiation tone. But with Senna, he was discovering, one did not necessarily get what one demanded with one's tone.

"Oh, but Finian," she protested, plucking at the damp, bedraggled rags barely reaching to midthigh. A feminine, curving midthigh he wanted to run his hand up, then his tongue. "Everything's wet, and—"

"Put them on, or I'm not going any farther." He also wasn't looking at her. How long could he do that, avoid making any sort of perusal of his companion's burning, curving, pink-tinged body? A minute? Three?

They had *days* ahead of them. He groaned.

With poor grace, she flung her leather tunic and leggings on, grumbling. "Is that better?" she demanded when she was done.

How would he know? He wasn't looking at her.

"'Tis just fine," he replied shortly.

She sat back in the boat and glared.

Chapter 22

Senna's glare, set and determined though it was, did nothing to provide a solution to a single problem in her life.

She did not want to be in this boat, with Finian, not being touched. And that was madness. But something burning and insistent had been awakened inside her. She wanted him to touch her, was practically desperate for him to. That was ridiculous, and perhaps a sign of impending madness.

Rather than worrying about Rardove and his fury, or how she was going to salvage the business, or how she would ever get home again, and if she had a home to go to in any event, all her attention was focused on how to get this Irishman to touch her.

Damn the whisky.

All ensuing conversation that afternoon was desultory at best. It was getting toward late afternoon, and Senna was dying of heat. And boredom. The boat slipped effortlessly down the small river. Whenever a village appeared in the distance, Finian made her lie down flat again. Otherwise, nothing happened. Little talking, no touching.

And the heat.

"Can we pull to the side?" she suddenly asked.

He looked at her like she was mad. "Are ye mad?"

"No," she said very slowly, as if he might not understand. "I am mucky. I stink."

He sniffed. "Ye do not."

"*You* are mad. I've been lying in muck."

"We're not stopping."

Dour silence ensued.

"Just the tunic," she said a few moments later.

The look he shot her was murderous. "Don't."

She threw him an equally warning glance. "I'm hot."

And it was hot. At this moment, probably the hottest it would be all day.

"Don't."

"I'm dying of the heat." She panted plaintively, to demonstrate. He looked away.

"If any of yer clothes come off, Senna, I'll roll ye into the river."

She gasped. "Just the—"

"Splash," he said ominously. She drew back. "Have ye learned to swim yet, in the last hour or so?"

"Of course not."

"Then sit back."

"I am sitting back," she retorted sourly.

"We'll be there soon."

"Not soon enough."

He snorted.

"You really do snort a lot."

"Ye complain a lot." He nailed her with a look. "Why don't ye take a rest? Lie on the packs, close yer eyes?"

And my mouth, she thought crossly.

In the end, they came to an unpleasant compromise, wherein Senna perched over the side and washed her face and armpits and everything she could reach by pulling things aside but not actually disrobing, while Finian sat backward in his seat and stared the other way up the river.

"I'm all done," she sang out.

He turned in stony silence and started paddling again.

An hour later she was about to go mad. No conversation, all heat and boredom, and the only reason her belly wasn't heaving dried bread and cheese over the side was because the tributary they traveled was shallow. The boat didn't rock much, and rarely shot forward with any purpose. But still, it was *not* comfortable.

She shifted for perhaps the hundredth time, levering herself to her knees, which creaked. She groaned and put a hand to her spine. "I think my back is broken." Her leg suddenly cramped. She grabbed it and tried to pound it out.

"Do ye know much about boats, Senna?" he asked sharply.

She eyed him. The cramp was fading. "Some."

"Then ye likely know ye don't want to fling yourself about like you're in a mad carol. Or you'll tumble over the side."

"Is that so?" she said derisively.

A cool Irish gaze sailed over her. "Keep jostling and ye'll find out."

She looked at the shoreline, sliding away. "I can help, you know."

He barely glanced at her.

"With paddling. I can take a turn."

"No."

"Why not?"

"Because we're almost there."

In her excitement at the news, she tried to turn and kneel on the small wooden bench. The boat eddied around a little cove just then and hit a rock, unseen beneath the water. The boat lurched, Senna slid off the bench, her foot hit the bottom of the old boat hard, in just the right way, and went straight through into the water below.

She stared in shock at her left foot, now ankle deep in the river. Water began burbling up through the hole. She turned and looked despairingly at Finian.

He had risen, paddle in hand, staring if possible with even

more shock than she at the damage done. The small craft was starting to take on a significant amount of water.

"Finian," she said helplessly.

He sighed and, dropping the paddle, gently extracted her foot from between the shards of wood. The water was filling up the craft as high as their ankles. Finian bent and lifted her into his arms, which sent a *whoosh* through her belly. Then he swung her over the side.

"No!" she cried out, grabbing for his shoulders.

"It's not so high as yer knees," he said gently enough. "And the shore is not ten feet away."

She let go, and that's how she came to be standing in two feet of water, a pack on her back and a sack of otter hides clutched in her hands, when the English soldiers appeared at the edge of the forest.

Chapter 23

She froze.

"Finian," she muttered, barely moving her lips. His back was to her as he heaved their packs and the last sack of hides over the side of the boat, onto the grass. Then he turned and froze, too.

"Shite," she heard him mutter. He came to shore, shaking water off himself.

"They have quite a range, don't they?" she said, trying to keep her voice light, panic at bay. Truly, this was not what she'd been about when she agreed to come to Ireland. How had it gone so wrong? Seasickness or terror, she was going to vomit from one thing or the other before the day was through.

Seeing as they were now off the boat, that left just the one option.

Finian's eyes never left the soldiers' helmed, featureless figures. He moved about, tossing Senna her pack, picking up one of the sacks and resting it on his shoulder. He squeezed the slack neck of the other sack in a wide palm and, bending slightly, sailed it up onto his other shoulder.

"I wouldn't suggest trying yer previous trick here," he said. "They might insist on seeing the whole show."

She shivered. The sun was hot and she was freezing. "What do we do?"

"Act like a poacher." He started walking.

She hurried behind, lugging the heavy sack. They crossed the meadow at an angle. The soldiers made their way to intercept, getting closer. She could see their eyes beneath their helms, their unsmiling faces and sharp swords. Hear the creak of leather and the hard thud of wooden bootheels on the earth.

Finian finally stopped and dumped his bag to the ground, waiting for them. "How are ye feeling, lass?"

She jerked her gaze over. He looked like he was waiting for mass to begin.

"How are ye feeling?" he said again.

Terrified. "Fine."

"That's my girl."

Four grim-faced soldiers stopped in front of them and fanned around to form a perimeter circle. Silence descended, then one of them, obviously the leader, spoke.

"What are you about, on this fine day?"

"Walking."

He poked at the packs with the tip of his sword. "What's in the sacks?"

"Otter hides," Finian said.

She wasn't surprised that Finian didn't break gaze with the leader. She wasn't surprised he could act so calm in the face of such danger. But she was *stunned* to hear a West Country accent come out of his very Irish mouth.

The soldier looked up sharply, too. Finian was dressed like an Englishman, as that's what she'd grabbed for him from Rardove. But nothing about him bespoke the civilizing influence of the most predatory English. Long dark hair, sloping Celtic bones, those ever-blue eyes, his tall, muscular body, less accustomed to wearing mailed armor than to wielding a huge blade, or running for hours on end, or cutting peat out of the earth for winter fires.

Finian was as wild an Irishry as they could ever want to destroy. Even the young soldiers up the riverbank had known that.

But, just now, he sounded like an Englishman from Shropshire.

"You're English," said the soldier. Suspicion hung from his words like moss.

Finian nodded.

"You don't look like it."

Finian shrugged. "Would you? Out there with them, trapping?"

This was a convincing argument, apparently. The soldier grunted in what she supposed was approval. Men grunted a lot. His eyes slid to Senna.

"And her?"

"She's mine."

"She's pretty."

"She's pregnant."

The leader's brow took on a suspicious winkling above the eyes. "And she was out there, trapping with you?"

Finian's jaw set. "I just got back."

The soldier stared, then lifted his gaze over Finian's shoulder, to his men.

Finian shifted slightly, a small, unprovoking action, but Senna realized he widened his stance as he did so. He was getting ready to fight. And if she noticed it, they surely would, too. She felt the potency of the masculine posturing vibrate through the air, like she was in a room with a wave.

"Richard?" she said softy, touching Finian's arm. "Why don't we just let the good king's men lighten our load, and be on our way?"

He ripped his arm away and looked at her derisively. "And give the lot of 'em an entire winter's worth of work?" He glared at the soldier, who was eyeing the sacks.

"They look familiar, Jacks," muttered one of the soldiers. "That green stamp on the sack."

"Aye," agreed the leader. "They do at that."

"O'Mallery's," replied Finian in a tight voice.

Cold chills ripped up and down Senna's chest, like invisible, saw-edged stripes. This was going to end badly.

"Gaugin's," countered the soldier, looking at Finian slowly. A corner of his mouth curled up. "The fur trader in Coledove. Them's his sacks. And he don't lend 'em out."

"And that's just where we're headed," Finian retorted. The tension spiraled thicker.

"Take them," Senna said hurriedly. Panic jabbed at her belly with cold, stabbing pokes. She pushed her toe into the sack she'd dropped to the ground. "Take them to Gaugin for us, why don't you?"

The leader looked at her, then back at Finian ever more slowly. "I think we'll take you instead." A brief pause. "O'Melaghlin."

Finian knew a moment where his heart stopped beating, for the first time in a dozen years. He didn't pause to consider *'why now?'*

He kicked out his boot and stepped in front of Senna, unslung his sword and, before the leader could even lift his own sword, Finian had sliced his through the soldier's belly. Below the jutting iron nasal of his helm, his face looked surprised, then he toppled over, dead.

Finian spun to deal with the others with deft, rapid sweeps of his blade. His mind closed down during the battle, as always; it was all silence inside, narrowing attention and the feel of the earth under his boots.

But, in complete opposition to 'always,' he was for the first time aware of a person who wasn't about to bring a blade down on his skull. Senna's lithe form bobbed just outside their ring of battle, in danger, handling . . . was that a knife?

God save them.

He snapped his attention back and, with grim focus, absolutely overpowered the wiry young Englishmen, taking them down with quick, merciful strokes. And when the four of them lay like downed scarecrows around him, he held his sword hanging by his side, breathing rapidly.

Blood surged through his limbs, wicked fast pounding, urging him on, go, go, get more, *now.* Climb the side of a cliff, swim to the Aran Islands. It was at these times he knew he was an animal first, whatever God intended for his soul.

Gradually his breathing slowed. When his hearing returned, too, he looked over at Senna.

She was standing, mouth open, as if to make a very important point. Her chest was heaving, her breath short and swift. In her right hand she held a blade by its carved hilt, still hovering at shoulder height, as if she were about to throw it.

"I—I. Y—you. But, th—they . . ."

She was babbling.

"Ye're all right," he murmured, keeping his speech low and calm, to bring her back from the fringes of panic. "We're well. 'Tis over."

Her gaze was locked on him, wide, staring. She still held the blade, shivering, near her ear. He reached out and slowly pushed it down.

"Ye didn't have to use it," he said quietly, calmly. "Ye're a'right."

"I would have," she whispered, vehement. Her voice shook. "I would have used it. I just didn't want to . . . strike you. By accident."

"My thanks." He looked down at the soldiers, scattered in a semicircle, bleeding in the sun. Rardove's men. Soon, someone would find the bodies. They had a day now, maybe half again, until the baron knew they were not headed north, but south.

Would he figure out they were going to Hutton's Leap? Had Turlough, his captured kinsman, finally broken and revealed their mission to retrieve the dye manual? No way to know. And it didn't matter. Nothing would stop him.

"Let's go," he said.

They left the sacks of skins. Someone would be along. And whomever it was, Finian had no desire to meet them.

Chapter 24

"You saw them where?"

Rardove repeated the question slowly, as if the newly sworn-in soldier was stupid. Which, Pentony decided, he probably was. They usually were. Stupid enough to swear fealty to Rardove for a position or some land.

Some might say the same about him, of course. But then, Pentony was doing penance.

"By the river. He was Irish, for certain. But she was, too, my lord," the young soldier added weakly. He looked at his equally shamefaced companion, then tugged on the belt around his waist. The belt came with the hauberk, their lord's livery as their mark and first payment for service. It looked cracked around the edges, old. "She was Irish. I'd swear to it."

"Would you?" Rardove snapped. "Was she comely?"

"Oh, as anything."

"Red hair? Long?"

"Well, mores like yellowy-red, all curvy—"

"That's my goddamned dye-witch!"

The soldier's pimply face was not glowing red just from the sun he and his companion had endured all afternoon on their lark by the river, derelict in their duties at the keep. But what a gift, this truancy. Pentony was as certain as Rardove: these two sluggards had encountered O'Melaghlin and Senna.

"What were they doing?" Rardove demanded.

"Stealing a boat."

Rardove stopped his furious circuit while behind the table. He leaned across its wooden width. "And you didn't stop them? You let them just"—he flicked his fingers—"sail away, to go downstream and kill four Englishmen?"

"We thought they were delivering goods for the old man," the other unhelpfully piped in. Rardove's eyes snapped to him. "We thought she was his flaming doxy."

The baron went still. A muscle ticked by his jaw. "What did you say?"

The soldier swallowed. "No offense, my lord. Now that we know . . . 'Tis just she was, was . . ."

His voice trailed off.

"She was what?" The baron's voice was thin and low pitched. Pentony felt the urge to cover his eyes.

"Aw, bollocks," the soldier muttered. "She was sucking the Irishman's cock, and they—"

Rardove exploded. He bent his knees and upended the huge oaken table with a roar. A jug of wine and half a dozen scrolled parchments careened into the air, held a moment, then came crashing back down into the rushes Rardove was now stomping across, hurling curses and objects through the air as he went. The jug smashed, and pottery shards skittered everywhere. The table came crashing back to the ground, too heavy to be overturned completely. It trembled on all four legs.

"God's bloody *bones!*" Rardove punched the door of a wardrobe that held parchment and inks and wax for seals. It bounded open, the iron lock cranking wildly. He spun back and tried to yank the door off its hinges, then flung himself away, stalking across the room.

"Goddamned *whore!*" He picked up one of the fallen earthenware jugs and threw it back onto the ground. It shattered into a hundred pieces. "She will kneel at my feet and *beg*—" He smashed his hand into a tallow candle hanging on the wall. It fell, still aflame. Pentony put out a toe and quietly extinguished it. "She will bend that godforsaken head and—"

Rardove went still and spun to the soldiers. "They were going downstream?"

The soldiers, now utterly pale and huddled together like ducklings, nodded energetically. "Downstream, indeed. Far downstream."

"Just so, milord. Downstream."

Rardove looked sharply at Pentony. "South. They're going south."

Pentony nodded.

"But, why?" His voice quieted, as if on some inward journey. He felt for the edge of the bench and sat. "Why south? O'Fáil is to the north. What is O'Melaghlin up to?"

A few candles sputtered in their holders on the walls, casting pale, angular wedges of light across the room. One still huddled on the table, plunged deep enough in a puddle of tallow to have withstood the earlier quake. Its small, wavering light was almost depressing; it had no chance against the surrounding darkness.

Rardove stared at it, then cursed quietly.

"He's going to meet with the spy Red." His voice was hushed, perhaps in awe. "O'Melaghlin's taken over the mission. God's teeth. But . . . where? Where were they to meet? South. What lies south? Near enough for a foot journey, safe enough for the Irishry near my borders?"

His forearms were laid flat across the width of the huge oak table, a foot apart. The candle flame sucked and sputtered a few feet away as he sat, deep in thought. Then he lifted his head with a smile.

"Is not the abbess at Hutton's Leap an Irishwoman?"

But they both already knew the answer to that.

Rardove actually threw back his head and laughed. Another candle flickered out. Only one burned now, a fat tallow one, guttering in its iron holder on the wall.

Rardove called for one of his captains and gave his orders. "Any guests of the abbey, be they cleric or lay, round them up. Question them, break them. Find out if one is the elusive Red. Then bring him to me. Be quick about it. I expect you back by Sext on the morrow."

The guard nodded and spun on his wooden heel. Turning back, Rardove sailed a brief look over the young, derelict soldiers. "Return the armor and find another lord."

Their mouths dropped open. "But sir—"

Rardove turned on them. "You were not at your posts. You were playing at shuttlecocks, jacking off while an escaped prisoner sailed by your stupid faces. You do not know Finian *fycking* O'Melaghlin when he's standing right in front of you. You are of no use to me. Begone. Or stay," he added, turning away, "and if either of you are here by *couvre-feu,* it shall be your last."

Pentony watched as they made their dazed way out, escorted by one of Rardove's faceless helmed guards. The baron had taken to keeping his personal guard with him at all times, even about the castle. Perhaps that was wise. There might be need for such caution. Especially if Balffe succeeded in bringing Lady Senna back.

Rardove reached for the candle on the wall and pinched it out.

Chapter 25

"Why is it so dark?" Senna mumbled under her breath as she tripped over yet another tree root. But darkness wasn't the problem. It was her body.

Finian had healed her fingers, but the rest of her felt as if it had undergone a beating. Her hand was at the small of her back, cradling it as they scrambled up yet another hill. Her hips felt like they'd been stretched on a rack, or at least what she imagined such a torture would feel like. Her thighs actually burned, as if hot coals were ablaze under her skin. And her back . . . best not even to think of it.

"I believe I am somewhat the worse for wear," she said.

This time Finian replied, which he had not been doing for the last hour of hiking. Still, though, he was exceedingly curt, which he had been ever since the river.

"Ye'll be better off by tomorrow," he said. Curtly. "Three days is the charm. Yer body will get used to this manner of traveling."

"Ha." She flung knotted curls over her shoulder, spitting a tendril of hair out of her mouth.

He glanced over his shoulder. "Ye did fine back there."

Still curt, but communicative. She did not take her eyes off the treacherous, root-strewn ground below. "So did you. I had no notion you could mimic a man from Shropshire."

"I don't often find the need."

"No," she agreed ruefully. "I expect not."

He grunted. Senna scowled. Back to that, were they?

They walked for a long time, and Senna soon found that ignoring her painful muscles was one thing, but ignoring her growling stomach was quite another. By sunset her belly was reprimanding her at regular intervals.

She hadn't filched half enough food for them. She'd planned a quick trip to Dublin, not this trek across the marchlands. Cheese and dried meat were good, but they were almost gone, and she was hungry for real food, and above all, fresh meat.

He turned back regularly to watch for her welfare. Once he pulled her up the other side of a steep stream embankment, another time pushed her away from a deep crevasse she was about to blunder into.

"Sooth, woman," he growled from a few feet ahead after one such incident. "Can ye not keep your eyes open?"

"Sooth, woman," She mimicked his impatient tone, then stumbled and stubbed her toe. She hopped around on one foot, muttering.

He didn't look back and he didn't stop walking, but he said over his shoulder, "'Tis yer penalty for being contrary."

She glared at him. "'Tis, is it?"

"Aye."

Too weary to summon the strength for a good inhalation, she certainly could not come up with a good, biting retort. She yanked a tree branch out of her way then let it go. It slapped her bent backside as she walked under. She rubbed her nose and blundered on, each step a leaden effort, eyeing his back with an evil glare.

Long dark hair swung down past his shoulders. His chin was up, his shoulders back, and his gaze moved in a constant sweep of the land. The plated muscles of his thighs worked tirelessly, eating up the miles between them and a modicum of safety. He hopped over a downed tree trunk and, pushing lightly on the balls of his feet, leapt the width of a small creek. Landing without a sound in the thick, fecund earth on the far side, he turned and extended a hand for her.

Accursed Irish.

She glared at his upright figure across the creek. Her spine was curved in an endless, creaking bend. Her feet were screaming, her thighs burning, and if he did anything else agile or energetic, she would cuff him. Simply reach out and smack him on the back of the head.

She crawled over the greening stump, her nose pressed into the moss. Disdaining his help, she leapt over the creek, tripped as she took off, and landed smack in the center of the babbling stream, wetting herself to the knee.

Cursed Irish.

He said nothing as she slogged up beside him, squishing and squeaking. Slanting evening light sliced between the tree branches and lit up the contours of his impassive face, but as soon as she opened her mouth, he shook his head and turned away.

Some time later, he finally halted them. "We'll camp here for a meal," he announced curtly.

All in all, he was being very curt, which she considered highly unfair. She was the rejected party. Curtness was hers.

She sat down beside the pit as he gathered wood. Sleep would solve a few of her problems. For a little while.

But when Finian sat down nearby, even sleep became a lost cause. "Let me see yer fingers," he said. Again, curtly. He extended his hand.

She retracted hers, holding it to her chest. "They are hale."

He regarded her with a disheartening mixture of disgust and perceptiveness. "Senna—"

"Grand."

Had her teeth just gritted?

"What was that?" he said, looking around.

She glanced over her shoulder, as if seeking the source of the strange, creaking noise. "Perhaps another bird. Some are ground dwelling, build their nests in rocks and such."

His gaze swung back around slowly. He pinned her with a long look, then got to his feet. "I'll have us some food before we hike out tonight."

"Tonight?" Her voice curved up high with incredulity. Horror. "We walk more this night?"

He paused in the act of bending to sweep up the bow he'd set on the ground. "Ye had a different plan?"

"Sleep?"

He cradled the smooth curving wood of the bow in hand. "Not ours yet. Just a few more hours." He turned away.

"Where are you going?"

"Hunting." He started out of the clearing, into the woods beyond.

"Wait. I can help," she called, furious to be so expendable, to be treated in such an offhand manner. To be so. . . left behind.

He drew to a halt, his wide shoulders almost, if she was seeing correctly, slumping. He turned around slowly. "What did ye say?"

"I can help." She gestured toward his bow. "Hunt."

His glittering eyes held hers. "Is that so?" he said, in such a low, feral tone it didn't sound like a question at all. It didn't even sound like he was the least bit pleased. "Then by all means, come."

He extended his hand in a mockery of politeness, allowing her to go first.

She swept haughtily by. "I've no notion what this mood is about, Finian, but I do wish you'd scratch whatever itch is causing it, for your mood is most foul."

Before she could finish the L in *foul,* he had her arm locked in his grip and her body backed up against a tree.

"Scratch my itch, is it?" His eyes glittered dangerously, and Senna recalled he was a warrior first.

Then he spoke again, and in the onrush of deep, tempting fear, she understood he was a man first and last. A prime specimen of raw masculinity, virile, potent, hunting.

"*Ye're* my itch, Senna. I want to scratch *ye.* No notion?" He stepped closer, his fingers gripping her arm like a vise. "Shall I give ye a notion? Shall I give ye some small inking of what I want to do to ye?"

And like that, she was panting, her head spinning. One of his hands was on her arm, the other fisted against the tree over her head. In the dimming light, he was all solid, dark outline, his body taut, looming over her, closing in on her, dark, male energy about to consume.

He bent close to her ear. "Shall I tell ye, Senna, what I want?"

She whimpered something. Was it *yes*? *Please*? Whatever it was, he mustn't stop. She would die from the want of him.

"I want to run my hands up your side, take ye in my mouth. I'll start wherever ye want. I'll kneel down before yer body and worship ye."

Her knees weakened. He caught her and his hand moved just as he'd said, up her ribs, so tightly she felt he was lashing her with rope. His powerful thighs bunched and he pressed forward.

"I want to taste ye. Can I do that, Senna? Will ye let me do that?"

"Oh, Jésu," she whispered.

"Can I slide my hand up yer leg? Can I feel how wet ye are? Can I be inside ye? I want to be inside ye. Hard." His voice was like dark, perfect fury. He pushed his hand across her belly. "Do ye want me inside ye?"

"Aye," she said in a hot whisper. She threw her head back

and banged the tree. His thighs were hot on hers, then his erection pressed against her belly. She pushed back urgently, recklessly, one wrist hooked around his neck, her body moving of its own accord, her breath coming out in hard, sharp pants.

"Do ye have a notion now, Senna?" he growled, his voice thumped by the rocking of her hips.

"Aye."

"Do ye want more?"

"Aye."

He slid his hands under her buttocks and lifted her, so she was sitting on his hips, her thighs parted, dangling over his.

Trapped between the tree and his hot, sculpted body, she went senseless. Dimly, she heard herself whimper. The long, hard length of him pushed up between them, sliding over everything that throbbed in her body. Her hips pumped forward and he shoved into her, so every inch of them touched from hips to chest. Then he growled in her ear, "Do not move."

She went still. Every toned muscle of his body was rigid against hers. He shuddered slightly, and they stood absolutely still for half a minute. All she could hear was his ragged breath and the blood thudding inside her skull. Then he bent his head, his mouth by her ear, his words a dark, sensual threat. "I'll watch ye come, lass."

Rampant shuddering chills jammed down her body as his mouth claimed hers in a deep and savage kiss. She returned every plunge of his tongue with one of her own, her fingers twisting into his hair. Her tongue, her teeth, her lips, he claimed everything, relentless in his pursuit, drawing senseless gasps and whimpers from her body until he finally came up for air, and dragged his lips along her neck and shoulder, leaving behind an amoral trail of heat.

He yanked down the collar of her tunic, revealing the tops of her breasts. She leaned her shoulders back to allow him access, her fingers in his hair, inviting him to do more, much more.

His eyes held hers, level and unreadable, as he pushed his hand up under her tunic, over her hot skin. Then his thumb brushed roughly over her breast. She closed her eyes, arching up. With a muted curse, he shoved her tunic up as high as he could, bent slightly to the side, and closed his hot mouth over her nipple.

Her breath came exploding out. He locked his hands around her hips, his mouth claiming her breast with confident, damaging skill. Dark hair fell down over his face as he licked her and, gripping her hips with both hands now, holding her immobilized, he tilted his hips, sliding his erection in a long, slow skate against her leggings and the shuddering, quivering, questing flesh beneath.

Her world exploded. Hot, rippling undulations rode through her muscles, fast and greedy. Her head dropped forward, then back, as she cried out, stunned. Nothing like the explosive power of this man had ever entered her life before. Nothing so potent, nothing so vital, not in her fettered life.

When she finally stopped shuddering, he lowered her feet to the ground. But he didn't step away, and he didn't let go. He just gave her a moment to gather herself, without allowing her to crumple into a boneless heap on the pine needles and dirt. How chivalrous.

His body was still taut with restraint. His breathing was still ragged, his muscles gilded with sweat, his eyes hard and merciless, which he'd never been before, so she was really rather concerned to find both those things now directed at her.

She pushed away. He stepped back. She stumbled only once, over nothing, then righted herself and gave her tunic hem a sharp tug down.

The world looked much the same as it had a few minutes ago. How peculiar.

Had it even taken minutes? she wondered helplessly. Or had he done that to her in mere seconds? It felt like he'd simply breathed on her and she'd come apart for him.

"Wait by the fire pit," he said curtly. She was dearly weary of curtness.

If I take off my clothes and let you have me, will you smile at me again? is what she wanted to say, which was so pathetic she almost hated herself for it. How weak she'd become in the face of Finian.

"I'll not wait by the fire," she retorted, keeping her eyes slightly averted, her chin slightly aloft. The latter helped to remind her to maintain at least the semblance of dignity. "I'll be eating some of that game, so I'll help bring it down. I told you before, I was taught to use a weapon."

His darkness regarded her. She could feel it. "Ye also told me ye were no good at it."

She almost laughed. "I'm not good at so many things, Finian, I cannot let that stop me anymore." She turned on her heel and walked into the forest. His measured footfalls followed behind.

"In any event, I said I was no good with the *bow,*" she added, clarifying.

He pointed over her head to the right, where the sunsetting light coming down through the trees was a bit brighter. A clearing must be nearby. He looked down at her. "Meaning?"

"Meaning," she said, turning to look in his eyes, which she had not done since he made her world explode into the hot, perfect waves of pleasure still shuddering inside her, "I am fairly skilled with a blade."

He paused. "How do ye get close enough?"

"I don't." He stood with his hands at his side, bow light in hand, his eyes unwavering on hers. "I throw it," she said, and turned away.

"Senna."

She stopped but didn't turn.

"I'm sorry."

Oh, sweet Mother. He must have seen the hurt in her eyes. He was addressing it. Could she be more shamed? Perhaps she should just paint the words in her blood, to show how exposed she was. How on earth had that happened? In a matter of days. For shame. For shame, for grief, and the love of God, what had happened to her?

She nodded, her back still to him, her turn to be curt. There was a small squirrel in the tree before her.

"Did I frighten ye?"

No. I manage that quite well myself. "'Tis naught. We lost our heads."

"I didn't lose my head." His low voice rode through the trees and over her shoulders.

"No?"

"Nay."

"What was that, then?"

A pause. "That was hardly my head."

"Indeed."

She heard him take a deep breath, let it out. "I think we've to admit, Senna, that touching is a rash and dangerous thing."

"Exceedingly."

"We will not anymore."

She nodded crisply. "Of course not."

"And ye've to stop . . ." His voice faded away.

"Stop what?"

Silence.

She raised her eyebrows at the squirrel.

He gave what sounded like a ragged sigh. "Senna, ye have to see, I'm at yer mercy."

She swallowed thickly. "One could be excused for not seeing it that way. Considering you have a bow and a sword and all sorts of muscles."

"Aye, well, this is a more difficult matter than swords and bows."

"Not to you."

For a moment, he was quiet. "Aye. To me."

She inhaled deeply, cool evening air. She let her breath out slowly, as he had, in measured degrees. "Not to me," she said, lifting her chin that extra little bit. It so often helped. It failed so miserably.

"Nay?"

"No. I trow, I can hardly recollect what we were speaking about. Can you?"

The invitation to conspiracy came out sharply. Silence stretched out between them like an open range. Her breath sounded loud in her ears. She looked over. The bow hung from his fingertips as he watched her. She could divine nothing of what went on behind his eyes.

"No," he agreed slowly. "What were we speaking of?"

"Muscles, itches, I can hardly recall."

With the casual grace of a predator, he pushed off the tree. She realized she was trembling. Her hands, her legs. He stopped inches away.

"Bows," he murmured. He swept his palm across her cheek, a swift, gentle touch, then dropped his hand. "We were speaking of being mean with a bow."

She sniffed. "Were we?"

A small smile edged up a corner of his mouth. "I am certain of it."

She met his gaze, his perceptive, ever-blue eyes, and she started to smile back.

"Oh, indeed, I am quite terrible with a bow, Finian. But then, you should see me with a blade."

Chapter 26

The easy, sense-damaging smile expanded across Finian's face. He approved. Jésu. She was lost. It was hardly his fault she'd fallen so hard. Was he to be disapproving, so as to call up her instincts for self-preservation? Those were bobbing in the Irish Sea, fifty leagues away.

"A blade, ye say?"

Was that incredulity in his voice? Better than pity, and she did appreciate a challenge. There'd been so few to live up to of late. Despite the constant struggle of keeping the business afloat, the last true, blood-pounding challenge had come when the business had been saved, twice, when she was fifteen.

But best not to think of that rescue just now. Or ever again.

"You sound doubtful," she said instead.

His lips pursed, but his fine eyes contained a smile. An appreciative, if slightly incredulous one. "Not many people can toss a blade, Senna."

She arched an eyebrow. "Watch," she said, focusing on the goodness of his smile in this moment, not all the terrible things that could be, that had been, that would, no doubt, be again one day soon.

"Oh, lass. Ye've no idea how I watch ye."

She turned away, her cheeks flushing.

"There's a meadow ahead," he said. "Come sunset, it should be filled with—"

"Rabbits."

She cut wide around the meadow, keeping to the wood, and emerged at the edge of the small clearing. Like a miracle, four or five hares sat in the center. They nibbled at the grass and hopped lightly about in the slanting golden light.

Moving stealthily around a tree trunk, Senna positioned herself in a crouch, squinting against the evening glow. The now-ubiquitous tall grasses hid her as she knelt and pulled the long leather thong from her pouch. Somewhere in the woods, Finian was also fitting his bow. Who would bring down supper first?

She lifted her face and felt the breeze while she pulled out the curved hilt from its sheath, feeling with her fingertips, unconsciously recalling lessons from her youth. Her injured hand healed apace since Finian's ministrations. And she hardly noticed it now. A long wavy reed brushed against her cheek as she made final adjustments to the curved wood handle in her palm.

Slowly she stood, lifted her arm, elbow bent, blade by her ear. One of the rabbits stopped, his black nose in the air, sniffing madly.

She half closed her eyes, all her attention narrowed into that one small spot. In her mind's eye, she sighted a line between the blade and her quarry. Her body hummed. The rabbit seemed to freeze. He looked huge. Unmissable.

She snapped her arm forward. The blade hurtled across the clearing, tossing off orange glints as the blade caught and reflected the sunset. Its humming thrummed in her ears, then the rabbit thumped to the ground with nary a sound.

Senna was rather more noisy.

She leapt up and screeched. The remaining rabbits scattered like swarming minnows, and she danced in a wild, high-stepping little circle, laughing. After years of minimal practice, through the turmoil of the past few weeks, and before the uncertain future that was now her life, she could take care of her own needs and survive.

Beholden to no one.

Finian watched from beneath a tree on the opposite side of the clearing. As she floated back into the woods, rosy with pride and clutching the rabbit by the ears, he moved soundlessly to intercept her. Every so often she lifted the rabbit level with her eyes and stared at it with profound satisfaction.

Her grin stretched from ear to ear when he stepped into her path, bow in hand. The sandy yellow haze of sunset lit her in a latticework of golden green dapples.

"Good God, woman," he said in a husky voice.

She nodded happily. "I know."

"Ye're good," he said. But what he was thinking was, *You're marvelous, magnificent, frightening.*

He wanted to pull her to him, make her remember very well what they'd been talking about in the wood, relight the fire in her that would make her body melt for him again. Instead, he simply said, "Very, very good."

She grinned.

"All I ask is that, next time, ye try to *not* alert the English garrison in Dublin as to our whereabouts."

She blushed around her smile. He reached for the rabbit and she passed it over, long ears first.

"That was foolish of me, Finian. I was far too loud. I simply felt so, so . . ."

"Just so," Finian echoed, smiling faintly.

She began to reach for the rabbit, but he lifted it into the air, just out of her reach. "Ye brought him down," he said. "I will clean him up."

She stood and stared, then her grin grew. "Irishman, I believe you are right."

He strode back to their camp. "Usually."

After cleaning and skinning it, he spitted and cooked it over their small fire. Senna leaned so far forward to watch she was practically sitting in his lap. Finian did not ask her to stop.

"Mmm," she sniffed, her nose in the air. "It smells good." She pulled her pack close and loosed the leather thong tie. She fumbled inside and extracted a small pouch. "Herbs."

"Herbs? You've got herbs in there?" He tried to peer down into the dark, shapeless leather satchel, but she playfully snatched it away and held it close to her chest, as if to hide the contents. "What else have you got, Senna? I could use a pot, for boiling water."

"Next time." She slid the tips of her folded hands into the warmth between her thighs and leaned forward demurely. "For now, you'll just have to make do."

With ye? he thought. Make due with her vibrant, spirited, startling self?

This had gone beyond playful flirting; what he was doing with Senna had a rock-hard purpose. He had no idea what it was, but he recognized the feel of it. It was memorable. Like going to war. Like preparing for battle by painting himself for the journey to the afterlife. Like diving off the cliffs near his home into the churning blue sea below when he was fifteen, with his mates, and knew he was invincible.

But still, those moments took decision. The plunge had been intentional. And always, there was no turning back.

He did not want that. He could not swim back up from these depths.

Cutting several slits crosswise along the cooking hare, Finian shoved handfuls of the herb mixture inside the marbled meat, then smeared a thin layer over the outside with his palm. With a flick of his wrist, he turned the hare. A bit of fat dripped off into the fire, where it sizzled and flashed into a brief flame. Out of the corner of his eye, he saw Senna lick her lips.

"Ye didn't seem afraid when the English soldiers came."

"I wasn't." She looked up. "I was terrified."

He smiled faintly. "But now, now that ye watched me kill them, ye don't seem too terribly wrought up."

She didn't meet his eyes this time. "I raise sheep," she mumbled. "I've hunted rabbits. I've seen things die."

"These weren't rabbits."

"I did not learn to throw a knife in order to kill rabbits," she replied in a clear voice, and looked at him. "But they make good practice targets."

He turned the rabbit again, very carefully. "Have you killed a man, Senna?" He said it casually, like he might ask if she'd brought the wash in from the line.

There was a long pause. "I've done everything once."

Once? *Everything?* What on earth did that mean?

He turned the rabbit again, unnecessarily. It would be the most evenly cooked piece of game on earth. He did not ask any more questions.

When it was done, he flipped it onto one of the bordering stones, and when it was cool, they ate with relish, licking their fingers. Then they sat in a companionable silence for a while, under the darkening trees.

Soon it would be time to leave the clearing for a few more hours of travel, but for now they sat, the world hung in a bleached transition, timeless and clear. The sky was laced with steel.

"I do believe that was the best meal I've ever had, Finian," she said. He looked over as a deep sigh brought her lush mouth fully into a yawn. She sighed again and slid her hand down her thigh in an unconscious, highly sensuous movement. Finian wrenched his eyes away.

She was alone in the world, and far too easy to take advantage of.

Too stunning in spirit, too comely in form to trust his motives around. He might lose his wits, go mad like his father, let her tromp all over him, rip his heart out one day when she decided someone else had more of whatever it was she wanted.

Women wanted. 'Twas their nature. Their duplicitous, fomenting, desirable nature. He'd learned that the long, hard way. No more lessons, ever again.

Chapter 27

They sat quietly in the growing darkness, Senna sitting with her knees clasped between her arms, Finian flat on his back as twilight took its flat, pale shape.

Shades of pearly gray and pale blue slunk across the bowl overhead, but under the trees, it was darkly shadowed. The birds had stopped chirping. A frog could be heard in the distance, searching for a mate.

An owl swept low over their clearing, his big round eyes reflecting moonlight as he searched for prey. A tiny bat skittered and clicked in a jittery trajectory overhead.

"What made ye come to *Éire,* Senna?" Finian asked, breaking the silence.

Senna jumped at the sound of his voice, although he'd spoken quietly enough, in that low, resonant voice which did not carry far into the air, but deep into her. Like it was made of earth.

She'd felt it the other night, too—it seemed a year ago—when he'd stood beside her in the bailey, his hand hooked over her shoulder. He'd murmured to her in that soil-voice, and it felt like he was breathing for her.

"Business," she replied. "I came for business."

He'd been leaning forward, and his arm paused in its reach

for a stick on the ground, muscles stilled in their silky slide beneath his skin. He continued reaching forward. "Ye mean money. Ye came for money."

"Why else would someone do such a thing as this?" she replied in a flat voice, carefully leeched of any emotion.

"Why indeed."

"You don't understand," she said angrily. Angry she felt the need to explain herself. Angry that he did not approve.

"I understand 'twas a piss-poor notion."

She gave a snort of derisive laughter. "You've no idea. My family is famed for piss-poor ideas. We ought to have a chamber pot on our coat of arms."

He sat back and uprooted a small plant near his hip with much more force than was necessary. Small clumps of dirt went flying. She listened to them land, tiny, swift, muted thumps falling on soft leaf fronds. A miniature army in sudden retreat.

It was getting harder and harder to keep the emotion from her voice. She snatched an innocent stick off the ground and began peeling it, cutting into the soft flesh under the bark with vicious stabs of a fingernail.

She felt Finian studying her face. "Had ye heard of Rardove, Senna? His violence?"

She waved the stick through the air. "No. Not enough to know all . . . this."

All this indeed. How could anyone ever know what awaited her outside the door? It was a dangerous business, stepping out into the wide world, and she was sorely sorry she'd done so. Whether it was done to save the business, or her father, or her wretched, empty life, she was all sorrow now.

But mostly, at the moment, she was sorry for the way Finian was looking at her, with something akin to disappointment in his eyes. She squared her shoulders in the steely gray light filtering down through the trees. "You do not understand."

An edge of his mouth lifted, but there was nothing amused

in the grating voice he answered with. "Oh, I understand, Senna. My mam had the same choice to make."

"What choice?"

"The one women always have to make." He stared into the dying fire. "Her heart or the money."

Senna almost couldn't see the earth below her anymore. Her eyes were filling up with shocking tears, fed by unfamiliar, impotent fury. What would he know about the choices a woman had to make, in the dark, when the papers were sitting there in the fading light, and no one spoke a word? When no one cared for the lifetime of moments before the decision, simply the consequences that followed behind?

"How fortunate for your mother," she snapped. The emotions would not be contained anymore. Sharp and fast, they shot out. "To have a choice. Many women do not enjoy such liberty. So tell me, when she married your father, was it for love or his money?"

"She did not marry my Da," he said in a cold, impossible voice.

Senna went still.

Finian shut his eyes. Why in God's name had he revealed that? He gritted his teeth. It would only mean curiosity, then questions, and perhaps sympathy, and from this homeless waif—

"I assume she had her reasons."

Her voice was cool, but soft. The dirt under his fingers was cool. Soft, too, like silt. Like her voice.

What an unexpected reply. It barely stemmed his anger, though.

"Aye," he retorted, feeling his mouth twist derisively. "She had her reasons. And fine ones they were. A beautiful big castle, a fine English lord, coffers spilling coin and jewels."

He pushed abruptly to his feet, surprised to find his head was a bit spinny. Up too quick, in a prison too long. That was all. Soon he'd be right again.

"And that's enough of that," he said firmly.

She swallowed. He could see her slender throat work around it. "I assume she did what she felt she needed to do," she said stiffly, as if he hadn't spoken. "The . . . taking care of things. One takes care of things. One manages them."

"Is that so?" He stared at her. "Ye call it *managing*?"

"I most certainly do."

A sad pride filled her voice, which under normal circumstances he would have heard. But just now he barely noticed it, because anger was foaming so high against his own shores.

"Tell me, Senna," he asked in a low, steel voice. "What do you think of yer masterful managing now, sitting here on the Irish marches?"

She yanked her head up, a jerky movement. "An error." Her lips barely moved. "A terrible mistake."

And as he stared longer into her beautiful, staring eyes, sense finally routed anger. He muttered a curse. "That was wrong of me, Senna—"

"No. You're right. Absolutely correct." She gave a brittle, bright smile. Each of her words had a precise point, and her voice was hard like stone. He could climb all over it and never find a way in. "We both had mothers who left. How peculiar. And sad. And, as I observed about your mother, so it must be true of mine: they had their reasons. Your mother left for pennies. Mine for passion. Reasons, nevertheless. How old were you when yours left? I was five. My brother Will was but a year. My"—she gave a tight little laugh—"was he heavy. To me, at least. But we managed."

She looked over. Her eyes had turned into bright, staring gold stones. "Although, as you've pointed out, not so verily well."

"Senna," he said slowly in a voice he hardly even recognized.

"But then, one does what one can."

"Senna."

"Did your mother ever return? Mine did not."

"Senna."

"Did she, Finian?"

He crouched down in front of her and pressed his fingers under her chin, turning her face up. Small tendrils of coiled curls shivered by her cheeks; she was shaking, very slightly. Her eyes were staring straight ahead, bright, shimmering.

"Senna, heed me."

The shivering coil of amber stilled. Her hard gemstone eyes slid to his.

"Did she, Finian?" she asked, but though her words were as brittle as before, he heard the plea inside them now: she very greatly wanted to hear a tale different from hers. "Did your mother ever come back?"

Something heavy dropped off a cliff inside him. "Aye. She came back, and killed herself. I found her hanging from an oak tree."

Everything went still.

"Oh, this accursed world," she whispered. She wrapped an arm around his shoulders and he dropped to his knees before her, their heads bent close, pocketed by her outstretched arm and falling hair. For a while, they just breathed together.

"She oughtn't to have done that," she whispered.

"Nay." He cupped the nape of her neck and, in the small pocket of space between them, felt their heat mingling together. "I'm told she's paying for it now."

"Do not say such things. She is not."

"Ye think not?"

She rested her forehead against his. "I have a heresy in my heart, Finian," she confessed quietly. "I have met ever so many priests and abbots in my travels. Some have been gentle hearts, others with a brutality to depths I cannot fathom. At times, I was of the opinion they must worship different gods, because they have told me such different things."

He smiled faintly. Senna would have an opinion about dirt.

"They all said the same to me," he said. "Ye think some of them may be wrong?"

"I think," she replied slowly, "if there is a place in Heaven for each of them, how could there not be a place for each of us?"

He scooped up her free hand as it dangled off her knee in the small pocket of space between them. "Ahh," was all he could say, surprised to hear his voice had gone hoarse.

Her free hand, the one he wasn't holding, scuffed and dirty, rested on her knees. Her braid fell over her shoulder, trailing into the space between them like a rope lowered down the side of a castle.

She was succoring him, and all he wanted was to rescue her. It was enough to make you weep. He, who was filled with so many holes he didn't know why his ship hadn't sunk thus far, *he* wanted to rescue *her*. A woman who shone like the sun. He'd bared his deepest shame, the horror in his dreams, and all he could think was, *How could your mother have left you behind?*

"You see?" she asked.

"I see." Lifting her delicate hand in his callused one, he pressed a kiss to her knuckles, then let her go.

"Finian—"

He got to his feet. "Ready, Senna?"

She had her mouth open, as if to say something more, then she closed it and got to her feet. Wise woman. "I am ready."

"Just another hour or so."

He turned and began trekking a path into the woods. He heard her swing the pack over her shoulder and follow behind. They didn't speak of missing mothers again. They didn't need to.

Chapter 28

Battered, weary, and waterlogged from crossing yet another river—"Stream, whichever," she'd snapped when Finian tried explaining the difference—Senna would have praised him as a god, if it were required, when he halted them after another two hours of hiking. She was literally stumbling from exhaustion.

They came to a small clearing, he stopped moving forward, and her knees slowly buckled. She looked up at him.

"We're done for the night, Senna." His tone was gentle.

She half smiled, rubbed her shoulders wearily, then threw her bag on the ground and slumped on top of it. She cried out briefly as her fingers took some of the impact, then was asleep before she could finish the cry.

Finian watched her, curled around the satchel—a pack full of knobbly objects and sharp edges—like a nestling cat. Her knees were by her chin, her arms clutched around the bag, hair tugging free from the braid and spilling over her face until only the profile of a small, delicate chin could be seen.

Turning on his heel, he walked to a small rise in the land and began his watch.

The moon rose to its heights and a small wind blew by in gentle gusts, pulling the soft, wet scent of loamy earth and growing things behind. He ran his hand through his hair, drew a deep breath, and began a slow reconnoitering around the perimeter of the clearing. In the center of his sweeping circle, Senna slept.

Nothing moved in the dark world. Years of practice made him move soundlessly through the sticks and leaves covering the ground. One circuit, two.

An owl hooted.

He froze.

In the treetops to the west, the rapid beat of wings shuddered briefly, then a bird shot out of the dark greenery, squawking.

Moving swiftly and soundlessly, he pushed his spine up against a tree trunk. Another small sound far to his left disturbed the night silence. His body was frozen but for his hand that swung to his sword hilt.

Again it came. Shuffling, heavy hooves. Far away but far too close. The murmur of a voice speaking in hushed tones, racing through the night air. Creaking leather, jangling spurs.

Soldiers.

Bending low, he slid his sword free and crept back through the trees, moving from shadow to shadow, making no more noise than a bat winging overhead. When he reached Senna, he crouched down, mouth by her ear.

"Up, lass. We've company."

Her eyes shot open. Her startled, bright eyes were inches from his.

"Unwelcome guests. I've need of yer talents with a blade," he whispered, rising and pointing to a far tree, indicating where to position herself.

She scrambled to her feet, feeling in the sheath lashed around her waist, pulling out the knife. Her other hand briefly touched a second blade strapped to her leg, then she slunk across the shadowy glen to where he had pointed, bending low.

The sound of hooves crunching on sticks suddenly stopped.

Every muscle in Finian's body rippled in readiness. He threw his head back, his mouth slightly parted, every sense alert to scent, sound, motion. At his side, his sword hung still. The dull silver plane of steel shone in the slatted moonlight.

A nicker broke the tense silence, then a muffled snort. Two voices, speaking in thick, almost unintelligible English accents, prickled the hair along the back of his neck.

Sweeping his sword up, he crept closer, moving from tree trunk to tree trunk like a slinking shadow. His blood welled thick and sluggish in his veins, an icy, solid feeling. Planting the heel of his hand on the gnarled bark of one tree, he edged his head around and squinted, trying to pierce the darkness.

The night was too thick, the woods too dense. He couldn't see anything. Behind, he heard the uneven whisper of Senna's breathing.

The soft clop of hooves began again, moving slowly away. An exchanged curse or word occasionally floated back to him. He let another moment pass. Then, to comfort Senna in her fear and ensure her continued silence, he turned to her, a finger at his lips.

Astonishment dropped his hand to his side. Was this not the woman he'd awoken two minutes ago from a dead slumber, telling her their lives were about to be shortened? Nay, it could not be. She did not look in the least afraid.

To the contrary, she radiated power and energy, and she was marvelous. Having nailed her lithe torso against the trunk of the tree, she peered around with one chestnut eye, her cheek pasted to the rough bark. Curving and tense, her body was finely tuned, her head thrown back. Masses of tangled dark curls slipped over her shoulder and along her arms. The blade hung deceptively still by her thigh, dripping from her fingertips.

The taut lines of muscles in her arm were defined by the filtered moonlight. Broken fingers did not seem in any way a hindrance. Her eyes glittered as she met his startled gaze, and she flashed him a bold, intrepid smile.

"We are alive yet," she whispered with an exultant look.

Partner. He had a partner. Sweet Jésu, when last had he such a thing?

Never. Never, and always sought it.

He forced his gaze back to the woods. The sound of the soldiers was farther away and continued to grow more distant. Motioning for Senna to stay where she was, he crept after them.

Half a mile of stealthy hunting assured him they were indeed headed away, and would trouble them no more. He turned back. Upon reached the clearing, he saw Senna had done as he bid, waiting motionless by the tree.

"They are gone," he whispered.

Her body was trembling with repressed excitement. He could scarcely fathom it. This was a dangerous world, and she was a small woman in its merciless midst. The crown of her head barely topped his shoulder, although the fuzz of untended hair added a good half inch, and he could nearly wrap his fingers twice around her slender wrist. With a twist, he could snap it. She was defenseless, really.

With weapons or without, she was no match for a soldier, no match for him. And she could have been killed a moment ago.

But she was smiling, God save him, with an untamed, fearless grin that smashed through the base of an untended wall of his heart and entered in.

He kept expecting Senna to be a simple matter: a smart, sensuous woman with some surprising, engaging traits. But that all lay in the dust of the past. In the damp, impressionable here and now, she was coming together as a human being in such startling and unexpected ways he was quite helpless before it.

He couldn't think of a single thing to say. The moon was setting.

"Were they searching for us?" she whispered.

He shook his head. "No way to know. I doubt it. That is a rarely used path between two towns."

"Is it safe to stay here?"

"I don't want to chance it. Can ye walk some more?"

She nodded. No semblance of a braid anymore, she was a sea of wild red-brown curls he could dive into. "All night, if we must. But, the moon has set," she pointed out. "It will be ever dark."

"I can see us through. Yer hand?" he asked, gesturing.

She looked at it as if surprised, then grinned. "I do not feel a thing."

They were very quiet as they shouldered their packs and started off. They hiked until the sun rose, when russet light fell like rain through the emerald tree branches. Scented with pine needles and forest resin, the triangulated rays of gold and dusty red drifted between the branches, humming faint light.

They passed through this furred illumination, their bodies alternately light and shadow, chilled to the bone and alive. It would be another glorious day.

They stopped twice—once to rest for a deep, hard sleep at midday, and one other time for a quick scrub in a stream.

But mostly they walked. And talked, although not of the nights before. Finian told her about his extended foster family and his love of music, and she might have mentioned something about a few be-knighted daydreams of her youth.

And he watched her. Endlessly.

Every time she bent her body, he followed the curve. When she laughed, he watched her mouth stretch up into that bewitching grin. When she looked up to ask him a question, he was already watching her with a slow regard that brought a blush to her cheeks.

At which point he would jerk his gaze away. The feeling was indescribable, akin to being stoked by fires that had been long banked. Something like coming home.

When evening finally turned honest eyes unreadable, she brought up their brush with the soldiers.

"Have you ever felt that way before, so alive when you are so close to dying?" Her voice was so low it barely disturbed the air. She could have been talking to herself.

He nodded silently, a bit alarmed by the feelings coursing through him. It brought life to her blood, did it? That pleased him. He knew the feeling well: the waterfalling sensation, the tumbling exhilaration of facing death alongside the inner certainty, *'This moment is mine.'*

There were few enough people who had such a response, with hearts who liked to live near the edge of unseen cliffs and fling themselves over the side, *knowing* they could fly.

Maybe *pleased* wasn't the right word.

He'd stood within inches of her body when it had come alive, when he'd told her their lives might be about to be shortened. Peered into her eyes when they'd sparked with fire. He'd known exactly how excitement pounded through her body, made her shimmer like a warrior-sprite. It left him breathless.

She was like some creature from a mythical land, and she did not even realize it, how uncommon she was.

No, he corrected himself. She seemed to know quite well she did not belong anywhere. What she had no idea of, was how perfectly she fit into the echoing, empty spaces of his heart.

Chapter 29

Senna stayed awake long after Finian had fallen asleep. Too much excitement, excitement that ought to be scaring her witless. Instead, she felt . . . excited. Alive. Reckless.

She rummaged about in her pack and came out with one of the flasks. She took a great draught and glanced at Finian. He was dead to the world. She regarded such peaceful repose glumly, then took another swig. His dark head was resting on the pack, his fingers interlaced over his broad chest. A steady, low rhythm lifted and lowered his hands. One knee was bent and resting against a small sapling.

She took another swallow, then corked it, still looking at Finian.

Devouring him, she admitted, since no one was inside her head to witness the admission.

She did like this whisky.

She was contemplating some rash, risky things just now, but for what reason urge herself to caution? She'd been dying inside for half her life, and Finian was the only thing that had ever made her even want to be renewed. Did one just toss that aside? She'd gone beyond the Pale in every way since coming to Ireland. She was hungry in a way she'd never been before. Sore in a way she'd never been before.

Alive in a way she'd never been before.

She set the flask down and crawled closer. All she wanted was to touch him. Not even to have him touch her. Just to feel his body. Touch. Be touching.

Not be alone.

She knelt beside him, her feet tucked beneath her. Planting a palm on each side of his chest, she leaned low and inhaled.

Finian opened his eyes to find her leaning over him, her hair tickling his arms. The curve of her body was clear as anything, the rise of her breasts just inches from his nose.

"What are ye doing, Senna?" he asked carefully.

She didn't leap back, as he'd expected. Instead she straightened and knelt, knees tucked under. So prim and proper, her stance. An instinctive seductress, to the tips of her dirty fingernails. And she was smiling. He frowned.

"Ye're a'right?"

"Finian, I wanted to ask you something."

She sounded shy. He closed his eyes and said a brief prayer. "Aye?"

"Do you remember what happened? Before?"

"Before, when?" he asked warily.

"Before," she waved her hand. "Before we hunted, before. After the boat ride, before." Her words slowed. "Against the tree, before."

He groaned and wiped his hand over his face, his shaft already hard.

"Do you?"

"Jésu, woman," he rasped. "Do ye expect me to forget?"

"I was thinking."

"Stop, then."

She leaned down a little closer. Her hair tickled against his neck. "I was thinking, that thing that happened to me," he groaned, "I don't think that happened to you, too."

He gave a muffled curse and threw his arms up, over

his face, bent at the elbows. "Senna," he said through gritted teeth.

"Did it?"

"Nay," he grated. "What's got into ye, woman? I can't take this, ye know."

"I know," she crooned, then bent to his ear. "'Tis the whisky."

"Not the whisky," he said grimly.

"The yarrow, then." Warm feminine curves pressed onto his inner arms, his cheek. Her breath came into his ear. "Finian, I would like that thing to happen to you. I would like to watch it happen to you. Like you watched me."

There was absolutely no defense against this. Her lips fluttered over his arms, and he let his elbows drop to the earth. With her hair a curtain around them, she kissed him in the moonlight, slow, light kisses over his cheeks and nose and chin, and finally, his lips.

And although he wanted to descend upon her, grasp the back of her neck and pillage her rampant femininity, he held himself in check, letting her hesitant, testing kisses inflame him to the point of pain. All he did was bend his arm and rest his palm against the curve of her hip, not guiding her, not caressing her, just holding on.

She knelt facing into him and slid her lips down his neck, her mouth leaving soft butterfly kisses behind, then to his collarbone. She glanced up, eyebrows arched in query, and tugged on the edge of his tunic.

"If you're cold . . ."

He ripped it off in a quick second, and listened to her slow exhale as her gaze traveled across his body. She bent low and breathed deep, then her tongue slipped out and licked across the smooth side of his rib cage.

"Senna," he managed between gritted teeth.

"My turn, so hush," she whispered. Then she licked his nipple.

He suppressed a growl and ran his palm up the curve of her buttocks. She froze, except for her breath. It came out in a hot rush over everything she'd just licked wet.

"Don't stop," he murmured thickly.

She opened her mouth and flicked her tongue. She slid one hand up his bent leg, ankle to knee, then down his thigh, to his groin. Unable to resist, he clamped his hand over hers and held her to his erection. Her slender fingers closed around the length of him, her mouth hot and panting on his nipple. He made her squeeze him tighter. He slid his other hand up and over her bottom. Then he floated his fingers slightly down the seam between.

"Oh," she exhaled hotly, all over him.

"Off," he growled, tugging on her leggings.

She was already pulling on the ties, and he was fumbling, too, propped up on an elbow, and then they were free. He slid them down to her knees, so her bottom was exposed, pushing up to the sky as she bent back to him.

She slid her mouth down the center of his belly then, fast and wet, kissing and nipping and licking, until he was so hard he thought he'd explode. He slid his hand across her belly and up between her thighs. She was wet. Slippery, hot. He pushed one finger high, searching for the crest of her.

She threw her head back, gasping. Hot, wet, damaging, good, this angel was everything he'd never hoped for. He folded his finger and slid it forward, over the slippery folds, pushing until he felt the circular bud. Another shocked, gasping whimper shot out of her. He fluttered his finger again, and she dropped her face into his chest, moaning. Hard, hot, churning lust pounded through him. He could barely see straight. He wanted this woman like no other, ever, not even in erotic dreams.

He tipped his wrist and pushed hard with the heel of his palm, pressing against her pulsing wet heat. She threw her head back and exhaled in hot, gasping moans, rocking back and forth on his hand.

She started trying to untie his leggings. Cursing, he did it for her, his one slippery hand still working on her, her rocking becoming more frenzied, her head dropping lower, until she was on her elbows, her face inches from his erection. Together, one hand each, they pushed open the ties of his leggings, just exposing him. Her shadowed face, curtained by windswept hair, turned to him as he was furiously grappling to slide his wet hand back up between her thighs. He was practically light-headed. More heat, more sex, more Senna.

"I don't know quite what to do," she whispered, her voice a mingling of panting arousal and blushing embarrassment.

In a heartbeat, he was on his knees, flipping her onto her back. He rested his forearms beside her hips, his face between her thighs.

"Like this, love," he rasped, and bent his face to everything hot and wet between her legs. He flicked his tongue once, snapping it lightly against her. Her hips instinctively rocked up into him.

"Oh, please," she cried, tossing her head.

A slow, charging, explosive descent into the pits of passion. Finian could barely hear her, he was so violently aroused. He sent his tongue in another long sweep up. Wet, hot honey.

"Spread yer legs. Farther," he demanded hoarsely.

She whimpered and did, until her heels were planted in the earth and she had her fingers entwined in his hair, restlessly tugging. He took two fingers and slowly spread her slippery wet folds wide, exposing the hard, slick nub to the cool moonlit night. With his thumb he brushed it, then followed with his tongue, fast and hard.

She gasped and froze, her fingers locked in his hair, her hips pushed up. At once he changed his pace, to slow and languorous, taking long, slow sweeps of her. His head was starting to spin, she tasted so good. So ready, so wet. His thumbs spread her flesh apart and he sunk his tongue deep inside her. One thumb circled her swirled nub lightly, then pressed in hard.

"Oh, no," she breathed, long-pitched and smoky.

"Oh, aye," he whispered, and rose to his knees.

She grabbed for him but he caught up her wrists and trapped them on the ground over her head.

Kneeling, his leggings unlaced but still around his waist, he straddled one of her restlessly bobbing legs. He pushed his hand hard up between her legs and without pausing, slid two fingers inside her.

Crying out, she arched her shoulders into the air, her pelvis down low, so Finian had to reach down to keep his fingers inside her, to keep prodding her, which drove him mad, to be so stretched out over her body, one hand trapping her wrists high above her head, the other plunged deep inside her. Her knee came up between his legs in a restless motion, and he rocked his hips, sliding his erection along her thigh. She pushed back, hips up, a rippling, undulating curve of flesh in the moonlight, heedless and reckless, whimpering and tossing her head, making her hair spill out all around her head so it looked like she was floating underwater.

He drove her hard, his fingers confident and sure, his thumb hot amid her folds. She pushed against him, feminine curves thrumming with the pounding sexual rhythm he was playing on her body.

"Do ye like this, Senna?" he whispered roughly.

"Oh," she exhaled, pushing up on her elbows, trying to kiss him.

"Do ye like what I'm doing to ye?"

"Aye, aye. I want more."

He bent to her ear. "What more, Senna?"

"You," she panted, lifting her hips in a wild, bucking motion. "I want you. Inside me."

His head was spinning. "No," he rasped, shaking his head. "I'll not take yer maidenhood."

She gave a shaky explosion of laughter. "Oh, Finian. I'm not a virgin."

He lay low over her body and rasped in her ear, "What?"

"I'm not an innocent. And I cannot have children. Finian, please."

That was all he needed. Another time for the mind. Now was all about the need.

"I'll devour ye, angel," he growled in a ragged whisper, bending his mouth to her skin. "Ye'll never know what's run through ye."

Senna's blood throbbed, molten iron churning through her veins. He covered her with his body in one simple movement. The curling hair of his thigh scratched against her inner thighs. She could feel his bunched muscles nudging her apart for him. Invading her. She lifted one leg and hooked it around his hip.

"Now," she panted, her hands sliding over his back, gentle against the scars but still feeling every vertebra, every curve of muscle sliding beneath his warm skin. She slid farther under him, the ground solid and cool beneath, Finian demanding above, solid and hot.

Dark hair fell around the planes of his face, fixed in determination as he reached down to position himself. She felt the edge of his hand, hard and hot, brushing against her wetness as he grasped his erection and slid it to her. The rounded wide tip of him pushed in. She closed her eyes, her hands clasped at the back of his neck, an ankle at the small of his back.

Holding himself on one knee, Finian thrust himself into her waiting heat, feeling her hot passage constrict around him, yielding, slippery, tight. He sank in a little deeper, his gaze locked on their union, watching himself disappear inside her. He wrenched his eyes away, determined to hold himself in check, and looked up. Senna's eyes were open, watching him.

"Ye're a'right, lass?"

"'Tis good," she said, half laugh, half cry, her words shaky.

Using every fragment of self-control he'd ever possessed, he stopped his long, slow penetration. With soft whispers, he kissed her nose, her chin, each flushed cheek and her forehead, until she was soft and sighing again.

"Did Rardove . . . ?"

"Nay," she whispered. "He never even tried. I think I scared him."

"Ye terrify me," he murmured and moved inside her again, holding back, filling her in long, slow strokes so she could grow used to the feel of him. It was exquisite torture. Wet and tight, her flesh was hot, swelling, sweet womanly depths. The muscles of his back and legs were taut with restraint. Her small heel pressed into the flesh beside his spine, almost hurting, and he wouldn't have asked her to move it if it meant an extra dozen years of life.

He pushed his hips forward again. She sighed, a breathy, wanton thing. The small, aching whimper pounded lust through his blood. He growled and shifted his hips, nudging in farther.

"Oh, that feels good." Her voice came up like a sigh, and she lifted her hips, widening his entryway.

She was a hot, swelling cradle of tight perfection and he could do nothing but throw his head back and roar as he plunged into her again and again. The earth started to spin beneath his knees and palms, his breath coming in short, raspy breaths.

Senna lifted her hips in howling, bucking thrusts, and Finian's penetration grew more firm and long, each time filling her more fully, sheathing himself deeper in her hot, shuddering wetness. He dropped his head onto her neck, his palms splayed on the earth beside her, his hair swaying beside his face as his hips moved in an ancient, throbbing rhythm.

Each perfect move he made sent a fresh wave of pleasure

shuddering through Senna. Her skin was humming, her blood roiling. Her hands were greedy in their touches, wanting to be everywhere, wrapped around his shoulders, sliding down the muscles of his back, brushing aside his hair so she could watch as passion closed his eyes and made him throw back his head.

His hand suddenly swept down to the small of her back and fitted her rocking hips tightly against his. Bolts of thudding, intense pleasure skidded across her belly and somehow her legs were wrapped around his hips and no part of her touched the ground. It was all masterful touches and the hot, sweaty, sculpted body of Finian.

With a muffled curse, he clamped his arm around her waist and hoisted her up, swinging them over so she sat astride him, his torso supported on a sharp rise of grassy earth. He looped cords of her hair around his palm and pulled her face down to his.

"Spread yer legs," he said in her ear, his free hand spread possessively across her back. She did as he bid and he sank in farther, pushing hard. "I've only got so much more," he said hoarsely.

"Getting tired?" she asked, her voice just as ragged as his, but laced with laughter.

"No. Getting close to coming inside ye. Ye'll like it."

She dropped her head back, rocking her hips in rhythm on top of him. When he spoke so, she felt like her body could do all the things he promised from the pleasure of his words alone.

Plunge, thrust, retreat, plunge. Her head spun and her body sang. Senna gripped his shoulders and leaned into him, her chin by his forehead, her knees digging into the earth. Their passion hammered to a violent crescendo.

Her eyes flew open. "Oh," she whispered, startled. Another thrust of Finian's hips, another perfect, thick penetration. She threw her head back and moved her body in unbridled lunges, her lower lip locked between her teeth.

"Don't stop," she whispered. A wickedly carnal undulation

of pleasure vibrated through her pulsing body. Up along her back, down her legs, along her neck rippled the Finian magic. Another . . . quite something . . . stretching . . . quiver. Her body lurched to a halt, yanked to the edge. Her face contorted.

He grinned crookedly.

"What is it?" came her wild whisper.

"Let it be," he coaxed, holding her hips into the rocking rhythm.

"Oh, please, oh please, don't stop."

"Never. I will never stop," came his ragged reply.

She tipped toward some inevitable precipice. Hesitating at the edge, he surged into her again and touched some mad, spiraling pleasure point deep inside her. A wave of shuddering wetness crashed through her body, flaming white heat and long, undulating quivers. She leapt off the cliff and flew, throbbing and shuddering and *now* alive.

Finian felt her release ripple along him and his hands flexed around her hips as he plunged into her one last time, exploding into his own quaking, rocking fulfillment. He held her shuddering in his arms—copper hair, parted lips, and burning spirit—and felt his heart shift.

The moment lasted forever. She mewed his name in helpless repetition, each whimpering cry accented by a shudder of warm flesh along his quivering length. He held himself deep inside her, spent, satisfied, and shocked.

Chapter 30

"Shocked?"

Pentony, seated at the table, nodded.

Rardove groaned. His eyes were red rimmed, and the small beard he usually kept so carefully trimmed was rough edged and uneven. "That's what he says?" he asked Pentony, who was reading from the scrolled missive which had just arrived, pressed with red wax in the image of a sword-wielding, helmed horseman that marked King Edward's seal. *"Shocked?"*

"And displeased," Pentony added.

"Displeased."

Pentony nodded without looking over again. No need to witness the deterioration with every sense. Hearing it was quite enough for now.

Rardove cursed and reached for the jug of wine and poured. Just what was required: more drink.

All the nights since Senna left had been filled with sleeplessness, fury, and flagons of wine, evidenced by the roars that exploded from Rardove's bedchamber and sent maidservants scurrying. This morning had not brought much different, except that his rage seemed muted by a monstrous hangover. Even now, by candlelight, his eyeballs were obviously swollen and red rimmed, his nose mottled with little red spots, his cheeks ruddy red. He was a study in crimson.

Mayhap he would kill himself with drink. Today.

Pentony turned back to the royal missive in his hands. "The king is on the Welsh border, waiting for a good wind. When he gets it, he'll sail for Ireland and march here. He's sending Wogan the justiciar, governor of Ireland, on ahead to speak with you. When the weather cooperates, he will come himself."

Rardove swept up a mug of wine and drank the dregs, then simply dropped the cup. It clattered to the ground. "Good," he snapped. "The royal hound will learn how difficult it truly is, guarding his marches against the accursed Irish."

"He will also learn you made the Wishmé dyes without telling him."

Rardove scowled, but it was bravado, and Pentony knew it. Rardove had cause to fear. The king of England, Edward Longshanks, Hammer of the Scots, had an uncanny way of finding out who was inciting rebellion in his lands. It was the reason there *was* so little rebellion in his lands. Aside from the spy Red, that is, who must be mad to court the fury of this royal will. Edward was a terrifying enemy. Acquisitive, determined, brutal.

And he seemed to have found out that Rardove was trying to make the legendary dyes behind his back.

No, shocked and disappointed were probably pale versions of what Edward Longshanks was feeling. Enraged. Murderous. These were more the thing.

Especially when he learned Rardove knew the legend of the dyes to be legend no longer, but fact. Rardove had samples to prove it, made by the only dye witch who'd been able to produce the coveted dyes in the last five hundred years: Elisabeth de Valery.

Senna, her daughter, was Rardove's last chance to make them again.

A long shot, by all accounts, Senna was like a single arrow

winged over the ramparts from a hundred yards away, but there you had it. She was whelped from a long, ancient line of dyers, and while she claimed she had not been trained, that might not matter: legend said it was a talent carried in the blood.

The mother had it, for certes. She'd rediscovered the ancient recipe, written it all down, then run away.

That, at least, ran in the blood, Pentony thought. Mother and daughter, both had the wits to flee as soon as they were able. Unlike Senna, though, Elisabeth had taken the secret of the dyes with her.

Also unlike the daughter, Elisabeth had been married, to a wool merchant. Gerald de Valery, a man she apparently loved to great depths—deeper than Rardove. Love triangles were never good things.

But then, Pentony suspected Elisabeth had never been triangulated whatsoever. All her love had been for de Valery. Why she'd come for the dyes still baffled him.

But come she had. After she was wed, after there were children whelped and homes to keep, Elisabeth left Gerald de Valery and came to Rardove. To the Indigo Beaches. The promise of crafting the legendary dyes apparently proved a greater temptation than heart and home.

Temptation, passion, craving. Fatal weaknesses for the family. The mother: dye making. The father: gambling. Senna appeared to be the strongest branch on that family tree.

A shadow suddenly appeared at the door. The baron didn't look up. The soldier peered nervously between Pentony and Rardove. Pentony waved him in.

Armored from heel to neck in plate and mail, he glittered dully in the flickering candlelight. He strode to the front of the table where Rardove slouched, his gaze riveted to some invisible spot on the far wall.

"My lord, we found a man who may be Red."

Rardove's spine unbent as he sat up, looking at the soldier, then behind him. No six-foot Irishman lurked in the shadows. His gaze came back to the fore. "Where is he?"

The soldier stared intently at the wall directly above Rardove's head. "At the abbey."

"What? What is he doing there, and not here?"

"She . . . kicked us out."

"She?"

"Mother Superior."

Pentony was shocked to find his lips twitching into a grin.

"She did what?" Rardove repeated, incredulous. "Kicked you out? She's a *woman,*" he sputtered, waving his hand at the soldier's belt. "You have a sword."

The soldier cleared his throat. "Aye, my lord. But she has God."

Rardove's face went absolutely unreadable. It looked like he didn't best know how to explode. His face turned slowly, like an autumn oak leaf, into a bright, flaming red.

"Get out!" he roared. The soldier skittered backward and fled the room before the echoes faded.

Pentony rose and began assembling the sheaves of parchment scattered across the table. "Ireland has become quite a hotbed of treason of late," he observed mildly. "You, O'Melaghlin, Red."

There was no verbal reply, but it felt as if a towering presence had suddenly built in the room, like a stack of storm clouds. Pentony looked over his shoulder. Rardove was staring at him. Pentony stilled, sheaves of paper in hand, while the strangest combination of amazement and . . . joy dawned on Rardove's face, as if Pentony had beautiful, naked women dancing behind him. How terribly odd. Or perhaps just terrible, for no reason he could name.

"God. Damn," Rardove exhaled.

Uneasy, Pentony dropped the scrolls and let them roll over on themselves, like small flat creatures nesting.

The baron got to his feet. "Goddamn, you're goddamned brilliant, Pentony."

God had been damned quite enough in the past minute, even in this place of sin. Something was amiss.

Pentony was surprised by the cold, wavy sensation moving through his chest. Was that nervousness? Worry? It had been too long to know for certain.

"My lord?"

Color was flooding back into the baron's face, florid, healthy, disturbing. He snapped his fingers. "Sit. Write."

Pentony did neither. "Write what, my lord?"

"Write about treason," Rardove retorted, almost gleeful. "As you said, terrible treachery abounds in Ireland. The Irish have grown far too bold, and this intrigue with Red proves it. 'Tis time to crush them."

"Crush them?"

The soles of Rardove's boots cracked against the wood planks beneath the rushes. "This alliance between Red and the Irish threatens the king's peace along every shore of his realm. Edward will not like to hear of it."

Pentony had a flash of understanding. Hear of *this,* rather than of the fact that Rardove had both found and lost a dye witch, all without mentioning it to his liege. Putting out the hue and cry on someone else was an excellent way to deflect attention from one's own crimes.

It was a frighteningly clever maneuver.

"Edward will be enraged to find more Celts aligning against him, with what he has brewing in Scotland." Rardove looked over, saw Pentony staring, and waved his hand through the air. "Write, man. Write!"

Pentony sat and dipped the tip of the quill in the inkwell, more by long years of habit than obedience. "Who?" he asked, although he already knew. He wrote slowly.

"Wogan, the justiciar. He is riding to us? Well, let us send riders to intercept him along the way, and tell him of the intrigues of the Irish."

Pentony's pen scratched across the parchment.

"No, I shall not wait placidly for war to be launched upon me," Rardove said, in a voice as close to thoughtful as he could come. He ran his fingers through his beard. "Send word to all the neighboring lords as well. And all my vassals."

Pentony's pen scratched to a halt. He looked up slowly. "Why, my lord?"

Rardove strode to the window. He moved in and out of the narrow bands of sunlight that squeezed through the shutters. Flipping the rusty iron latch up, he flung them wide. Sunlight poured in. It hurt Pentony's eyes.

"The lord governor of Ireland marches north," Rardove said loudly. "The king of England is marching too. The harvest is in. It is time to make war on the Irish."

Chapter 31

Finian lay on his back and stared at the stars. For almost twenty years, he'd devoted himself to a two-fold goal. Recover Irish lands, notably the Wishmé beaches, and never, ever get entrapped by a woman.

Yet here he was . . .

What?

Bedding a woman. He threw his arm over his face and thought it again, liking how it sounded. That's all he'd done. Bed a beautiful and intelligent woman. Nothing else had happened.

He groaned into the bend of his arm. There was no fooling himself here. Nothing would ever be the same again. Because he'd more than bedded her. He'd possessed her. Dived into her like she was a river and he the rain.

And he was not done yet. Like water on parched skin, he was absorbing her, never even knowing he'd been dying of thirst.

She lay collapsed atop his chest, her legs draped on either side of his hips like streamers, trembling slightly. He was still inside her, and had no desire to pull out. Even now, minutes later, soft quivers still occasionally rippled through her body, caressing him softly as his fingers curled around a length of her hair, idly lifting it, then letting it fall. Even in sleep, her body still responded.

He felt her shift. She lifted her head and looked at him. He smiled faintly.

"Ye're awake."

She nodded.

"Will ye tell me something?"

"I will tell you anything."

No, he thought. *Do not say such things.*

"What did ye mean," he tucked a strand of hair behind her ear, "when ye said ye're not an innocent?"

She nodded, as though this was what she'd expected. "I was married before."

"When?"

"Ten years ago. I was fifteen."

He digested this tidbit. He found he did not like its flavor. "For how long?"

"One night."

A corner of his mouth curved up. He ran the tip of his thumb across the edge of her lips. "Ye seem destined for short relationships, lass. Why so brief?"

"He died."

"What happened?"

She shrugged. It was hard to see her face. He shifted slightly, so the moon would shine across her features, and then he saw she looked sad. "Me. I happened. He was old, and cruel, and that was that. I was with child, but lost it. It was . . . a terrible time. The physick said I could have no more."

"Och, lass," he murmured. He reached up and brushed the whole of his palm and fingers across the side of her head. Warming her cool cheeks, not asking anything more.

Senna didn't want talk either. She didn't want anything of the world, and certainly not the old world. She didn't want anything but Finian.

"'Twas a wondrous thing you just did to me," she said into his neck.

He ran his hand down her side, over the dip in her waist. "I'm pleased to hear it," he rumbled in that calm, playful, seductive voice. "What ye did to me was most fine, too."

"When will you do it again?" Senna whispered shyly, glad of the curtain of curls that had fallen over her face.

Strong fingers parted the curtain and Finian's dark eyes peered in at her. "When do ye want me to do it again?"

Shocking herself, she tightened her inner muscles around him and squeezed.

He closed his hand around the back of her head and pulled her slowly down. His eyes were dark and inscrutable but they did not hold humor, Senna saw that much. There was something other, something solid, considering; as she had never seen such a look before, she didn't understand it.

And as hot and passionate as had been their previous encounter, this one was gentle and solemn.

His tongue touched hers as if seeking something delicate, something that might be swept away if he moved too quickly, like a glistening in a spiral of sand under clear water, or a feather on a rock. Senna's heart flipped over and she responded in the same slow way. His eyes held hers as his tongue slid into her mouth, his thumb caressing her chin.

It was, in fact, a reverent kiss.

He explored her with erotic tenderness, gliding over her tongue, her teeth, every inch of her mouth, kissing her until she was breathless and hot and whimpering. Slow and languid, tender and sweet, the gentle kiss ignited the same fires as the explosive ones had before. His manhood grew heavy and hard inside of her, and she sighed.

A morning breeze crept up the hill. It lifted her hair, insinuated itself between their sweaty, passion-burned bodies. Senna kissed his eyes, his cheeks and high forehead. Her fingers danced over his eyebrows and lips. Sweet, good, peace. She knew she was lost. Utterly lost.

He stroked her cheek and traced soft kisses across her jawline until she begged for more, until the tenderness evolved into raging passion yet again. He lifted himself inside her, plunging deep, over flesh already quivering in readiness. His thrusting hips pushed her legs apart, his hands gripped her hips and pushed her farther down onto him. Then, without warning, he rolled them over and propped himself up between her bent knees, keeping up a measured, rocking penetration.

She gripped his hips, trying to make him move faster, but he kept his movements deliberate and slow. He buried his shaft deep inside her then pulled himself out slowly, so slowly she keened. With only the thick tip of him resting inside her, she squirmed and writhed.

"Don't torment me, Irishman," she reprimanded, reaching for him.

Clasping her hip in one hand, he dragged her up against him, the long, slow ride enough for her body to begin humming again. The hum quivered out of her lips as senseless purring. Hot and possessive, he was like a velvet rod, burrowing into her swollen, heated flesh.

He whispered in her ear of how she pleased him, told her how to move, asked her what she wanted. Bending slightly on his knees, he fitted his hips hard into hers and moved his body from side to side. When her hips bucked against his, a corner of his mouth lifted in a crooked smile.

"Tell me, Senna, does this please ye?" he demanded, knowing she was quivering from her toes to the ends of her bouncing chestnut curls.

"Finian," was her only gasped reply. The trees marching down the side of the valley learned his name. She whispered it like a mantra and he grew satiated on it, affirming him as the only thing in her world, the center of her universe.

'Twas more than good.

Slipping his hand between their locked bodies, he pushed her hips to the ground with the back of his hand. Sliding his thumb between them, he flicked once against the nub at the crest of her.

"Oh," she cried out, never having imagined such an intense, specific, hard, good feeling.

"Aye," he agreed in her ear, and did it again.

Senna threw her head back and panted. What she'd done to herself was *nothing* like this. Her head spun, and the slow, huge wave of pleasure rode up her legs and down her back.

"Why don't ye come for me, lass?" he murmured, his finger massaging her. Over and over, his fine touch stroked her pleasure point as his thick shaft thrust deep into her swollen warmth. Deeper he moved, his thumb wicked in its fluttering, sensual torment. Out from this radius her body flamed, burned, knew only his touch.

"Finian," she gasped between rasping breaths.

"Aye, like that." He removed his hand and, with a savage tug, lifted her hips and plunged into her. Now he pleasured her with his body, and the wave began to crash again. Her body and mind exploded into a million starry shards of sensual fulfillment, her body pounding out the rhythm.

He erupted within her, drowning his hard manhood into her until she was spread-eagled beneath him, her arms flung wide, her hips pounding up to him, mouthing his name. Swollen pink flesh shuddered around him like a tight fist, pulling him in, draining him. His explosion rocked him to the core, and he held her trapped against his chest, tripping into a well of affection he'd never known existed.

He rolled them over so she was atop again and held her, his slick, shuddering length still buried deep within her womb. His head fell back, his arms around her back. She rested her chin on his chest and closed her eyes.

For Senna, it was enough to keep breathing. Forget sense or reason. There was only Finian.

He who knew too much of women's bodies. He whose careless charm assured her he had dozens of women to warm his bed, none needed to warm his heart. He who was only trouble. Danger and unseen cliffs.

And she had fallen in love with him.

They lay together in silence, their limbs entwined, feeling each other breathe. Then they fell asleep.

Dawn crept stealthily over the horizon, throwing the world into the sharp, musky relief of breaking rose and misty green.

The mounted party was spread out in a thin uneven line that stretched half a mile wide. On their tunics was stitched a diving bird, a raven, descending with claws extended. Sharp knightly eyes pierced the ever-present mists from under their helms. If she was here, she would be found.

If the Irishman was with her, he would die.

Chapter 32

The next day, they crouched outside the town of Hutton's Leap when the sun was at its highest, just inside treeline where the shadows were their shortest, and watched the steady flow of people in and out of the town.

"Do you know this town?" Senna asked quietly.

"Somewhat," he evaded. It probably sounded like an answer. "I've had a few meetings here."

"Certainly there are people here who are friendly to the Irish? Sympathetic?"

"Not friendly," he assured her.

"But there are Irish people here," she protested. "We're in Ireland. *Éire*. These are your people, Finian. They must be sympathetic. Given sufficient," she paused, "cause."

He angled her a flat look. "Ye mean coin. Given sufficient coin. Senna, for most souls, money does not weigh more on the scales than their lives. And to abet me, 'twould be their life."

She gave him a derisive look. "I do not believe money matters more than one's life. And I do not say others think so, either. What I am saying is, I believe people can be persuaded."

"I know exactly what ye're saying." He reached over and smashed a wide-brimmed hat down on her head. He'd pinched it off a rouncy pony left by his owner outside a village hut.

She adjusted it with a swift, unconsciously feminine move. "How do I look?"

He glanced down. "Ye look like a crystal, flashing fire. So keep yer head down."

"Will do," she whispered. "You too. You shall likely draw more attention than I. You look important. Or at least," she eyed him, "tall."

"Och, well, I'm training to be a king."

She snorted.

They walked nonchalantly to the road and joined the steady stream of fair-goers entering the town. At the gates, there was a throng of people bustling in and out.

"It's so loud," she murmured.

Finian eyed her, satisfied with her disguise. The hat covered her face admirably. A few wipes of river mud across her cheeks, and the cloak draped around her despite the warmth of the burgeoning day, and the disguise was complete. She looked like a tall young squire.

Not that Finian expected any problems this far south and west, not so soon. Rardove would expect them to go directly north, to the O'Fáil king, not detour south to this small but bustling English town. And truly, so *many* Irishmen might have been moved to kill four English soldiers beside a river. There was no certainty Rardove would place Finian near the crime.

But even if he did, Finian had no choice. Red was waiting, with the precious dye manual.

"Loud?" he repeated distractedly. He turned to study the sentries patrolling the walls. His heart beat strong, pumping blood to the parts of him that would most need it: legs, arms. He forced himself to look down at Senna. "Ye're always traveling to towns, are ye not? Signing contracts, breaking townsmen's hearts."

"I try to avoid towns." Her gaze was darting around. "As I said, they're so . . . loud." She glanced up into a flood of sunlight illuminating her face. She squinted into it and gave a stiff smile.

"Keep your head down," was all he said.

Behind them another party of fair-goers arrived, clogging up the gate path. Good. The more distractions, the better. This group looked like entertainment: minstrels dressed in bright, beribboned, flowing clothes, and a monkey perched on one of their shoulders. They'd have stories to tell and tricks to perform.

Senna looked around, her eyes wide. "Is that a monkey?"

Her words were low, but while probably intended to disguise her voice, succeeded mostly in making her sound throaty. Seductive.

The minstrel overheard and laughed.

"Indeed, 'tis, mistress."

Finian groaned inwardly. Senna's disguise would work only if a man didn't come within ten feet of her. Any closer, and Finian could hang her with leeches and a man on the hunt would still know she was a woman to be hunted.

"Come to our show this evening, in the market square," said the minstrel, smiling. He was more interested in a customer than a woman, Finian realized, the tension lessening somewhat. "You'll see a fine show. Half a denier."

Then he bent forward slightly at the waist and winked. "And we're always needing pretty volunteers, maiden. No deniers required for them."

So he was *somewhat* interested in a woman, Finian amended dourly.

A smile tugged her lips upward. She shook her head shyly and turned back to Finian. "I've never seen a monkey," she whispered, grinning at him from under her half-tipped hat.

He resisted the urge to kiss the tip of her exceedingly dirty nose. Wouldn't do to draw attention by kissing his squire.

They drew nearer the gates. The porter stood, an armed guard on either side, giving desultory inspections to the packs and wagons entering the town for the fair. Someone jostled them from behind and then, there they were, standing in front of the porter.

Every muscle in Finian's body was stiff, ready to fight or flee. He nodded, opened his mouth to say God knows what, when the warden waved his hand impatiently, already looking at the minstrel group behind.

"Get on with you, Irish dog," he barked, and for once, Finian wasn't overcome by the urge to smash a vulgar Englishman's face into a wall.

He hurried them through the winding, crowded streets of the town, Senna close as a skirt hem. The sun was high and hot, heating the busy, bustling world inside the timber walls. Dust rose up under the boots of men and women. The main street was partly cobbled, and lined with shops. Everywhere craftsmen peddled their wares. Leather saddles and embroidery needles, candles and silverwork were on display. In the distance, the distinctive sound of metal striking metal rang out; the blacksmith was hard at work.

Finian propelled them past all these riches, hoping Senna wouldn't stop to haggle simply to stay in practice. He hurried them into the town square.

A riser stage was set at the far edge of the cobbled area. In good times, outdoor feasts were held here, the stage serving as the scene for great tricks and storytelling. In bad times, it served as a gallows. Right now, there was a crier strolling by it, calling out who was selling new wine today. No one appeared to be listening. Perhaps they already knew. Perhaps they had already imbibed.

"Wait here," he said to Senna, motioning to one of three mounting blocks near the town well.

It was shady there, positioned out of the line of slop buckets and chamberpots that might be emptied from second- and third-floor windows, but still within the shadow that projected out from them.

She nodded and slipped wordlessly over, attracting no more attention than the flies. There she stood, hands crossed in front of her waist, feet slightly spread, looking blankly over the crowd. A young, dullard squire, waiting for his master.

He wanted to kiss her.

A line of storefronts ran behind them, in front of which a line of human traffic moved like a winding serpent. In the center of the clearing before them were jugglers telling bawdy jokes, packing people in around them. Pasty makers walked in and out of the crowd, selling meat and cheese. Anyone might stop in this shady spot, idling away an afternoon, for hours at a time. He would be back sooner than that. She would be unnoticed.

If anyone so much as breathed on her . . .

"I will be back," he said grimly.

She gave a confident, careless nod without looking over. Such insouciance must have taken a great deal of effort, considering how tightly her jaw was clenched. Affecting to lace his boot, Finian bent over, motioning for her to follow him down.

When they were both bent well below the eye level of the crowd, he leaned forward and kissed her lips, swift and hard.

"Ye're stronger than ye know, lass, and I'll be back for ye sooner than ye know."

He straightened and, without looking back, started for the abbey where his spy was waiting.

Chapter 33

It was cool inside. The knobbly stone walls of the abbey kept the heat at bay, and the dim, chilled air wafted like vapor over his forearms and face. There was a short nave, the chancel at the opposite end. Finian bent to one knee, lowered his head and crossed himself, kissing his fingertips lightly. Then he rose and turned to face the small sound that had hissed behind him.

A robed figure moved closer.

"Mother."

The abbess briefly touched his bent head. "This way."

Finian followed her through the nave, through a small door, and out into a sunny courtyard. They crossed it and entered another building. The door slammed shut behind them. It took a moment to adjust to the darkness, but when he did, Finian saw they were in a large room, strewn with fresh rushes. This is where the nuns transcribed and illustrated their magnificent illuminated manuscripts.

Mother Superior turned. "My son, you are late."

"I was delayed."

"Mayhap too late."

"I couldn't help it."

She eyed him severely. "What matters that, to the Lord?"

"It mattered to me," Finian muttered, and glanced around.

Her square-cut veil framed an impressively stern face. Tanned, from working outdoors in the gardens, he assumed. "They came."

He looked back sharply. "Who?"

"Someone who wanted whatever he had as much as you do."

"Mother, where is he?"

She pointed to a doorway on the other side of the room. The wide sleeve of her robe gaped open, revealing a surprisingly muscular forearm. Finian was taken aback. "Down the stairs, through the cloister, straight across to the dormitory. Last door on the right."

She regarded him somberly. Her finger rotated and indicated Finian's sword. "That stays with me."

Finian handed it over without protest. The three other blades tucked in various folds of his clothing and buckled to his arm should serve at need.

He passed swiftly through the open-aired cloister, where nuns moved like floating blue bells in the bright sunshine, murmuring in quiet conversation. One swept the stone-laid walkway with a whisk broom. She glanced over, then quickly away. Finian leapt up the short stairwell to the dormitory and strode down the corridor.

He gave a perfunctory knock, already pushing open the door. "Red?"

He slammed to a halt.

Red was lying on the floor. A trail of drying blood marked a narrow stream that flowed directly from his bashed head.

Finian dropped to a knee.

"Red?" He slid his hands under the man's head, disregarding the blood that smeared his palms. "Jésu, Red. What are you doing out of bed? Red!"

He went cold in the silence that followed. A fly buzzed by the small window. He could smell the old, cold wood of the shutters. Finian's bootheel slid across the grainy floor of the chamber, gritting loudly as he lowered himself to the floor. He hauled on Red's torso, pulling him into his arms. "Red!"

Red's eyes flickered open.

"Oh, Jésu, man," Finian exhaled. He lifted him up farther, stretched his own legs out and rested his compatriot on them, cradling his head.

"Are you a'right?"

"Good God, Irish," Red croaked. "No, I'm not all right. I'm about to die. I'm just waiting on you." He swallowed around what was obviously a parched throat. "Trust the Irishry to be late." He squinted at him. "Why you? Where's Turlough?"

"Dead."

"Poor bastard."

Finian reached to his side and yanked free the leather skin of water. He held it to Red's mouth. He drank deeply, but slowly. Most of each suck went sliding down his cheek and chin. He was fading fast.

"Haven't the sisters been seeing to ye?"

"For whatever good it's done, aye. The Mother Superior though," Red gave a grim smile. "She was bloody wonderful." Red's eyes met his, half-lidded from weariness and pain, but sharp as ever. "Five days ago, when I got here."

"Forgive me." Finian shifted him and he groaned. "I was captured."

"I suppose that'll do. Quickly, now. I was out of bed, trying to get it before I go to meet my Maker. You'd never have found it otherwise. It's over there." He pointed to the wall. "There's a spot, low. Dig it out."

"The recipe?"

"In all its fatal glory."

Relief heated Finian's limbs. It felt like the old days, when he and Red would meet, their interests crossing paths; and trading intelligence, Finian for Ireland, Red for Scotland, both against Edward. Ever against Edward's insatiable appetites for kingdoms that weren't his.

Finian lowered Red to the ground when it became obvious he could never endure being lifted back to the cot. Then he dug where Red had directed him, with careful movements, excavating a small hollow in the stone walls that separated the *dormir* rooms. A stream of rubble funneled onto the floor, making a little dusty pile. He shoved his hand into the hole, the skin of his wrist scraping against the sharp, gritty stone. He pulled out a small manuscript, like a miniature treatise, bound between thick wood covers.

"This is it?"

Red nodded weakly. His eyes had been shut, but he opened them. "Aye. The recipe, coded."

"How did you find it, after all these years?"

Red closed his eyes again. "Doesn't matter. Open it."

A strange reluctance stayed Finian's hand, then he swept the bound pages open.

The colors hit him first—the reds and yellows and blues of the illuminations filled not only the margins, but entire pages, bright and brilliant. Images of plants in all shapes and colors, beaches and shells. Birds. Deep bowls and pestles and huge vats. Oak trees and burl wood, and tiny insects crafted with lines so small and precise he had no idea where they found a brush so fine. And . . . dancing.

Dancing women and men, strands of flowers and curving lines and copulation. Heads thrown back, in various poses of pleasure, their bodies were so skillfully painted they actually looked to be gleaming with sweat.

These illustrated figures were having more fun than some living souls did. The abbess would not be pleased to be the conduit for passing it along.

Finian looked up, brows raised. Red nodded, then shrugged.

He kept turning pages, focusing on the text because the drawings were not, at least initially, informative. They were arousing, though. He focused on the words. Flowing Latin script, letters and words, hugged corners here and there, and occasionally filled the center of a vellum sheet. Numerals as well, surprisingly . . .

"Arabic," Red croaked, following the direction of Finian's perusal.

"Aye," he said, feeling slightly tossed about.

But whether in Roman or Arabic, they were certainly measurements. Distances, miles, amounts, dilution rates. Everything was figured here.

But erotic imagery and computational guide aside, most of the work was sketches. They looked like architectural blueprints, of castles and water wheels and mills. Trajectories and trebuchets. Explosions.

This was a military manual.

"The mind that made this was lethal," said Finian grimly.

"Dyer had a genius," Red croaked.

Nobles in robes, dropping to their knees. Various sketches showed this. A man, a crowned king, wore a cape in one drawing. The bottom half of him was slowly fading out, disappearing. It looked as if the ink was fading, or as if water had been accidentally mixed with the ink and the image was washed out. But the whole thing was far too intentional for that.

"What is this?" Finian murmured.

"What does it look like?" Red's words were quiet, his eyes closed. But he seemed to know exactly what Finian was looking at.

"It looks like a man disappearing."

"Or being made invisible."

Finian looked up sharply. "That's madness."

Slowly, Red pushed himself up a bit and stuck his hand inside his leather gambeson. He pulled something out and extended his hand as if handing something over, but Finian couldn't make out what he was seeing.

He blinked and looked closer. Some kind of shimmering was on Red's upturned palm, like faraway butterfly wings over water. He reached out, touched Red's palm, and then he felt it. He was touching something he could hardly see.

Each time he tried to focus on it, it shifted, emitted that shimmering effect. But Red was holding something very solid, very definite in his hand.

"Take it," he rasped weakly.

Finian did, lifting the nothing-that-was-something. "What is this?"

"This is that." Red pointed to the image of the disappearing figure in the dye manual. "See what it can do."

"Madness," Finian said again, as precious time flowed away. But he had to understand. "As a powder, they're explosive. As a dye, 'tis the royal indigo shade—"

"And true-dyed onto a certain type of wool, in a certain weave, it can do that."

He could feel the wool's weave, sitting lightly in his hand, its draped edges ruffling down over the edge of his palm, but he could not see it. Not truly. And the more he tried to focus on it, the harder it became to detect.

"It appears some parts are there," Red rasped. "As if little specks of the fabric are visible—"

"But all the surrounding spots are not."

"As if one point in ten is showing."

"'Tis almost as if . . . it's picking up—"

Finian shook the fabric into the air, held it by his fingertips with the dun-colored wall behind it. For a brief second, it was visible as just what it was, a piece of pale weave, the size and shape of a child's tunic, not indigo alone, but with a slighter, redder hue.

Then, before his eyes, it seemed to disappear again, blending in with the wall behind it except for those few little spots of distinctive, steady color that made the shimmering so disorienting.

"'Tis magic," the spy said.

But Finian's concerns were much less enchanted. "And that manual tells how to do this?" he demanded.

Red nodded his head once, an effortful move. "Aye."

"But how? The secret of the Wishmés has been lost for hundreds of years." Finian held up the shimmering, vanishing fabric, evidence that someone, somewhere, had known how to conjure this dangerous magic.

Red met his gaze. "The manual in your hand is not a thousand years old."

"No, 'tis not. God save us," Finian said, his mind already integrating the information and finding the ramifications bone chilling.

Red summoned energy from somewhere, enough to scowl at him and sit up a little straighter. "You hope for God, O'Melaghlin. I've learned we've to make our own means in such matters. Now, listen. I'm giving this manual to you Irish for one reason."

Finian stiffened. "I didn't know there were conditions."

"I'm going to die. I make conditions if I want. You need to use that." He pointed to the manual.

"What do ye mean?" Finian set the fabric down and stared at Red. "Why now? Why are ye giving this to the Irish *now*?"

Red sat up a little more. It must have taken great effort, because his words came out more harshly, his sentences broken up by short, pained breaths. "The Scots have signed a treaty . . . mutual aid with France. Longshanks is like a tornado touching down, he's so furious. The Scots, straining at the bit. Come hell or high water, King Edward . . . will invade Scotland. Surely as I will die." Red grabbed his arm. "Do not let him."

"How am I to stop him?"

"Goddamnit, Irish," he said with a sudden flash of anger. "I just gave you the 'how.' Set off a few explosions. Get his attention. Draw his eye, away from Scotland."

"Draw his eye," Finian repeated slowly. "Straight to Ireland."

"Scotland will fall, O'Melaghlin. And then Ireland shall,

too. Either Longshanks looks to you now, or he looks to you later, but look he shall, and one by one, we will all fall under his boot." His eyes were furious. "Scotland is weary of going to the Continent for aid. France is a thousand leagues away. We need Ireland."

"We?" Finian echoed. "Ye are English."

In a rush, like air from a bellows, all the anger and its energy blew out of Red. His head dropped, the fire faded from his eyes. "My wife was Scottish."

They sat in silence, Red's breathing labored, until Finian said in a low, measured voice, "I will not promise a war to save Scotland, not if I have to offer up Ireland as payment. I cannot."

"Bastard," Red rasped. "Suspected that. One more. Condition. Most important." His words were getting quieter, his sentences more abbreviated, staccato. "Rardove sent for . . . dye-witch."

Finian's body rushed with cold. Rivers of coldness, washing through his limbs. "Who?"

"From England . . ."

The rivers of coldness turned to ice.

"Get her out."

"I think I already have," he replied grimly.

"Good. Protect her above all else. Now, Irish . . . get out of here. The men who attacked . . . were Rardove's. They'll return."

Shite.

"Get out. Now."

"I'll not leave you—"

"Christ on the cross, man, I'm already dead. Go." Red's eyes closed for the last time.

Finian lowered himself back to the ground and held the greatest English spy for Scotland's cause on his lap until the life passed out of him in invisible ribbons of steam, dispersing his spy heat into the ether.

Chapter 34

The sun was dipping low by the time Senna finally broke. It was the smell of pasties that did it. Cooked food. Warm mashed bread crumbs and egg, with bits of pork, mayhap. Or ham. Which? She was almost frantic to find out. Someone walked by with one, and she leaned forward to sniff.

The man tossed her a startled look. She tipped back into position, practically in tears. It was ham. Salted, warm ham, with cheese, spiced perhaps with basil or sage. The wafting scent of warm pastry and hot cheese made her stomach clench painfully. Basil. It was basil.

She broke and bought four of them, taking coin from the purse tucked between her layers of clothes. Inhaling one, she ate the other more slowly, shoving the remaining two in a pocket for Finian. Calmer now, she stood as twilight deepened, smiling at the antics of a small boy doing handstands while his elders juggled beside him, occasionally tossing items for him to bounce off his feet. Tinkling music from a flute filled the bustling square.

Finian appeared beside her, sidling up like smoke. He pressed up close, his body warm, the urgency in his words chilling.

"We have to get out of here."

He didn't look at her. He was scanning the crowd. His hand was on her upper arm, turning her slowly away, when a ruckus disrupted the pleasant, bustling mood of the square.

A group of armored soldiers climbed the platform. A well-dressed, portly man hurried up ahead of them, as if he was being herded. Likely the head of the largest merchant's guild, de facto mayor of the town. Finian's fingers tightened around Senna's arm. He guided her backward, until they were up against the corner of a chandler's stall. The scent of warm wax was strong.

In the square, people stopped chattering and turned. One of the soldiers nudged the mayor, who stepped awkwardly forward and unscrolled a document.

"Lord Rardove has pressing need of this town's service," he announced in a loud voice. "Six nights ago, an Irish prisoner Lord Rardove was holding on charges of treason escaped."

No one seemed particularly impressed with this, Senna decided, looking around. But then, no one knew how terrifying the whole thing had been.

"This Irishman abducted Lord Rardove's betrothed when he went."

This got the crowd's attention in a more riveting way. Senna and Finian stared at each other.

"Lord Rardove is offering a bounty for the return of the Irishman and his betrothed." Senna noted the order of those events. "Any goodman who brings them back will receive a gold coin." The crowd was getting excited, elbowing each other and nodding. A few youngsters ran from the square, likely to spread the news to all the destitute and ambitious of the town.

The mayor was wrapping up his appalling, instigating decree. "News alone will earn pleasure for any past debts or allowances owing to his lordship."

One of the soldiers stepped forward, elbowing the mayor aside. His loud, commanding voice rose over the crowd.

"Lord Rardove wants them above all things. Find them. If someone does before we do, this night, five marks to him."

Now it was like a celebration. People pushed closer, tossing questions at the soldiers. A few farther back hurled insults, then quickly melted into the background.

Finian squeezed Senna's arm and they backed away from the square, while others pressed forward. Once clear, they turned down the main road, toward the west gate. She could feel the breeze rush by her flushed cheeks.

"Not too fast," Finian said, his fingertips on her arm, "or we'll draw attention."

Just then, a soldier wearing a Rardove surcoat stepped out from an alleyway. A hot stream of fear swept up Senna's throat. She smashed her hat down farther on her head and stared at the ground under her boots as they walked along at a screamingly sedate pace.

The soldier crossed the road and disappeared into the deepening purple-blue shadows behind another row of homes. Night was coming up fast.

"Finian?" she murmured.

"What?"

She tried to keep panic out of her voice. "They're going to close the gates."

"I know."

If they closed the gates, whether to trap them or for *couvre-feu,* they'd be locked in the city all night. With Rardove soldiers on the prowl. All the citizens, too.

They ducked around people and two-wheeled carts, increasing their pace, moving forward with intent focus, keeping to just under a trot. Finian bent his head beneath eaves when they had to walk close to the buildings. A horn suddenly sounded, a long, sustained note that rose at the end.

It sounded again.

They broke into a run, dodging a crowd that was suddenly streaming drunkenly out of a tavern. They spun to the right, turning onto the long, partly paved hill that led steeply down to the southern entrance. Then they skidded to a halt and watched as the huge oaken gates, studded and banded in iron, swung shut. They crashed with a resounding shudder.

Senna wanted to scream.

Soldiers stepped forward to slide the long bolts across its width, locking the gate with a huge, four-inch-thick wooden bar. The guards stepped back to their posts, small stone alcoves beside the gates. Above the gates, on the walls, was the alure, the stone walkway where armed sentries went on their ceaseless patrols.

Senna stood in the middle of the road, stunned and disbelieving. People flowed around her.

"Come," Finian murmured, putting his hand on her arm. She spun toward him.

"We can pay them," she said urgently. "I have money. For a small bribe, they'll let us through."

"Aye. And for a larger one, they'll turn us over to Rardove."

He nodded toward one of the numerous small alleyways all around, like warrens. They slunk into its dark closeness, hands skimming the wicker-and-wattle sides of homes to guide them straight.

"Where are we going?" she asked, stumbling beside him.

"Nuns."

"What?"

"To the nuns."

But they weren't, in fact. A quick detour by the back gates of the miniature abbey allowed Finian to see the abbess standing grimly aside as three soldiers shoved by her, into the warm golden light inside.

Finian slunk back to where Senna was waiting, a shadowy, lithe figure, kneeling amid the sharp branches of a yew tree.

"Not safe?" she asked.

"Not quite."

Footsteps sounded. He put his hand on the top of her head and pushed her down farther. He crouched beside her, under the copious foliage of the tree. A moment later boots marched by, their ankles at knee level. Three soldiers passed, lanterns held high, Rardove devices on their tunics, grimly surveying everything they passed.

Finian and Senna held their breaths until they passed.

"Come, then," he murmured. "Let's get out of here."

She took the hand he extended and got to her feet. Small and slim, her hand fit perfectly. Her cool fingers curved around the outer edge of his palm. A wisp of hair slid out from her hat, and even that was like tamed fire in the twilight. He tucked it back up with his free hand, and she followed him through the dim evening.

Every so often a page would hurry by, holding a lantern high in the air, while behind would follow rich burgesses. From shuttered windows, candlelight shone down, making pale yellow stripes on the ground. But soon, all over the town, wicks would be pinched out, to prevent fire.

A few shops remained open, alehouses and whorehouses, open by special license and a hefty fee. Finian hurried toward one, its wooden sign THISTLE swaying in the breeze. They ducked inside.

Chapter 35

"This is not what I thought you meant when you said *Let's get out of here,*" Senna murmured.

They were in a tavern. A whorehouse. It was clear as anything.

"Is this the sort of place a king-in-training ought to spend his time?" she inquired.

"I'm educating my squire," he retorted, and propelled her toward a small table in the shadows at the back.

The room was wide. At one end ran a long series of boards, set upon trestles. Behind them, wine barrels sat on their sides, corks plugged on one end. Ale ran freely, too. A few rickety tables were scattered about the room, joined by a few even more precarious-looking stools, but as a general rule, men usually stood and drank until they passed out or won enough in bets to purchase an hour or two with one of the prostitutes.

The place was absent patrons, except for one other table. It was early in the evening yet, and Rardove's pronouncement had ensured most of the town's inhabitants were at present bobbing through alleys, hoping to find the fugitives and earn coin they could spend here, no doubt.

That other occupied table was wreathed by a group of three loudmouths, talking about the bounty laid on the Irishman, and of their earnest, enthusiastic dedication to finding him and kicking his teeth in.

Yet here they sat, in a tavern-cum-whorehouse, tossing back ale until their bellies must be small, alcoholic lagoons. Soon enough the three of them stumbled to the rooms upstairs, a woman with swaying hips guiding them. Two other women followed behind. A few moments later another woman approached with a tray with two mugs for Finian and Senna.

Senna kept her head down until the waitress left, but it was a pointless effort. Even with a dirty, pale face, her hair tucked up under the floppy brimmed hat, smeared with dirt and sweat, to him, she would always be the brightest thing about. She was a woman from her booted heels to the knotted ends of her hair, and she terrified Finian in a way the prospect of death never had.

And she was a dye-witch? Madness.

But of course, it was true. Now that Red had said so, 'twas clear as anything. She was filled with fire, passion. A dye-witch could not be made from a lesser woman.

"So, what do you think of Eire, Senna?" he asked suddenly.

She shifted her gaze back. "Do you mean the marauding soldiers or the mad barons?"

He crossed his arms. "I mean the rivers."

She laughed, quiet, circumspect. Intimate. "They're long and wide and deep. And they make my belly spin."

"I mean me."

Her lips curved into a smile that would send a monk running for a brothel. "Long," she replied, her voice deep with the burgeoning mischievousness he liked so much. "And wide."

He grinned back. "And deep?"

She pursed her lips and shook her head. "Shallow as a stream."

He scooped up his mug and tipped it her direction. "I'll show ye shallow, later."

She flushed a deep shade of pink and looked away.

The room was deserted now, but for a handful of women clustered at the far end of a high counter, a long flat board set on trestles. Behind it on a high stool sat a tall, striking, but tired-looking woman who had been eyeing them suspiciously since they entered.

"What are we doing here?" Senna asked.

"Rardove's men are searching all the homes. We'll wait here until some fat, rich merchant comes, then we steal a few of his things while he's otherwise occupied upstairs."

She lifted an eyebrow. "Have you always been so enamored of thievery?"

"A lifelong dream."

"What sorts of *things*?"

"Cloaks, coin. Whatever might allow us out of these gates at night, appearing to be someone other than ourselves. We'll not last the night within the town walls."

She scowled. Finian sat back, kicked his boots out under the rickety table, and crossed his arms over his chest. "Ye have a better plan?"

"Well, not a plan, per se."

"Desperate straits require desperate measures, Senna."

"Indeed. I simply don't like the idea of robbing merchants, no matter how *fat* or *occupied* they may be."

"Ye wouldn't, seeing as ye are one."

She gave him a level look. "As a last resort," she allowed. "If it proves necessary. But if there is some other way . . ."

Her gaze traveled over the room and settled on the proprietor and the circle of pretty, painted women clustered around her.

He hoped Senna wasn't getting ideas about *whores*.

A loud clatter of something falling drew everyone's attention to the top of the stairs at the far end of the room.

A man stood there, glaring at the pitcher that had sailed

over the edge and smashed, spraying shards of crockery all around the feet of the prostitutes. He swung drunkenly toward the room he'd just left.

"Crazed wench," he shouted, his words slurring together. "I'll not come here again."

"That's for certain, ye won't!" shouted a female voice. "Not if ye don't pay for what ye took!"

The man staggered down the narrow hallway that paralleled the hall below. He pounded on another door, shouting vilely. The door ripped open. Two men came out, plucking at their tunics and hefting breeches up around their waists.

"Let's go," he snarled. The other men followed as their leader stumbled down the stairs, grasping the railing with a fat, white-knuckled hand. He threw up a palm as the tall, stately patroness took a step in his direction.

"I'll not be treated that way, Esdeline," he said in a pompous, drunken voice. It sounded like 'Ess-dull-leen,' and was followed by a violent belch. "Either that wench goes, or I do."

He waved his hand through the air, as if that would enhance the dire nature of his threat, when in truth it made him look like he was fanning away the belch. And with that, the men all staggered out the door.

The three girls who had been upstairs—the one who'd apparently thrown the jug and the two who'd been in the room with the others—came downstairs. Their faces were furious, although one looked close to tears, and not from anger. Finian could overhear them talking, their angry conference loud in the empty tavern. The defeated tone in their voices carried farthest.

"That's the third one in a sennight," muttered one. "Left without paying."

A few disgruntled *ayes* followed. The statuesque owner, Esdeline, her name as French as her bearing, sat on a tall stool, presiding over the conference, silent and utterly still, her graceful features rigid and stony.

"With the regiment that's been about the past few days, things have been better 'an usual." That from the small one who'd looked scared coming downstairs. Finian heard Senna shift on the bench beside him. "They always pay, and good."

Another girl looked at her pityingly. "Aye, but they shan't be camped here forever. They'll move out, and just come back every now and then, like usual. Maybe once a moon."

"Balffe always comes back regular," said the shy one softly.

Senna's face shifted around to look at Finian. It was paler than a moment ago. *Balffe,* she mouthed silently. Finian shrugged.

Esdeline reached out a long arm and brushed a wisp of hair off the girl's pale face. "Go wash, Máire," she ordered, but her voice was soft. She added, "Use my soap, the lavender."

Máire's face lit up. Senna shifted again, more sharply.

Someone else grumbled, not cruelly, but in an angry, disheartened tone, "Och, we could bathe in lavender every night and that wouldn't make 'em pay us."

More grumbles.

"I am not surprised to hear that," Senna said suddenly, quite loudly. "Sad, but not in the least bit surprised."

Chapter 36

Finian turned in shock. Senna was already on her feet. He grabbed for her arm, but she started across the room before he could make contact.

He shoved his heels into the floorboards and willed himself to keep his seat. Leaping up and clapping his hand over her mouth as he dragged her upstairs would probably draw too much attention. And if he dragged her outside, they'd be captured in seconds.

Every one of the prostitutes was staring at her as she marched across the room. They looked about two steps removed from anger, more shocked at the moment than anything.

"Sad?" snapped one of the prostitutes. What was once probably a very rosy, bright complexion appeared gray and washed out. "What the 'ell are you to be sad over? What business is this o' yours?"

"None of it." Senna reached the bar counter. "And 'twill not be any of yours, either, given another twelvemonth."

"What are you talking about?"

"What I am talking about is that this is no way to run a business."

A few of the more experienced women formed a tuneless Greek chorus of shock. "What?"

From the background, the tall, regal-looking woman watched in silence.

"That is, if things keep up this way," Senna clarified. "If they deteriorate even a dram, I give the place six months."

"Some of us 'ave been 'ere three years," wailed one young woman plaintively.

"Six months," Senna said firmly, then looked at the owner, who sat regarding her with a graceful face that might have been carved from marble.

"Hush, Mary," said the woman who'd thrown the jug at the officious debtor. She turned to Senna, interested but wary. "I suppose you know a lot about running a business?" Finian, back at the table, groaned. "What would you have us do?"

"Charge more," Senna announced.

A dumbfounded silence swept the room. *"What?"*

"Most assuredly," Senna said, and even from this distance, Finian could tell that her gaze went a little distant, as she started figuring. He settled back in his seat. There was nothing he could do to stop this from unfolding however it was going to unfold.

And truly, he admitted, his plan had very little chance of success. He had no idea how provoking these prostitutes offered a *better* chance, but, to his own surprise, found he was content to trust to Senna in this.

"Yes," she said more firmly. "You need to charge more."

"They're not even paying now," laughed one of the women. "And you'd have us charge more? As if they have more."

"Oh, they have it," Senna said in an ominous tone.

Finian took another sip of his drink. It wasn't bad ale; someone here knew her business.

"The rabble-shite that come 'ere?" snapped one of the prostitutes. She leaned her thin elbow on the bar and shook her blond head. "Money? Pah. They've got bollocks, that's what. Not coin."

"They have it," Senna demurred, "and if you demand it,

they will pay. You've simply got to charge more for yourselves than you do for a mug of this ale—no offense meant, madame." Senna sailed the apology over to an old woman who, Finian suddenly noticed, was sitting on a crate in the back room, just beyond the counter.

The old woman, face cragged, waved off Senna's words with a bony hand.

"And this business of collecting payment after the service is rendered . . . ?" Senna shook her head sagely. "That is poor practice indeed. You collect beforehand. In your business—not that I know much of it," she added quickly, "but I've a brother and a father, and I know them rather well. You simply cannot expect their assessment of the value of the . . . goods to remain as high after they have . . . sampled."

Finian smiled in the shadows.

"Och, well, then they won't be sampling at all," protested one of the women. Irish. This group was a mix of Irish and Saxon, he realized, and a few Scottish flowers as well.

"I wager they will," Senna countered. "You're the only . . . establishment . . . in the town, is that so?" A few affirmative nods. "Then they'll be back. But if you make it harder to get, they'll want it even more."

"And I want food to eat every day," muttered one of the more heavily painted women. A cobwebbing around the edges of her eyes bespoke an age older than most of the others. "The less I have, the more I want it. And if they don't come in, I won't have it a'tall."

The tall, willowy owner spoke then, her voice like smoke, low and sultry and just a little hoarse. "They always come back."

Finian watched Senna smile at her with the full force of her accountant's mind, which was quite a shining thing, even here in this dingy tavern.

"Of course they'll be back," she agreed.

The owner extended a long, elegant arm and lifted a cup to

her lips. Wine. Finian knew it without seeing inside. The way she lifted the cup, the way she swallowed, everything about the woman said she was drinking very good wine.

Senna leaned her side against the counter, totally absorbed in the impromptu business meeting. Finian put his boots up on the bench across from him, crossed his arms over his chest, and leaned the back of his head against the wall.

She met their eyes, one by one. "Your customers know exactly what they're asking you to sell. And they'll pay for it, if you make them."

The group fell silent, considering this.

"There is not a great deal more to be gotten out of our current clientele," observed Esdeline in her smoky, thoughtful voice.

"You're right," Senna allowed after a moment's reflection. "You'll eventually need to move the operation to a larger town or a city. Where there are lords. Merchants. Soldiers of fortune. Ones who've actually experienced fortune." The willowy owner smiled in a mysterious way but said nothing. "But in the meantime, you really should aim higher."

Confused silence.

"There are soldiers about here?" Senna persisted. "Well, look to their captains. A shire reeve, mayhap? The bishop—"

A gasp went up and Finian opened his eyes. Three of the girls had thrown their hands over their hearts. Senna's eyebrows went up, but she obviously decided not to have that conversation. The tall owner's smile expanded. Finian half closed his eyes.

"Perhaps not the bishop. But his steward. Do I misdeem the matter? Or is this conceivable?"

"You appraise rightly." The owner's low, sultry voice lifted like smoke. "I do believe I had forgotten it."

Finian swept up his drink and downed the last of it.

"You'll have to pay your girls more," Senna said.

Esdeline looked at her sharply. "They are not mine. My

conscience is a reservoir for no one's soul. They do this themselves."

"No. Indeed. That is as it should be. You are a . . . a business commune. What you need is money. And you must bring in pretties, hangings and the like, to enrich this place, so it's nothing they've ever encountered before, not even in their dreams. And yourselves. New dresses. Ribbons. Throws on the floor." Someone gasped. She paused before returning to her original and most important point. "And you need to charge more. A great deal more."

"Och, as if we can afford such things as you're speaking of," muttered one of them.

"I've a few pennies," said the shy one.

"Aye. Myself, I've a few, too," said another, stepping forward.

A gnarled old hand appeared in the midst of their little group and dropped a handful of bent coins onto the wooden counter. "That's all you'll get from myself."

Everyone looked at her in astonishment. "Grand-maman," murmured the tall owner. "Where did you get that?"

"You don't know everything about me," she muttered, and that cryptic phrase was the most anyone could get out of her.

"That's a good deal of money," observed the owner, considering the pile with a knowing eye. "But 'tisn't enough."

Senna looked up from the pile. Their eyes met.

"No," Senna agreed slowly. "Not enough by far."

She tromped back to the table and began rummaging through her pack. "Do we have a pressing need for money just now, Finian?" she asked, her head to the side as she peered into the bag.

"We've got to pay for these." He tapped the rim of his mug.

"Aye. The drinks. But other than that, do we need money for anything?"

His eyes swept across her dirty face, her ripped leggings. He pictured her in a green dress, with ribbons in her hair. And a jewel around her curving neck. On a bed. With fur covers. And the dress coming off. The necklace staying on.

"A few dozen things come to mind, aye," he said slowly. "Have ye more coin, then?"

"A little."

His gaze slid up. "Ye're like a treasure trove, Senna. Where did you get all that?"

She slid her hand from her pack, clutching a small pouch in her palm. "I brought some with me from England."

"Ye did?"

She shrugged. "Some. The rest is from Rardove's coffers. 'Tis recompense for my physic expenses." She paused. "What is your rate of pay?"

He gave a slow smile. "A powerful lot."

She smiled back.

"Ye've the makings of a very fine thief, Senna. How much coin did ye take?"

"Just one scoop." She cupped her hand and swept it through the air, like she was scooping a handful of water.

"Just one little scoop, is it?"

"Just one. Out of each coffer."

He laughed.

She held up the purse. "So, do we need this?"

"Aye, lass."

"As much as they do?" she asked, and flung her hand out behind her.

Finian followed the invisible trajectory drawn by the toss of her hand, to the small cluster of women, some barefooted, watching them in silence.

"No," he said slowly. "Not nearly so much."

Her bright smile nearly blinded him. If she'd been within reach, he might have swept her up in his arms for a kiss. But she turned and walked back to the cluster.

"We have to pay for our drinks, and we'd like two more,"

she said. "This should settle for those, and mayhap just one more thing."

They stared at the lumpy purse like a cat had just delivered kittens on their counter. The owner reached out and swept it up. She peered inside, then lifted her head.

"What do you want?" she asked slowly. Suspicion filled her already guarded eyes.

"More drink," Senna said. "And a way out of town, without being discovered."

Silence reigned. No one asked how she came by such a rich bag of coin, out of the nighttime, and yet had no horse of her own. A handful of causes would certainly have already come to mind. But they did not ask a single question. They did look at Finian, though.

"Who's he?" asked the owner, hooking her head his direction.

Senna glanced over briefly. "He's my . . ."

Finian waited to see how on earth she would describe him.

"My Irishman."

He grinned.

The group of women giggled, sounding genuinely, playfully feminine for the first time since they'd entered the tavern. "Where can I get one of them?" one of the girls whispered, and the group broke into tinkling laughter again.

Senna bent closer. "We're in Ireland," she murmured. "They're *everywhere.*"

"Not like that," one said.

The owner was holding Finian's eye. He nodded, acknowledging her silent regard. For a moment she didn't move, then a slim, elegant fingertip lifted briefly off the counter. She turned back to Senna.

"The guards change their posts in about an hour," she said, her voice like plush felt. "Ofttimes, we have need to escort guests home after the gates are shut for the night."

Senna looked shocked at the extravagance. "How much do you charge for *that?*"

Esdeline smiled her mysterious smile. "Indeed, they pay."

Senna harrumphed. "I should hope so."

"My wagon coming through the gate should not draw any undue attention. Tonight, you"—she pointed to Senna—"will escort him." She gestured to Finian.

When Senna came back to the table, he reached for her hand. She slid it into his, and he stroked his thumb over the center of her palm slowly.

"That was a kindness," he said quietly.

She shrugged, but shifted her eyes away. "'Twas only coin." Her voice hardly caught at all. "And truly, Finian, it hardly seems likely that—"

She stopped. They all heard it at the same time.

A low rumble, coming closer. The clatter of hooves into the stable yard, the sound of men, drawing nearer.

One of the women hurried to the door and pulled it open an inch. She slammed it shut at once and spun around, her face frightened. "'Tis the whole bleedin' regiment!"

"Quick, get the bag," snapped the owner, and the women went into motion, hurrying the pouch of money off the counter. One woman beckoned to Senna and Finian, by the back door. Senna hurried over while Finian strode deliberately to Esdeline.

"Lady," he said in a low, swift voice, "all those things ye spoke of, if Senna says ye need them, then so ye do. But I'm telling ye, ye also need a protector. Send word to The O'Fáil. Mention my name. Say I told ye I owe a debt, and to send a guard. One of my personal guard. Ask for Tiergnan—he's a monstrous hulk of a beast, but gentle inside."

"I will," she said in her throaty voice. "And what name shall I mention, Irishman?"

He lifted her hand to his mouth, his eyes on hers. "I think ye know that."

He pressed a kiss to the back of her hand, then followed Senna out the door.

Chapter 37

Their dour-faced wagon driver took them much farther than they'd have hoped, in a straw-filled, two-wheeled contraption that clattered and clumped and drew less attention than a bat. Then he dumped them on the side of the track and drove off without a backward glance.

Finian hurried them deep into the woods, where no Plantagenet soldier would dare to go. For an hour they walked, then Finian let them stop beside a river, where they rested and allowed Senna to wash off the mud he'd streaked over her face earlier in the day. He sat down as she knelt beside the bubbling creek.

"Tell me about yer wool, Senna."

She looked up quickly. Her face gleamed with wetness. "My little bleaters?"

He smiled a little. "Is that what ye call them?"

"I call them hope." She dried her face on her tunic. It left a smudge, visible even through moonlight. Beckoning with curled fingers, he had her bend low so he could wipe the dirt away with the bottom of his tunic.

"They are a very certain kind of wool?" he asked.

She sat back. "Very certain."

He felt colder than the air around them should warrant. He

lowered his tunic and sat back. "And why did yer particular wool matter so much?"

She looked affronted. "I created it. I spent years breeding for this strain. Its softness, its ability to absorb dyes, the way it melts apart for weaving. There is nothing like it in all the world."

"Nothing in all the world," Finian echoed. "That's just what I thought."

Rardove knew.

He forced himself to breathe slowly. Rardove could know as many truths as his cunning, corrupted mind could withstand. Without the means to create, he was as helpless as a lamb. Finian now possessed the last remaining dye manual. And . . . did he have a dye-witch, too?

"And you, Senna? Ye said Rardove wanted to dye yer wools." She nodded. "Did he just want the wool, or did he want yerself to do the dyeing?"

She looked away sharply. "He is mad."

"Aye. But can you make the Wishmés bleed blue?"

She shook her head vehemently. "No. I will never make them."

Interesting. "No?"

"No."

"Ye never will?"

"Never."

"But *can* ye?"

She opened her mouth—to protest, likely—but to his surprise, she shut it again, then looked at him for a long time. Long enough for him to start feeling a kind of discomfort he was unused to. Usually he was the one questioning others, making them squirm under his suspicious gaze. Just now, he felt like he was being assessed, appraised.

"I doubt it," she finally said in a low voice.

"But that is why Rardove brought ye here," he pressed.

"Aye."

"And are ye? Are ye a dye-witch?"

Her eyes narrowed. "Such names can get people killed, Finian."

"I vow, I'll only kill ye if ye don't answer me. Are ye a dye-witch?"

Another long considering regard, then she said in a rush, "No but my mother was."

He nodded, holding his face in a neutral way to avoid displays of amazement, hope, or any other emotion that might make her leap up and run away, because the look on her face seemed very close to panic.

Good God, he had a dye-witch.

For hundreds of years, there had been none. Bred out by invasion and the fear of discovery, caution had won over passion and the Celts let the knowledge of crafting the Wishmés die. Lost the secrets, splintered the lineage. Mothers no longer taught daughters, and somewhere in the dim past, four, maybe five hundred years ago, a branch of that tree had been allowed to wither.

But it had not died. And now he had the last fragile branch in his possession, his very own dye-witch.

Who didn't want the task at all.

What mattered that? he thought, surprised to notice that bitterness fueled the inner query. Who had such luxury to choose against a destiny? His parents had been weak, of course, frail, unable to prevail over overwhelming desire or strong emotion, but he had been raised by The O'Fáil. Taken in by a king, lifted up. That was a rare thing. There was no cause for the taste of bitterness to be in his mouth.

No, all he had to do was consider Senna. What to do with her. Return her home as promised, or tell the Irish who she was?

It would be disloyal at best, treasonous at worst, to withhold this knowledge from his king. But Senna had no interest in dyeing. And if he told The O'Fáil about her, dye she would.

Her circumstances would not be so bleak as with Rardove, not by a bow shot, but still . . . she would be held against her will. Made to dye. Forced. Captured. Impinged upon.

All conditions she did not prefer.

Then again, who had the choice of what their life held? He looked at her, face damp, eyebrows pinched together like they had not been since that first morning on the ridge, when they spoke of Rardove and her father and her acumen for business.

But mayhap . . .

"Surely, dyeing for Rardove would be a repulsive thing," he said mildly, giving her a chance to say she'd do it for *him.*

Inwardly he shook his head at the awkward gambit. Outwardly, he peered at her expectantly.

She peered back, less expectantly. "I cannot make dyes."

"But ye can, lass. Ye don't even know what ye're capable of. Rardove was right, the first time in his accursed life, Senna. Such things are in the blood."

She gave a small, dismissive shrug. "So says legend."

"No, Senna. *I* say."

The look she gave him was derisive at best. "And how do you know such things?"

"These stories have been in my family for a thousand years."

She waved her hand. "You do but prove me true. They are *legends.*"

He squinted at her. "Aye, legends. But why do ye think that makes them untrue?"

She looked startled. "Forsooth, I assumed. Legends after all are of a legendary nature—"

"I'm telling ye, Senna, if ye want to craft the Wishmés, ye can. Nothing could stop ye."

"Not having the knowledge might stop me."

He fell silent, finally.

"I do not have it in me."

"Ye can tell yerself that until hell freezes over, Senna, but ye're too scared to even try, to know what ye're capable of," he rejoined with a hard edge in his voice. She was to have a choice no one else did? One does not wish to do a thing, and so one doesn't? Not under this sun. Only in dreams. "Just so ye know."

Senna turned and looked at him, and he became quite sure she would not be making dyes for anyone.

"You think you can tell me something of my life, Finian? I do not need to know anything better than I do. My father made certain I was well aware what I was capable of. The same things as my mother." She paused then, and her face paled. "Oh. Do the Irish want the dyes?"

He just looked at her.

A bitter smile crossed her face. "Of course. Of course the Irish want the Wishmés."

"The question is, Senna, can ye make them?"

"No, Finian. The question is, are you going to tell them?"

Chapter 38

Dawn had not yet crept over the battlements when William de Valery arrived at Rardove Keep.

He was led into the hall, asked to see Senna, and when she wasn't brought immediately, demanded in a loud voice to see Lord Rardove. Servants scurried in all directions as if to do his bidding, but no one entered the hall for three quarters of an hour. By then the de Valery knights' heads were bent in a tight, murmuring circle, their hands by their sword hilts.

A servant poked his nose in the baron's bedchamber, his brow already scrunched up to ward off any objects that might be sent flying from his lord's ill humor. "My lord?"

"What the hell is it?" he snapped.

"Sir William de Valery, my lord."

Rardove's eyes snapped open. He looked up into the gray light. "What are you talking about?"

"Sir William de Valery is in the hall, my lord. A bit angry at being kept waiting."

Rardove sat up straight. "De Valery? Waiting? What is he waiting for? What is he *here* for?"

The servant cleared his throat. "He wants to see his sister, sir."

Rardove entered the great hall five minutes later and found a circle of six or seven knights standing in the center of it. His gaze swiftly scanned the group and settled on the one who looked most like Senna.

Gauntlets stripped off and held in one hand, the knight had also removed his helm, holding it under one crooked arm, and pushed the mail covering back from his head, revealing damp, matted blond hair. Leather boots, rising to his knees, were coated with mud. His surcoat was barely visible beneath an equally impressive layer of muck. The rest of the group looked in the same state, as if they'd ridden hard and long without stopping.

Rested or no, though, the blond-haired knight turned at the first sound of boots scuffing the rushes. His eyes were alert and infinitely wary as he crossed the hall in long strides.

"My lord?"

"Sir William?" inquired Rardove, nodding. He smiled, but the young cub did not seem inclined toward social proprieties, for he pointedly did not return the smile.

"My sister."

"Ahh." Rardove turned to wave a servant into bringing refreshments. "Senna."

"No one has brought her to me."

Rardove clasped his hands together like a monk and sighed. "There's been a slight problem."

"Problem?"

"She's . . . gone."

The hazel eyes shaded darker in confusion. "What?"

"She's been abducted by an Irishman."

"Abducted?" His voice was incredulous.

"Aye. This is a brutal land, and—"

"What the hell are you talking about?" William demanded, his hand flexing over his sword hilt, brushing against the simple clasp at his left hip. Rardove dropped his gaze to the sight, then lifted it deliberately.

"Nigh on a week ago, while I was sickened in bed, an Irish prisoner I was holding in the cellars escaped. He took Senna with him."

"Took Senna with him?" de Valery echoed, his face a study in confusion and anger.

"Snatched her up and took her away."

"Why?"

Rardove spread out his hands in a gesture of helplessness. "'Tis unfathomable."

"To where?"

"Finian O'Melaghlin is councilor to the O'Fáil tribe. We assume they went there. We've men out searching, but the castle . . . it's unassailable."

"Finian O'Melaghlin?" de Valery asked, his gaze sharp. "I've heard of the man."

"Ah, yes." Rardove exhaled in a disappointed sigh. "He's gaining quite a reputation. But the Irish are a twisted race and do not abide trust well. Upon a time, I tried to make an alliance with them, which they spurned. One cannot rely too much on alliances in these dark days."

William paused through the length of a breath. "No, my lord. One cannot."

They held one another's gaze, then Rardove broke contact and reached for a tray of mugs the servant had just set on the table.

"You know little of this land, Sir William," he said over his shoulder. "You might find it burdensome to scorn what friends you have."

"I will recall that to mind."

"Be sure you do." Wine gurgled from the flagon into his cup, the sound of splashing loud in the quiet hall. "As for your sister, let me assure you, I am doing everything I can to secure her return."

De Valery's reply was pitched low and harsh, carrying no farther than the two men. "Let *me* assure *you,* Rardove, I will see someone pay in blood if anything happens to Senna."

Lowering the cup, Rardove placed it on the table with deliberate slowness. "Alas, your dear, *docile* sister is not in my keeping at present, so I've little to say on the matter."

Rardove elongated the word *docile* to a number of extra syllables. De Valery's jaw tightened. He swiveled and looked to the circle of knights, who stood watching him with hooded eyes.

De Valery turned back. "I cannot see for what reason the Irish would take her," he said with a mistrustful glance down at the cup of wine on the table.

"They are fiends," Rardove explained in a magnanimous gesture, then followed de Valery's gaze to the goblet. "Care for some?" He raised the flagon. De Valery said nothing. "Your men, perhaps?"

Rardove held the vessel higher so the knights in the background could see. Ten pairs of eyes stared back, five armored knights and five muscular squires, none a day under seventeen. Not a muscle moved. Rardove cleared his throat and set the pitcher down.

"Explain to me why O'Melaghlin would take my sister," de Valery said grimly.

"Because they are savage barbarians," Rardove snapped. "All of them, with as little honor or sense of right as a sheep. I had a few of their men in my prisons and I expect when O'Melaghlin saw a chance to escape, he saw taking her, too, as a matter of pride."

De Valery's gaze slid slowly up Rardove's robes, to his face. "Aye. I expect he did."

Rardove's face grew hot at the insolence, but the cadre of sword-bearing knights kept his tone quiet as he leaned forward and spoke near William's ear.

"Woe to you, young cub, if you become the object of their

enmity as have I. You know nothing of this land, and happens your arrogance will bedevil you as much as the Irishry."

"Happens it may bedevil you the more if Senna is not returned in pristine condition."

Rardove set the pitcher down. "And there we come to the heart of the matter. The Irish are a changeable race, untrustworthy and as likely to turn an alliance as to spit."

De Valery's jaw flexed. "What is your plan, then?"

"There is no way around it. I've summoned my vassals to the muster. The justiciar Wogan is coming. Edward, too."

De Valery stared. "The king of England is riding here to rescue Senna?"

"The king of England is riding here to prevent a rebellion on his Irish borders while he tries to quell the one in Scotland."

"A rebellion? Senna is *out there*."

"I know. We march for the Irish come three days."

De Valery paused long enough for several thoughts to have flickered through his young mind. Rardove waited, wondering which he would choose. If he was anything like his sister, William de Valery was probably not going to make a wise choice, a political choice—

The cub leaned forward until the tip of his nose was practically touching the baron's. "Be assured of this, Rardove: I'll march straight over your bones if anything happens to my sister."

No. Not politic at all. Rardove ground his teeth.

He could cut this one to the ground with a few deft words if he wished, fling out a few memories of his mother, here in Rardove Keep, bending for Rardove, but for now such things needed silence. De Valery would not be pleased to learn his mother had been here, died trying to escape. And he preferred de Valery's alliance to his enmity. For now.

De Valery gestured to his knights and the troop moved out of the hall. The sound of booted feet on stone thundered through the room as the herd of armored men ascended the stairs.

"I can count on your presence at the muster?" Rardove called after.

De Valery paused with one foot on the top step. He half turned to glance over his shoulder, mail basinet clumped around his neck. "I think you know what you can count on from me, my lord."

Rardove smiled thinly. "Twenty-four knights and their retinues."

De Valery swung away. "I'll be there," he said without looking back. The mud-soaked knights disappeared in a swath of golden sunlight as the door swung open, then slammed closed again, leaving the great hall in blue-black shadows and moldy intrigue.

The de Valery horses were assembled outside the covered stairwell leading to the keep. As the men dropped down the stairs, puffs of dirt billowed in small clouds. Low-angled dawn light mingled with the hazy grit floating in the air, making amber swirls of grime that rose around their steel-encased legs.

Will dragged his mail hood over his head and stuffed a padded layer of cloth between his hair and the protective iron links, then swung up into his saddle. He shoved the helm onto his head and latched the slotted visor upright with a twist of his fingers, exposing his face.

His men watched him in silence. With a curt nod, the cavalcade moved off, riding slowly across the bailey.

Will held himelf straight and silent as they passed under the rusted fangs of the raised portcullis. The gate was slung so low he would have lobbed off an ear if he'd risen in the stirrups. The squeal of grinding winches lifted the draw after they'd passed.

His hands held the reins as lightly as ever; his words, the few he used, were as impassive as a monk's upon hearing the tally of the rectory's in-kind offerings at Michealmas. Indeed, nothing about him betrayed anger. He could have been a wooden wagon-wheel, rolling across the land. But he was far past anger. Nigh onto a noxious rage that needed to be tempered to prove useful.

Christ's mercy. Senna kidnapped by an Irishman. Only Senna. She'd come to conduct a business deal, and was caught up in an intrigue so large it would rock this war-torn land for a generation to come.

And now, the land Will had earned with a great deal of blood was at risk. He said frequently that he cared naught for land, but that was only because he had no land to care for. The manor would have come to him, of course, but he would never have taken it away from Senna.

Not that he could now in any event. The business was hers, ever since she bought out her father's debt with her very own dowry, after her husband died. With a blade through his heart.

Robbers, she'd said, and had called out the hue and cry. The culprit had never been found.

Will would gladly have done the deed himself if Senna hadn't. The way her face looked after a single night wedded was enough to bring murder to anyone's mind. It was more than sufficient to spur Will into teaching Senna every skill of blade and bow he had in his considerable repertoire.

But now, Will had land. *Land.* And despite his nonchalant claims to the contrary, he wanted it badly.

He was quite conscious of the fact that he did not know much about Ireland, certainly not enough to know if Rardove was telling the truth about the Irish and their lack of honor. It mattered little. They had Senna, and he would run his sword through them, every one, to get her back.

With a gentle prick of his spurs, he lifted his horse into a canter. His men followed suit and the land fell away under the smooth, rocking motion as they made for the de Valery keep.

Chapter 39

Finian stopped them on a small rise of land. In the distance, Senna could see occasional glints of silver, as the currents of a small watercourse flowed between trees.

"Up, Senna."

She looked around. The leaves of the trees were obviously green, but in the night, the branches were more of a dark black mass. "Up what?"

He pointed high, to a small wooden platform set in the upper branches of a tree.

"A deer blind!" she exclaimed.

"One thing I can honestly give thanks to an Englishman for."

They climbed the rope ladder leading up to the blind. Senna pushed through the hole at the top and scooted backward to make room. His head popped up through the opening in the platform. He pushed the rest of the way through, then pulled the rope ladder up behind and shut the trap door.

It was a wooden platform, about three long paces wide, cut out like a crescent moon around the huge bole of the tree trunk. The leaves rustled every so often on a light breeze. Otherwise the night was utterly still.

He sat at the edge and hung his feet over the side, as the

nighttime winds swept over the land like feathers. He looked at Senna, lifted an arm, half curved, and crooked a brow. She smiled and scooted to his side. He dropped his arm over her shoulder and lifted his hand, pointing into the valley below.

"Do ye see those lands, Senna?"

"I do."

"They're yer brother's."

Her smile faded. "What?"

"Did ye not know he has lands here?"

"No." She looked over. "Will does not speak of his pursuits, ever. I know nothing of what he has gained. Or lost."

"No? Well, I do not need anyone to tell me. Yer king took the land, gave it to someone he owed a favor to. Yer brother, in this case."

They stared at the manor below. The forests around had been hacked back a good league. A tall motte was built up in the center of the clearing, and atop its rounded hump sat the manor house. A spiked wooden palisade encircled it.

A few outbuildings showed here and there, and a few homes and barns—a small village—huddled at the base of the motte. No villagers could be seen at this late hour, but evidence of their existence was in the tipped cart, which was spilling hay, outside a small stable.

"Why are you telling me this?"

"Do ye still wish to go home, Senna?"

"Oh."

"What's it to be, lass? Run yer business, count yer coin?"

"'Tisn't like that," she said dully. It was exactly like that. "What other option have I?"

"Ye could stay with me."

She knew she must appear shocked, lower jaw dropped, her eyes wide, but she couldn't hide it. Finian returned the look, utterly impassive. He might have just asked her to pass a plate of bread.

"Pardon?" she managed.

He scooped a heavy swath of hair into his palm and leaned forward to kiss the side of her neck, soft as mist. Whispered, rough-edged, his words came against her skin as he moved down her neck. "Will ye stay with me?"

"I—I—"

He ran the tips of his callused fingers down her neck, stopping just in the valley between her breasts. "Is that an *aye*?" he asked, smiling.

How shameful, to have all her wits melted like ice by a single Irishman. Stewards from the royal household and chancellors from St. Mark's Abbey had bent before her negotiating talents. Finian simply said *Will you?* and she'd practically wept her *Yes*.

He leaned forward to lay claim to her lips. She poked her index finger into his chest, holding him at bay.

"No," she corrected. "'Tisn't, actually. Why are you asking?"

He looked startled. He scratched his forehead. "*Why?* Ye're asking *why?*"

Now here was a phenomenon; an intelligent man laid low by that simple query.

"For certes," she assured him. *"Why?"*

"Why"—he looked around incredulously—"because 'tisn't safe at yer brother's manor."

"Then why did you offer in the first place?"

"So ye'd have a choice," he grumbled. "So I might be a modicum different to ye from other men."

A modicum. She felt like laughing. He was like a star might be viewed through one of Bacon's optics, brought close and placed in her palm. It was hopeless—she was in love with someone who had no need for the kind of fumbling attempts at affection she could bestow. Why would he need her?

And therein lay the truth: he didn't. He might want her, but he didn't need her, so it was only a matter of time.

She had no words to describe how she felt about him.

When he smiled at her, teased her, listened to her with patient regard. And there *were* no words to describe how she felt when he touched her. When he looked at her with desire and affection mingled. It almost made her heart break.

And now he was offering it to her, giving her the chance to have him hand back her heart, broken anew, each morning, when she woke up and recalled he would never truly be hers. Had he not made it plainer than daylight? Only a fool would believe it wasn't so.

He might wed, some day, for position and heirs. But it would not be for love. And it would not be to her.

He was distracting her, running his hand up her leg. He bent and brushed his lips over the vulnerable part of her neck, the center of her throat, where every swallow had to nudge by his lips. The blunt tip of his index finger slid over her thigh, and backward, brushing across the top of her buttocks.

"Is this about the dyes?" she asked outright, almost hoping it was. If so, it would be a black mark, a smudge on a man who was, to her, so gleaming bright it almost hurt her heart.

"No."

"Then why?"

He finished the kiss she'd stopped him from before, and she didn't stop him again. Up her neck he pressed kisses—small, hot raindrops—every so often followed by the smallest nibble, his teeth holding back their bite, just enough to raise shivers of pleasure across her breasts, hardening them. Then he moved to her lips.

His mouth slanted gently over her, his touch so gentle she felt his warm exhalation more than his kiss. As if they had all the time in the world, he kissed her, like she was a savory, a new taste for his lips and tongue.

He coaxed her mouth open and launched a slow, irresistible invasion, his tongue plunging deep in the wet recesses of her mouth. His hands slid over her hips and, with a confident tug, pushed her leggings down to midthigh. Then he positioned one knee between hers, his sculpted body and hard erection pressing against her groin.

"Staying, then, are ye?" he murmured against her ear—hot, masculine breath.

"You're muddling my head," she complained.

"I'll muddle ye straight through to yer center. Stay with me."

"Why are you asking?"

He shoved his muscular thigh up between her legs, pressing roughly against everything in her that was throbbing and wet.

"For this," he growled. He sounded certain. She was. Certain she could not live without him.

He bobbed his thigh up and down and she arched to him, entwining her fingers in his hair.

"For this." He kissed her earlobe, sending shock waves down her belly. She arched up into it. Shameless, and lost. "And this."

He fitted his palm into the small of her back and made her arch farther, so only the top of her head and her heels were on the wooden platform. Everything else was pressed up into Finian or supported by his hand on the back of her spine. His other palm pressed into the wood, holding them up, one knee shoved between her legs.

"'Cause I want to watch ye like this, Senna," he said, almost in a snarl, and bending his head, he took her nipple between his teeth, still beneath her tunic, and bit down, just shy of pain.

She exploded into full readiness, and without realizing how, she was ripping at her leggings with him, pushing them aside. But when he started to push inside her, reality intruded with a hot, raw flush.

She put her hands on his chest. "I'm a bit sore," she whispered.

Immediately he pulled back, and the hot, long length of

him slid out. She was relieved and frustrated, and whimpered her ambivalence.

"'Tis a'right, lass," he murmured, and went back to kissing her. That was purely unacceptable. If she was choosing the descent into the hell of perfect passion and uncertain futures, she was not about to settle for half measures.

"But I might like to try something else," she mumbled.

His lips paused on her neck. "Such as?"

"To try what I tried before. To do . . . that."

Now she could feel his lips curve into a smile against the warmth of her neck. "To do what, Senna?"

"To do to you . . ." her voice trailed off. "I never got to do to you . . . what you did to me. With your mouth." She was mumbling into her own chest now, she'd turned her face so far down. "We did . . . other things. But I did want to try . . ."

"So try," he said, his voice fierce and low-pitched.

She scrambled off him. Finian propped his back against the tree trunk and Senna knelt beside him. She unlaced his leggings and drew them open, sighing when his erection fell out, hot and heavy.

She slid tentative fingers over the long length of him, over the satiny skin, feeling it move like silk over the hard flesh beneath. His sculpted body shuddered slightly. She looked up.

"Can I—"

"Anything," he rasped. His spine was propped against the tree trunk, one knee bent, the other leg stretched out. He had a hand gently on her waist. "Ye can do anything ye want."

She smiled and bent back to him. She breathed deeply, inhaling the warm, almond scent of him. Then she opened her mouth and ran her tongue slowly down his erection.

He let out a long breath, but his hand on her waist did not move.

She grew bolder. Propping herself on an elbow, she bent very low and cupped him with her other hand. The heavy sacks of him, weighted in her palm and against the inside of her fingers, were hot and covered with dark wiry hair. Her hair fell down around her face; she felt like she was in a room alone with his maleness. Impatiently, she tipped her head to the side and ran her teeth against the length of him, very gently.

He sucked air. "Do that again," he ground out.

She shifted slightly.

"No," he ordered, his voice taut. He brushed her hair back, lifting it away from her face. "Keep yer head to the side. I want to watch ye."

Hot shivering ribbons shot though her body. Between her thighs she was pulsing, hot and ready. She ran her teeth against him again, her mouth open a little wider, sliding and tugging at the silk skin with gentle, threatening sharpness. She nudged her tongue behind. His hand tightened on her back.

She looked up. He watched her almost distantly, his body curved deceptively still against the tree. But she could hear his quickened breath, feel the quivering restraint of him, in all the bunched muscles he'd given over to her keeping.

"Like that?" she whispered, loving the feel of such power.

"Nay," he murmured, but his voice was thick. His dangerous eyes were intent on her, darkened by desire.

She shivered.

"Take me in yer mouth."

Heat jammed into her womb like a whip, snapping and demanding obedience to the craving.

She opened her mouth and took the wide, rounded head of him in, and then the hand on her back shifted. Pushing her leggings down, confident and certain, he unlaced her in seconds and had his hand between her thighs, slipping his thumb into her wetness, making her whimper. She slid her mouth along his length, up and down, moving her body back and forth, no longer aware of the hard wood beneath her knees.

"Hold yer hair up," he said, his words low and demanding.

She did, lifting one hand and pushing it back, so he could watch the side of her face as she licked up the length of him.

"Suck on me."

Hot, trembling desire shot through her body. She knew she was whimpering, rocking on her knees, helpless before their passion. She sucked him into her mouth—her mouth filled with his thick heat, inhaling, devouring the full, hard, pulsing male presence of him.

She felt his wicked hand between her thighs. His thick finger pushed inside her, his thumb nudging just across the slippery circular nub, and she moaned around his erection.

With a low sound in his throat, he suddenly moved. Nudging her aside, he repositioned them so he was lying flat, Senna kneeling beside him. Then he nudged her hips around, toward his head.

"Go back to what ye were doing before," he ordered in a thick voice. Panting, she bent to him. "And straddle me," he added.

She froze and looked over her shoulder, shocked. He wanted to be in that warm, tight space between her thighs. He wanted her to kneel over his face.

"Senna," he almost growled. He brushed his fingers between her thighs again, circling her nub with his thumb, then suddenly pressing in hard. She whimpered and dropped her head to his groin. He slid his hand under her belly and exerted pressure on her far hip, forcing her to shift closer. Then he took one of her knees in his hand and lifted it over him, so she was straddling him.

"Finian?"

"Just enjoy," he rasped, and, pushing himself up on his elbows, licked along the hot wet curve of her, flicking his tongue.

Her body started humming, cords of fire whipping though her body. She leaned on bent elbows, breathed deep his warm musky scent, and sucked him into her mouth again, thick and full, as much of his hard, pulsing length as she could.

His tongue worked with erotic confidence on her, licking in long, smooth strokes, then flicking fiercely, confident such abruptness would serve. It did. He suddenly sucked her flesh deep into his mouth and pressed the tip of his tongue into her. And again. The rasp of his teeth sliding by her most sensitive spot, danger held at bay, a ragged nip, then he sucked again, harder, pulsing tugs, harder, dragging her down to nothing but need.

The reality of this, imagining just for a second how he must look, on his elbows, face to her, sent her diving into a shattering, explosive climax. She threw her head back, crying out, and didn't remember anything except the total ecstasy of the sensations he'd mapped out through her body.

When she came back to sensibility, she was cradled in his arms, sitting sideways on his lap, her leggings tossed aside. He had his back to the tree again. She was still shuddering, but he seemed totally still. Rock hard, composed, self-contained, masculine power, his arm around her shoulder.

"Well, I know I did," she said in a whisper. "But, did you?"

"Don't ye recall?" Amusement tinged his words.

"Not exactly."

"No one had a better view than yerself." His arm tightened around her shoulder.

She almost choked. "I'll have to pay better attention," was all she could say.

"I'll have to impress myself upon ye more."

She leaned the top of her head against the V formed by his collarbones and mumbled into his chest, "I think you've impressed me quite enough."

Chapter 40

Finian gave a weary chuckle.

The air had a soft coolness to it; it had been a mild autumn. The harvest had been good. The cows would be *booleyed* down from the upper pastures where they summered. The piles of square peat bricks would be stacked under wooden lean-tos and eaves, waiting to serve as fuel to warm cold winter nights. And the smell of the sea would come pouring like a wave over the land.

He never knew why it came so strongly in the fall. Perhaps the leaves falling from the trees opened pathways for the salty, wild scent.

It would quicken his blood, and as everyone was closing in for winter, Finian would find himself restless. Discontent to repair harnesses or tell stories around the fire. Discontent to listen to the traveling *Seanchuich* weave their poetry and tell their histories and sing their laudatory tales to whichever king could pay them the most. The simple, quiet joys of the winter held no allure for him.

Then again, every season brought the racing, churning blood, the desire to be on the go, to move, to see and touch and do.

And every year, for the last half decade or more, it had

been a wearying thing. Not the exhilaration of finding and experiencing. Not the thrill of the new, just a disillusioned realization that this was no way to live a life. At some point, he'd be skimming the surface of it all, no matter what others said. The tales of Finian's exploits, on the battlefield, in adventurous, dramatic ways, were almost legend. The next crop of boys—young men, he supposed—looked at him with something bordering on awe.

It simply made him tired.

The way Senna looked at him, though, made him feel wide awake. Alive. Engaged. Met and seen.

She did, indeed, fit so well into every hidden corner of his heart. Even the ones he hadn't known were there.

She moved against him then, her rounded bottom cool as it slid across the top of his thighs. She swung a leg over his, straddling him.

His hand tightened around her hips. "I thought ye were sore."

"I am. But more, I am this." She shifted her hips and with him not guiding at all, she maneuvered just right for the tip of him to slip into her waiting heat.

"I am *this* as well," he murmured. She smiled and kissed his forehead. He kissed her chin. She kissed his nose. He nuzzled her neck.

For a few moments they moved together, holding each other, slow. He cupped her breast, kissing, slow again and more slow. It was a loving slow, languid and attentive, one hand on her curving spine, one on her breast, then tangled in her hair, his gaze intent on her face, her eyes half-closed, all in him and open to him, and it was beyond good.

Then she leaned down to kiss him and opened her eyes fully. Her face washed white.

That's when he heard them.

Soldiers. Marching. An army.

* * *

Her legs tensed, but otherwise they were motionless. A rider shouted to another. Someone was coming into the clearing.

"Scouts," Finian whispered into her hair, which was shivering, because her body was trembling. Minute vibrations of terror. He knotted handfuls of her hair in his fist and pulled her close to his face. Their lips brushed.

"Silence."

The riders trotted into the clearing. The only sound was their horses' hooves on the loamy ground. It sounded like hammer blows on old, rotting wood. An occasional clink of metal on metal, and the ever-present groan of leather. Saddles, pouch ties, armor, everything creaked like old doors.

"Nope, 'tis better down in the valley," one said. "There's water close, and a few village houses we can commandeer."

His companions reined around. "This ridge has a better vantage point."

The three of them lined their horses up and stared at the lands below. Almost right under the tree. They were off to the side enough so that Finian could see them. So that they could see Finian, should they glance up.

For the first time, he felt regretful that Senna's hair was so dazzling.

Muscles frozen, lungs barely expanding, they sat and waited. Finian's thigh muscles began to ache as he held them, knees half bent, Senna sitting astride him. He could feel her inner thighs, trembling ever so slightly against his. Her knees were pressed onto the wood, holding her in a half-risen position. Their faces were close together, lips almost touching, Finian's hand still fisted in her hair.

"My knife," she whispered against his lips, "is just by your right hand."

Their eyes, inches apart, met. He nodded slightly.

For another few minutes, all was motionless. Even the soldiers. Then their horses shifted, pawing, pulling their necks to get at the grass under their hooves, but otherwise moonlight was the loudest thing about.

"C'mon," muttered one suddenly. "The river is better, sheltered."

The others agreed, and they attempted to convince the sole holdout, the one with the chestnut mount who seemed skeptical and must be their leader.

"I dunno. 'Tis a rare view, up here," he said reluctantly.

"Whadda we need a view for?" one of the others scoffed. "Think you're gonna spot bleeding O'Melaghlin on the horizon?"

They busted up at that.

"And his whore."

Finian didn't even realize his body had stiffened until Senna pressed her hips down, dampening his unconscious movement.

"Whore, traitor, I do not care," snapped their leader. "Rardove wants to pay twenty French *livres* to anyone who brings them in before battle? I bring them in."

Finian heard the word *battle,* but he didn't need words at all to understand what he was seeing. This was not a scouting party, not a group of loosely aligned riders on a treasure hunt for outlaws. This was the contingent of an army on the muster, and there was only one man powerful enough to summon it: Rardove.

He was also fairly certain Senna would not be unaware of any of this.

The riders reined their horses away. The sounds of a small army were louder now, bootheels and muttering. The scouts met up with someone halfway down the hill.

"The river," Senna chanted against his mouth, willing them to choose away.

"Here in the clearing," the chestnut rider called out.

"Mother Mary," she exhaled.

Within fifteen minutes, the small army had tromped up the

hill and encamped themselves on a meadowlike clearing just outside the treeline, eighty feet from where Senna and Finian sat frozen, mid-coitus.

She pulled back an inch and stared into his eyes. Hers were terrified.

"They'll be gone with the dawn, Senna," he said quietly, "and never even think to look up. We're safe up here."

"I know," she replied, and the sadness in her voice came from the kind of deep reservoir only very old women should have had the time to dig. "Up here, I am safe."

He tightened his hold on the knot of hair in his fist. "With me, ye are safe."

Her thighs were trembling. "With you, I am safe."

He dipped his head. Their foreheads touched. Just outside the line of trees, the army camped, coarse voices and weapons everywhere, like a foul river murmuring. The moon rose.

She finally moved, lowering her body, which of course she had to do. She could not hold herself up all night.

She slid her hips forward and back, rocking on him. That, she did not have to do.

His fingers tightened on her hips to stop her. "Senna—"

"I'm afraid." Her voice was so low it was almost breath.

"I know," he whispered back, running his hands over her cheeks, cupping her face.

"I do not like being afraid."

Her hips rocked again and slowly, Finian became aware tears were slipping over his fingers, down her cheeks.

"Shite," he rasped, and pulled her to him.

Slow and almost motionless, they rocked together, very slow. For a long time she just rested her forehead on his, and he kept his hands on her spine, and they moved, not wanting anything more than to just hold and be held.

But as the length of him was deep inside her, sliding over slippery, sensitive flesh, she started pressing down in harder thrusts, pushing for more. She didn't move faster—they dare not—just harder, more desperately, pushing with more force. She spread her legs as far as she could, pressed down as hard as she could, and it was not enough.

He lifted his hips ever so slightly, trying to meet her obvious, desperate need, but they couldn't risk any more movement than that.

"More," she whimpered.

He gave a ragged, whispered laugh. "Jésu, Senna, my hands are tied here." A tiny but vicious pump of his hip only made her writhe more.

"More." She bent to his ear and begged, "I need more."

His wide palm suddenly pushed her back a few inches. Dark and moonlit, his face looked dangerous as he met her eyes, his gaze predatory and appraising. He grabbed both her wrists and pulled them behind her back, held them locked in his grip.

The other hand he closed around her throat very gently but very powerfully, exerting just enough pressure for her to feel his restraint. Dangerous and erotic. Then he leaned forward and sucked her breast into his hot mouth.

She dropped her head back and moaned silently. Her hips slid on him, and with another small, violent shove up, he jammed himself farther up inside.

It was like he knew her body from the inside out, because the changed angle increased the feel of him, touching her high inside. He was pushing against shuddering, trembling flesh, a slow, torturous slide. Each small plunge tightened some silken cord that ran from her womb to her breasts, down the back of her legs and up her spine. It connected her to his pleasure.

He tightened his hold on her wrists and on her throat, his eyes never looking away, pressuring her, pushing her. Hot, flat jolts of energy shot though her. She whimpered and arched her back. He closed his teeth around her nipple and flicked his tongue, hard touches just shy of pain.

She leapt in his arms, quivering.

"Is this good to ye?" he growled.

"Aye," she whispered. "More."

"How much more?" he rasped.

"Don't stop. Much more."

She heard a low growl, as if he'd turned animal, then, releasing her wrists, he sat up a little straighter and slid his hand down the sweaty curve of her back, over her bottom. Every movement was slow, torture slow, painful slow, safe, undetectable movements. He slipped his hand between her thighs, between his, to where they were joined. His fingertips circled through the slippery wetness, then he trailed them back and nestled them between the seam of her buttocks. Slow, never-stopping.

She whimpered, her forehead rolling on his shoulder. He nuzzled the tip of a finger between her smooth rounded cheeks and pressed up.

"Oh, sweet Lord," she exhaled in a hot rush, so he did it again, slid his finger up a little farther.

"Ohh," she whispered in a choked voice, and Finian didn't know if it was pain or pleasure, or both.

"More, Senna?" he grated, and he almost didn't recognize his own voice, it was so clouded with violent passion. "Do ye want more?"

Her breath exploded out of her and her teeth closed on his shoulder as her hips slammed against him very, very slowly. His head was spinning now.

She leapt in his arms, quivering. Her knees pushed out, so she was sprawled against his chest. Her buttocks, soft and yielding, gripped his finger tightly as her body trembled and rocked.

"Do ye like this?" he growled.

She was sobbing against his shoulder, biting him, quivering, tiny, frantic shoves of her hips, opening her to him.

"Feel all of me inside ye," he rasped.

His finger, slippery with her juices, pressed up a little farther and held there as she threw her head back in a silent scream. He pressed and released, steady, ever-more pressure on the sensitive opening of her, until his finger was inside her and he could feel the orgasm begin in her womb with his finger and his cock.

He locked his mouth over hers as they erupted together, her explosive orgasm clenching him in hard, rhythmic pulses as he released deep inside her, utterly silent but for her sobs, which he swallowed, and the words she was crying into his mouth, *"I love you."*

Later, when he could, when she was cradled in his arms, limp and sweaty, he lowered them by degrees to the floor of the deer blind and tugged her into the curve of his body. The army was almost silent now. Only a few small fires burned. A guard or two sat around them, desultorily on watch. No one else was awake but Senna and Finian, and an owl perched on the longest branch of their tree, blinking bright green eyes, waiting for unwary creatures to show themselves and become prey.

Some time later, she pushed up slightly and peered over her shoulder at him. Damp tendrils of hair curled beside her face, and her eyes were heavy lidded with passion. She looked exhausted and sated and magnificent.

"You heard, did you not?" she whispered. "What I said."

He pulled her back down, pressing a kiss to the top of her head. He wrapped an arm around her belly and pulled her back into his chest. "Sleep if ye can. I'll keep watch. Tomorrow, we find a horse. We'll be at The O'Fáil's by nightfall."

As if that would solve a single problem.

Chapter 41

In the mists of a Dublin dawn, a troop of mercenary soldiers grumbled onto their horses, but every one of them knew things could be worse. The pay was good and the plunder better. There were worse professions than employment with the king's governor in Ireland.

Motionless, the justiciar, Wogan, watched from horseback, supervising the muster as the soldiers mounted up. The sound of heavy boots and creaking leather bounced back off the wall of mist.

Always a march and battle, taking here and giving there, only to have it taken back again. Irish king-making and deposing, releasing men held hostage and rescuing besieged ones, appointing good men and burying dead ones. His face revealed nothing; he was a chiseled sculpture whose craggy presence made his men mount up more quickly when his gray eyes settled on them.

King Edward would follow shortly, but Wogan had orders not to wait. The king had received news that greatly displeased him. Wogan was to begin settling the matter. Soon the Irish would understand the king's terms. They would capitulate, or they would die.

Wogan's fingertips were damp and chilled, and he blew on

them absently as he straightened in the saddle. His gelding nickered at the sudden movement and skittered sideways over the wet cobblestones. Wogan spoke a soft word, and the horse quieted.

Turning, his hand in the air, he swept his arm down in an arc, and the retinue headed off into the mists. They would make good time, bound for northern Ireland where the deviltry dwelt.

They wouldn't see him coming for a long time. When they did, it would be too late.

When the sun was midway through its western arc the next afternoon, Finian lifted his hand and pointed into the valley below.

"O'Fáil lands."

Senna nodded calmly, belying her fluttering heart. Her entire life had been spent on a remote manor, locked away with profit sheets and a stylus. Exactly as she'd planned it. Finian seemed to feel sad about that, that she'd somehow been injured as a result, that a loss had been suffered. But she'd never seen it that way.

As a widow, she'd made the final decisions about her life. Bought a dying business and made it thrive, raised her brother and, until their father gambled it away, ensured a rich manor remained for the ensuing generations—that would probably never come, she suddenly realized, because neither she nor Will seemed inclined toward unions. Marriages, children, that sort of thing. Being connected.

They'd been ruined for it.

Each of them lived ferociously solitary lives, connected only to each other by steely thin threads of devotion, and to their father by knotted ropes of dismay. Dread. Desolation.

Until now. Senna had let go the rope and gone over the edge of that particular, spectacular cliff with Finian.

She tried frantically to straighten the wild curls of her hair into a semblance of a braid. It helped little to realize now that she was terrified of meeting people. That her self-imposed sequestration had not simply been a preference for numbers or the clarity of a contract. It had been—and was—fear.

She admitted it now: fear had ruled her life. For good reason. There was much to fear, and it was all inside her, flowing like blood. Just like blood.

The same blood that gave her powers to create the most rare, coveted dyes in the West. Dye-witch, indeed. A dye-witch was someone who courted terrible, dangerous things, who let passion rule her life. Senna knew now she was no better than her mother.

They were met long before the castle gates by warriors who obviously knew Finian on sight. Solid muscle locked on muscle as the long-lost warriors pounded each other on the back, hooting and hollering.

"Finian O'Melaghlin, ye crooked Irishman," roared one voice above the others.

"Ah, Saint Pat, Finian, we thought ye were dead," said another, and she could hear the despair the thought had conjured.

A burly arm wrapped around his shoulders, and her escort disappeared beneath the hearty welcoming of those who flocked to the gates.

Someone pounded Finian on his shoulder and roared, "'Tis more than good to have ye back. 'Twas grievous when we thought ye were captured and killed with the rest."

"'Tis grievous enough that the others were killed," he replied grimly.

"Aye, that it is," the other man said. "But the king has need of all his nobles, and to lose a great lord and councilor like yerself would be a loss too tremendous to bear."

Finian grunted noncommittally, but Senna's weary eyes were yanked open by the recognizable English words. Great lord? Councilor? Her great, hulking warrior? What, with his irreverent jokes and earthy ways, favored by a king?

Lord Finian. Good Lord. He was noble.

The rest of the household greeted them just inside the inner bailey gates. Older men, women, and a bevy of children swarmed into the bailey or hung out of windows, waving and calling. Afternoon shadows stretched across portions of the bailey, and a golden glow of firelight formed a backdrop for the silhouetted figures.

Women of the household flitted and fluttered nearby, bright Irish butterflies. Senna was quick to note them pinch their cheeks and brighten their smiles when Finian's gaze turned to them. A chill of worry slunk across her breast.

Someone approached. Tall, long-haired, and kilted, he nodded levelly at Finian. "Our king will no' believe me when I tell him you made it out of yet another close call, O'Melaghlin. I was just on my way to save your sorry arse."

Finian turned. "The day I need a Scot *gallowglass* to save my arse 'twill truly be a sorry day."

"A regular day," retorted the other, crossing his arms. "A day like any other. I've saved you too many a time to count."

Finian snorted. "Ye've drunk me under the table too many times to count. Saved me? I think not."

"Saved you, indeed. That's why The O'Fáil was sending me out, to save you. As usual. I was just leaving."

"Aye, well, ye're too late. As usual."

They stared for another moment, then suddenly embraced with hearty thumps on the back. These men did like to thump. Senna couldn't help smiling, but the smile fled when she heard Finian's low-pitched words. "The O'Fáil received word of my capture, then?"

The other man pounded him on the back, replying in a voice just as low, "Aye, we've a word: bastard."

"I've two," Finian said as they released. "*Dead man.* Where is the king?"

"Inside. He's been worried like a sick cat, Irish. He'll be glad you're here."

"Maybe," Finian said flatly. "Until he hears my news."

"We've had some news ourselves," said the tall Scotsman.

Finian looked at him sharply. "Of what?"

The Scotsman's eyes drifted in Senna's direction for a moment. "Rardove has spun a fascinatin' tale about your escape."

"Is that so?" he replied grimly. "I've a tale as well. But for later," he said, passing a sharp glance around the circle of warriors. "For now, all ye need to know is that this," he reached out to Senna, "is my savior." He tugged her into their circle.

"This comely vision was yer wings, ye lout?" one man roared in laughter and turned to her in mock reprimand.

Finian took a deep breath. "I'd have you meet Senna de Valery."

Stunned silence swept through the group. Someone said in a quiet voice, "Rardove's betrothed?"

He jutted his chin out. "She never was."

"Rardove says she was," another man said grimly.

"Rardove lies when he breathes."

"Sweet Jesus, O'Melaghlin, why is she *here?*" someone else demanded.

"She's here because I've brought her here." Finian's gaze glittered dangerously over the group, and Senna felt the tension ratchet up another notch. Her heart started that familiar thundering, and the resultant dizziness tingled at the base of her neck. The Scot who'd embraced Finian turned to her with a smile.

"Now, why would you have done such a thing as that, lass, setting a scoundrel like Finian O'Melaghlin free?"

She gave a weak smile. "Had I known the depths of his depravity, rest assured I would have found another."

The crowd broke into noisy, if tense, laughter and turned to enter the keep. Finian looked down at her.

"They don't want me here," she whispered.

Chapter 42

"Not to worry," Finian said. "I'll see to ye."

He slid his arm around her waist, laying claim in a way that might, he hoped, ward off any problems. But then, there was a war at hand, and women never fared well in them.

By keeping his arm tight around her waist, Finian was privy to every quivering muscle in her body as they climbed the stairwell into the keep. Her backbone ran in an unerringly stiff line from neck to buttocks. He pursed his lips as they topped the stairs.

"Do ye know where my favorite place in this hall was, when I was young and fostered here?"

She jerked her head up. "Nay." Her voice was barely a whisper.

He gestured with his chin. "See if ye can pick it out."

Her gaze swept the large room as they stopped in the arched doorway of his long-ago home. The great hall, three broad steps below them, was wide, clean, and bright, lit by evening light coming in through high windows and rushlights burning in iron sconces. A huge fire roared in a recessed firepit along the far wall, a blaze of light and heat. Fresh rushes covered the floor, and the room smelled comfortably of faint herbs and warm bodies.

People were everywhere, in pairs and threesomes, talking, eating, and laughing. A young couple was having a lovers' argument in a far corner, the disagreement evident by a quivering lower lip and dewy, tear-filled eyes.

A group of youngsters huddled at a far table, playing some kind of game. One lad exploded into such raucous laughter he rolled backward off the bench. The others erupted after him, little volcanoes of good spirit.

Two dogs lolled comfortably by the roaring fire, crunching bones. The outline of a cat was frozen in midstride, her bright green eyes fixed on some unseen rodent threat beneath the rushes.

A herd of young men, not yet warriors but no longer boys, loitered near a group of men. They weren't watching their elders though, who were, at the moment, the most boring creatures imaginable. They were espying a bevy of young females chattering at another table, lasses who hid their lips behind slender hands, eyed their admirers, then giggled and looked away.

Senna's gaze swept back to him. "At the head of that table where the maidens are?" she asked, the tremor gone from her voice.

He smiled, pleased his gambit had proven successful. "Guess again."

"At the center of the dais table, then, being self-assured and commanding."

He shook his head.

"Tell me, then."

"No. Ye're to figure it out yerself."

"I will." She accepted the challenge with bright eyes.

"Och, how could I doubt it? Ye're quick-witted, and if ye cannot figure it out yerself, all ye've to do is pull out that pretty smile and lure the truth out of some poor unsuspecting."

It was indeed a pretty smile that brightened her now-relaxed face as Finian led her into the hall, battling back the wave of protectiveness washing through him. There were more important things to attend to just now, such as recovery of ancient Irish rights and onrushing war. He must not get distracted by Senna.

Just then, the king looked up and saw him. He went still, then got to his feet, slowly. Tablets on his lap crashed to the floor.

Finian started forward, toward the man who'd taken him in when everyone else was willing to say he was a lost cause, who'd believed in something the others hadn't seen. To them, he'd been the son of a mother who committed the sin of suicide, right now burning in hell, and a father who'd melted away after it happened.

But The O'Fáil had brought him in, raised him up, called him son, councilor, friend. Finian had not exaggerated a whit; he owed The O'Fáil more than his life. He owed him his reason for living.

Finian reached out for his foster father's hand.

"Jésu, Finian," the king muttered, grasping his wrist and coming around the table. "I thought ye were—" And then The O'Fáil, one of the greatest Irish kings since Brian Bóruma, came forward and crushed Finian in a bear hug.

If Senna had seen glimpses of love from the corners of her life, then this was it in full force, bursting and unreserved. And it fell down all over Finian like rain.

The king pulled back, bearded and smiling. His hands continued to grip Finian's shoulders. "So. You decided to visit."

"In truth, my lord, I had nothing better to do for the night."

The king laughed heartily, then looked around swiftly. Almost the entire hall had their eyes shifted toward them, but no one was nearby. Only Senna. His gaze flitted over her, paused momentarily, then returned to Finian. "Your mission?"

"Done, and then some," Finian assured him in a low voice.

"Good. Good." The king swept his piercing gaze back to Senna. "And who is your astonishing escort?"

"Senna de Valery, my lord." Finian grabbed her hand and dragged her forward.

Above his gray-shot beard, the king's perceptive eyes appraised her in seconds. She felt the inspection as if a hook had been laid into her, poked about, and extracted. Then the king smiled. He gestured for her to sit beside him. She did so shyly, ducking her head.

"Lass, you ought not to bend your head so," the king said. "Makes it hard to see your beautiful eyes."

Finian rolled his eyes.

"So you all do that," she replied softly, her voice a blend of seductress and innocent, so that Finian didn't know whether to guide her from the room to protect her from the onslaught of masculine attention that was about to come her way, or lay her out on a table and claim her with a roar: *She's mine!*

Doubtful she'd see it as a compliment though. He kept his hands to himself.

The O'Fáil scratched the top of his ear, then wiped his hand along the back of his neck. "What is it we do, lass?"

"Charm. You charm us."

The O'Fáil grinned. "Aye, we like to think we do our part. As do you ladies."

Senna lifted her eyebrows a delicate fraction, conveying exactly a blend of innocence and feminine command. "I do not think I have ever made Lord Finian blush, my lord, and I quite doubt I could do it to you."

Finian crossed his arms over his chest, an impermeable barrier of confident, careless warrior. The king grinned broadly at him, then turned back to Senna. "Well, you'd never know if you did it to me, now would you, under all this fur." He tugged on his beard and she smiled. The king leaned a bit closer. "But with Finian, lass, you just might be able to tell."

Finian unslung his arms and stepped forward. "That's enough," he announced, putting his arms under Senna's armpits and practically lifting her off the bench.

The O'Fáil was still laughing as Finian said, "The king has a council to attend, and you need to eat, Senna."

She batted his hands away long enough to turn and bow her head. "Sire, I am not accustomed to being indebted, and suspect I do not do it very well, but know this: I am grateful beyond words, and indebted to you for my life. I vow to repay it."

The O'Fail regarded her a minute before nodding, too, then Finian guided her away and sat her at another table on the other side of the room. He felt The O'Fáil watching the whole time. He tromped back and they walked out of the great hall together.

"She's filled with fire," the king observed as they strode down the corridor.

"Ye've no idea."

Up ahead was the meeting chamber. Other men, young and old, were already filing inside. No one had to officially call this meeting; Finian's arrival had been summons enough. The O'Fáil stopped and turned to him.

"Son, do I need to say it aloud?"

Finian met his hard gaze with one equally unflinching. "What?"

"She's got to go back."

Chapter 43

Around the table sat The O'Fáil, his chief councilors, a priest, and a group of Irish nobles. Finian lounged on the bench beside Alane, his relaxed pose at odds with the roiling tension in the room.

Everyone waited when the servants brought food and drink. No one touched theirs except for Finian, but they waited as he drank half a tankard of ale. They waited as he scanned the room after meeting each man's gaze, and they even waited through his subsequent sigh.

"Rardove is amassing an army," he said. "He wants a war. I say we give it to him."

The room erupted into shouts and curses.

"There's more," he added, pushing into the noise. The room quieted. "He knows. Rardove knows about the dyes."

Silence poured out of the cold walls. He could hear the sharp drops of fresh water in a cistern at the corner of the room.

"How much?" the king asked. "How much does he know?"

"He knows they explode."

More curses, hands scrubbing jawlines, shuffling boots. Men growing more tense, wanting action. Finian let them sit with the news a minute, then said, "We've one thing in our favor."

Someone snorted. The king looked up. "And what is that?"

"This." He took the dye manual from its pouch and held it up. Bound in wood, with pages that could burn, it was as fragile as a leaf. Everyone stared as if he were holding a flame in his hand.

"Good Lord," the king breathed. "The dye manual. Turlough was sent to retrieve this."

"Aye, well, I got wind of Turlough's fate while in Rardove's care."

"And did the rendezvous yourself." The king looked at him. His bearded head nodded, the traces of a smile evident. "Well done." He paused. "You missed the wake, Finian. 'Twas a worthy one."

Finian nodded roughly. "I wish I'd have been here."

"I know."

Finian swept on. No time for mourning past losses, else there'd be many more to come. "Without that"—he indicated the manual—"Rardove cannot make the dyes. Not unless he has a dye-witch. And he doesn't."

He didn't bother to point out that they did. That he had brought back both the dye manual and a dye-witch.

The first breach in his wall. He felt the crack of disloyalty shiver down his bones.

The king reached for the bound booklet. "Hundreds of years," he said reverently, "and we have the Wishmé recipe again." He cracked it open and touched the scalloped and tattered edge of a page. "Saint Brendan, Finian, this is well done." He looked up. "What else did Red say?"

"Not much. He died in my arms."

The room exhaled a reverent breath of male air, filled with the heady juxtaposition of murmured prayers for his kin and descendents to the fourth generation, fervent signs of the cross, and a boatload of creative curses, which seemed like they ought to cancel out the prayers.

"Which brings us to the only other thing we've got in our favor," the king said finally. "Rardove will not want anyone to know about this recipe. Can you fathom a hundred rebellious Englishmen in on the hunt for the legendary Wishmés?"

He looked around the room at the grim and angry faces.

"No," The O'Fáil said firmly. "He shan't even want it breathed about. Which means, if we return his excuse for a war, we'll buy much-needed time."

Finian looked over slowly. "What do ye mean, *return his excuse*?"

"I mean Senna de Valery."

He shook his head. "Not a chance. Not if my head were on the block."

"'Tis."

He looked over. "Chop it off, then."

"'Tis all our heads, Finian. Every Irishman living in northern Ireland."

"Christ's blood, man," Felim, a noble, muttered. "What would ye have us do? We haven't the men, our castles are in disrepair. Ye said yerself that Rardove was amassing troops. We've no way to hold them back. We need time."

"Time for what?" Finian asked sharply.

"Jesus, O'Melaghlin, what don't we need time for? To call up allies. To placate, negotiate, convince him we're not wanting to fight."

"Well, we haven't got that kind of time," Finian said tightly.

Everyone was quiet a moment. Then the king said what they all were thinking.

"We do if you send the woman back."

Finian ripped his gaze away. Firelight flashed off his sword hilt as he leaned his spine against the wall and kicked out his booted feet, crossing them at the ankles.

"What do ye expect from us, Finian?" someone demanded. "That we fight for our lives to save an Englishwoman?"

"Nay," he retorted. "Fight to save yer own."

"They'd be in little enough trouble if it weren't for her," Brian, an Irish warrior with a sullen frown on his face, observed.

Alane suddenly leaned forward, shaking his head. "The Irish have been coasting on top of a very deep current for a very long time. Sure as anything, the waves crashing at our shores are no' caused by the lass." Alane made a sound of disgust. "You send her back, she's like a rabbit in a glade: dead in her tracks."

"As we will be," shouted someone, "if Rardove calls up even half his vassals."

Alane sat back and shrugged. Finian sailed him a grateful look.

"And that's just what he'll do. He'll want war," a noble said in a grim voice.

"Aye, because he wants her back—"

"Nay! Because he wants our *lands*." Finian was practically shouting and it was helpful to have Alane's hand clamp down on his forearm briefly.

"And I think you ought to let him have her," Brian finished irritably.

"And I think ye ought to fall on yer blade for suggesting such a thing, Brian," snarled Finian. "Have ye heard nothing of what I've said? *This has naught to do with her.* Rardove has been looking for an excuse to launch a campaign against us for twenty years now."

"And 'tis a most perfect opportunity ye're giving him," the first noble said.

Finian swung his head around like a raging bull. "And if Senna hadn't given him such a *perfect opportunity,* Felim, I'd be dead."

That brought silence.

"She's the reason I'm alive. She's brave—"

"And beautiful," Alane chimed in cheerfully.

Finian retracted his previously grateful look. "The drink has addled yer mind. Yer mother said 'twould not be long in coming." He looked back at the others. "'Tis wrong to return her to the maggot. She's gotten caught up in something larger than herself."

"Aye." A few heads nodded around the table, mostly the younger ones. Alane's was among them.

Brian, the young, argumentative one, pushed back the bench and rose. "And I say curse ye, O'Melaghlin, if this doesn't go well."

"And curse ye," Finian growled, rising, too, "if ye could leave a maiden to be eaten by Rardove. She's alone, and brave, and without her I wouldn't be alive. She may be a spark, but Rardove has been laying this kindling for some long time."

He slammed his fist on the table. It lay there, a sturdy, clenched reminder of his inclinations on how to deal with the matter. He went on, restraint evident in every taut syllable.

"Do ye think I'm putting anyone's life in danger without a thought, Brian?" Finian's eyes glittered hard as he pinned each member of the gathering in his glare. "He imprisoned me and my men, have ye forgotten? He killed every one of them. My men. My responsibility, and they died, to a man. Some were hanged, and that was the kindest way to go."

His voice quaked for the briefest moment, then rode on, hard and harsh. "The ones I wasn't forced to watch, I couldn't miss hearing. And 'twill be on my conscience long after I tread on my sod of death, ye bastard."

The room reverberated with silence.

"I'd as soon rip his heart out as spit across the room, and I will. *I will.*"

"We're not forgetting yer capture," Felim said into the heated tension, and rubbed the back of his neck. "Ye do well to remind us of the travails of leadership, for those of us who've had them, we'll not soon forget the grief of it."

Finian threw his chin up and looked around the room, incensed, belligerent, wont to fight.

There were no takers. After a minute of quiet, during which

pages tiptoed in and poured more drink, then slunk out again, O'Hanlon spoke.

"I agree with O'Melaghlin. Rardove is on the hunt for the dyes, and he's got to be taken down. What better excuse than us retaliating in a war he's launched on us?"

"Ye speak well. 'Tis best to deal with the worm on our own terms." Lifting his mug, Finian threw back his head to down a swallow of ale, then passed it to Alane.

"Ye speak of Rardove as being an insect," grumbled Brian from the shadows. "But a bug at least is predictable. Ye know what it will do, when, and why."

His sullen words caught Finian's attention. "Ye know a great deal about bugs, do ye, Brian?"

Brian scowled from across the table. "Aye, I do. 'Tis certain men who are more difficult to understand."

Finian laughed. "They are as predictable as mist in the morning, they are. Money, power, and women."

"And no' in that particular order," Alane chimed in.

"And yerself, Finian O'Melaghlin?" snarled Brian. "Is that why ye're at doing the things ye're doing? For I don't like the idea of having my head served up to some Saxon king because of yer aching rod."

Finian's hand flashed out around Brian's neck, then dropped immediately when Alane's elbow nudged his ribs. But he did not turn his fury. "Ye're not listening, Brian. 'Tisn't her. She matters naught. She's *nothing*."

From the shadowy darkness, the king cleared his throat. All heads swiveled to him. "Then why did ye not take her to her brother's manor, and leave her danger there?"

"No one was in residence," he retorted. That wasn't, precisely, the reason, but no one needed to know that.

"Oh, but aye, someone is very much in residence there now."

"I saw no sign of it." It wouldn't have mattered though.

"Well, we did. Smoke. Not three hours ago our scouts reported smoke rising from the de Valery keep."

"What of it? His reeve."

"And a whole lot of horses milling around. War horses. And someone shouting orders."

Finian narrowed his eyes. "I saw no one."

Brian shrugged, stretching out his hand for the vessel busily making the rounds through the room. Alane intercepted it, took an unhealthy draught, then handed the empty vessel over with a broad grin. Brian scowled and dropped his hand.

Finian grabbed the other flask and splashed drink into his cup, the gurgling loud. His elbows came to rest on his knees as he bent at the waist, the hardened leather of his outfit creaking as he went. Holding the cup between callused fingertips, his hair swung alongside the pewter cup as he studied the ground.

Brian shook his head in disgust. "So now we'll have de Valery and his knights joining the godforsaken Saxon throng looking to cut us down. Well done, O'Melaghlin. Ye're at making us enemies near as well as ye used to make us friends."

"And ye're at making yer life in peril, Brian," Finian retorted in a dangerously smooth voice.

Alane unraveled from the bench to stand beside Finian. "Shut your mouth, pup," he said to Brian smoothly, but with a snarl underlying.

The O'Fáil spoke up from the shadows. "I'll have no disrespect in my home, Brian O'Conhalaigh. Lord Finian deserves no less, and a good deal more. Have you a word to say, say it, and I will consider it 'ere I make my decision. But when I decide, 'tis what we will do. What we will all do."

The room grew quiet. Everyone watched the king, the king watched Finian, and Finian stared at the wall. He knew that look very well. He'd been the recipient of such considering appraisals for many years, usually after he'd done something remarkably risky and reckless, like indulge in cliff diving, or visiting the grave he'd dug for his mother, when the priest denied her burial in the churchyard.

"I know what I am doing," he avowed in a solid, steely voice.

"So ye say," allowed his king. "'Tis the rest of us who don't."

The rest of us, meaning him. The O'Fáil. The man who'd saved Finian's life and heart, and was now looking at him in deep disappointment. Could such things cross the border into regret?

The king got to his feet, in a royal enough way to bring the room to silence.

"This is your battle, Finian," he announced, looking around the room and meeting the eye of every uncle or cousin or other claimant to the throne—and there were multitudes of them, not just in this room, but scattered across northern Eire, full or half-blood descendants of the reigning king—before settling back on Finian.

"You lead the men. 'Tis what you've been trained for. Yours, to win or lose. I give it to you."

Finian got to his feet slowly. How many years had this been coming? And now the moment was to hand. Kings were not chosen solely by being the last one standing at the end of in-fighting or intrigue, but they were never chosen without it. Being handed battle command by the standing king settled the matter in a way councils never could.

Hot and cold, the cord that ran through Finian's core resonated at the words. Started so low, to have risen so high, and have his foster father and king's belief in him—it was a potent dénouement to a suicidal life. Finian reached out and clasped his king's fist. "*Onóir duit,* my lord."

"Nay, Finian. The honor to you. Win this war."

They laid their plans swiftly. Word was already being carried to the other Irish of the region by swift runners, female Irish couriers who could move between mountains without even the trees knowing they had passed. The disparate Irish armies would head to their traditional muster point for northern campaigns, a burned-out old abbey on a hill above Rardove Keep.

The room fell silent after the planning. Each man stared into the darkness, wondering if he would again see his family and friends, if he would be alive to watch summer come, or to reap the harvests in fall.

Finian sat with his head bent, the burden of the future weighing down his shoulders. The men began milling, heading for the door, talking as they went, slow and roundabout, like water eddying amid the rocks.

Senna. He would go to Senna, for just a moment.

Chapter 44

Sitting alone in the great hall, Senna listened to the unintelligible conversations swarming around her. The great hall was filled with people, the din of conversation almost deafening to her untrained ears. She was more accustomed to the wailing winds and pattering of rain against the windows, not the sounds of people talking. Laughing.

She leaned forward, chin in her hand. The content was lost on her, as it was in Irish, but she found herself enchanted by the strange, lyrical language. And she did not need to know the words themselves to know this was a gathering like those she used to witness when she left her empty manor and visited others on business. A night where kinsmen passed along tales of politics and gossip of family, accounts of happenings both great and small.

She'd always sat stock-still in her seat, trying to be as invisible as a bug. She never knew any of the people being spoken about, and none of the happenings were ever hers. No one spoke of her, ever. She'd been as alone in her homeland as she was here, where she didn't speak the tongue.

That was a disquieting realization.

Remaining motionless, she shifted her attention whenever necessary, attending whoever was talking the loudest, laughing the hardest, or had the most people standing about, smiling. Perhaps if she listened well, tried to attend, learned how they did it . . .

A woman sat down beside her.

"Mistress de Valery?"

The accent was so thick it took Senna a moment to understand her own name.

"I am Mugain," the beautiful woman said, tapping her chest lightly.

Senna smiled in reply. Her first lesson in being the sort of person who could hold a conversation that didn't involve ledgers or sheep barns.

"You are in Finian O'Melaghlin's company."

She nodded.

The Irish woman's eyes traveled over her appraisingly. "I know Finian."

A creeping chill slunk across Senna's chest like a nocturnal claw. "Indeed? I know little of him, and do welcome your words," she lied with a faint smile.

Mugain smiled back. Senna's heart dropped. Here was a prime specimen of an Irish butterfly. Dressed in a red-dyed gown, while Senna sat in dirt-caked leggings: Raven-haired and glossy, where Senna's knotted brown hair dragged by her dirty ears. Curving where Senna was unerringly straight.

"You would do well to stay in his company," the woman suggested. Her eyebrows lifted significantly.

Senna blushed. "'Tis not like that."

"Och, but it should be," she scolded, and leaned forward. "You trust me. I know: it *should* be."

Senna almost groaned in misery.

The Irishwoman lifted the ladle from a vessel on the table and poured a portion of meaty stew over the day-old bread that served as a trencher, while peering at Senna. "We will talk? I would like to get to know you."

"Indeed." She smiled weakly, and ate with a rapidly

diminishing appetite while Mugain fluttered at her side, each minute ticking by like an hour in the company of the suspiciously friendly Irish butterfly.

Half an hour later Lassar, the king's wife, approached the table. A wave of relief washed through Senna, and she almost tipped the bench getting to her feet. Lassar extended a hand and touched Senna's gently in greeting.

"A room has been prepared for you," the king's wife said softly. "And a bath."

A bath.

"A warm bath?" she asked without thinking. Warm water. Soap.

Lassar exchanged an amused glance with Mugain and nodded. "'Tis quite warm."

Senna bowed her head. "I am most indebted, my lady. When Finian returns . . . ?"

Lassar smiled faintly. "He knows where his room is."

"His room?"

"Where Lord Finian stays when he's to visit. He said to put you both there."

Her cheeks flamed. "I see."

Lassar smiled gently. "'Tis said you sprouted Lord Finian a pair of wings. For that, we are all indebted."

Senna's mouth was locked shut. This was awful and yet . . . what did she expect? And what did it matter in any event, her reputation? She had no life anymore. No home, no business, no lands, no coin, no relationships. She had nothing but Finian, who seemed to have everything, and need her not at all.

She studied the floor, knowing she was red-cheeked with embarrassment. But deeper than that was a chilling sort of disquiet. She was, at this moment, beholden.

A decade of her life spent ensuring she would never be indebted, never be needful, and here she was, full of nothing but need.

Food, shelter, safeguarding. Finian.

She brought nothing, could offer nothing, had nothing. *Certainly nothing,* she thought with a tired glance around the hall, *nothing Finian could not already find, in great, willing abundance.*

She was precisely what she'd spent her life endeavoring not to be: unwanted and beholden.

"Come," Mugain was saying and, gesturing for Senna to follow, began walking away.

"My thanks," Senna murmured to Lassar, touching her hand before following behind.

As they crossed the hall, she took malicious inventory of each seductive sway in Mugain's hips and sinking notice of the appreciative masculine glances that followed her across the room.

"Finian's room is in the tower," Mugain announced over her shoulder as they crossed the bailey to a doorway set within the battlement walls.

"Is it?" she snapped.

'Twas quite an extravagance to have a room set aside in a castle that must be bursting to the seams with householders, retainers, and servants, never knowing when that guest might visit again. But Finian could melt the heart of an icicle, and it was clear he held an especial place in the king's heart.

They climbed the curving, narrow staircase and entered a small room set in a turret of the battlement walls. It was a medium-sized room with closely-woven wicker walls, warmed by a fire in a brazier. A narrow wardrobe sat against a wall, and on its shelves was a richly dyed tumble of linen, dark red. Block gilt embroidery decorated one visible hem, a rich extravagance. A pair of polished leather boots stood at attention beside the shelves, leather laces running up the sides, awaiting their owner.

But most wonderful, the room boasted a low-slung bed piled high with coverlets and pillows, a soft haven of scented distraction. And a bath, just as Lassar had promised. A steaming, scented tub of water that almost brought tears to Senna's eyes.

"I will help you, Mistress de Valery."

She spun around. "No! I mean, nay, my thanks. I find myself weary," she stammered. Good heaven, the last thing she needed was Mugain watching her undress.

"You would like to rest," Mugain agreed amiably, with a glint in her eye.

"Aye. That's it. Rest."

"I will go, then. I will be busy." She winked conspiratorially.

Senna smiled in confusion. "With some secret, it looks like."

"A secret. A present."

"A gift? For whom?"

"For Finian O'Melaghlin."

Her smile faded. "I am sure he will like it."

"Och, he always does like my presents."

Senna stilled. "Really." Her lips froze in a glacial smile. Mugain dripped with hot honey as she returned it.

"Indeed, Mistress de Valery."

"Senna," she corrected vaguely.

"Lord Finian is fond of presents, Senna. I tell you this because once he and I were close, but are no longer."

"Indeed." She sniffed. "You tell me because you were close, or because you are no longer?"

"Both." The raven-haired vixen leaned closer. Her smile bespoke friendship, but her eyes held an unfriendly shine.

"I thank you, I think."

"Och"—Mugain leaned back with a flutter of her hand—"no need to thank. Finian will tell you all that he likes and dislikes." Her gaze grew closer. "You look so much like Bella."

"Bella?"

Mugain nodded and plucked at an invisible piece of dust on her bodice. "Bella."

"Bella." Senna echoed everything: the word, the inflection, the hinted seduction. The only thing missing were the claws.

"Bella was his woman for many long years. Years it has been though, and there have been others since. Strange it is, how they've all looked like her." Mugain smiled. "Excepting me, of course."

"Of course."

"You know his history, do you not?"

She shook her head wordlessly.

"Mayhap I ought not be the one . . ." She glanced around conspiratorially. "He works his way through women like a hot knife through butter, Mistress de Valery."

"Senna," she choked.

"But if you stay here, you will find that out soon, and 'tis wrong of me to speak of it." She leaned closer. "The women's looks when they saw Finian—you did see them?" Senna nodded dolefully: how could she have missed? "Once, many of them were on his arm, and do ache to be there again. Except me." Mugain smiled brightly. "Does he find you special names? Och," she went on, clucking at Senna's miserable, confirming nod. "Careful you, Senna de Valery. He is a good man, but a wolf with women."

Mugain got up and shook out her skirts. "Please you to tell Finian I've a present for him?"

Senna could not even look up, let alone nod. She stared at the place Mugain's eyes had been, her heart quivering in the bottom of her chest.

Chapter 45

Senna bathed, then, still damp, stood peering out the small slitted window when she spotted Finian coming across the bailey toward the tower.

When he entered the room, it was dusky with nighttime and candle glow. The scored candle on the tabletop showed it was somewhere between Vespers and Compline.

She turned and smiled. He did not.

In fact, he scowled, then stalked to the narrow wardrobe and pulled out the layers of dark red cloth. Likely one of the knee-length *léine* she'd seen the other men wearing. He glanced at the tub briefly, walked back to the door and wrenched it open, hollered for wine, then slammed it shut again. He turned and scowled at her. Again.

"Sit, Senna. Be at ease."

She did neither. He barely spared her a glance, just began stalking the room, a large male presence moving almost soundlessly between the shadows. After a while, the wine came, and he poured them each a cupful. He set his down without drinking.

Depositing himself on a bench, he reached for the pair of clean boots she'd seen earlier. His hair swayed beside his face, and he swept it back with an impatient, callused hand—so careless with something she loved so well.

How many nights would be like this, quiet moments spent watching Finian undress, knowing he would come soon and hold her in his arms? She could probably have dozens of them, mayhap hundreds, before he moved on to new conquests, if what Mugain had said was true. And she saw no reason to think otherwise.

To the contrary, everything Mugain said confirmed every unsettling suspicion in Senna's mind.

She picked up her wine cup. "I spent time with some people while you were in council, Finian."

He looked up sharply. "Were they good to ye?"

"Indeed. Lassar was most kind."

He seemed to relax and tugged off one of the old, scuffed boots he'd been wearing. "Aye. Lassar is the kindest sort of woman. I'm pleased ye passed some time with her."

Taking a sip to steady her nerves, she cleared her throat. "I spent time with many people, Finian, not just Lassar."

"Good."

"I met Mugain."

The earth-shaking news did not seem to effect any great change. He tugged the other boot off and stood.

"She said she has a present for you."

He grunted again and unbuckled his sword belt. Off it came, followed by various other blades, all tossed with careless skill onto the bench, until it glittered with steely, deadly things.

"She said you always like her presents."

His gaze finally flicked over. "The last gift Mugain gave me was when she was ten, and 'twas a cold shank of lamb in my bed one night."

Senna smiled but the chill in her chest did not warm. "She is fond of you, like many others. You are well loved."

"I grew up here, Senna." He tugged his tunic over his head.

His body was naked and perfect except for a few scars, whitened and puckered in various places across his ribs and belly. She hadn't seen them before; it had always been dark, or perhaps she'd been too distracted by the gleaming power of him. "The bonds from fosterage are ofttimes stronger than blood ties."

She dragged her gaze from the scars. "And now you are the king's advisor. How did that come to be?"

"I advised and he found it good." He reached for the clean boots.

She wrinkled her nose. "From a race of storytellers, that was poor indeed."

And finally, like a rainstorm that comes in the dog days of July, he laughed. One of those deep, carefree masculine rumbles that made her heart lift and sink all at once. He got to his feet and reached for her. She went. He swept up her hair in his hand and studied her as if he was seeing something new. Then, wordless, he cupped the side of her cheek and ran his face down her neck, *inhaling her.*

Something was wrong.

"Finian?"

He dropped her hair.

"Your council was troubling."

"The times are troubling," he replied, his voice so low she ducked closer to hear, but she almost stumbled, because he released her and stepped away, back to the bench, where he started pulling on the clean boots.

"Has this to do with Rardove, Finian?" she asked slowly.

He didn't answer.

"It does," she said fiercely. "In which case, it has to do with *me.*"

He looked up, but his eyes were unreadable, closed off. He may as well have been gone from the room. "It has nothing to do with ye."

"Finian, I can help. I can *do something*. What is happening? Tell me."

"I came only to make sure ye were settled," he replied gruffly. "Stay here in the room. Ye'll hear people going into the hall. There's a feast tonight, but I'd rather ye stay here."

"A feast—?"

"Lassar will see ye've got a pretty skirt or two, and clean things, and she'll look out for ye. We leave in the morning."

"Where are we going?"

"Not ye." Finian yanked on the other boot and rose. Swiftly he tugged on the dark red *léine* and belted it.

"Pardon?" she asked.

"We're going to war." He knew his speech was clipped and brusque, and it was the only way.

"Oh, no," he heard her whisper behind him.

"I leave first thing in the morn." He grated the words out, glanced at her briefly, then turned for the door. "I may not—. I will not see ye before I go."

"Oh."

That brought him swinging back around, shocked at the fury she'd conjured with such a simple word and all its complicated implications. "I am doing my duty, Senna." He had to smash the words out through his clenched jaw. "My duty. There is nothing else, do ye not see that? Have I not made that clear?"

She lifted her chin. "To the contrary, you've made several things abundantly clear. One, you are capable of great stupidity. Two—"

His jaw dropped.

"You have obviously been spoiled terribly, to have the arrogance to don clean clothes over that dirty body. Thirdly, you demonstrate a streak of stubbornness I had not—"

He started for the door. "Stay here."

He made it to the threshold before he felt her light touch on his arm. "Do not leave me in this manner."

It could have been a plea. But it wasn't. It was clear and fierce and bright and exactly what he wanted from her, and it made him turn, when what he ought to do was smash through the door and never stop going.

He had no choice. *Clear and fierce and bright* would get her killed. She would be noticed. Already the murmuring was beginning, that she'd started a war. Things could go badly. Quickly. So he met her gaze dead-on, cold and challenging, ignoring the urge to lose himself in her feminine strength.

"Listen to me, Senna," he said coldly. "Stay in the room. If it pleases ye more, I will try to see ye before I leave."

He pulled open the door but she appeared in front of him, blocking his path. He could plow her over, of course, but she was small and—God save him, was that a blade in her hand?

"Jesus, woman," he snarled, but he snarled it while frozen. The blade tip hovered just beneath his chin.

"Try to see me?" she echoed his words, rather coldly, he admitted. There was a glint in her eye that harkened to violence. Fortunately, much as she might throw a blade with skill, she was inexperienced with combat and far too furious to be effective. Or focused.

He snapped his hand up and clamped his fingers around her wrist, then yanked down. He gave a fierce shake and the knife broke loose, clattering to the floor. Still holding her wrist, he propelled her backward. When she hit the wall, he bent to her face.

"Do not ever raise a weapon to me."

"Do not ever abandon me." She was breathing fast, her face flushed, but her words came out slow and precise.

The wrist trapped in his grip was delicate—he could snap it with a twist—but she was staring at him with ferocity, and she seemed, as she always seemed to him, magnificent as the sun.

With a muted curse, he dropped her wrist and threaded his fingers violently through her long, damp tresses. His hands caught on knots, but he simply fisted them into handfuls and dragged them up, beside her jaw. He did not want to talk to her, answer her questions, feel anything at all. Senna's every fiber quivered for connection, and he did not want it. He was going to war. All he could manage of Senna de Valery right now was her body.

But that—that he suddenly needed with a desperation he'd never known before.

Before she could utter another maddening word, he plowed her mouth open beneath a kiss and backed her up to the low bedstead. She sat down hard on the mattress. Standing before her, he pushed her legs apart with a knee and stood between them, shoving aside the robe covering her damp body. She already had one hand on his head, pulling him down to her. He bent his hips, but remained standing. She scraped her other hand up his chest, her tongue hot in his mouth as soon as he was close enough. They were like mad things, touching each other, each feel of skin wanted and insufficient, left behind as they reached for the next.

He clamped her hips and dragged her to the edge of the bed, sliding her naked body over the furs, stretched out like a gift—a river of damp hair across the furs, her slightly rounded abdomen, long, muscular legs, and the tangle of reddish blond curls between her legs. He dragged a single callused fingertip between her breasts, down her belly, to the curls, raising throaty whimpers.

She flung herself up and impatiently fumbled with the folds of his *léine,* fingers trembling. He watched, motionless, letting her fumble with the unfamiliar layers, then he loosed the belt and stepped between her thighs. He cupped her cheek and pushed her back to lie flat on the bed, while he stood before her.

"Raise yer knees," he ordered.

She lifted one, but before she could get it fully bent, he had his palm under it, pulling up. Her chest fluttered in unsteady panting as she tried to reach around to the curve of his buttocks to pull him forward. He bent enough to plant his free hand onto the mattress beside her head. Eyes locked, he entered her in one slow, relentless thrust. Her lips parted in a low keen.

No more questions, no more wondering on the future or the meaning of things. There was only this one perfect moment, where she would mouth his name and let him rule her. He rocked his hips forward in long, relentless thrusts. She met each one with furious abandon, her mouth open, her eyes locked on his, every shadow of her lit for him.

Her surrender came on every level, and a wave of respect corded with guilt rose inside him. She had given herself over completely to this thing with him. It felt as if he were being drowned in her; there was no breath that was not Senna-filled. She was his, to do with as he would.

He plunged again, feeling her hot, throbbing passage constrict around him. "'Tis good," he muttered against her swollen lips. *His.*

He straightened and reached for her other knee, holding it as he did the first. Standing between her thighs, her knees dangling from his upturned palms, he threw back his head and closed his eyes, centering on the feeling of being deep inside her, of loving her without words. His penetrations became rocking, furious, powerful thrusts, and she stopped even trying to meet him at the crest. She took each one with a deep-throated moan of pleasure, eyes pressed shut, neck arched, arms stretched on the bed above her head, twisting through the furs.

The muscles of his neck and arms strained, each sinewy fiber outlined and bulging as he pounded fiercely into her wet heat, hips against hips, a groan for each mewling cry, as he drove her riotously into a savage, unbridled climax.

It came quickly. She staggered over the edge and fell headlong into her shuddering orgasm, crying his name. Finian roared as he found his own cliff and tipped over it, into her, kissing her, losing himself in this brave, unexpected woman.

There was nothing he was more afraid of. Weakness followed directly from this sort of thing.

They disentangled their sweaty bodies far enough for him to fall on the mattress beside her. She smiled tiredly, but the look in her eyes closed his. He rolled onto his back and stared up at the smoke-blackened beams bisecting the ceiling.

Senna wielded some warped, shining notion about him as a man, what he was capable of, and she believed in it the way others believed in God or the power of rain. That would never do. He was built to lead his people, then self-destruct.

There was still time to make her understand there was nothing else inside him, nothing at all.

He pushed away the furs and propped himself on an elbow, then ran the back of his knuckles down her cheek in one gentle stroke.

"Ye oughn't to ever have let me touch ye, Senna," he said quietly. "I'll ruin ye."

She rolled toward his soft, warning words. "No."

"There's naught to be done, lass," he said and, pressing a kiss to her forehead, rolled off the bed and threw on his *léine.*

"Finian—!"

"No more, Senna. I haven't any more." She'd begun to rise, but stilled at his words. Her face looked shocked. Not even to sadness yet. He turned away. "Stay here in the room."

He turned, grabbed his weapons, and swung out of the room.

Loud shouts erupted in the bailey. Finian paused, then clattered down the stairs and flung open the door just as a page appeared at the bottom of the tower, looking up, hands cupping his mouth, his face flushed red with exertion.

"A runner," he shouted. "A runner has come! The king wants his council. Now!"

The cry was echoed through every corner of the bailey.

Boots thumped and buckles clanged as men everywhere swung away from whatever task they were engaged in and made for the keep. Finian stood frozen for half a second, then swung inside and launched himself up the stairs, four at a time. He flung the chamber door open.

Senna, half-draped in furs at the window, spun, her eyes wide, her face washed white.

"Do as I said, lass," he ordered swiftly. "Stay in the room, lock the door. And *keep yer blade to hand*."

Then he was gone, striding out of the chamber without looking back. Something cold folded over Senna's collarbone and shoulders like a frozen cape.

Two things warred for her attention. The realization that Finian might have just admitted he would fail her. And the certainty that he was afraid. *For* her.

Balffe drew rein. The line of soldiers beside him halted in unison. It had been hours since the sun had set, but Balffe had pressed on despite the darkness and cold. A hunter in these regions for nigh on thirty years, Balffe knew the Irish well. Knew O'Melaghlin well.

Of course O'Melaghlin would come here, dragging the de Valery whore behind. Straight to The O'Fáil, the man who'd first dragged O'Melaghlin out of the muck years ago, when his whore of a mother killed herself.

Which is why he wasn't entirely at ease, riding ever closer to the Irish keep. Finian O'Melaghlin was in there, but he would come out, too, and when he did, it would be at the head of an army. An army that might be poorly equipped, but would be outfitted with a commander who possessed the keenest leadership abilities and the most impressive warrior skills known in the Irish marches.

Balffe was all too aware of these particulars. He had come out on the losing side of too many encounters over the years to underestimate either the Irishman's intentions or his abilities.

Aye, O'Melaghlin would come out, he decided with a quick righting of his codpiece. And Balffe would be waiting.

No one escaped a castle of which he was guard, at least not without sacrificing a few vital body parts as payment. Certainly not the Irish dog who had debased Balffe's very own sister some ten years earlier with his contaminated charm. My, yes, their history went back some, and O'Melaghlin would die with a slow twist of a knife plunged in his chest.

Balffe would see to it himself.

But first, he would take Senna de Valery, more witch than woman, back to Rardove with a malicious pleasure.

And if she caused him any trouble, *any at all,* she would be pitifully sorry. As would anyone close enough to hear him extract her useless screams for mercy.

Chapter 46

The men stood in the king's chamber just as the runner stumbled in, sweaty and harried. It was half a minute before they could get the news out of her. During that time the men stood, the silence dense. She clutched her side, doubled in half and panting.

"The king's governor of all Ireland is marching north with a massive hosting." She gasped for another breath.

"Wogan?" The shocked murmur swept through the room. The justiciar? The governor of all of Ireland? The hand-picked servant of Edward, Hammer of the Scots and bleeder of the Irish, was marching north?

"They must be over four thousand strong."

Someone cursed. It seemed to come from far away. Finian said hoarsely, "How long until they get here?"

"Two days, mayhap half of another."

Two days to muster as many divergent, loosely allied Irish and any loyal English they could to their cause. A cause which was looking more bleak as news of the English arrayed against them grew. Not only Rardove and his vassals. Now 'twas the governor of the isle, King Edward's lieutenant, John Wogan.

And that about does it, thought Finian.

"There's more," panted the messenger, folding to her knees. "The Saxon king is coming, too. His muster is in Wales, waiting for a good wind. When they get it, Edward Longshanks will march on Ireland."

The room dropped into shocked silence. Everyone turned to Finian, who was staring at the far wall. He could feel every ponderous beat of his heart as it slowed, as his body closed in on itself, as everything went cold.

"Leave us," he heard The O'Fáil say.

The room cleared of men until it was only Finian and the king, who stood staring at him with sad eyes.

A clamor outside the window made Senna start, drew her out of her simmering reverie. The hem of the dark blue undertunic Lassar had given her picked up stray bits of rushes as she walked to the slitted window and leaned her elbows on the knobbly ledge.

People were laughing and exchanging friendly insults as they darted across the bailey from one doorway to another, dashing to and fro, readying themselves for the evening entertainment. New people meant new ideas, new conversations, new stories, new dalliances, most of all. And that the fine-looking, charismatic Finian O'Melaghlin was one of them was almost too thrilling to imagine.

Better than stories, Finian himself, in all his glorious flesh, was to be there, to flirt and entertain.

My, how did they bear it? she thought acidly.

Down in the bailey, someone pulled open the door to the main keep. Yellow light and laughter spilled out into the chilled blue twilight.

"Come see Finian!" someone shouted, laughing. "He's already here!"

People scurried in and the door slammed shut.

Come see Finian, indeed.

He'd come to see *her,* when the mood had moved him. But Senna was simply not capable of sitting like a rocking horse in the room, for Finian to come and ride when the mood spurred him. And this *I'll ruin you* notion of his, that was madness. He was simply not capable of ruining her, nor, for that matter, protecting her. These things had already been done, by Senna herself.

This matter between them had nothing to do with ruination or fortifications. It concerned something else entirely. And 'twas time for him to acknowledge it, before he left her behind, lying to himself as he broke her heart.

Then, by the window, she heard the others. Small groups of men, talking, murmuring among themselves, like the buzzing of bees. Or a stampede from far away. She tipped her head out the window and listened hard. They were talking about war.

They were talking about her.

She pulled her head back inside, threw on a yellow overtunic, flung a cape over her shoulders and marched down to the hall.

She did, though, do one thing Finian had bid. She kept her blade close.

"I'll not return her," Finian kept repeating, after the other men had left. Each time he repeated it, his heart sank further. Until finally the king nodded grimly.

"So you love her."

Finian threw up his hands. "Why does everyone keep saying that?"

The king lifted his shaggy brows. "Because you're willing to take us to war for her."

Finian stared, unwilling to repeat, yet again, that this war had been coming for some long time. He said only, "She saved my life. I'm not sending her back."

"She's distracting you. Weakening you."

Like your father.

Which was exactly his deepest fear. The O'Fáil didn't say the words, but he didn't need to. They reverberated in the air between them, like waves of heat.

"I've never been distracted before," he replied in a low voice, packed with fury.

"You've never run out on us before, either."

"I'm not running out on ye!" But he didn't meet his foster father's eye. "I'm *right here.*"

The O'Fáil looked at him for a long time. "Is there something you're not telling me?"

Finian took a deep breath. The king waited, he waited, and they stared at each other through the ensuing silence. Yes, Finian realized. Disappointment could pass into the territory of regret. At this very moment, his foster father was crossing the border.

"The reason ye cannot send her back," Finian said, hearing his own voice coming in from far away, "is because she's a dye-witch."

The king didn't say anything for a very long while. It gave time for the wrenching pain to twist around Finian's heart like a steel wire. Och, if this was loyalty, it was a hurtful thing.

The king ran his hand across his beard a few times, then over his knee. "I thought she looked familiar."

Finian looked up sharply. "My lord?"

"I suppose you were wise to not mention it earlier," The O'Fáil went on in a musing tone.

Finian felt the bite of impatience. Enough of intrigue. "And why was such a thing wise?"

"Because men have a way of going mad when dye-witches come around."

Finian nodded curtly. He hadn't held his tongue out of wisdom, seeking only a private moment with his king. He'd done it for very different reasons indeed. Ones he barely understood. If he'd been protecting something vulnerable, a creature weaker than himself, he could grasp the meaning of his silence, an action of near treason, certainly disloyal. But what he felt was nothing like that. Nothing at all. Protection, aye. But of an entirely different sort. And he had never felt it before.

He did not like it. It made him . . . weak. Just as his king had said.

The O'Fáil studied him, lips pursed. Then he ran his palm across the smooth tabletop. "Did you know Rardove had himself another dye-witch, decades ago? I saw her once."

Finian felt cold. "I did not know that."

"Aye, he did." The king stopped making palm circles on the table. "She looked an awful lot like the lass you brought to me."

The coldness went deep, into his bones. He hadn't brought Senna to the king. But she was his now.

And yet, just now, another matter wanted his attention . . . Senna's mother had been a dye-witch *for Rardove?* How much worse was this going to get?

"She died," the king went on, "trying to escape. Nineteen years ago."

Finian nodded silently as he leaned forward, elbows on his knees. He stared at the rushes on the ground. He could hear the people in the hall below, the loud buzz of their conversations coming up the stairs. Someone said something about Rardove, and there was a chorus of male shouts. He heard someone say "the Englishwoman."

"Bring her to me," the king said quietly.

A low fire was all that burned in the trough at the center of the hall at this late hour, but Senna's eyes were well adjusted to the dim light. She'd been waiting for a long time. Seen the men tromp through the hall to a guarded office chamber.

Seen them come out again. Waited while some came in to make their beds on the floor.

Now the hall was a huddled mass of sleeping male bodies, snoring and farting, scattered across the benches and rush-covered floor. A few men sat on a far bench beside the fire, talking in low tones, but otherwise the castle seemed to sleep. She couldn't stand in this corner all night, and was finally ready to admit defeat and leave, when the masculine voices by the fire rose in slightly slurred tones, just enough to be heard.

Light from the dying flames did not shine far, and while the fireside conversants were cast in flickering shadows, the rest of the hall was drenched in darkness.

Senna paused, her cheek by the wall.

"Och, and 'tis only the whole English army he's bringing down on us, it is."

"Ye're right. But I'll be glad of a reason to wield a sword well enough, whatever the cause."

"And this thing with Rardove has been going on a fine long time. O'Melaghlin says the Englishwoman has nothing to do with it."

"Naught to do with it, and naught to do with him, that's what he says all right," complained a younger, higher-pitched voice. "But still, we've an army marching for us sure as anything, and 'tis because *she's* here."

"Ye're right," agreed an older voice. "Maybe she t'ain't the reason, but she's sure enow the cause."

"Naught to worry on," said another voice. "O'Melaghlin loves the ladies, but he'll not endanger our lives and lands over one. They're for bedding, not politickin', and he knows that as well as anyone."

"Better."

"Still," said the young one, his voice a dark, drunken snarl. "We should go teach her what we think of women who start wars."

He rose unsteadily and tripped over his feet. The small group broke into predatory snickers and yanked him to his feet.

Senna backed up through the darkness, her hand at her chest. She waited until they were gone, then crept through the darkness, out of the hall, her heart and blood pounding. She staggered into the bailey and the autumn night.

She didn't belong here. They didn't want her.

The thought was so familiar it almost had taste. Metal, cold, rusty.

Now what?

She turned and slammed directly into Finian's chest.

Chapter 47

"What are ye about, Senna?"

She kicked herself backward, but he already had a hand on her arm, and stopped her completely.

He was frowning. Burnished black hair hung unfettered over his shoulders, one small braid dangling near his eye. Beneath the layered maroon *léine,* his powerful legs, covered with dark hair, disappeared into high boots. His wrap was belted at the waist, and a blade dangled at his side.

"I told ye to stay in the room. 'Tisn't safe out here."

She gave a wild laugh. "No. Not by half."

She yanked on her arm. He held firm, in fact pulled her a few inches closer to his body. Frantic and suddenly on the edge of panic, she wrestled, her right hand going instinctively for the blade strapped to her waist. He knew her that well, though, and before her fingers could touch her skirts, he had gripped her and spun her around so her back was to him. He folded her wrists together in one of his hands, and put his other palm behind the back of her now thrashing head.

"What the hell is going on, Senna?" He spoke directly into her ear.

She stopped thrashing. "Ah, so we both have the same question," she replied, keeping her voice low. Finian stood behind, warm and solid, listening. "You tell me nothing of what is afoot. You bring me here to this castle—for what purpose I know not—and your people are not glad to see me. I know a war is brewing, but can only guess at the whys, as you do little but bid me stay in the room. And take me on the bed." He stiffened, but she kept on.

"Then I hear men talking, about how I brought this war to their shores. *I* did this? You say it has naught to do with me, but of course it does. So I wonder, why would a wool deal matter so much?" She felt him breathing slowly by her ear. "It doesn't, of course. It did not matter to Rardove, and it does not matter to the Irish. 'Twas always the Wishmés." She didn't bother to ask if she was correct.

"So tell me, Finian: what is it about a mollusk that makes for a war?"

His breathing stayed rhythmic by her ear. He didn't reply, so she did.

"I do not know the whys or the hows, but this war is over the Wishmés, and that means over me. You see how it all comes together, neat as a weave? I am nothing but trouble, so I shall leave."

"No."

"You may fight your war over something else."

"'Tis far past that, Senna."

She tugged on her arm. "Let. Me. Go."

He looked down, as if surprised to see he was still holding her, then opened his fingers. She pulled free and turned to him. He'd shaved again at some point while he was not with her, so only a dusting now darkened his jawline. His eyes were shadowed and narrowed.

"They said they were coming to get me," she said in a calm voice, "to teach me a lesson about women who start wars. I know what they meant to do. My husband taught me that much." She lifted her chin a little farther. "So much alike, the men of Ireland and England. I had almost begun to suspect otherwise."

If the jab hit home, she did not know, because he grabbed her by the shoulders. *"Who tried to hurt you?"* he demanded in a voice devoid of anything but cold, honed fury.

She stared at the menacing transformation, then shook her head, sending hair tumbling over her shoulders. "I do not know. I do not care. They do not matter." She didn't say *only you matter,* but surely these things were clear. "I will not stay here and wait for such things, Finian."

Did he suspect what she would not wait for? That never again would she wait to be rejected, every sunrise additional proof of the never-ending rejection?

No more. Never again. Not her mother, not her father, and certainly not Finian. What she'd had with him was the only thing of real value in her life. If she let him abandon her, it would all be sullied, and nothing good could come out of those ashes. She would rather die.

But she had no intention of doing that.

She was going to build a business, if she had to swim back to England herself. She knew wool, and she knew how to survive. One could not ask for more than that.

But of course Finian understood all the implications of her words. She could see it mirrored in the pain in his eyes. He started to slide his hands from her shoulders to her face.

"Tell me what is happening, Finian. Or I will leave."

He paused. "I will not let ye."

She gave a bitter smile. "You would not be here to stop me, would you?"

"I'd put a guard on ye."

"I'd throw a knife in him."

He blew out an irritated breath and dropped his hands. "I told ye, Senna, the whole affair is a dirty river. Do not dip in."

She leaned close and said fiercely, "I was dipped on the day I was born, Finian. Do not think you can rescue me. But I can help you. In truth, I may be the only one who can. So tell me, what is it? Rardove wants the dyes, and the Irish want the dyes? Do they matter so much? So be it. I will make them."

She said it swiftly, plunging into the decision the way one plunges off a cliff; you'd seen it coming from a mile off, but in the end, you simply tipped over.

This time he did make it all the way to her face, cupped it between his palms and dragged her up onto her toes. "Ye would do that?"

"I would. I will. I will try, at the least."

"Why?"

She gave a sad smile. "You do not know?"

Their faces were inches apart, his eyes filled with fury. "Och, lass, why did you have to need me so much?" he muttered in a low growl, then forced her mouth open with a blistering, hot, hungry, angry kiss. Just as swiftly, he broke it off and dropped her back to her feet.

"I told ye men were fools, Senna."

The masculine rasp came by her ear. "I did not think you meant *you,*" she whispered brokenly.

"Och, I am the worst sort of all, *a rúin.* I look good."

He disentangled his fingers and everything was cold where he'd been touching her, even the strands of her hair. The back of her head felt as if a door had swung open, and everything dark and nighttime swooped in.

"'Tis time, Senna."

"Time for what?" she said dully.

Above his shoulder, the moon had risen above the squat round tower in the background, cut black against the sapphire sky. "To answer yer questions. And see the king."

"The king? Why?"

"The Wishmés." Whatever was going on inside him was unreadable through his eyes. They were as magnificent and remote as a mountaintop.

"You told him. You did not wait for my consent."

"It was that or have him send ye back to Rardove."

She looked at him for a long minute. Her fingertips were cold. "You knew I would, didn't you?" she said flatly. "You knew, in the end, I would make the Wishmés for you."

He turned away. "I knew nothing."

"No? Well, you know now."

Chapter 48

Finian escorted her to the king, not looking back to see if she followed. He could hear her well enough, and he couldn't show her his eyes just now or else the thin screen of control he'd erected by dint of controlled fury would be kicked to the ground, and he'd be naked before her, his every yearning and shame exposed.

He showed her to the king's bedchamber, which, like most bedchambers, doubled as an office. The antechamber held a fireplace, a cistern, a small table, and a few low benches. Finian invited her to sit, which she declined, invited her to eat, which she declined, and offered drink, which she vehemently declined.

"Whisky?" Finian suggested, trying to offer something that would alleviate a bit of the furious hurt in her eyes. Or perhaps lessen the blows to come.

She aimed him a withering look. "I think not."

"'Twill go easier . . ." He didn't finish. Senna did not take lesser blows. She stood straight, with that tilt of her chin, and got punched back by the waves of the world. And every time, she stood up again. Senna would not appreciate a 'lessening.' He could not change that. He did not want to.

The king was sitting back, watching their charged interchange. Abruptly, he leaned forward. "Why do you not sit with me, lass?"

She angled her chin up, lifted her skirts and sat. Finian shook his head.

"How much do you know about the Wishmés, Mistress Senna?"

"Nothing a'tall. As I told *Lord Finian.* And Rardove." She folded her hands primly on the table in front of her. She looked as prim as an iridescent dragonfly. "No one seems to believe me."

"I believe you," Finian gruffed. The king lifted an eyebrow and he subsided. He propped his shoulder on the wall and crossed his arms over his chest. Senna glared at him.

The king handed the dye manual to Finian. Senna was glowering directly into his eyes though, boring into them with silent fury, so she didn't witness the transfer.

"You wouldn't be able to decipher this, then, would you, lass?" the king prompted.

It took her a while to drag her enmity from Finian's eyes. The king pointed to the manual. She saw the pages and visibly started. She got to her feet in shock.

"Why, that is my mother's." Finian let the pages go when she reached for them. "Where did you get this? 'Tis Mama's."

"I know," he said thickly.

She looked up at him, her face pale amid her dark flaming hair. "You know? Where did you get it?"

"From my conduit. Red."

If possible, she looked even more stunned. Her free hand swung out slowly, as if it were moving through water, until it made contact with the table behind her.

"Red?" she whispered. "But . . . that's my father."

"He was a spy," Finian explained.

They were standing, he by the wall, Senna by the table,

where she'd been when the realizations hit her. The king had left them alone. The room was small, but warm. That is all Senna was certain she knew in the whole world, except that Finian was holding her gaze and not letting go.

"Your father was an Englishman," he said in that solid, earthy voice, slowing her down, pulling her back when her body was ready to float away, "but also a spy against King Edward and his ambitions. And," he added, "I suspect your mother was, too."

"Spies," she whispered, unable to acclimate to this knowledge in a normal tone of voice. This required whispers, like all secrets do. "I don't understand."

But she did. Some small, young part of herself understood exactly what he meant. Too many nights trying not to listen to arguments that didn't sound like debtors' arguments. Too many explanations that never came. Too many Scotsmen.

"My mother was Scottish," she said, as if that would explain . . . what? "Her mother—my grandmother—was sent to marry an Englishman. The family had just enough noble blood to be commanded about suchly. But my mother always called on Scottish saints to reprimand me, and claimed Scotland as her own. And my father—" Her voice broke. "My father always said, 'As falls Elisabeth, so fall I.'"

Her eyes filled with tears. Finian's face shimmered through them. "Why did they not tell me?"

He watched her for a long minute before speaking, and while she waited, her heart slowed. She felt calmer. "Perhaps they didn't want you to get caught up in it," he finally suggested. "Get hurt by it."

"Oh," she said sadly, "I do think that has already occurred."

"Yer mam is dead, Senna."

"I assumed as much," she said with as much cold dignity as she could wrap around her. No tears. Not for being left, never again. "Twenty years have passed. 'Tis quite reasonable to assume she might have—"

"She died trying to escape."

She looked away. Angled her eyes so they regarded the one part of the floor uncovered by rushes, underneath the king's chair, where he'd kicked them away. The stone looked cold.

"Escape from where?"

"From Rardove."

She wobbled. Her knees went weak. A dull thrumming started in her head. She started sliding down the wall. Her spine bumped over the uneven rocks. "No. Not Rardove."

"Aye. Rardove." He pulled her to her feet, brushed her bottom off for her, and sat her on a bench. "And now, mayhap because of what your mother and father did, the king of England is marching for Ireland."

She looked up, startled. "King Edward? Marching here?"

"Aye."

"That's *madness,*" she spat, for some reason furious. "Cannot one war be enough for him?"

"Not when those are at stake." Finian indicated the manual. "The secret of the Wishmés. Look."

She shook her head.

"Senna, this ye can't avoid simply because ye do not wish it to be."

She shook her head again, but Finian touched her chin and stopped the movement. He held out the book.

"Look."

Chapter 49

She took the book.

It looked just like the drawings on the sheaves she'd received from an unknown Scottish uncle on her fifteenth birthday, on the occasion of her betrothal.

And then, of course, she'd seen the book itself once, too, in her father's hand, as he hurried down the stairs one night to join the arguing men.

She turned the pages slowly, recognizing her mother's familiar hand in both the letters and the sketchings. She turned the pages slowly, then faster and faster. A shiver skimmed over her. The pictures were highly erotic. The formulas, the measurements and alignments, were remarkable. The computations vaguely terrifying.

She forced herself to look up. "What is this?" It was a flat query, like her heart felt right now. Stomped on and flattened.

"That is the secret of the Wishmés. They are weapons. They explode."

"Oh, dear God." Slowly realizations settled down on her, like rings on a tree, aging her. "No. My mother did not make weapons."

Finian was relentless though, pushing past her denial. "She

did. She rediscovered the ancient formulas and then she wrote them down. And she did this, too."

He handed her a child's tunic. Her fingers slid over it, touching what she could hardly see. It shimmered and almost flickered in his hand. Her heart was hammering in her chest and she had no idea why. "What is that?"

"Perfect camouflage."

"God save us," she whispered, touching it. "How?"

"With a certain dye. In a certain weave. On a certain wool."

Her fingers started shaking. "On *my* wool."

"Aye. Yours. Yer mother started the strain, did she not?"

She shook her head and found she couldn't stop. She just kept shaking it, back and forth. "No. She would not do that. My mother would not make weapons—"

"The explosions the Wishmés produce can bring down a castle, Senna. And that?" He gestured to the fabric. "With that, ye could get *inside* any castle. Anytime, anywhere. Anyone."

She stared at the tunic, then briefly touched the edge. "It looks like a child's tunic," she said dully.

Finian crouched in front of her and rested his fingertips on the top of her knee, a light, steady touch. "I thought the same. 'Twas for a little girl." He closed his fingers around her hand. "Would keep her safe as anything."

"Oh," she whispered with a watery laugh. "I suspect her coming home might have done that better." She swallowed and shifted on the small bench. "And Sir Gera—my father?"

"I knew him as Red."

She looked at him bleakly. "So did we."

The rushes under her feet were crunchy. The weight of Finian's hand on her knee was warm and comforting. "Red is the name he used to call my mother. Mama's red hair," she said, and like that, she was swept up by a vivid memory of her parents, so that every sense was awakened.

They'd been swimming in the pond at twilight, when Senna,

four years old, was supposed to be abed. Father sitting on the bank, leaning back on his palms, murmuring something. Her mother smiling and lazily making her way over to him, one pale, graceful arm stretched out in the green water, her long red hair streaming out behind. The world had smelled like roses and moss that night as Senna tiptoed out the back gate, and the white moon rose through the willow tree.

She took a deep breath and let the memory go. It floated away. She was back in a strange room, a hard bench beneath her, Finian's watchful, guarding gaze on her.

He prompted her gently. "Ye said he used to call yer mother Red."

She nodded. "It became a joke, to call Father that instead. All the Scottish uncles and Mama did so. Father, with his dark locks. What happened to him?" she asked abruptly.

He sat back on his heels, still crouched before her. "Ah, lass. He died."

She nodded. Of course he'd died. He'd lived a dangerous life, not of dissolution or excess, as she'd thought, but of intrigue and valiant causes, and heartbreak. He was committed to stopping Edward from subsuming his wife's homeland by simply opening his royal mouth and swallowing. Her father had been committed and in love, even after Mama was dead.

"My parents loved each other," she said dully. All this time, thinking her mother had abandoned them. Had not loved her father. What a shame.

"He wasn't alone, Senna," Finian said, and his quietly spoken words broke through the ether of her memories. "I was with him at the end."

Of course Finian was with him. Of course he had stayed. "That is good to know," she said, hearing the unfamiliar catch in her words.

"He spoke of ye, Senna. The last thing he said was about ye. Told me to keep ye safe. Protect ye above all else."

She bit her lower lip. And what was she to do with that? It

was probably sooth. Why would he want her hurt? He had loved her in his own way, she was certain. But what her parents had had, she now realized, encompassed only them.

After her mother's death, that devotion had gripped her father like an eagle on a fish, with great, curving talons, piercing any attention that wished to wander from this one screaming fact: his wife had been killed.

Of course, she'd been more than wife. Or more than solely a wife. She'd been compatriot, inspiration, spy-lover. How could a child compete with that?

And the one left behind could, she supposed dully, spend the next decades of his life pretending to be something else, letting vengeance and intrigue hold sway, while small children fell off the edge of his particular map, nothing more than sea monsters, while his dead wife, his Jerusalem, was inked at the center of it all.

And how did the sea monsters then decide to care?

"Finian?" she said thickly.

He was still crouched before her, watching her face and waiting. His forearms leaned against the edge of the bench, his palms lightly grasping her hips. One thumb stroked slowly, probably without him even realizing.

"Thank you for not letting my father die alone."

"Ye're welcome, lass."

And that released the tears. She leaned forward until her forehead touched his, trying to make the hard bones of him steady her spinning head. Dimly, she heard the door open, then a set of footsteps draw to a halt, but Finian did not move away. His touch helped, but it didn't shut down the waterfall of emotions. And with the cascade of tears came images from her mother's book. They flashed and tumbled through her mind.

As the fragments spun through her thoughts, rotating into position and sinking into her memory, she realized something wasn't right. Or rather, wasn't complete.

She pushed back from Finian. "Let me see that manual."

He handed it over. She flipped through it, to the end. Then back a few pages, then slowly again, forward to the end.

"What is it?" Finian asked, a note of urgency in his voice tamped down but still audible. "What is wrong?"

She looked up. "This is missing pages."

"How do ye know?"

She held it out. "See, here. 'Tis torn."

He ran his thick thumb over the faint, worn edge of a softly torn page.

"How much would that matter?" the king asked from the doorway.

She got to her feet and walked over. She flipped to the end and held the manual open between them. "See these numbers? And this grouping of words and symbols? They are ingredients."

The king looked at her, then Finian. "I thought you said you knew nothing of dyeing."

She heard Finian get to his feet. She gave a small shrug. "'Tis true. I've no notion how I know such a thing. I simply . . . know."

"'Tis in the blood, legend says."

Senna sighed deeply. "I am terribly tired of legends and things of the past. I do not know how I know these things. I simply do. And I can assure you the instructions on this page end too abruptly. There are more pages, and they are missing. And the *computare* for this"—she pointed to the shimmering tunic on the bench—"are on those missing pages."

Finian drew a sharp breath. The king looked at him, then the fur on the sleeves of the king's robe brushed against her arm as he turned to Finian.

"Anyone could have them," the king said. He started out the door, although Finian did not move. "But it must be someone Red knew well. Assemble a small group of experienced men, Finian, men who know how to keep their heads down and their ears open. We have another contact who might have heard—"

"I know where they are," Senna said in a clear voice. She felt like a bell ringing Prime. "I know where the missing pages are."

The king turned back in shock.

"Where?" Finian asked in a terrible, hollow voice.

"Rardove Keep."

Finian closed his eyes. Senna stared at the wall.

The king said simply, "We have to get them back."

Chapter 50

It was quiet in the chamber for a long time. Then, as if invisible words had formed in the air and drifted into Finian's ears alone, he turned and pinned the king in his sights.

"Nay."

The O'Fáil didn't shift his gaze away from Senna. Finian stepped directly into his line of sight. "No."

The king looked at him then.

"She's not going back there," Finian said curtly.

"She will buy us time."

"She has been used by too many people to buy off too many things."

"You don't see it, do you?" The O'Fáil said, the level tone of his words underscoring their seriousness. "First Scotland, then Ireland will fall to Edward, deeper and further, until they will never get out, not for a thousand years. If the Saxon king can get his men into any castle he wishes, unseen? If he can create small explosions in the bedchambers of any nobleman who opposes him?" The king's words slowed. "Edward cannot be given such power as the Wishmés, Finian. He must be stopped."

"So be it. I'll kill him."

The O'Fáil gave a bark of laughter. "If they have the recipe, you'd have to kill every king to come after as well, son. And in any event, you couldn't get within a league of Longshanks, not with you being the one who stole his dye-witch. You'll be killed on sight."

Senna lifted her head and the king glanced over. She looked away, picked up a piece of straw, and began knotting it, little knots up its length. The moon was rising higher. The rounded edge of it slid into view through the narrow window.

"Ye will not be sending her back," Finian repeated flatly.

The king studied Senna's profile. "No," he agreed slowly, looking back to Finian. "'Tisn't the sort of thing you do *to* a soul. They've to choose it themselves."

"Good." Finian stared at the king hard, his words slowing to the pace of the dripping water in the cistern. "We are in agreement. She stays."

The king lifted his eyebrows. "I'll not send her anywhere."

Finian nodded and turned. "Ye're not to worry, lass. Ye're not going back."

"Of course I'm not," she said agreeably.

He paused. "'Tis too dangerous."

"Of course it is."

His eyes narrowed.

"What could the lass do, anyhow?" the king interjected. His words were flat, his question was flat, his face was flat. Expressionless.

He wanted her to explain to Finian *exactly* what she could do.

"Just so, my lord," she said brightly. "There's little I can do. Except for the middling matter that I know where the missing pages were left. I could retrieve them."

"Or, we could burn his castle down," Finian suggested amiably. "As we were going to do anyhow. And that will take care of the missing pages."

"Very true. Unless, of course, Rardove has found them, and perhaps hid them away, in which case, I would have the best chance of finding them." Finian stared at her. "Alternately,

I could stall for time, let him believe I will make the dyes for him. He would give me the missing pages to do so, and then I could destroy them or bring them to you."

"Destroy them," the king said curtly.

"That is not yer duty," Finian said tightly.

She gave him a sad smile. "No, 'tisn't. Not a matter of duty."

He took a step toward her. She was certain it was intended to intimidate, to quash opposition. "We were going to fight this war before ye came, Senna. It has nothing to do with ye."

She nodded. "Just so. You are right."

He took another step closer. She put her palm on his chest and said in a highly aggrieved tone, "Becalm yourself, Finian. I say you are right."

They stared at each other until she coughed a little. Then a little more. She held her fingertips to her throat and coughed again, apologetically. "Might I have a drink?" *Cough, cough.* "In fact, I think perhaps a bit of that whisky now?"

He stared at her a moment longer, then turned on his heel, looking at the king briefly but significantly on his way by. "I'll be back."

He strode out, calling for a servant. She and The O'Fáil waited a minute, then the king turned to her.

"Do you know how kings are made in Ireland, lass?"

"Stop." She got to her feet. "I shall go. But not to make him a king."

The king rose, too, and they walked swiftly out of the office chamber. "You think you can locate the pages?"

"Aye." Her words sounded dusty and dull, but her heart, buffeted by terror, felt bright. Fear had come hunting, and she was not running. That had to be worth something.

The king gave swift instructions for a few of his personal guards. He sent someone to delay Finian. All the while, they walked swiftly toward the stables. "Are you certain on this, lass?"

"Can you win the war if I don't?"

He gave a grim smile. “It will not matter, if you don’t.”

“And then Finian will be killed.” Was that her voice, that thick, throaty sound?

The O’Fáil shrugged as they hurried into the bailey. “People die in battle, lass. One cannot predict such things. But if Rardove and Longshanks get their hands on that recipe, I can predict everything down to how they’ll tie the ropes around Finian’s wrists and ankles.”

“Then I am certain.”

Stars glittered sharp and bright above as they hurried to the stables. Yellow light spilled out of the windows, and the door was thrown wide, so the mud in the bailey glistened in the golden glow.

“I’ll have my men take you as far as the barrows,” the king said as they entered the stables, “and keep you in sight until you draw near the river, to make sure you’re safe.”

It was decidedly not funny, but the urge to burst into laughter almost overtook her. “Aye,” she agreed solemnly, “until I’m safe.”

Swiftly, the king had robes brought for her, as the night was chilled. Three Irish warriors saddled horses. They mounted and one extended a hand to Senna. She reached for it and he swung her up behind. The horse’s rump was warm. The back of the soldier’s armor was cold.

“Put yer arms around me, beautiful,” he murmured in his Irish lilt. “And I’ll not let ye fall.”

Oh, God, she was so frightened, it was possible she might dissolve from it.

The king reached up and took her hand, gave it a squeeze. “Balffe has been spotted on the riverbank not half an hour ago. If we leave you there, he’ll be on you in minutes.”

She nodded, since terror had snaked around her throat and made speech impossible. She shook free of it. “What will you tell Finian?” The world was spinning. Nothing that was happening seemed possible. How had she gone from tending sheep to saving Scotland and Ireland?

The king nodded to the riders. The horses started out of the stables. *Clop, clop,* over the packed dirt earth, into the glittering night.

"I will tell him," the king's words came drifting to her back, "that you are much like your mother."

"No." They were outside the stable. She didn't turn back, just raised her voice, expecting it to be wobbling and broken. It wasn't. It came out strong. "Tell him he is wrought of stronger steel than other people's errors. Tell him he will make a masterful king. And tell him I realize we were both in error. I did not need him a'tall. I simply chose him."

The Irish warriors dropped her, as arranged, at the base of a fat hillock. Less than half a mile off, the dark thread of a river could be seen, trees scattered around its shores like ashes.

The Irishmen waited as she slunk away into the darkness. She glanced back once to see them sitting motionless on their horses, dark silhouettes, watching her go. Clouds were piling up on the horizon.

The scouts had said Balffe was barely half a mile away, but Senna could feel him already, his enmity weaving like warp and woof through the dark night air.

Chapter 51

Finian came back into the chamber with a mug of ale and stopped short. The two servants in his wake, bearing trays of food and more drink, almost ran up his heels. The king was sitting exactly where he'd been before, but Senna was gone.

Finian set the mug down carefully. "Where is she?"

The king shook his head.

He turned on his heel, went to his bedchamber and started throwing on his armor.

The O'Fáil came in behind him a few minutes later without speaking. The news spread, and soon more and more men crowded into the chamber, to protest Finian's headlong pursuit of the Englishwoman.

"Ye should just let her go," ventured Brian, his sleepy eyes grown sharp with anger when, alerted by the shouting voices, he, too, had stumbled into the room. Already ten or so men were standing around the small space, bumping knees and arguing.

"And ye should watch yer tongue," Finian suggested, his words muffled by the hauberk he was tugging over his head.

Brian shook his head, rubbed at his eyes, and took the mug of ale a sleepy servant was passing around the impromptu council meeting. "We'll be better off without her troublesome meddling. I don't know why ye're going after her."

"And I don't know why I don't kill ye," Finian retorted amiably, bending to tug on his riding boots. Alane elbowed his way into the room, already dressed in armor and a grim smile when he saw the men crowded in the room.

Brian scowled and sat down on a small bench by the wall. "So ye're to start sniffing at bent grass blades, while the rest of us march to war?"

Finian ignored him, his hands taking unconscious inventory of the arsenal of blades strapped across his body as he strode toward the door.

Brian snorted before tipping the mug into the air. "I say good riddance."

Alane kicked the leg out from Brian's bench as he passed by. The bench overturned and the ale spilled. Brian sprawled on the ground a moment, then got to his feet, scowling.

Alane dropped onto another bench and swung his heels up on the small table, his gaze trained on the shadowy young warrior. Finian snatched up his gauntlets and headed to the door. "I'm off."

Ten heads dropped into twenty cupped palms.

"And the men?" someone shouted after. "The muster?"

"I'll be there."

"Ye cannot go without the king's leave," complained Felim. He was dressed in a long tunic whose hem was lifted by errant drafts surging through the darkened tower room.

"Who said 'tis without his leave?" retorted Finian. But he didn't look at the king. "And," he added as he elbowed through the men, pausing as he passed Alane, who, for all Finian knew, thought him as mad as everyone else did, "ye'll have Alane's gracious good company until then, so I don't know what ye're all complaining about."

"Och, they'll not have me," Alane demurred, still sitting with his boots up on the table.

"And why not?" Finian asked, glancing down at his lounging friend. "Ye're going to be real busy, are ye, these next few days?"

"I am."

"With what?"

"Guarding your sorry arse. Again." He started getting to his feet. Finian clasped his forearm and dragged him the rest of the way up, relief and gratitude rushing into all the cold hollow places that had formed when he realized Senna was out there alone, on her way to Rardove.

"My thanks, friend," he said in a low voice.

"You've saved my sorry arse a few times, friend, for much less noble reasons than rescuing an innocent. And anyhow," he said, nodding to the king, "The O'Fáil will no' let me leave you."

The king watched them but didn't say a word.

Amid the cries of their countrymen, they strode out of the room.

The O'Fáil tracked him and Alane down the stairs, past the flickering circles of torchlight and down into the darkness. When they reached the doorway to the bailey, he put a hand on Finian's arm. Alane ducked out the door.

"She said to say you would make a fine king."

Finian was running his hand over the various hilts and blades one last time, checking. He glanced up. "Ye told her?"

"Listen to me, Finian, ere you risk your life and the outcome of this war over a woman. You've been waiting for this moment for years."

Finian lifted his gaze from the hand wrapped tightly around his forearm. Long hair hung over the king's shoulders, but there were strands of gray shot throughout. Careworn wrinkles lined his face, and there was a light tinge of bluish haze in the eyes regarding him. In the dim, wayward light, his foster father looked old for the first time.

"You cannot go after her."

"I can, and I am."

The O'Fáil's voice dropped to a baritone whisper. "Finian, I'm asking you as a father."

The whetted edge of despair sliced a thin sliver off the surface of Finian's heart. Throwing up his chin he clamped a palm on the king's shoulder.

"Don't, then," he said thickly. "She's my debt."

"You haven't a bigger one than her?"

Finian's fingers tightened on the king's shoulder. "Would ye have me dead?"

"I'd have you recall your loyalties, Finian. She *chose* this. Let it be."

"And I choose this." He said it loudly, hearing the belligerence in his words. It blanketed the anguish.

"Finian," The O'Fáil said sadly. "You could be a king."

Silence boomed through the small antechamber.

"So we're losing you for a woman," he said bitterly, when it was clear Finian had already given his answer. "Who did I raise you to be?"

"Ye didn't raise me to abandon women, sir."

Darkness turned The O'Fáil's shaking head into a purpling transition of shadows, but there was no mistaking the warning in his next words: "I could stop you. Call up the guard, cut you down where you stand."

Finian turned and kicked open the door.

"She said she did not need you," the king called after.

"Aye, well, I need her." He leapt down the small set of stairs and started across the bailey.

Alane, who had paused outside the door, said in a low voice, "I'll watch out for him, my lord."

The O'Fáil turned dully. "It hardly matters now, does it?"

"We'll catch up with the *slogad* at the muster," Finian called over his shoulder.

"You will not," The O'Fáil said. He didn't bother shouting.

Finian was already halfway across the bailey and didn't stop. "I will."

Senna made her way toward the sound of running water. The thunder of the powerful watercourse grew loud, drowning out everything else. She picked her way amid the wet rocks, slippery with moss, intent on the ground lest she slip and tumble into the frigid water.

She did not note the shadowy figure tracking her. Kneeling on a boulder, she did not notice it creep up behind. They stifled her scream when they seized her from behind, a wide palm slapped over her mouth, the other sweeping her legs off the earth.

They lifted her over the large boulders that formed a makeshift bridge across the river and carted her away under the pines.

Chapter 52

She was half dragged, half carried, for about five minutes, then dumped in a small clearing where ten equines and an equal number of armed men milled about. In the center of the gathering was a fire, a circle of soldiers, and block-shouldered Balffe.

Senna's heart crashed into the pit of her chest. She kept her eyes down as she was shoved in front of him. She could see his boots and the stained breeches he wore. The tip of his sword dangled down beside these things.

"Mistress Senna," he said, his voice guttural. "Are you unharmed?"

Just keep your mouth shut, she counseled herself.

Clad in mail and as solid as a brick, Balffe's hand suddenly appeared before her downturned eyes. He lifted it to her face, pressing the links of metal against her jaw. The river of fear moved lower, pushing against her groin.

"Perhaps you did not hear my query, lady. Are you unharmed, happy and well?"

She gave a curt nod.

Pressing his fingers deeper into her skin, Balffe jerked her chin up and examined her face as if he were inspecting a horse. "Your eye is not so blackened as 'twas a few days ago.

That is too bad. Do not give me cause to bring it back to life, woman," he murmured, his words drawn out slowly, like a dagger being pulled from its sheath.

She nodded again, staring at the tarnished hook on the shoulder of his hauberk, bleak terror foaming on the shores of her heart. Another gust of odious breath gusted by her face. "You look well enough to ride."

"I am fine," she snapped. "Now unhand me."

He went still. "What?"

"You have captured me. There is nowhere I can go. Unhand me."

His hand slid farther along her face, until her chin was forced into the webbing between his thumb and forefinger and the flat of his mailed hand pressed against her throat. She tried to swallow but the heel of his hand was pressing hard. Any more and it would be difficult to breathe. He bent near her face.

"Say please."

Senna stared over his shoulder. Balffe tightened his hold.

"Please," she whispered. She had no idea how she'd accomplished it, but likely it was because pride was no longer an issue. Everything had narrowed to a small, bright band of purpose: retrieve the pages and save Finian.

Seconds ticked by, extending into a grim silence. "Do you know what my lord bade me do when I found you?"

At this scant distance, Senna could see the blotches of discoloration pockmarking his skin; huge, craterlike pores clotted with dirt and grime. Close-set eyes huddled together beside a misshapen nose. A score of old scars were seared across his face, shallow gutters of white-fleshed skin no sun could darken.

"I know nothing of what your lord bids or disallows."

He gave his hand a shove, pushing her against the tree. "Know this, lady: you are *mine*." Then he released her and stepped back, turning to his men, shouting.

"Mount up, sluggards. We're for Rardove Keep. *Now!*"

* * *

Finian and Alane caught up just as Senna was carried into the clearing. They watched helplessly from their hiding place under a bush as she was dragged into the circle of the twenty men-at-arms bearing the Rardove device. Exchanging one swift glance, they knew they would succeed only in getting all of them killed if they charged in.

Finian crept from beneath the bush to his horse, motioning to Alane. With a swift kick, he lifted the horse into a ground-eating gallop, whisking him toward the only hope close enough and sympathetic enough to offer succor.

"Are we going where I think we're going?" Alane asked in a voice only loud enough to lift above the rhythmic hoof-beats hammering on the grassy earth.

"Very likely."

"This is a bit dangerous."

"A bit."

"Her brother's?"

"Aye."

"I counsel against."

"Do ye now?"

"Seeing as de Valery has probably learned his sister is no' with the baron anymore, aye. 'Tis passin' likely Rardove mentioned she was kidnapped. By you."

"Aye, I doubt he'll have liked hearing that."

Their horses were loping easy now, side by side. "Your family's lands were taken by King Edward himself, Finian. Which means de Valery holds them direct of the king of England, who is now marching north to make war with us. And his justiciar's army."

"Aye, it's going to be a regular party. Have ye any other obstacles to throw in our path?"

"Oh, aye. I'm the one throwing obstacles." They slowed to navigate up a winding path. "Will we have enough time?"

"De Valery's manor is less than an hour's ride from here." Finian reined his horse up a low hillock. Alane kept his mount so close that muzzle touched rump as they climbed the small rise of land.

"I was no' worried so much about how long it would take us to get there," Alane replied dryly. "I was thinking more of how long it would take to convince him. Or to get killed."

"That shouldn't take long at all."

They galloped down the other side, into the dawning sunrise. It was so glittering bright it was hard to see any way ahead of them at all.

Chapter 53

"Someone comes, my lord."

Will de Valery turned to the sentry. Around him raged a cacophony of sound. Knights strode between horses, checking saddlebags and lance holders, soldiers in knee-high boots shouted to one another, leather creaked, and the dull clang of steel and iron sounded through the air. Even the hens were out, squawking and strutting. "Who?"

"Irishmen."

Will took the stairs two at a time and entered the guard tower. One of his soldiers gestured with an index finger. "You can see them over the rise just now, sir. It looks to be just the two of them."

"Irishmen? Coming here?" He glanced at the disorganized melee in the inner bailey; they were to be gone by Terce to join the Rardove muster. "Find out their names and show them to me in the hall. At blade point."

He disappeared into the firelit yard and strode through the shouting men and restive horses.

Finian and Alane were guided none too gently into the hall, on the point of four guards' blades. Their escort had originally consisted of two burly soldiers, but when Finian's name was known, the guard increased by half again, and only after sending word to de Valery, wondering if they ought not to escort their guests direct to the cellars.

Alane was considering taking the guards on bare-fisted when they were shoved in front of de Valery. Flames from a roaring fire leapt up behind his leather-clad figure, orange and blue behind a black silhouette. Men-at-arms lined up on either side and behind them. One stepped forward.

"These were taken from the prisoners, my lord." He dumped two broadswords and three daggers onto the floor. The light tinkle of the wickedly sharp misericorde clattered last.

De Valery's gaze lifted from the mound. "Finian O'Melaghlin."

Finian nodded briefly. Alane stood as still as a boulder beside him.

"I admit to being surprised to see you here."

Finian glanced around the room where more soldiers had grouped themselves. "But appear no worse for yer amazement."

De Valery smiled faintly. "I am not a fool."

"And I am not a prisoner. I came to talk, not be bound and stripped of my weapons."

"Weapons are allowed in my castle only with my permission and good cause."

"I have cause. Traveling over a hostile countryside to meet with ye in good faith."

"Where is my sister?" He flung the question like a knife across the room. Alane steeled himself. This was not going well.

"She's with Rardove, or soon will be."

Liam de Valery repeated in incredulous humor: "*Rardove?* Jesus Christ, O'Melaghlin, if she were back with Rardove, I'd have had you horsewhipped before you made it through the outer bailey."

"Be that as it may, she is on her way back to the baron."

De Valery let out a bark of laughter. "Indeed?"

They stared at each other. One moment ticked by. Two. Harsh, male breathing echoed against the stone walls. The Englishman stared hard, then snapped his fingers.

"Lock them up in the cellars."

Shite, thought Alane.

"And send word to Rardove, to see if, by some madness, what this Irishman says is true, that my sister is safely returned. If so," he added a small, grim smile, "I'll have them swinging from the walls by morn."

Finian shook his head. "That will be too late. Rardove's going to have yer sister back by evening, and by my reckoning, she'll be dead come morn."

De Valery took a step forward, leaving ten feet of rush-covered stone and a wall of disbelief to separate them. "What the hell are you talking about, O'Melaghlin?"

Alane straightened his spine. His right hand flexed around air, because his sword was distressingly absent.

"Mayhap you ought to tell me what is going on," de Valery snapped.

"Mayhap ye ought to call off yer dogs." Finian glanced at the men still planted a few inches away, their blades even closer. "And I'll tell ye everything."

De Valery paused, then made a gesture with his hand. The armed men reluctantly dropped back some thirty feet to line the walls of the cavernous but crumbling hall.

"Sit."

Finian dropped onto a bench lining one side of a rough-hewn table and casually met Alane's eyes with a brief but significant glance. The message was clear: it would be best if they were not in *exactly* the same spot if all hell broke loose.

Alane inclined his head the barest inch and locked his gaze

on the leader of William's household troops. Clad in scarlet and gray, he was the size of a small mountain and had one eye sealed shut, whether from royal retribution or ruthless healing, Alane did not know. Nor did he care. The mountain was the closest thing to Finian and his dagger was drawn.

Backing up a few steps, Alane positioned himself by the wall and stood, silent and vigilant, legs planted wide, arms crossed.

Darkness was the most noticeable thing about this hall; tallow candles sat at crooked angles in a series of holders along the wall, casting a dim, unwieldy light, and one off-center one graced the oaken table. It was a narrow, cold room, unlived in for a long time.

De Valery considered Alane's retreat to the wall in silence, then turned his attention back to Finian. Retreating to the far side of the table, he dropped onto the bench and crossed his arms with exaggerated leisure. "You have a tale?"

Finian considered de Valery before he spoke, as if planning an attack. When it came, it came bluntly. "She wasn't partial to the way he tried to force her into a marriage—"

De Valery half rose off his seat. *"What?"*

"And I admit, I saw her reasoning. So, she left. And freed me on her way. I was in the prisons."

"Why?" he asked sharply, keenly.

"That is a mighty long story," Finian said wearily, "and goes back to old days. I haven't got the time to tell it to ye now. Except to say, Rardove is about to get yer sister back, and there's no worse place in all the world for her to be."

A log exploded as the fire suddenly reached a pocket of air. Hissing red flames shot out of the monstrous fireplace opening, and the log thudded as it rolled over. De Valery's narrowed eyes never left Finian.

"That doesn't make any sense," he muttered, then got to his feet.

Finian shrugged. "'Tis the truth."

As de Valery paced, flames from the fire picked up glints from his armor and shot flashes of rust-white light across the room. "Ah, but so claims Rardove, which brings us full circle."

"Ye've a long way to fall, if ye're relying on Rardove for yer truths."

De Valery's step slowed and he looked over his shoulder. "If you have something else to say, O'Melaghlin, you'd best say it straight away."

"Yer mother was a dye-witch?" De Valery started. "Do not deny it. 'Tis the only thing that kept yer sister alive in Rardove's care."

The young de Valery exhaled around a curse and sat down opposite Finian, on the other side of the table. "Legend," he said.

Finian's gaze went hard. "We haven't time for that sort of thing. We've been here ten minutes, and that's nine too long. 'Tis not legend, and yer family knows it."

"What do you know about my family?" de Valery demanded.

"Och, I could tell ye things about yer family that would make yer head explode. But right now, I need yer help. There's going to be a war."

"I am well aware of that," de Valery said dryly.

"And ye're going to have to choose sides."

De Valery pushed back in his seat and shoved splayed fingers through his hair. "Christ on the cross," he exhaled in a stream of mutterings. "Senna has ever been trouble, and when I lay my hands on her again . . ." were the sorts of things they heard. Then de Valery looked across the table. "Do you know who my lord is?"

Finian nodded. "Longshanks."

The English knight lifted a brow and smiled sardonically. "I didn't expect you to say that. Not many people know."

"I make it a point to know about the men who are deeded

my family's lands. I surely know more about ye than yer sister does," he added.

De Valery sat back and gave him a considering look. "Do you know what I do for 'Longshanks'?"

"Ye kill, maim, and otherwise get people out of the way whom Edward deems bothersome."

De Valery gave a pale smile. "Do you know he is starting to consider *you* such a bother?"

Finian leaned his elbow across the table, closer to the candle flickering in the center. "Ye can tell him the feeling is mutual. I think he's a son of a bitch too."

De Valery threw his head back and laughed. A single bark of laughter, that was all, and before it finished bouncing off the stone walls, he was looking at Finian again.

"It wouldn't be sensible to join with you, O'Melaghlin, since my fealty for these lands lies with Edward."

"Aye. Treason it would be. Listen, English. I've need of speed just now, and ye're slowing me down. Ye'll have to look into yer own heart for the truth. Ye'll either join us, or kill us. But ye'll have to decide quick, for I'm getting up now."

The rumor of swords and violence was ringed around the hall. Finian pushed to his feet. The bench stuttered back across the floor, knocking into one of the soldier's shins.

Every man in the room strode forward and unslung his sword. The sound of sharp steel hissed against hardened leather, then shattered the air as blades sliced across the metal clasps atop their sheaths. Alane pushed off the wall. Liam de Valery got to his feet.

He reached out his hand to Finian. "I'm in on the hunt."

Alane shut his eyes briefly. Thank God Finian did not know how fast his heart was beating, or how icy was his blood. He'd never live it down.

De Valery turned to shout commands. Alane stepped forward. "Could you have pushed him any further, O'Melaghlin?" he asked quietly.

Finian grabbed his gauntlets off the table. "Aye. He's young though, and I felt pity."

Alane snorted as their swords were brought over. "Your sympathy is a frightening thing, my friend."

They started restrapping the sheaths and buckling blades around thighs and arms. "Ye're about to see my rage."

Chapter 54

De Valery's one-eyed captain was summoned forth. Half of his not-insignificant force was dispatched to the stables to ready itself for the sortie onto the Irish countryside. The others were told to hold at the manor, until de Valery sent word. Then the three of them strode to the stables, weapons slung and belted across their bodies.

"Tell me about Senna," de Valery asked as they crossed the courtyard. "How is she?"

"Reckless. Resilient. Startling."

De Valery looked over, his eyebrows raised. "I meant, is she hurt? She's bewitched you, has she?" They reached the stables and began saddling their horses. "Not many see the charm. But then, she terrifies them with her stylus. Wields it like a sword. Very dangerous."

"Yer sister is a force of nature. Most men hunker down."

Liam considered him. "How did she get recaptured by Rardove's men, anyhow?"

Finian shrugged. "She was out on her own."

De Valery glanced at Alane, then back. "How'd she manage that?"

Finian scowled. "How does yer sister manage anything, de Valery?"

Liam looked at him in surprise, likely at the vehemence of his reply. "By saying she's going to do it, then doing it. That's how Senna does everything."

Finian tested the cinch of his horse's saddle by slipping a finger underneath, just behind the gelding's front leg. "Aye. That's her."

"So," Liam said, his tone contemplative. "She left."

"Aye."

"What did you do, to make her leave?"

Finian returned his gaze with a level look of his own. He could almost feel Senna's presence under his skin, her heated touches, her roiling spirit. The eyes that peered at him were so much like her own they tugged at his heart. *Do*? God save him if he did anything but her bidding if he could only get her back.

"Whatever yer sister and I did, Liam, we did together."

Another suspicious slant of the hazel eyes. "What exactly did you do together?"

"Everything."

A pause. An arched blond eyebrow. "*Everything*?"

Finian swung up on his horse. "Everything she wanted to do."

"Mother of God," her brother muttered.

The sun was almost too bright, filled with petulant, gray-bottomed clouds. They gathered in small, patchy bunches, like young, angry men posturing and rumbling to themselves. They had a greenish tinge to them, and roiled within; a low rumbling sound they sent out made the ears hum. The three of them mounted up swiftly and reined toward the gate.

"So, do you know where this sortie is, the one that captured Senna?"

"Aye. By now, easily two hours north. Their leader is Balffe, and for the next few hours, we've need to worry about him much more than Rardove."

"You know Senna's captor?"

"Aye. I know Balffe."

"You know Balffe," de Valery echoed. "Why do I trow that has some significance?"

They passed under the small inner bailey gate. De Valery's men followed behind.

"Balffe has a wicked temper, and the temptation to right what he sees as an old wrong may prove too tempting for his conscience, which is a skinny thing in the best of times."

De Valery's glance moved to Finian slowly. "What old wrong has Senna done him? She can be more vexing than an infection, but she's only been here a week."

Finian shook his head. "'Tisn't her. She's been with me, and Balffe knows it."

"And?"

Finian plucked his lower lip between his thumb and forefinger and tugged before responding. "We've a score to settle from years back."

"Plague take me," he snapped. "'Tis like a hornet's nest out here, all this swarming of secrets. Is it not possible to meet someone who has no old scores to settle?"

"Aye." Finian tossed him a level look. "Yerself."

"Ah." He settled back and ran his hand over the hilt of his sword. "Well."

"Aye."

"So tell me: what did you do that knocked—what's his name? Balffe?—off his oats?"

"Bedded his sister," Alane piped in.

De Valery froze. "Do you do that a lot?"

Alane cocked an eyebrow, a weary, faint smile on his face. Finian shook his head and looked away, unamused.

"Balffe's sister was a waif, sad and slender, with less color than wheat powder. Years ago, when Rardove and my king still pretended to be allied, The O'Fáil hosted a feast. Rardove and his minions came. Balffe came. He brought his sister."

"And you slept with her?" de Valery finished incredulously. "By the arm of St. Peter, O'Melaghlin, couldn't you—"

"I did not bed her. I talked to her. She'd been betrothed to a man who was harder than Balffe. And I mentioned to her that her face need not be beaten at each mealtime to serve some dim-witted man's notion of knighthood, and that there were men who did not whip their women as a prelude to their evening entertainment."

De Valery considered this. "And?"

"She chose to not return with the rest of Rardove's party."

A smile crooked up the corner of Liam's mouth. "And?"

Finian shrugged, but Alane spoke up into the dark air. "She found a husband who does no' beat her, bore five children, all of whom have lived, and she gives Finian a hand-dyed cloak every Yuletide, smiling through her tears."

De Valery was quiet a minute. "Well, I cannot see why Balffe—what an ungodly name—would be angry with that."

Finian glanced over. "Because we are Irish. Because his sister defied their father. Because the father then proceeded to die an hour after the wedding, no doubt from horror."

"No doubt," he murmured as they rode under the outer gates. "So, you stole his sister and killed his father."

"Something like that."

They were quiet a moment. Liam observed, quite unnecessarily, "We'll hardly beat them to Rardove Keep. They've got a fearsome head start."

Finian gathered up his reins. "I know a shortcut."

The gate creaked shut behind and they galloped silently out under the storm clouds about to unleash themselves on the land.

Chapter 55

Senna pressed her eyelids shut but could not make the world dark enough to blot out what was happening to her.

By late afternoon the next day Balffe almost had them to Rardove Keep. He'd not let them stop all morning and afternoon long, most of it at a lope, and the tension in Senna's throat rose to almost throttling proportions as each mile disappeared behind them.

They climbed to the top of a rolling hill. The view lasted for miles, spilling greening hills into valleys and lowlands. Small blue watercourses sparkled in the distance. And all around the lowlands and draped up the hills like multicolored blankets, were armies. Armies mustering to decimate the Irish.

On the distant rise, swimming before her gaze, was the hated castle. Faded red pinions fluttered from the stone ramparts, snapping in the sharp breeze.

She could almost see the gate through which she and Finian had escaped, the moat where he'd tossed her to ensure their safety. Perhaps at this very moment the afternoon sun was hitting the spot where he'd acquiesced to her plea for a kiss, and she'd known everything in her life before Finian had been pale and flat.

She bent her face, her breath catching over and over.

Balffe grunted and stared determinedly ahead. Women's tears came cheaper than basil, and he was not going to be turned by the threat of them, not even if the fat, wet drops started dripping down her cheeks.

"Who are all those people?" she asked, pointing at the crowds milling on the plain before the castle gates.

But she knew. Villagers, fleeing the armies that were marching to war. Uninvited guests. They would not be asked in, not even when the battle began, nor would they be allowed to pass through the ring of any opposing army encamped outside the castle walls. They would hover in between the warriors, nothing but unwanted mouths. It was a killing zone.

Balffe's armor creaked as he turned to look at her. It was silent except for the sudden flutter of bird wings somewhere to their left.

Then, from out of nowhere and all around, came a pounding of hooves and rough cries. From behind and on each side galloped a muster of knights on horses, racing toward them with bright swords drawn, arrows fitted. Steel-tipped points whizzed by Balffe's head and bit into the earth beside them. The slender, graceful shafts of ash belied the death carried at their steel tips.

With a curse, Balffe whipped the horses into a wild gallop and they raced ahead of the armed throng. Senna screamed at the suddenness of the charge, tossed around on her saddle like a sack of wheat.

They sped across the open plain, racing for the castle that emerged from the evening mists. She clutched at the mane of her horse. Her knee smashed into the knobby pommel and her teeth clattered inside her skull, and through the vibrations, she espied her brother.

"William!"

Then she saw Finian.

"Oh, please Lord, no," she whispered, then screamed as a surge of scalding fire exploded across her scalp. Balffe was hauling her toward him with an armored fist, by her hair.

Dragging her back into the saddle, he wrapped the reins of her horse around his palm and hauled her close, until their horses' red-flared nostrils touched as they galloped like a devil's tongue across the plain.

Balffe contemplated stopping to do outright battle with O'Melaghlin, went so far as to sit upright in his saddle and rein in his stallion, when a small ax hurtled past his head, close enough to trim the day's growth off his jaw.

He crashed his nose into the horse's mane to escape death. An arrow skidded across the equine's rump and the horse bolted into a wild dash Balffe no longer had the inclination to oppose.

He urged his stallion into a pace violent enough to hurl rocks and small farm animals from under hoof, speeding toward the castle. Lifting himself in the saddle, he spurred the horse in a savage, reckless leap over a heather-strewn hedgerow, dragging Senna's mount behind.

The keep was close now, the draw only a quarter mile away. Flaring his nostrils like his frenzied mount's, Balffe pushed the pair of horses with his thighs, his arms, his fury, until they breached the wooden bridge and flew under the outer gates.

Guards stood in stupefied amazement, their jaws agape.

Balffe roared, *"Raise the fycking draw!"*

Like maggots on a mound of meat, the guards swarmed to their posts. Heaving and grunting and sweating to rival a seaman in a whorehouse, they dragged on the heavy chains, tearing open hardened calluses as they hoisted the bridge.

Balffe didn't wait to see the outcome. He urged his horse on, bending low over his withers, until they crossed over another bridge, under another gate. Another bellowing shout,

Chapter 56

She threw her hand out reflexively as Balffe propelled her to the top of the stairs outside the great hall. It was so brilliantly light outside, and so densely dark inside, she was blinded for a moment. Balffe dropped down the stairs into the hall, herding her before him.

Rardove sat in his chair on the dais, wrapped in a cape that grew his shoulders out like a crow's wings, watching their approach. His cold features—nose, chin, cheek—were set in a pinched, translucent mold. Whatever had been golden about his presence before was now tarnished. Only his eyes revealed life.

He rose from his seat like a bird taking flight. Senna wanted to fling herself at him, scratching and clawing. Or, preferably, throw a knife into him. Instead, she forced herself to stumble. Appear weak.

Balffe bent to her, hand extended, but a sharp glance from the baron drew him upright again.

It was utterly silent. Silence seeped from the walls, a wicked, waiting thing. No one spoke. The clatter of a dropped mug brought a clumsy maid to tears. The baron's furious gaze fell on her, which only made things worse. It took two varlets and a strong tincture to get her huddled, weeping figure out of the middle of the hall floor.

The hall was almost empty now. Only Senna, Balffe, and Rardove. And Pentony. She sensed him there, in the shadows.

"Sir," Balffe said, stepping forward. He pushed Senna out in front of him. "As ordered."

Rardove's gaze slid over her, from head to dirty yellow skirt hem. "Where?"

"Near The O'Fáil encampment, by the old barrows hill. No escort. She'd escaped, or left, or something. She won't say."

Rardove looked her over, his eyes glittering. "Certainly she will," he murmured, coming around the table and down the dais stairs.

She stared at the far wall, where a faded, limp tapestry hung behind the dais.

"So much trouble, over one small woman," Rardove mused, striding around her. Suddenly, his breath was on the back of her neck, sliding over her like smoke. His hand slid up under her skirts, up her thigh. She shuddered, but his fingers found the blade she'd lodged in a band there. He slipped it free and stepped back.

"I do not know why you came back, Senna—or were sent back—but I will learn. And you shall not like my methods."

She stopped breathing.

Balffe cleared his throat. Rardove's eyes darted from Senna's determined profile, still angled toward the wall behind the dais, to his captain, who obviously had more news to relay. "What is it?"

"They attempted a capture. Just outside your gates."

"Did they?"

"Aye. The Irishry. And her brother."

Rardove twitched slightly. "De Valery?"

"Aye. With O'Melaghlin."

Rardove contemplated this a moment, then swung out his

arm. "So be it. De Valery has made his choice. He shall die with the rest of them."

Senna swallowed thickly, her jaw set.

Rardove nodded to Balffe. "Ready the men. The plain is fat with villagers and their whelp. Gather every male over twelve and put him on the castle walls. Siege measures to be enacted, in the event. Send a messenger to the sortie we sent to intercept Wogan. Tell them to shoot de Valery on sight, should he try to establish communication with Wogan. Come dawn, the rest of the troops will arrive, and we shall be ready for battle." He looked down at Senna. "By then, who knows what my dye-witch will have done for me?"

No one moved. Balffe glanced at Senna. He shifted uncomfortably.

Rardove turned slowly. "Balffe?"

The soldier's gaze snapped from Senna.

"Why are you still standing there like a dolt? Round up the men."

Senna saw a telltale flicker shudder cross the veteran warrior's face. It was nothing of note, a flash by his lips, a tightening along his jaw. He turned to his men-at-arms, who were lined up along the walls.

"You heard what your lord said. Double the watches, everyone on half rations. Mac and Conally, round up the men from the rabble out front."

A slow groan rose from the war-wasted men, some of whom were only here on castle duty from their own lords, a service that was due to end for some of them within a dawn.

At the sound, Balffe turned back with a blank and utterly terrifying look. "You want for me to convince you?"

The men scattered. Wood-soled boots cracked stone as they barreled up the stairs out of the hall. Angry echoes bounced back into the hall as the soldiers passed along the long, dank corridors to the barracks.

Rardove turned to Senna. “And now, what shall I do with you?” he said, his tone contemplative.

“Do with me, my lord?” The interchange with Balffe had given her just enough time to gather her wits, and she needed them all to carry her next words into the air. “Why, you shall marry me.”

Rardove’s attention narrowed in on her like an archer’s. “I somehow doubt you will say ‘I will’ in front of a priest.”

“I somehow doubt you would have a priest who much cared. But I shall come willing enough.”

“You will?”

“Aye.”

Rardove’s hand shot out and gripped her shoulder. The pain had begun. “Willing? You lie,” he spat. “That is as big a lie as the other.”

Cold drops of fear slid down the back of her throat like medicine. “Aye, I lied. But we both knew that, did we not? I am a dyer. As skilled as my mother was.”

“You are like her in every manner,” he snarled, then reached into his tunic and slammed something into her chest. She toppled backward a few steps, gripping what he pressed there.

The missing pages. He’d found them.

Indeed, she found herself thinking—some rational, orderly part of her mind was still in working order—*no more concerns on how to proceed. We know just what to do.*

She pushed back her shoulders and said in a clear voice, “I will make you the dyes.”

He burst out laughing. “I know exactly what you will do, Senna. When, and how.”

“Do you?” She met his gaze. “Tell me, do you want them explosive or”—she paused for effect—“camouflaging?”

His face underwent a series of small metamorphoses, from startled, to impressed, to furious, to . . . desirous. She seized the moment.

"You call off this war, and I will make you the dyes."

His breathing, made unsteady by her admission, slowed. "I cannot. It has gone out of my hands."

"Retrieve it back into them," she said coldly. "Tell the king the dyes are only legend. A lie." She looked down at the pages in her hand. His tongue flicked over his lips as she smoothed them. She perused them briefly before looking up. "I do not want King Edward to know of this. Do you?"

His eyes were slightly distant as they met hers. He looked in the beginning throes of madness. Or passion.

"I do not want anyone to know," he agreed hoarsely.

She lowered her voice to match his. "No. 'Twill be our little secret. Tell Wogan, the governor. Send word to King Edward." She looked down at the manual languidly, ran one finger slowly over it. "Call them off, and I'll stay here with you. Willingly."

His eyes narrowed. "Why?" He might be pure evil, but he was pure cunning evil. Incipient madness—or lust—had been overtaken by scheming. "You do not want me to have the dyes."

She had to find a way to bind him to her more than Edward. More than his hatred. She took another intuitive step in the dark.

"This is what we do, the women in my family, is it not?" she murmured. "We start as de Valerys, but we end with you. I know my mother was here, with you." She took a step closer. Desire swept over his face, slackening his jaw. He nodded as if in a trance. "And now, 'tis I."

"You are mine," he said thickly. He shoved his hand through her hair, dragging her head back. "Your mother is dead."

"I know." She fought off the urge to mark him, to carve up his face. Ten years ago it had gone like this, and she hadn't known how to defend herself. The knife on the marriage bedstead had been a stroke of luck. Now, she knew very well how to defend herself. And she couldn't do it.

If she killed Rardove, if news went out that he was dead,

King Edward's men would crawl over the castle like fleas on a straw tick, and they would find the pages. They would find her. And they would find someone who, given time, could decipher the deadly recipe of the Wishmés. Then Ireland would fall, Scotland would fall, and Finian would have ropes tied about his wrists and ankles.

Rardove's vile lips were by her ear, breathing into her hair. "And I swear, Senna, I will kill you, too, if you do not craft the Wishmé dyes for me."

She gathered every scrap of reason and sense from the cold, trembling corner of her petrified mind, and drew herself up. "I will work on the dyes this night," she said, putting a hand on his chest. "In the morning, come to me."

In the morning, she would kill him.

Or he would kill her.

But really, it couldn't go on like this.

Twilight poured through the high, narrow windows of the empty great hall, creating a mingling of firelight and pale purple light, illuminating the spinning, dancing dust motes into an unearthly glow. Blue-black. Much like the Wishmés.

Pentony should know. He'd seen the color they made. And not the sample that was hundreds of years old. He'd watched a fresh batch be born, hatched by Senna's mother.

Sooth, he'd helped pound out mollusk shells himself, when the baron was out hunting one afternoon and Pentony had not yet fully adapted to the groaning silences of Rardove Keep.

Elisabeth de Valery had been like fresh air when she arrived, twenty years ago. She'd chatted and laughed in that winsome, unique dialect of hers, some melding of Scots and mid-England French—and her hair practically glowed red, and she'd cared not a whit for Rardove's rage or the gloomy Irish winters, which is probably why, when she'd handed him a mortar that dreary afternoon, Pentony simply took it and started pounding.

It is probably also why, when it became needful, a year later, he helped her escape.

And it is certainly why, when she entrusted him with the last copy of the dye manual, he did as she bid.

He'd sent it, along with a small sample of the dyed fabric, to her husband, de Valery. 'He'll either receive me or the secrets,' she'd said to him, smiling. Pentony knew which he would have chosen.

Then, the night she fled, she handed him a clutch of parchment sheets, scribbled over with her mad, beautiful sketches. *For my daughter, on her wedding day. Just in case,* she'd whispered, and this time her smiles were covered in tears.

Then she slipped out the gates and ran for her life.

Ten years later, Pentony had followed up on that final request. He had sent the parchment sheets to her daughter. Under cover of darkness and packaged to appear a gift from an 'unknown' Scottish grandfather, on her betrothal eve, Senna de Valery, at fifteen, became the possessor of the last secret of the Wishmés. The only person who could create the beautiful weapons.

Right now, Pentony knew two things with absolute certainty: Rardove would never call off this war—probably couldn't now—and Senna was a dead woman.

Just like her mother.

He stood a moment longer in his vantage point of shadows lurking at the corners of the hall, then stepped out and hurried across the room.

Chapter 57

The night dragged itself out without incident, the only remarkable thing about it being the armies encamped around the baron's keep. Tents and small fires lighted the plain before the castle, dark things disturbed now and then by shouts of male laughter.

To the west, on the abbey's hummocks and streaming down their sides for miles, camped the Irish. Pitched battle was not the usual state of affairs in Ireland, but then, the threat was not a usual one.

As midnight became a distant memory, Rardove sat in the great hall, slumped on a bench before the low trough fire. He drummed long, thin fingers on his stained breeches, drunk and incredulous. The events of the day were forcing upon him a self-examination he hadn't experienced since he exploded inside his first wench, thrusting and quivering, leaving him spent and sure that *this* was what he wanted from the world above all else.

He swallowed a bolt of wine, staring straight ahead. His entire world had crumbled. Everything he ever wanted had become a curse or been destroyed. Elisabeth, his only true love: gone, and in a sudden blaze of heartache that had never stopped thudding, even twenty years later.

How could she have preferred Gerald de Valery over him? For a short time, he thought he'd won that battle. She'd come to him, had she not? He'd secured these Irish lands, at great risk to himself, for *her.* She'd wanted dyes, and he'd got her the most legendary ones around. And, eventually, she came. Left de Valery for him.

Having her close was all he'd wanted from living. Listening to her, watching her move. And for one blessed year, he'd had his dream.

Then she fled. Dead on the Irish marches.

God, how he missed her. The bite was as sharp as the morning he realized she was gone. With the recipe. She hadn't wanted him after all.

Rardove had had to kill her, of course. Track her down and strangle her before she made it to the ship. He'd had no choice. He could not let her escape with the recipe.

But in the end, she'd had no recipe. He'd found nothing on her person, nor back at the castle. No coded instructions, no written clues on how to re-create the fabulous, dangerous dyes she, the last of the dye-witches, had crafted for him.

And now he had the daughter. She sat in a chamber above him, around a sweep of stony stairs, driving him mad. She was a living, breathing problem. A woman he couldn't possibly contain. She was nothing like her gentle, loving mother, except in looks and the capacity for treachery.

Except . . . she said she could make the dyes.

But in some dim, honest corner of his mind, Rardove knew even this would not assuage the awful, pounding pain in his heart.

His hands rose to cup the sides of his head, as if to ensure the insides did not spill out. The room was a melding of chalky light and bulky shadows. His pointed fingertips almost touched over the crown of his head as he bent under the pain.

* * *

That night, the winds blew chill and the stars sparkled brightly. On the hills with his men, Finian called for music. The king stood a few yards away, back in the shadows, silent. On the eager green turf the musicians worked their craft. Thoughtful looks were etched on their granite faces as the music spilled out, harvested from centuries of brave deeds done by men now rotting in their graves.

Finian stood at the edge, a moment of stillness amid weeks of action, and the realizations crowded in thick.

All these years, what every Irishman knew was that The O'Fáil had an expansive belief in Finian O'Melaghlin. Endless, enduring. But perhaps, after all, it had its limitations.

Or rather, perhaps it reckoned on *his* limitations.

Finian could wield any weapon, fight any war, carry any negotiation through to its unforeseeable end. He could make his mates laugh and his women swoon. He could sing a passing tune, lift bricks of peat, and he alone could provide the necessary leadership to guide the *tuatha* to safety and prosperity again. He had everything a king and councilor and warrior required.

He had not, though, believed he had what Senna required.

And mayhap the king had known that all along. Mayhap 'twas part of what *he* believed in. Counted on. That Finian was flawed.

Senna saw him not as a warrior, not a potential king, but as a man full. And perhaps it *would* do. Perhaps he did have it in him.

So he stood at the edge of the circle of warriors and stared across the windswept land, intent on a rescue.

Perilous and foolish, it mattered naught. He would claim Senna come high waves of protest from all the shores of his life.

In Rardove's chamber, bent over the long trestle counter, as she'd been for the last ten hours, Senna lifted her head. Every move she made, lifting and moving, measuring and boiling, was like a taste of her mother.

She felt like a wraith, a ghostly shadow of her own past, right down to how she pushed the hair off her brow with her inner forearm, the only part of her arm not stained with dye. Just like her mother.

The missing pages were laid out beside her, utterly, awfully comprehensible. Her mother had indeed been a weapons-mistress. A consummate one. And Senna understood the coded language as if she were reading a ledger. Such things *were* in the blood.

In front of her lay a small fragment of wool. Her wool. Her special crafted wool, from sheep that her mother had begun breeding twenty-two years ago, woven in the intricate pattern that had seemed simply complicated, not meaningful. Now it was dyed with the Wishmés.

It shimmered and guttered light and the absence of light as she lifted it between the tips of two fingers and held it in the air. You'd hardly know it was there.

It hadn't taken years after all.

Her eyes started filling with tears. Oh, she was filled with such awfulness. And such goodness. Like in her womb right now. That was goodness.

She'd not thought it possible. The ravages of a night of "wedded bliss" had resulted in three physicks concluding she was barren.

Finian brought her back to life.

She sat on the floor, settled her spine against the wall and pulled a lantern closer. Sliding out its horn covering, light blazed forth, spilling pale yellow light in a wedge. Her lap, the side of her leg and her low boot were illuminated. That's all she needed.

She would destroy the pages, for certes. But first, she planned to study them one last time, commit the entire thing to memory. Every image, sketch, word would be etched in her mind.

She was really *very* good with documents.

After, she would burn the pages.

Then she would escape. Because Senna had no intention of dying here.

But seeing as she hadn't a blade, a horse, an ally, or a plan, she wasn't quite sure how she would do it.

She rested her palm on her belly and, bending over the pages, started reading.

In the main hall, soldiers were lying down for the night, curled up against the walls and spread across the floor.

The hall was shadowy and warm. Pentony strode quietly across the room, nodding briefly to any sleepy eyes that he met. He froze when he spotted Rardove, bent over, elbows on his knees, head in his hands.

He looked dead. Then, a small groaning sound came from the lump of him. He didn't look up.

Pentony went into motion again, swift and silent. There was much to arrange before the dawn. He slipped outside and inched open the portal gate in the bailey wall. He nudged a rock in front of it with the toe of his boot, scratched a thick-armed Celtic cross into the wooden door, then walked back inside.

He'd have to hope that something inside him was aligned with something inside the man who'd already risked as much for Senna as Pentony had for her mother.

Hours passed. The strange, uninvited music drifted away. The night grew ebony and the moon set. Stars glistened and pale scents were carried on the rising wind.

Chapter 58

The dark of night was dislodged by the pearly gray of predawn. The bells in the chapel were beholden to another hour of silence before they rang out Prime. Down in the inner bailey there was a flurry of activity and sound, muted by the thin mists of night: hooves and hushed, masculine calls of one man to another.

Senna heard the heavy thud of a boot outside the door. She shot to her feet, pages in hand. Slow listening. Heartbeats thudding. Cold sweat shivered down her spine. A mouse could not have scurried by without her hearing. But there was nothing. Nothing.

She swallowed thickly and turned to the brazier, building it into a wild flame, not at all like a brazier was intended to burn. But then, it hadn't been intended to burn military secrets.

She leaned close to blow. The flames flared higher. She reached for the pages.

Rusty hinges creaked behind her. "So. You did it." Rardove stepped into the room.

She spun and tripped over the hem of her skirt. The pages went flying, but she couldn't look away from Rardove. His hair was in disarray, tufted and dirty. His face was flushed from drink, but it was his eyes that terrified her. They were mad. They looked coated in pottage, mealy and thick, but when they caught sight of the dyed fabric on the counter—the shimmering butterfly wing she'd made—they cleared.

He picked it up. Felt it all over, then set it down again and looked at her blankly. "These are the pages?" He gestured to the sheaves of parchment scattered across the floor.

She didn't reply. He unslung his sword and extended it, twisting the tip gently back and forth, as if admiring it. In the flickering candlelight, it cast flashing points of fire all across the room.

Her voice, despite all intention, dropped to a whisper. "What are you doing?"

He looked up. Mad, staring eyes. "Taking care of an inconvenience that has plagued me far too long."

He was between her and the brazier. Between her and the door. He lifted the sword.

Senna took a running leap, flinging herself past him. He wrapped an arm around her waist as she flew by and slammed her to the ground. Senna fell, but as she landed, she threw her knee between his thighs.

He grunted and his eyes glazed over. The respite was sufficient, allowing her to roll away. She banged into the brazier. It toppled over. She scrambled backward and flung handfuls of the pages toward the stream of chunky orange coals. The pages scattered like small birds, an arc in the air. They fluttered to the ground. None made it into the coals.

"You *bitch,*" Rardove snarled. He staggered to his feet and lifted his blade. She was still on the floor, trying to kick sheaves of parchment into the flames. His shadow rose up.

"No!" she screamed and threw up her hands to block the blow of his sword.

"If you do it, you will die," said a voice from the doorway.

Rardove's head snapped around. "Pentony," he rasped in amazement. "Get out!"

"No."

"Get out!"

"No."

Senna scrambled away, hyperventilating and staring in amazement at Pentony, who stood in the doorway with a sword. Rusty, aye, but lifted for a blow.

Without removing his eyes from the baron, Pentony reached behind him and locked the door. Senna almost cried.

A second later, from outside the door, loud shouts exploded, and fists pounded against the wood. "Lord Rardove!" a soldier shouted. "Are you a'right?"

No one even looked at the door. Sweat dripped down between Senna's breasts and made her palms slippery against the floor as she tried to scuttle backward another inch.

"Get out of here, Pentony," Rardove said, sounding tired, and turned to Senna. The appearance of Pentony's sword, lifted to hover, edgewise, just at the vein on his neck, stopped him short.

A bubble of foamy mucous gathered in the corner of the baron's mouth. The spittle from his lips flicked into the air and exploded in invisible bursts. "I will kill you," he wheezed in fury.

"I know."

Rardove began choking on his words. They squeezed out in meaningless sounds of rage. His face burned a fiery red, his fingers twitched on his sword, but he dared not move.

"I gave you *everything,* Pentony," he spat. Senna could feel his eyes following her as she scrambled to her feet and stood behind the gaunt seneschal. "Money, a free hand with the finances, direction over all my lands—"

"I found I had lost my soul," Pentony said in a quiet, dignified way.

Rardove's face contorted. "You lost that some thirty years ago, when you trussed up the skirts of that nun and defiled her—"

"She was not yet a nun," he whispered hoarsely.

"You escaped punishment, of course, due to your royal connections, but I heard hers was severe indeed. More like torture, with the stones and the—"

Pentony's face lost all semblance of being a blooded thing. "She was my wife."

"Nay, *priest.* She was to *become* your wife, if only you could have waited. Waited for her to leave the nunnery, for you to renounce your vows. But you could not, and I was told the baby's screams could be heard at all five Cinque Ports, if the peasants can be believed."

Pentony's blade twitched against Rardove's throat. "She was my wife in mine heart, and I have carried her there all these years."

Rardove barked in laughter. "She must have been a rare beauty, then, for the only thing I have seen you hold tight to in all the years I've known you is money, steward."

Pentony paused. "In truth, she looked like Lady Senna. And her mother." He half turned his head to her. "Go. Go now."

Senna's chest started heaving, holding back the sobs of fear and sorrow punching at her heart. Tears blocked her vision; she could barely see the floor. Her head was roaring, her heart hammering. She stared at Pentony, slowly shaking her head.

Rardove struck without warning. He took a sidearm swing at Pentony's torso. The blade cut true, and it split open the tunic and the flesh beneath. Pentony's bloody body collapsed on the floor.

She screamed, her hands by her cheeks, unable to believe what had just happened.

"Get out!" Pentony called hoarsely to her. Rardove kicked him flat onto his back. Pentony's head lolled to the side. A trickle of blood seeped from his lips.

For a moment she and the baron stood there, staring at the steward, then Rardove turned, sweat rolling down his cheeks and neck.

"You're next," he rasped.

She leapt back, spinning, trying for the door. She crashed into the table instead and fell, her legs tangled in the wooden posts. Rardove lifted a foot to step over Pentony and towered above her prone body.

She pushed backward. He stopped her by planting a boot on her belly.

"No," she screamed, thrusting her palm outward. "No! *The baby!*"

Rardove faltered, his face bleached white.

Then, with a tumultuous, thundering racket, the door suddenly cracked and was flung open. A black silhouette stood in the battered frame with a drawn sword.

It paused for the briefest moment, then Finian vaulted over the threshold and into the room.

Chapter 59

Finian wrenched Senna away by her wrist just as Rardove's blade came whizzing by in a horizontal swipe that would have severed her head from her shoulders. Flinging her behind him so she fell and sprawled on the floor, Finian turned to the baron.

Rardove stared at him with red-rimmed eyes. Finian bent at the knees and reached behind him. Grasping Senna's arm, he yanked her to her feet. "Go. Now."

She didn't. Instead, she reached down, felt along Finian's thigh, and yanked out a blade—the long-handled knife she and Finian had stolen from Rardove's armory, a hundred years ago.

"Had I known you were planning a visit, O'Melaghlin," Rardove snarled, his gaze trained on Finian, "I would have arranged a more fitting welcome."

"This will do nicely." Finian circled the perimeter of the room, keeping Senna tucked behind him as he maneuvered her toward the door. Rardove followed their progress, turning in a slow revolution.

"But now that you are here, I shall give you a choice much like the one you offered me: you can stay and have my men slay you slowly—"

"Which men would those be, *cruim?*"

Rardove flicked a wary glance at the door. Two armored bodies were slumped one on top of the other, swords not even drawn. The edge of a third boot nudged in the doorframe. It was attached to a body bathed in blood.

"Or," Rardove finished slowly, turning back, "you can leave now and meet the armies at my gate for a quicker death."

Finian kept backing toward the door, Senna behind him. "I would weep for yer soul, if I thought ye had one."

While the men taunted one another, Senna squinted an eye and lifted her arm, testing the weight of the blade versus the weight of the hilt, shifting it between her fingers. *Rardove's neck. That was the only thing not armored. No. Too narrow. Move lower.*

The baron smiled thinly. "English rage will be murderous."

"Ye're about to get a taste of Irish rage."

Rardove glanced over Finian's shoulder. She had the blade up, her arm cocked. Their eyes met. Rardove's mad gaze didn't leave hers as he said to Finian, "Your woman is going to try to kill me." He sounded amused.

Senna couldn't see Finian's face, but she felt him grin. "She's not going to *try*."

Rardove lunged. Senna snapped her arm down, launching the blade. It sank into his belly. The force of her throw through his armor was not quite equal to his furious momentum, but it slowed him down. And he no longer looked amused.

Finian pushed Senna away and crashed his sword against Rardove's, smashing it aside. The baron lifted his again and their blades met in a *V* in the air, holding. Finian moved relentlessly forward, propelling his weight against the baron, then suddenly stepped to the side. Rardove went stumbling forward.

"Quickly it is," Finian muttered and, taking his sword in two hands, he spun in a full, howling circle, sword outstretched, and swung it into Rardove's torso.

Rardove staggered back a few steps. A bubble, a wet gurgle. Gasping for air, he dropped to his knees. His hands clutched to his belly. He stared down in amazement, then tumbled in a heap to the ground, dead.

Senna looked to Finian, who stood watching Rardove and slowly fell to her knees. It was dark in the room; the candles had all blown out. All she could see was his gleaming eyes. Just as in the prison, when she'd first truly met him.

His gaze shifted to her. Slowly the haunting gleam dimmed and he went down on a knee. One wide hand reached out to her, stretching across the shadows. She reached for it.

"Well, you have, in truth, rescued me," she announced in a wobbly voice, then gestured to the shattered door frame. "But that was purely showing off. I could have managed better."

Finian knelt on his other knee and folded her into his arms. He rested his chin on the top of her head for a brief second. "I know, lass. Ye do everything better."

Then, because it was needful, he pulled her to her feet, placed a hard, swift kiss on her lips, and led them away from the dead bodies and blood.

They crept through the dim castle. At times he jerked on her hand sharply, and they would both halt and press their backs against the wall, their eyes wide, breath stilled, as from another corridor they heard fragments of rough conversation, heavy boots pounding, frenzied cursing. The search was on.

Shouts and the sound of hurrying feet bounced and echoed throughout the stone and wood castle, making Senna feel crazed. They rounded another corner. Finian threw his head into the air and froze.

At the end of the corridor stood Balffe. Armored, sword in his grip, and he stared directly at them.

All the breath left Senna's lungs. The world slowed, each moment ticking by like an eternity. Colors were surprisingly bright; the fiery glow of torchlight, the black of Balffe's scuffed boots, forest green breeches, the dull, sand-colored tunic under the red Rardove surcoat. Balffe's belt buckle and sword gleamed dimly, and the vein on his neck pulsed.

It was silent. Someone held their breath, someone let theirs out in a long, slow hiss. There was a single intersecting place in the corridor, a point where the lines of their sights crossed. Invisible vectors ran at odd angles across the stony space.

A scuffle came from behind Balffe on the curving stairwell.

"Balffe?" a hoarse voice called up.

"Aye?" He threw the word over his shoulder.

"Any sign?"

His eyes held Finian's. "Nay." A series of curses floated up. "Search the stables."

Senna squeezed her eyes shut. Finian nodded once and turned her away, guiding her down the stairs behind them.

"My sister," Balffe called out quietly.

Finian craned his neck to look over Senna's head. "Is well."

Balffe nodded.

Finian turned and guided Senna away. Balffe watched from the shadows. A gleam of reddish light from a torch shone on the side of his face, then he turned away.

Chapter 60

Out on the fields, the grass was a bloody mattress where dead men lay. Brian O'Conhalaigh, locked in a death struggle with an English soldier, gripped the hilt of his sword tighter with a sweaty hand and swung. The blade met bone and the man fell over, his last words an unintelligible groan.

Brian was pulling his sword free of the body when, out of the corner of his eye, he saw a mace being lifted, hurtling toward his head.

With a shout, he threw himself to the side. He fell across the body of the man he had just killed, and found himself staring into the sightless eyes of another dead man. Beyond him lay another, and another.

He rolled to his feet. The iron ball was coming again and he couldn't move away fast enough. It barreled toward him.

Something changed its trajectory. Instead of smashing into his skull, it blew by, an inch from his nose. Its owner dropped to the ground in an openmouthed scream that never made it out. Above stood Alane.

Grim-faced, he stuck out a hand.

"Jesus," Brian muttered, grasping it to rise. "I owe ye my life."

"I'm no' worried of that debt. Stick close and you'll repay

me soon enough." He turned back to the chaos raging around them.

Brian looked around in stupefied amazement. The carnage seemed to stretch for miles. The stench filled his nostrils, his feet walked on blood-sodden ground. His arms, his legs, were leaden weights, dragging on him, as if he'd been dropped into an ocean fully clothed. The muscles were cramping and shuddering, but he couldn't stop lifting his blade. He couldn't stop killing them or they would kill him.

A horse galloped by, jarring him. He stumbled and dropped to a knee.

"'Tis only de Valery," Alane's voice said from behind.

"Oh," Brian replied dumbly, stumbling back to his feet. He was so thirsty his throat crackled when he inhaled. When he exhaled, it was like hot wind blowing over a burn.

"We're outnumbered," he muttered.

"Aye," Alane agreed. "Let's go," he said, and plunged down the small hill back into battle.

Weary hotness filled Brian's eyes as he followed him down, but Alane was only approaching a small group of Irishmen who stood in an area the fighting had passed by. Brian followed. In the distance, he could see the de Valery knight urging his horse up a hill, straight for the justiciar's standard.

"He'll get himself killed," he croaked.

The Irishmen turned.

A small band of horsemen appeared on the far hilltop. At its head rode Will, flying through the butchery, seeking Wogan.

His one-eyed captain looked over as they galloped up the hill. "Sir? Is this the wisest thing to do?"

"No."

He kicked his horse into one last gallop. At his side rode his squire Peter, the king's crest prominently displayed. The pennant snapped in the morning breeze. Hands were raised, pointing at them. The justiciar's guard turned their horses and unsheathed their swords. Two men wearing Rardove's livery lifted longbows and aimed them at William's head.

The justiciar threw out his arm and shouted something. The bows hovered a moment, then lowered.

"Wogan!" Will shouted, hauling on his horse's reins as they crested the hill. The stallion slid in on his haunches, tossing his head.

"Who the hell are you, and what the hell is going on?" the justiciar demanded.

Will swung off the horse, ignoring the battle behind them and the swords angled at his neck. "I've a story to tell, my lord."

When Finian walked out of Rardove Keep with Senna, Wogan, the king's governor, stood atop the hill, his pennants blowing in the breeze. He was not on his horse. Senna's brother Liam and The O'Fáil stood beside him, talking. There was no fighting. Everything was quiet. Even the birds flew away when battle came.

Finian stopped, stared at the sight of the men talking on the hill, then simply dropped to the ground where he stood, holding Senna's hand. She sat down beside him. It was a long time before anyone spotted them.

Senna dragged Finian to Wogan's tent, not so much because she wanted Finian to meet the governor, but because he would not let her out of his sight. And when it became clear Senna was going to speak to the justiciar come a plague of locusts, it became evident Finian would be meeting the king's governor, too.

"There is no such thing as Wishmé dyes," she insisted, after every moment of her time with Rardove had been explored and exhausted in excruciating detail. "Lord Rardove was mad, I am sorry to say. The Wishmés are mollusks, not some mythical dyes. And certainly"—she gave a tinkling laugh—"not *weapons*."

Wogan did not have a hard time believing her report. But after an hour of nonstop conversation and a few cups of wine, he did see fit to say, "You're not quite what I expected from a wool merchant."

Finian, sitting in the governor's tent beside The O'Fáil, replied with feeling, "Ye've no idea."

Wogan nodded at Finian, a slight smile lightening his somber visage. "I've found some women can hide many layers."

"Have you found that to be a problem?" Senna interjected brightly.

"I have found it," he said, shifting his gaze her direction, "to be invigorating."

She smiled even more brightly. "The highway back to Baile Átha Cliath is a long one, my lord governor. If I may, I would suggest a small detour. To the town of Hutton's Leap."

Wogan lifted a cup of wine to his mouth. "And what might I find in Hutton's Leap?"

"Oh, anything the lord king's governor wants, I should imagine." She smiled. "Jugglers, fine embroidery needles, and the most delicious ham pasties. And a . . . shop"—she stumbled very slightly over the word—"called Thistle, I believe, with a proprietress from the south of France who I suspect has *many* layers. Tell her I sent you."

Over the rim of his cup, Wogan watched her a moment, then smiled.

Within half an hour, the English army was wheeling out of the valley, leaving only bird calls behind them as the sun set.

Epilogue

Winter, Scotland, 1295 A.D.

Will de Valery stood before Robert the Bruce. A pithy Scottish winter sunset had come and gone before they finished the wine in their wooden cups.

"I think we're safe from the threat for now," Will said.

The Bruce looked at him thoughtfully. "No secret weapons for Longshanks, then?"

A fireplace roared in the far wall, but most of the heat went sailing up the chimney or into the stone walls. Both men wore fur pelts, even inside.

Will shook his head. "Legends. That is all the Wishmés are."

And, really, Will had decided, that was all anyone needed to know. Senna was the only person on earth who could craft the deadly dyes, and she insisted she had no interest in doing so.

"Perhaps the children," she allowed when he'd demanded to know her plans. "But I will neither insist nor deny, Will. All I will do is explain. Never fear," she'd added when he'd opened his mouth to protest that his concern was neither of those things, "I will always be here, so nothing, ever, will go unseen."

And that, he decided, was perhaps better than a spy network. Senna being watchful could bring down a kingdom, if she wished it. Or save one.

And even so, Will thought, what benefit could come from a king of Scotland knowing about the thing?

The Wishmés had been lost for centuries, until their mother and father had resurrected them. For good cause, perhaps, but all that could come of them was evil. Scotland had enough perils facing her, without the dubious advantage of the Wishmés added to her strain.

"You told King Edward they were more than rumors," The Bruce said, watching Will closely. "You told him Rardove had the dyes, that they were real, that they were weapons, and that he'd better hie himself over there right quick."

Will gave one of his calculated shrugs. "I tell King Edward many things. 'Twas necessary to bring him hammering on Rardove's door."

Being a double agent for Scotland's cause required saying many things to many people for many different purposes. The trouble came only in trying to remember it all.

"And why did we want him hammering on Rardove's door?" The Bruce asked, his regard watchful.

"We did not, my lord. I did. My sister was there, and in danger."

The Bruce lifted a cup in a mock toast. "I did not realize my spies used their contacts for personal good."

"Then you are not very wise, my lord." Will poured himself a cup of wine. "But I still think you ought be king."

Robert laughed. "As do I."

Will drank. He only thought The Bruce should be king because he *could* be king. 'Twas possible for this nobleman to rule the beautiful, scarred land of his heart, the country his mother and father had loved so well. But it was Scotland *go braugh,* not Bruce *go braugh.* Never for a man.

They were so fallible.

"And I do believe it benefited Scotland," Will added

quietly. "Edward turned his eye elsewhere for a few months. We might have been saved an invasion before we were ready."

"And now, we are ready," The Bruce said. He pushed open a shutter. The sound of sleigh runners hushed into the courtyard outside. Winter had come, cold and white and bright. "So, what of your sister?" The Bruce asked.

Will waved the parchment in his hand, the latest missive from Senna. "Rardove's lands were taken back into the king's hands, of course. And, oddly, deeded to a commune."

Robert the Bruce raised his eyebrows. "Truly? A business commune?"

"So she says. I can hardly make it out," he added, bending over the missive for perhaps the tenth time. He walked to the window and held the parchment under the spill of cold winter sunlight pouring into the room, but still it was hard to be sure he was reading it rightly. "A commune of . . . *bellas?* Can that be right?"

The next king of Scotland shrugged, but he was grinning while he did it. His beard gleamed brown and red. "I do not know, de Valery, but I would surely like to visit a commune of pretties."

"Aye," Will said absently. "An Italian word, is it not?"

The Bruce nodded. "Or Southern France, perhaps."

"Indeed," Will said, as baffled as ever. "Senna reports Wogan, the Irish justiciar, put in a word to Longshanks to give it over." He shrugged and set the letter on the table. "No mind. I will go when I can, and figure it out."

"Good. Because right now, we have an invasion to plan."

Will nodded as they opened the door and strode to their horses. "And I must return to the king, ere he wonders why his spy is taking so long to reconnoiter the northern borders."

Finian put his arm around Senna's shoulder and pulled her closer to his side. They stood on a stone embrasure on the walls surrounding Castle O'Fáil; the day, while brilliantly sunny, was windy and chill. The O'Fáil, down in the bailey, glanced up and lifted his hand. Finian returned the gesture before bending to place a kiss on Senna's head.

After two months among the Irish, Senna had almost memorized the array of names and faces and lineages stretching back far too long.

"Sooth, Finian, why do we need to know about poets from the fourth century?" she had asked in a fit of irritation earlier that afternoon, which is why he'd finally led her out to the walls, to stare down at the sea below and calm herself. They'd done this several times since they'd returned to O'Fáil lands and realized Senna was no longer quickening.

"It happens all the time," she'd said, smiling through her tears on the night she understood.

"Aye, it does," he'd agreed.

She was thinking of it now, he knew, and a moment later was proven right when she said quietly, "A week along is all I was. Ofttimes, one never even knows so soon."

"No." He kissed the top of her head again, and rubbed his palm over her upper arms, warming her. "We will have children, Senna."

She smiled. "You will give me children."

He paused. "I'm fairly certain I'm supposed to say that to *ye,* lass."

"But," she went on, lost in thought, "if I do not quicken right away, that will do for now. I must get my sheep over to Ireland, and the king has told me of your astonishing weavers. I believe we can gain them franchise in the towns. But, before all, I must meet with the mayor of the wool staple in Dublin."

"Och, well, the woolly mayor it is, then," he said lightly.

She narrowed her eyes. "Therefore I do not understand why you wish me to learn the names of the poets—the *file?*" She lifted an eyebrow to question if she was pronouncing the term correctly. He shook his head. She narrowed her eyes again. "Why must I know the names of poets from so long ago?"

"Because it matters," he said. And he said it in such a simple, calm way, she believed him.

He was including her in every aspect of his life, his heritage and his future, sharing everything with her, accepting her involvement as natural. Desired. Which was, Senna realized, what she'd wanted all along: to be cherished, as she was.

In return, she was willing to offer much, including attempting to learn the names of centuries-dead poets. Or the entire Irish language. It was a beautiful tongue, but perilous, she realized with trepidation as she waded in to lessons each afternoon. Finian was a patient teacher. She tried to be a patient student. Her fingers had healed. Pentony was dead.

"I hope he did right by himself," she murmured, her gaze drifting down the sloping hill below them. "I do not like to think of him suffering anymore."

In part, she wished that because if Pentony was not suffering anymore, despite his sins, then perhaps Finian's mother was not either. And one day, that thought might bring Finian peace.

He stood near her, towering to his full rangy height. Black, windswept hair fell across his shoulders, and he was as magnificent to her now as when she'd first laid eyes on him.

"You sent a trunkful of coin to his illegitimate child in England, didn't you?" she said abruptly.

He started shaking his head, but she held up her hand.

"I know you did. I heard Alane speaking of it."

He shrugged. "Ye'll believe what ye want, Senna. Ye always do. I've given up trying to change ye."

"You never began." Her breath caught in her throat. "You are a good man, Finian O'Melaghlin."

"And ye," he whispered close to her ear, "are the most beautiful woman I ever did see."

She feigned shock. "You say nothing of my goodness."

"Aye, for I've nothing good to say of it."

She laughed as he pulled her back into his embrace and they both looked out over the walls. He breathed into her hair as the chilled winds swept up from the hills below.

"Yer father asked me for something, Senna," he said quietly a moment later. "Before he died."

She looked over her shoulder. "Indeed? What was that?"

"To help save Scotland."

She looked away sharply. "You owe my father naught."

He turned her by the shoulders and peered down with those dark, perceptive eyes. "Just so. This is not a matter of a debt or a duty. Ye taught me that much."

She nodded solemnly. "I see. Will the king allow it?"

He nodded gravely. "We've already spoken of it."

"But I thought— You were to be . . ." Her words trailed off.

"I'll never be king here, Senna. I made my choice."

She stared at the castle behind him, then forced herself to meet his eyes. "A choice between a woman and a kingship. Some would say 'twas an easy choice."

"Oh, aye. Simple enough for me." He ran his palm over the side of her head. "I suppose ye'll have to make yer choice now, Senna, knowing I'm not to be a king after all."

She pursed her lips, as if considering the matter. "I have always heard 'tis best to keep royalty at a distance."

"Have ye?"

"You, I shall keep close."

He slid his hand to the back of her head and pulled her forward. "Will ye, now?"

She rested her arms around his shoulders. "I made my choice in a stinking old prison. I'm fairly certain you were there. Do you not recall?"

He smiled faintly, but, still cupping the back of her head, looked down into the valley below. "A prison is a prison. Free air has a different odor. I've seen men in cellars make vile, regretful choices."

She entwined her fingers behind his neck. "But, Finian, what you saw was a *woman* in a cellar."

His blue gaze came back down, his smile deepending as his eyes searched hers. "Well now, that is so. And she was a fair staggering thing."

She disentwined her fingers to wave her hand, her face flushing. "Enough of that."

"Nay, not enough." He ran his hand down her neck to her shoulders in a manner she knew far too well.

"Cease," she protested, but she didn't mean it, and he knew. He caressed her shoulders in deep, circular motions, massaging. A prelude.

She bent her head to the side and closed her eyes, but still said sternly, "You shall not be let off so easily. We were speaking of plans. Instead of being a king now, you shall be a spy?"

"Tend toward calling me a diplomat when we travel. It'll sound less treasonous if anyone asks."

She opened her eyes, smiling widely. "I am to come with you."

He cocked an eyebrow. "For certes." He ran his lips over her cheek, then slid them down to her jaw. "I've been looking for ye my whole life, lass. Dye-witch or no, I'm not letting ye go. Kings can want ye; I have got ye."

"Good," she whispered.

He bent to her lips but she put a hand on his chest stilling him.

"And are you never going to ask?" she said in a low voice.

"Nay."

"You do not want to know how I did it?"

He was quiet, then reached into his fur and held up the small scrap of Wishmé-dyed fabric she'd carried out with her that day at Rardove's, and given to him. A gift of nothing, she'd laughed. He had not joined in, she recalled.

"I think the dyes are a thing rare and astonishing," he

replied slowly, handing it to her. "Like their maker. Ye wish to tell me, so do."

"'Tis a secret. You cannot tell a soul."

He smiled faintly.

"I followed my mother's recipe. 'Twas the simplest thing in the world."

"Is that so? Five hundred years of Irish dyers do not agree." He rested his hand between her shoulder blades, a gentle touch. Unconsciously, she was certain, he started rubbing.

"Perhaps they must not have been women," she explained loftily. "One must have a willing woman."

"Ah." He kissed her cheek. "I like that."

"I thought you would."

He moved lower, kissing her earlobe. He seemed to be losing interest.

"Have you even a notion what that means?" she demanded.

"Nay." He kissed her neck, and his hand slipped lower. "Keep yer secrets, woman," he murmured into her hair. "I want only yer body."

She laughed and turned, resting her hand on his upper arms, holding him slightly at bay. "Are you not the least bit curious?"

He pushed the warm fur away from her shoulder, pressed a kiss to her bare skin. She shivered. "For ye, I shall be the least bit curious."

She smiled. "The secret of the Wishmés is that the woman has to be in love."

He paused, looking vaguely impressed. "How?"

"Urea."

"Fascinating," he said after a moment's reflection, and met her eye. "But then, willing does not always mean loving."

She touched his cheek with her fingertips. Her heart actually hurt from the fullness of loving him, of knowing he loved her equally, of contemplating all the things that could be with this man.

"For the Wishmés, it means just that," she said softly. "A woman must be deeply in love. No other will do."

He pulled her to his lips once and for all, his arms tight around her body, his fingers tangling in her hair.

"I agree, lass. None other will do."

Author's Notes

Pronunciation and Translation of Irish Words

uisce beatha (fire-water—whisky) /eesh-kee ba-hah/
bhean sidhe (woman faerie) /ban shee/
a rúin (My love) /AH-rune/
Dia dhuit (God be with you) /jeeu which/
Onóir duit (Honor to you) /on-yay which/

Dyes

There are no Wishmé mollusks or dyes. But elements of them are modeled after something based in reality. And the rest is just pure fictional fun.

I based the color on the famed Tyrian murex purple dye of ancient Rome.

As far as its explosive nature, I modeled this after picric acid, a yellow dye that, in its powdered state, is explosive.

And the "chameleon" effect . . . that's pure fiction.

A little about chameleons: They do not really "reflect" their environment. They have a limited repertoire of colors which change based on mood—they're more like living mood rings. With three layers to their skin, light waves from the surrounding environment get filtered through these, bouncing off underlayers, reflecting some and absorbing others.

In fact, cuttlefish are actually more chameleon-like than chameleons when it comes to camouflage, changing their chromatophores to blend in with their environment.

I started wondering, *Well, why can't this happen with wool fibers?* Senna's wool. What if a certain sheep's wool had the capacity for such qualities? Tri-level cells that continue to "read" environmental input after fleecing, and shift in response. Of course, it would be impossible to create such an effect with dead wool.

Wouldn't it?

Characters

None of the primary characters are real. Some of the secondary characters, including the the justiciar of Ireland (steward, governor) John Wogan, King Edward I of England ("Longshanks"), and the Irish tribe O'Melaghlin were real, vibrant peoples in Ireland in the late thirteenth century.

Weather

Autumn is often quite stormy in Ireland. I needed it to be calmer, and drier, though, so I played with this.

Illegitimacy and Suicide in Medieval Ireland

Illegitimacy had not yet gained the social stain it would in years to come, and already had in England. It was certainly no barrier to kingship; rival claimants to the princedoms of Ireland often were sons of kings by various mothers, fighting one another for supremacy, and no less legitimate for it. But while illegitimacy may not have hindered political aspirations, a mother abandoning her family would cause great pain, and shame, just as it would today. Particularly for a son left behind in the care of an enervated father.

Suicide, on the other hand, was cause for shame all around, and was a very public debacle. No burial in church grounds was allowed, and in fact, corpses were often debased, burned, and otherwise disgraced, a physical mirror of the abasement believed to have been done to the soul.

Fictional Kingdom

I wanted to base the Irish tribe in this story on a real *tuatha,* specifically the O'Neills. For years, in the working manuscript, that was my default kingdom and king. The O'Neills were the dominant Irish tribe in the north for thousands of years. All I needed to make it work for the story was a relatively stable period of kingship about the time that the Auld Alliance was being forged in Scotland.

Such periods are hard to find in medieval Irish history. If the story had been set a few years earlier, my aging king could have been Brian mac Neill Ruiad Ó Néill, who reigned in relative stability from 1238 until 1260. But alas, the Scots had not yet rebelled so openly, and Edward "Longshanks" was not yet king of England, so out with Brian mac Neill.

Set a few years later than Brian's reign and I could have used Àed Buide. His term certainly endured the ups and downs of an Irish kingship, but in the end, he served as a relatively stable king, from 1263 until his death in 1283.

But following Àed Buide, there were too many violent transitions of power, too many coups, for me to have a "good king" who was old enough to serve as Finian's mentor.

Thus was born The O'Fáil. The name Fianna, inextricably linked to *fáil,* has a long and rich history in Ireland.

A *fian* is group of soldiers. Mythically, the Fianna were a great tribe of Irishmen, known from the Fenian Cycle, led by the greatest Irish warrior, Fionn mac Cumhaill (pronounced *Finn McCool*). In ancient Ireland, the Fianna was also a name given to semi-independent warrior bands, often made up of noble-born men not yet come into their inheritance, who lived apart from society in the forests as mercenaries, and often bandits, but still served their ruling king in wars. And in contemporary times, the name Fianna has been used by a great number of organizations, right up to the Fianna Fáil, the largest and most influential political party in the Republic of Ireland.

Fianna Fáil is commonly and usefully translated as "Soldiers of Destiny." But *fáil* is a rendering of the ancient pre-Christian word for Ireland.

Music I Listened to While Writing *The Irish Warrior*

"The Space Between," Dave Matthews Band
"Hallelujah," Jeff Buckley
"One Thing," Finger Eleven
"You and Me," Lifehouse
"Better Days," The Goo Goo Dolls
"I'll Be," Edwin McCain
Far too many Irish songs to list

Bibliography

Annals of Innisfallen.

Barry, Terry B., Robin Frame, and Katharine Simms, eds. *Colony and Frontier in Medieval Ireland: Essays Presented to J. F. Lydon*. London: The Hambledon Press, 1995.

Otway-Ruthven, A. J. *A History of Medieval Ireland*. 2nd ed. New York: Barnes & Noble Books, 1980.